'There is a reason why Gary Shteyngart [...] Granta's Best Young American Noveli[...] narration, is witty, intelligent and has an a[...] left me helpless with laughter ... Shtey[...] apparent ... This is a wonderful book' Da[...]

'Misha is one of the greatest comic creations in recent fiction ... Like a victorious wrestler, this novel is so immodestly vigorous, so burstingly sure of its barbaric excellence, that simply by breathing, sweating and standing upright it exalts itself' *London Review of Books*

'Shteyngart writes a vulgar, carefree kind of humour, wildly politically incorrect, vicious, jeering and ribald ... His imagination – like the best imaginations – seems completely unfettered. He writes with vim, zest, gusto, zeal and élan' *Irish Times*

'An almighty laughing horror of a book ... read it – not only for a lethal satire on globalized values, nor for a stream of immoderately good jokes, but for a demonstration of the kind of unabashed comic maximalism that's been next to non-existent in American fiction since *Catch-22*. So far, I think, this is by far the funniest novel of the 21st century' *Independent on Sunday*

'Gary Shteyngart's brilliant, scathing new novel ... is a satire, an irrepressible, fiery and hilarious one, but it's also surprisingly sensuous ... Shteyngart evokes Joseph Heller and Evelyn Waugh and more than bears the comparison' *Guardian*

'You're unlikely to read a wittier book this year than this mind-boggling satire. The images tumble forth, as Shteyngart skips effortlessly from gangsta rap to Russian literature. Shteyngart's novel is a rip-roaring farce' *Irish Examiner*

'Reviewers of Gary Shteyngart's 2002 debut novel *The Russian Debutante's Handbook* compared him with Bellow, Nabokov, Rushdie, Roth, Miller, Franzen, Richler, Martin Amis and Evelyn Waugh ... [*Absurdistan*] is full of beautifully lucid touches ... [and] the dazzling convolutions of Shteyngart's writing' *New Statesman*

'Shteyngart brings a ... viciously clever humour to ... the tragicomedy of current international relations' *Observer*

'This is a staggering knock-out bull of a book ... It is a substantial work of shuddering importance ... Funny as hell and profound as well, this is as rewarding a read as you'll be offered this year' *Big Issue Scotland*

ALSO BY GARY SHTEYNGART

The Russian Debutante's Handbook

ABSURDISTAN

Gary Shteyngart

Granta Books
London

Granta Publications, 12 Addison Avenue, London W11 4QR

First published in Great Britain by Granta Books 2007
First published in the United States by Random House, 2006
This edition published in 2008 by arrangement with Random House,
an imprint of Random House Publishing Group,
a division of Random House, Inc.

Portions of this work were originally published,
in significantly different form, in *The New Yorker*.

Grateful acknowledgement is made to Bug Music for permission
to reprint an excerpt from 'Ass-N-Titties', written by Craig Adams,
copyright © 2000 by Intuit-Solar Publishing (ASCAP)/Million Dollar Man Music
(ASCAP)/administered by Bug. All rights reserved. Used by permission.

A CIP catalogue record for this book
is available from the British Library.

5 7 9 10 8 6 4

ISBN 978 1 84708 006 6

Printed in the UK by CPI Bookmarque, Croydon, CR0 4TD

PROLOGUE

Where I'm Calling From

This is a book about love. The next 338 pages are dedicated with that cloying Russian affection that passes for real warmth to my Beloved Papa, to the city of New York, to my sweet impoverished girlfriend in the South Bronx, and to the United States Immigration and Naturalization Service (INS).

This is also a book about *too much* love. It's a book about being had. Let me say that right away: *I've been had*. They used me. Took advantage of me. Sized me up. Knew right away that they had their man. If "man" is the right word.

Maybe this whole being-had deal is genetic. I'm thinking of my grandmother here. An ardent Stalinist and faithful contributor to Leningrad *Pravda* until Alzheimer's took what was left of her senses, she penned the famous allegory of Stalin the Mountain Eagle swooping down the valley to pick off three imperialist badgers representing Britain, America, and France, their measly bodies torn to shreds in the grasp of the generalissimo's bloody talons. There's a picture of me as an infant crawling over Grandma's lap. I'm drooling on her. She's drooling on me. The year is 1972, and we both look absolutely demented. Well, look at me now, Grandma. Look at my missing teeth and dented lower stomach; look at what they did to my heart, that bruised kilogram of fat hanging off my breastbone. When it comes to being torn to shreds in the twenty-first century, I am the fourth badger.

I'm writing this from Davidovo, a small village populated entirely by the so-called Mountain Jews near the northern frontier of the former Soviet republic of Absurdsvanï. Ah, the Mountain Jews. In their hilly isolation and single-minded devotion to clan and Yahweh, they seem to me *prehistoric,* premammalian even, like some clever miniature dinosaur that once schlepped across the earth, the *Haimosaurus rex.*

It's early September. The sky is an unwavering blue, its blankness and infinity reminding me, for some reason, that we are on a small round planet inching its way through a terrifying void. Roosting atop the ample redbrick manses, the village's satellite dishes point toward the surrounding mountains, whose peaks are crowned with alpine white. Soft late-summer breezes minister to my wounds, and even the occasional stray dog wandering down the street harbors a satiated, peaceable demeanor, as if tomorrow it will emigrate to Switzerland.

The villagers have gathered around me, the dried-out senior citizens, the oily teenagers, the heavy local gangsters with Soviet prison tattoos on their fingers (former friends of my Beloved Papa), even the confused one-eyed octogenarian rabbi who is now crying on my shoulder, whispering in his bad Russian about what an honor it is to have an important Jew like me in his village, how he would like to feed me spinach pancakes and roasted lamb, find me a good local wife who would go down on me, pump up my stomach like a beach ball in need of air.

I'm a deeply secular Jew who finds no comfort in either nationalism or religion. But I can't help feeling comfortable among this strange offshoot of my race. The Mountain Jews coddle and cosset me; their hospitality is overwhelming; their spinach is succulent and soaks up their garlic and freshly churned butter.

And yet I yearn to take to the air.

To soar across the globe.

To land at the corner of 173rd Street and Vyse, where she is waiting for me.

My Park Avenue psychoanalyst, Dr. Levine, has almost disabused me of the idea that I can fly. "Let's keep our feet on the ground," he likes to say. "Let's stick to what's actually possible." Wise words, Doctor, but maybe you're not quite hearing me.

I don't think I can fly like a graceful bird or like a rich American superhero. I think I can fly the way I do everything else—in fits and starts, with gravity constantly trying to thrash me against the narrow black band of the horizon, with sharp rocks scraping against my tits and stomachs, with rivers filling my mouth with mossy water and deserts plying my pockets with sand, with every hard-won ascent brokered by the possibility of a sharp fall into nothingness. I'm doing it now, Doctor. I'm soaring away from the ancient rabbi clinging warmly to the collar of my tracksuit, over the village's leafy vegetables and preroasted lambs, over the green-dappled overhang of two colliding mountain ranges that keep the prehistoric Mountain Jews safe from the distressing Moslems and Christians around them, over flattened Chechnya and pockmarked Sarajevo, over hydroelectric dams and the empty spirit world, over Europe, that gorgeous polis on the hill, a blue starry flag atop its fortress walls, over the frozen deadly calm of the Atlantic which would like nothing better than to drown me once and for all, over and over and over and finally toward and toward and toward, toward the tip of the slender island . . .

I am flying northward toward the woman of my dreams. I'm staying close to the ground, just like you said, Doctor. I'm trying to make out individual shapes and places. I'm trying to piece my life together. Now I can spot the Pakistani place on Church Street where I cleaned out the entire kitchen, drowning myself in ginger and sour mangoes, spicy lentils and cauliflower, as the gathered taxi drivers cheered me along, broadcasting news of my gluttony to their relatives in Lahore. Now I am over the little skyline that has gathered to the east of Madison Park, the kilometer-high replica of St. Mark's Campanile in Venice, the golden tip of the New York Life Building, these stone symphonies, these modernist arrangements the Americans must have carved out from rocks the size of moons, these last stabs at godless immortality. Now I am above the clinic on Twenty-fourth Street, where a social worker once told me I had tested negative for HIV, the virus that causes AIDS, forcing me into the bathroom to cry guiltily over the skinny, beautiful boys whose scared glances I had deflected in the waiting room. Now I am over the dense greenery of Central Park, tracing the shadows cast by young matrons walking their bite-sized Oriental dogs toward the communal redemption of the Great Lawn. The murky Harlem River flies past me; I skirt the silvery top of the slowly chugging IRT train and continue northeast, my body tired and limp, begging for ground fall.

I am over the South Bronx now, no longer sure if I am soaring or hitting the tarmac at Olympic speed. My girlfriend's world reaches out and envelops me. I am privy to the relentless truths of Tremont Avenue—where, according to the graceful loop of graffito, BEBO always LOVES LARA, where the neon storefront of Brave Fried Chicken begs me to sample its greasy-sweet aromas, where the Adonai Beauty Salon threatens to take my limp curly hairdo and turn it upward, set it aflame like Liberty's orange torch.

I pass like a fat beam of light through dollar stores selling T-shirts from the eighties and fake Rocawear sweatpants, through the brown hulks of housing projects warning OPERATION CLEAN HALLS and TRESPASSERS SUBJECT TO ARREST, over the heads of boys in gang bandannas and hairnets jousting with one another astride their monster bikes, over the three-year-old Dominican girls in tank tops and fake diamond earrings, over the tidy front yard where the weeping brown Virgin is perpetually stroking the rosary round her blushing neck.

On the corner of 173rd Street and Vyse Avenue, on a brick housing-project stoop riddled with stray cheese puffs and red licorice sticks, my girl has draped her naked lap with Hunter College textbooks. I plow straight into the bounty of her caramelized summertime breasts, both covered by a tight yellow tee that informs me in chunky uppercase script that G IS FOR GANGSTA. And as I cover her with kisses, as the sweat of my transatlantic flight soaks her in my own brand of salt and molasses, I am struck stupid by my love for her and my grief for nearly everything else. Grief for my Beloved Papa, the real "gangsta" in my life. Grief for Russia, the distant land of my birth, and for Absurdistan, where the calendar will never pass the second week of September 2001.

. . .

This is a book about love. But it's also a book about geography. The South Bronx may be low on signage, but everywhere I look, I see the helpful arrows declaring YOU ARE HERE.

I *Am* Here.

I Am Here next to the woman I love. The city rushes out to locate and affirm me.

How can I be so fortunate?

Sometimes I can't believe that I am still alive.

ABSURDISTAN

1

The Night in Question

June 15, 2001

I am Misha Borisovich Vainberg, age thirty, a grossly overweight man with small, deeply set blue eyes, a pretty Jewish beak that brings to mind the most distinguished breed of parrot, and lips so delicate you would want to wipe them with the naked back of your hand.

For many of my last years, I have lived in St. Petersburg, Russia, neither by choice nor by desire. The City of the Czars, the Venice of the North, Russia's cultural capital . . . forget all that. By the year 2001, our St. Leninsburg has taken on the appearance of a phantasmagoric third-world city, our neoclassical buildings sinking into the crap-choked canals, bizarre peasant huts fashioned out of corrugated metal and plywood colonizing the broad avenues with their capitalist iconography (cigarette ads featuring an American football player catching a hamburger with a baseball mitt), and what is worst of all, our intelligent, depressive citizenry has been replaced by a new race of mutants dressed in studied imitation of the West, young women in tight Lycra, their scooped-up little breasts pointing at once to New York and Shanghai, with men in fake black Calvin Klein jeans hanging limply around their caved-in asses.

The good news is that when you're an incorrigible fatso like me—325 pounds at last count—and the son of the 1,238th-richest man in Russia, all of St. Leninsburg rushes out to service you: the draw-bridges lower themselves as you advance, and the pretty palaces line up alongside the canal banks, thrusting their busty friezes in your face. You are blessed with the rarest treasure to be found in this mineral-rich land. You are blessed with respect.

On the night of June 15 in the catastrophic year 2001, I was getting plenty of respect from my friends at a restaurant called the Home of the Russian Fisherman on Krestovskiy Island, one of the verdant islands caught in the delta of the Neva River. Krestovskiy is where we rich people pretend to be living in a kind of post-Soviet Switzerland, trudging along the manicured bike paths built 'round our *kottedzhes* and *town khauses*, and filling our lungs with parcels of atmosphere seemingly imported from the Alps.

The Fisherman's gimmick is that you catch your own fish out of a man-made lake, and then for about US$50 per kilo, the kitchen staff will smoke it for you or bake it on coals. On what the police would later call "the night in question," we were standing around the Spawning Salmon pontoon, yelling at our servants, drinking down carafes of green California Riesling, our Nokia *mobilniki* ringing with the social urgency that comes only when the White Nights strangle the nighttime, when the inhabitants of our ruined city are kept permanently awake by the pink afterglow of the northern sun, when the best you can do is drink your friends into the morning.

Let me tell you something: without good friends, you might as well drown yourself in Russia. After decades of listening to the familial agitprop of our parents ("We will die for you!" they sing), after surviving the criminal closeness of the Russian family ("Don't leave us!" they plead), after the crass socialization foisted upon us by our teachers and factory directors ("We will staple your circumcised *khui* to the wall!" they threaten), all that's left is that toast between two failed friends in some stinking outdoor beer kiosk.

"To your health, Misha Borisovich."

"To your success, Dimitry Ivanovich."

"To the army, the air force, and the whole Soviet fleet . . . Drink to the bottom!"

I'm a modest person bent on privacy and lonely sadness, so I have very few friends. My best buddy in Russia is a former American I like to call Alyosha-Bob. Born Robert Lipshitz in the northern reaches of New York State, this little bald eagle (not a single hair on his dome by age twenty-five) flew to St. Leninsburg eight years ago and was transformed, by dint of alcoholism and inertia, into a successful Russian *biznesman* renamed Alyosha, the owner of ExcessHollywood, a riotously profitable DVD import-export business, and the swain of Svetlana, a young Petersburg hottie. In addition to being bald, Alyosha-Bob has a pinched face ending in a reddish goatee, wet blue eyes that fool you with their near-tears, and enormous flounder lips cleansed hourly by vodka. A skinhead on the metro once described him as a *gnussniy zhid*, or a "vile-looking Yid," and I think most of the populace sees him that way. I certainly did when I first met him as a fellow undergraduate at Accidental College in the American Midwest a decade ago.

Alyosha-Bob and I have an interesting hobby that we indulge whenever possible. We think of ourselves as the Gentlemen Who Like to Rap. Our oeuvre stretches from the old-school jams of Ice Cube, Ice-T, and Public Enemy to the sensuous contemporary rhythms of ghetto tech, a hybrid of Miami bass, Chicago ghetto tracks, and Detroit electronica. The modern reader may be familiar with "Ass-N-Titties" by DJ Assault, perhaps the *seminal* work of the genre.

On the night in question, I got the action started with a Detroit ditty I enjoy on summer days:

> *Aw, shit*
> *Heah I come*
> *Shut yo mouf*
> *And bite yo tongue.*

Alyosha-Bob, in his torn Helmut Lang slacks and Accidental College sweatshirt, picked up the tune:

> *Aw, girl,*
> *You think you bad?*
> *Let me see you*
> *Bounce dat ass.*

Our melodies rang out over the Russian Fisherman's four pontoons (Spawning Salmon, Imperial Sturgeon, Capricious Trout, and Sweet Little Butterfish), over this whole tiny man-made lake, whatever the hell it's called (Dollar Lake? Euro Pond?), over the complimentary-valet-parking-lot where one of the oafish employees just dented my new Land Rover.

Heah come dat bitch
From round de way
Box my putz
Like Cassius Clay.

"Sing it, Snack Daddy!" Alyosha-Bob cheered me on, using my Accidental College nickname.

My name is Vainberg
I like ho's
Sniff 'em out
Wid my Hebrew nose

Pump that shit
From 'round the back
Big-booty ho
Ack ack ack

This being Russia, a nation of busybody peasants thrust into an awkward modernity, some idiot will always endeavor to spoil your good fun. And so the neighboring *biznesman,* a sunburned midlevel killer standing next to his pasty girlfriend from some cow-filled province, starts in with "Now, fellows, why do you have to sing like African exchange students? You both look so cultured"—in other words, like vile-looking Yids—"why don't you declaim some Pushkin instead? Didn't he have some nice verses about the White Nights? That would be very seasonal."

"Hey, if Pushkin were alive today, he'd be a rapper," I said.

"That's right," Alyosha-Bob said. "He'd be M.C. Push."

"Fight the power!" I said in English.

Our Pushkin-loving friend stared at us. This is what happens when you don't learn English, by the way. You're always at a loss for words. "God help you children," he finally said, taking his lady friend by one diminutive arm and guiding her over to the other side of the pontoon.

Children? Was he talking about *us?* What would an Ice Cube or an Ice-T do in this situation? I reached for my *mobilnik,* ready to dial my Park Avenue analyst, Dr. Levine, to tell him that once again I had been insulted and injured, that once again I had been undermined by a fellow Russian.

And then I heard my manservant, Timofey, ringing his special hand bell. The *mobilnik* fell out of my hand, the Pushkin lover and his girlfriend disappeared from the pontoon, the pontoon itself floated off into another dimension, even Dr. Levine and his soft American ministrations were reduced to a distant hum.

It was feeding time.

With a low bow, manservant Timofey presented me with a tray of blackened sturgeon kebabs and a carafe of Black Label. I fell down on a hard plastic chair that twisted and torqued beneath my weight like a piece of modern sculpture. I bent over the sturgeon, sniffing it with closed eyes as if offering a silent prayer. My feet were locked together, my ankles grinding into each other with expectant anxiety. I prepared for my meal in the usual fashion: fork in my left hand; my dominant right clenched into a fist on my lap, ready to punch anyone who dared take away my food.

I bit into the sturgeon kebab, filling my mouth with both the crisp burnt edges and the smooth mealy interior. My body trembled inside my leviathan Puma tracksuit, my heroic gut spinning counterclockwise, my two-scoop breasts slapping against each other. The usual food-inspired images presented themselves. Myself, my Beloved Papa, and my young mother in a hollowed-out boat built to resemble a white swan floating past a grotto, triumphant Stalin-era music echoing around us ("Here's my passport! *What* a passport! It's my great red *Soviet* passport!"), Beloved Papa's wet hands rubbing my tummy and skirting the waistband of my shorts, and Mommy's smooth, dry ones brushing against the nape of my neck, a chorus of their hoarse, tired voices saying, "We love you, Misha. We love you, bear cub."

My body fell into a rocking motion like the religious people rock when they're deep in the thrall of their god. I finished off the first kebab and the one after that, my chin oily with sturgeon juices, my breasts shivering as if they'd been smothered with packets of ice. Another chunk of fish fell into my mouth, this one well dusted with parsley and olive oil. I breathed in the smells of the sea, my right fist still clenched, fingers digging into palm, my nose touching the plate, sturgeon extract coating my nostrils, my little circumcised *khui* burning with the joy of release.

And then it was over. And then the kebabs were gone. I was left with an empty plate. I was left with nothing before me. Ah, dear me. Where was I now? An abandoned bear cub without his li'l fishy. I splashed a glass of water on my face and dabbed myself off with a napkin Timofey had tucked into my tracksuit. I picked up the carafe of Black Label, pressed it to my cold lips, and, with a single tilt of the wrist, emptied it into my gullet.

The world was golden around me, the evening sun setting light to a row of swaying alders; the alders abuzz with the warble of siskin birds, those striped yellow fellows from our nursery rhymes. I turned pastoral for a moment, my thoughts running to Beloved Papa, who was born in a village and for whom village life should be prescribed, as only there—half asleep in a cowshed, naked and ugly, but sober all the same—do the soft tremors of what could be happiness cross his swollen Aramaic face. I would have to bring him here one day, to the Home of the Russian Fisherman. I would buy him a few chilled bottles of his favorite Flagman vodka, take him out to the farthest pontoon, put my arm around his dandruff-dusted shoulders, press his tiny lemur head into one of my side hams, and make him understand that despite all the disappointments I have handed him over the past twenty years, the two of us are meant to be together forever.

Emerging from the food's thrall, I noticed that the demographics of the Spawning Salmon pontoon were changing. A group of young coworkers in blue blazers had shown up, led by a buffoon in a bow tie who played the role of a "fun person," breaking the coworkers up into teams, thrusting fishing rods into their weak hands, and leading them in a chorus of "Fi-ish! Fi-ish! Fi-ish!" What the hell was going on here? Was this the first sign of an emerging Russian middle class? Did all these idiots work for a German bank? Perhaps they were holders of American MBAs.

Meanwhile, all eyes fell on a striking older woman in a full-length white gown and black Mikimoto pearls, casting her line into the man-made lake. She was one of those mysteriously elegant women who appear to have walked in from the year 1913, as if all those red pioneer scarves and peasant blouses from our jackass Soviet days had never alighted on her delicate shoulders.

I am not enamored of such people, I must say. How is it possible to live outside of history? Who can claim immunity to it by dint of beauty and breeding? My only consolation was that neither this charming creature nor the young Deutsche Bank workers now shouting in unison "Sal-mon! Sal-mon!" would catch any tasty fish today. Beloved Papa and I have an agreement with the management of the Home of the Russian Fisherman restaurant—whenever a Vainberg takes up a rod, the owner's nephew puts on his Aqua-Lung, swims under the pontoons, and hooks the best fish on our lines. So all Czarina with the Black Pearls would get for her troubles would be a tasteless, defective salmon.

You can't ignore history altogether.

On the night in question, Alyosha-Bob and I were joined by three lovely females: Rouenna, the love of my life, visiting for two weeks from the Bronx, New York; Svetlana, Alyosha-Bob's dark-eyed Tatar beauty, a junior public-relations executive for a local chain of perfume shops; and Beloved Papa's twenty-one-year-old provincial wife, Lyuba.

I must say, I was anxious about bringing these women together (also, I have a generalized fear of women). Svetlana and Rouenna have aggressive personalities; Lyuba and Rouenna were once lower-class and lack refinement; and Svetlana and Lyuba, being Russian, present with symptoms of mild depression rooted in early childhood trauma (cf. Papadapolis, Spiro, "It's *My* Pierogi: Transgenerational Conflict in Post-Soviet Families," *Annals of Post-Lacanian Psychiatry,* Boulder/Paris, Vol. 23, No. 8, 1997). A part of me expected discord among the women, or what the Americans call "fireworks." Another part of me just wanted to see that snobby bitch Svetlana get her ass kicked.

While Alyosha-Bob and I were rapping, Lyuba's servant girl had been making the girls pretty with lipstick and pomade in one of the Fisherman's changing huts, and when they joined us on the pontoon, they reeked of fake citrus (and a touch of real sweat), their dainty lips aglow in the summer twilight, their teeny voices abuzz with interesting conversation about Stockmann, the celebrated Finnish emporium on St. Leninsburg's main thoroughfare, Nevsky Prospekt. They were discussing a summer special—two hand-fluffed Finnish towels for US$20—both towels distinguished by their highly un-Russian, shockingly Western color: orange.

Listening to the tale of the orange towel, I got a little engorged down in the circumcised purple half-*khui* department. These women of ours were so cute! Well, not my stepmother, Lyuba, obviously, who is eleven years younger than me and happens to spend her nights moaning unconvincingly under the coniferous trunk of Beloved Papa, with his impressive turtlelike *khui* (blessed memories of it swinging about in the bathtub, my curious toddler hands trying to snatch it).

And I wasn't hot for Svetlana, either; despite her fashionable Mongol cheekbones, her clingy Italian sweater, and that profoundly calculated aloofness, the supposedly sexy posturing of the educated Russian woman, despite all that, let me tell you, I absolutely refuse to sleep with one of my co-nationals. God only knows where they've been.

So that leaves me with my Rouenna Sales (pronounced *Sah*-lez, in the Spanish manner), my South Bronx girlie-girl, my big-boned precious, my giant multicultural swallow, with her crinkly hair violently pulled back into a red handkerchief, with her glossy pear-shaped brown nose always in need of kisses and lotion.

"I think," said my stepmom, Lyuba, in English for Rouenna's benefit, "I thought," she added. She was having trouble with her tenses. "I think, I thought . . . I think, I thought . . ."

I sink, I sought . . . I sink, I sought . . .

"What are you *sinking*, darling?" asked Svetlana, tugging on her line impatiently.

But Lyuba would not be so easily discouraged from expressing herself in a bright new language. Married for two years to the 1,238th-richest man in Russia, the dear woman was finally coming to terms with her true worth. Recently a Milanese doctor had been hired to burn out the malicious orange freckles ringing her coarse nubbin, while a Bilbao surgeon was on his way to chisel out the baby fat flapping around her tufty teenager's cheeks (the fat actually made her look more sympathetic, like a ruined farm girl just coming out of her adolescence).

"I think, I thought," Lyuba said, "that orange towel so ugly. For girl is nice lavender, for boy like my husband, Boris, light blue, for servant black because her hand already dirty."

"Damn, sugar," Rouenna said. "You're hard-core."

"What it is 'harcourt'?"

"Talking shit about servants. Like they got dirty hands and all."

"I *sink* . . ." Lyuba grew embarrassed and looked down at her own hands, with their tough provincial calluses. She whispered to me in Russian, "Tell her, Misha, that before I met your papa, I was unfortunate, too."

"Lyuba was poor back in 1998," I explained to Rouenna in English. "Then my papa married her."

"Is that right, sister?" Rouenna said.

"You are calling me *sister*?" Lyuba whispered, her sweet Russian soul atremble. She put down her fishing line and spread open her arms. "Then I will be your sister, too, Rouennachka!"

"It's just an African-American expression," I told her.

"It sure is," Rouenna said, coming over to give Lyuba a hug, which the temperate girl tearfully reciprocated. " 'Cause, as far as I can tell, all of you Russians are just a bunch of niggaz."

"What are you saying?" Svetlana said.

"Don't take it the wrong way," Rouenna said. "I mean it like a compliment."

"It's no compliment!" Svetlana barked. "Explain yourself."

"Chill, honey," Rouenna said. "All I'm saying is, you know . . . your men don't got no jobs, everyone's always doing drive-bys whenever they got beefs, the childrens got asthma, and y'all live in public housing."

"Misha doesn't live in public housing," Svetlana said. "I don't live in public housing."

"Yeah, but you're different from the other peeps. You're all like OGs," Rouenna said, making a ghetto gesture with her arm.

"We're what?"

"Original gangsters," Alyosha-Bob explained.

"Look at Misha," Rouenna said. "His father killed an American businessman over some bullshit, and now he can't get a U.S. fucking visa. That's, like, hard-core."

"It's not all because of Papa," I whispered. "It's the American consulate. It's the State Department. They hate me."

"Again, what it is 'harcourt'?" Lyuba asked, unsure where the conversation was heading and whether or not she and Rouenna were still sisters.

Svetlana dropped her line and turned on me and Alyosha-Bob with both hands on her negligible waist. "It's your fault," she seethed in Russian. "With all of your stupid rapping. With that idiot *ghetto tech*. No wonder people treat us like we're animals."

"We were just having fun," Alyosha-Bob said.

"If you want to be a Russian," Svetlana told my friend, "you have to think of what kind of *image* you want to project. Everyone already thinks we're bandits and whores. We've got to rebrand ourselves."

"I apologize with all my soul," Alyosha-Bob said, his hands symbolically covering his heart. "We will not rap in front of you from now on. We will work on our image."

"Damn, what are you niggaz going on about?" Rouenna said. "Speak English already."

Svetlana turned to me with her fierce off-color eyes. I stepped back, nearly tipping over into the Spawning Salmon waters. My fingers were already skirting Dr. Levine's emergency speed dial when my manservant, Timofey, ran up to us in great haste, choking on his own sour breath. "Ai, *batyushka*," my manservant said, pausing for air. "Forgive Timofey for the interruption, why don't you? For he is a sinner just like the rest of them. But sir, I must warn you! The police are on their way. I fear they are looking for you—"

I didn't quite catch his meaning until a baritone yelp from the neighboring Capricious Trout pontoon caught my attention. "Police!" a gentleman was braying. The young bank workers with their American MBAs, the old czarina in her black pearls and white gown, the Pushkin-loving *biznesman*—everyone was making for the complimentary valet parking where their Land Rovers were idling. Running past them were three wide gendarmes, their snazzy blue caps embossed with the scrawny two-headed Russian eagle, followed by their leader, an older man in civilian clothing, his hands in his pockets, taking his time.

It was apparent that the pigs were headed squarely for me. Alyosha-Bob moved in to protect me, placing his hands on my back and my belly as if I were in danger of capsizing. I decided to stand my ground. Such an outrage! In civilized countries like Canada, a well-heeled man and his fishing party are left in peace by the authorities, even if they have committed a crime. The old man in civvies, who I later learned had the tasty name of Belugin (just like the caviar), gently pushed aside my friend. He placed his snout within a centimeter of my own, so that I was looking into a grizzled old man's face, eyes yellow around the pupils, a face that in Russia bespeaks authority and incompetence both. He was staring at me with great emotion, as if he wanted my money. "Misha Vainberg?" he said.

"And what of it?" I said. The implication being: *Do you know who I am?*

"Your papa has just been murdered on the Palace Bridge," the policeman told me. "By a land mine. A German tourist filmed everything."

2

Dedications

First I would like to fall on my knees in front of the INS headquarters in Washington, D.C., to thank the organization for all its successful work on behalf of foreigners everywhere. I've been welcomed by INS representatives several times upon arrival at John F. Kennedy Airport, and each time was better than the last. Once a jolly man in a turban stamped my passport after saying something incomprehensible. Another time a pleasant black lady nearly as large as myself looked appreciatively at the outer tube of my stomach and gave me the thumbs-up. What can I say? The INS people are just and fair. They are the true gatekeepers of America.

My problems, however, rest with the U.S. State Department and the demented personnel at their St. Petersburg consulate. Since I returned to Russia some two years ago, they've denied my visa application *nine times,* on all occasions citing my father's recent murder of their precious Oklahoma businessman. Let me be frank: I feel sorry for the Oklahoman and his rosy-cheeked family, sorry that he got in my papa's way, sorry that they found him at the entrance of the Dostoyevskaya metro station with a child's amazed expression on his face and a red gurgling upside-down exclamation mark on his forehead, but after hearing of his death *nine times,* I am reminded of the guttural old Russian saying: "To the *khui,* to the *khui;* he's dead, so he's dead."

This book, then, is my love letter to the generals in charge of the Immigration and Naturalization Service. A love letter as well as a plea: *Gentlemen, let me back in!* I am an American impounded in a

Russian's body. I have been educated at Accidental College, a venerable midwestern institution for young New York, Chicago, and San Francisco aristocrats where the virtues of democracy are often debated at teatime. I have lived in New York for eight years, and I have been an exemplary American, contributing to the economy by spending over US$2,000,000 on legally purchased goods and services, including the world's most expensive dog leash (I briefly owned two poodles). I have dated my Rouenna Sales—no, "dated" is the wrong term—I have *roused* her from the Bronx working-class nightmare of her youth and deposited her at Hunter College, where she is studying to become an executive secretary.

Now, I am certain that everyone at the Immigration and Naturalization Service is deeply familiar with Russian literature. As you read about my life and struggles in these pages, you will see certain similarities with Oblomov, the famously large gentleman who refuses to stir from his couch in the nineteenth-century novel of the same name. I won't try to sway you from this analogy (I haven't the energy, for one thing), but may I suggest another possibility: Prince Myshkin from Dostoyevsky's *The Idiot*. Like the prince, I am something of a holy fool. I am an innocent surrounded by schemers. I am a puppy deposited in a den of wolves (only the soft blue glint of my eyes keeps me from being torn to shreds). Like Prince Myshkin, I am not perfect. In the next 318 pages, you may occasionally see me boxing the ears of my manservant or drinking one Laphroaig too many. But you will also see me attempt to save an entire race from genocide; you will see me become a benefactor to St. Petersburg's miserable children; and you will watch me make love to fallen women with the childlike passion of the pure.

How did I become such a holy fool? The answer lies rooted in my first American experience.

Back in 1990, Beloved Papa decided that his only child should study to become a normal prosperous American at Accidental College, located deep in the country's interior and safe from the gay distractions of the eastern and western seaboards. Papa was merely *dabbling* in criminal oligarchy then—the circumstances were not yet right for the wholesale plunder of Russia—and yet he had made his first million off a Leningrad car dealership that sold many wretched things but thankfully no cars.

The two of us were living alone in a tight, humid apartment in Leningrad's southern suburbs—Mommy had died of cancer—and were staying mostly out of each other's way, because neither of us could understand what the other was becoming. One day I was masturbating fiercely on the sofa, my legs splayed apart so that I looked like an overweight flounder cut precisely down the middle, when Papa stumbled in from the winter cold, his dark bearded head bobbing above his silky new Western turtleneck, his hands shaking from the continual shock of handling so much green American money. "Put that thing away," he said, scowling at my *khui* with red-rimmed eyes. "Come to the kitchen. Let's talk man-to-man."

I hated the sound of "man-to-man," because it reminded me once more that Mommy was dead, and I had no one to wrap me up in a blanket at bedtime and tell me I was still a good son. I pocketed my *khui,* sadly letting go of the image that was driving me to pleasure (Olga Makarovna's enormous ass hanging over the wooden chair in front of me, our classroom rank with the farmer's-cheese smell of unattained sex and wet galoshes). I sat down across the kitchen table from my papa, sighing at the imposition, as would any teenager.

"Mishka," my papa said, "soon you'll be in America, studying interesting subjects, sleeping with the local Jewish girls, and enjoying the life of the young. And as for your papa . . . well, he'll be all alone here in Russia, with no one to care if he is dead or alive."

I nervously squeezed at my thick left breast, funneling it into a new oblong shape. I noticed a stray piece of salami peel on the table and wondered if I could eat it without Papa noticing. "It was your idea that I should go to Accidental College," I said. "I'm only doing as you say."

"I'm letting you go because I love you," said my father. "Because there's no future in this country for a little *popka* like you." He grabbed the floating dirigible of my right hand, my masturbatory hand, and held it tight between his two little ones. The broken capillaries of his cheek stood out beneath his graying stubble. He was crying silently. He was drunk.

I started crying, too. It had been six years since my father had told me he loved me or wanted to hold my hand. Six years since I had ceased being a pale little angel whom adults loved to tickle and school bullies loved to punch, and turned instead into a giant florid hymie with big, squishy hands and a rather mean-looking overbite. Almost twice the size of my father, I was, which stunned us both pretty hard. Maybe there was some kind of recessive Polish gene on my miniature mother's side. (Yasnawski was her maiden name, so *nu?*)

"I need you to do something for me, Mishka," Papa said, wiping his eyes.

I sighed again, slipping the salami peel into my mouth with my free hand. I knew what was required of me. "Don't worry, Papa, I won't eat any more," I said, "and I'll do exercises with the big ball you bought for me. I'll be thin again, I swear. And once I get to Accidental, I'll study hard how to become an American."

"Idiot," Papa said, shaking his double-jointed nose at me. "You'll *never* be an American. You'll always be a Jew. How can you forget who you are? You haven't even left yet. Jew, Jew, Jew."

I had heard from a distant cousin in California that one could be both an American and a Jew and even a practicing homosexual in the bargain, but I didn't argue. "I'll try to be a rich Jew," I said. "Like a Spielberg or a Bronfman."

"That's fine," my papa said. "But there's another reason you're going to America." He produced a smudged piece of graph paper scribbled with outlandish English script. "Once you land in New York, go to this address. Some Hasids will meet you there, and they will circumcise you."

"Papa, no!" I cried, blinking rapidly, for already the pain was clouding my eyes, the pain of having the best part of me touched and handled and peeled like an orange. Since becoming gigantic, I had gotten used to a kind of physical inviolability. No longer did the classroom bullies bang my head against the board until I was covered with chalk as they shouted, "Dandruffy Yid!" (According to Russian mythology, Jews suffer from excessive flakiness.) No one dared touch me now. Or wanted to touch me, for that matter. "I'm eighteen years old," I said. "My *khui* will hurt terribly if they cut it now. And I like my foreskin. It flaps."

"Your mama wouldn't let you get circumcised when you were a little boy," Papa said. "She was afraid of how it would look to the district committee. 'Too Jewish,' they would say. 'Zionist behavior.' She was afraid of everyone except me, that woman. Always calling me 'shit eater' in public. Always hitting me over the head with that frying pan." He looked toward the cupboard where the dreaded frying pan once lived. "Well, now you're my responsibility, *popka*. And what I say, you will do. That's what it means to be a man. To listen to your father."

My hands were now shaking rhythmically along with Papa's, and we were both covered in sweat, steam rising in invisible white batches from our oily heads. I tried to focus on my father's love for me, and on my duty to him, but one question remained. "What's a Hasid?" I said.

"That's the best kind of Jew there is," Papa said. "All he does is learn and pray all day."

"Why don't you become a Hasid, then?" I asked him.

"I have to work hard now," Papa said. "The more money I make, the more I can be sure no one will ever hurt you. You're my whole life, you know? Without you, I would cut my throat from one ear to the other. And all I ask you to do, Mishka, is get snipped by these Hasids. Don't you want to please me? I loved you so much when you were small and thin . . ."

I recalled how my little body felt when encased in his, his wise brown eagle eyes eating me up, the worsted bristles of his mustache giving my cheeks a manly rash I would treasure for days. Some wags say that men spend their entire lives trying to return to their mother's womb, but I am not one of those men. The trickle of Papa's deep vodka breath against my neck, the hairy obstinate arms pressing me into his carpet-thick chest, the animal smells of survival and decay— *this* is my womb.

• • •

Several months later, I found myself in a livery cab, roaring through a terrifying Brooklyn neighborhood. In the Soviet Union, we were told that people of African descent—Negroes and Negresses, as we called them—were our brothers and sisters, but to the newly arriving Soviet Jews at the time, they were as frightening as armies of Cossacks billowing across the plains. I, however, fell in love with these colorful people at first blush. There was something blighted, equivocal, and downright Soviet about the sight of underemployed men and women arranged along endless stretches of broken porch-front and unmowed lawn—it seemed that, like my Soviet compatriots, they were making an entire lifestyle out of their defeat. The Oblomov inside me has always been fascinated by people who are just about ready to give up on life, and in 1990, Brooklyn was an Oblomovian paradise. Not to mention the fact that some of the young girls, already as tall and thick as baobab trees, their breasts perfectly shaped gourds that they regally carried down the street, were the most beautiful creatures I'd seen in my life.

Gradually, the African neighborhood gave way to a Spanish-speaking section, equally disheveled but pleasantly coated with the smell of roasted garlic, and that in turn gave way to a promised land of my Jewish co-religionists—men bustling around with entire squirrels' nests on their heads, side curls flapping in the early-summer wind, velvety coats that harbored a precious summer stink. I counted six tiny boys, probably between three and eight years of age, their blond untrimmed locks making them look like infant rock stars, running around a deeply tired penguin of a woman as she pattered down the street behind a scrim of grocery bags. *What the hell kind of Jewish woman has six children?* In Russia, you had one, two, maybe three if you didn't care for constant abortions and were very very promiscuous.

The cab stopped in front of an old but grand house whose bulk was noticeably sinking into its front columns the way an elderly fellow sinks into his walker. A pleasant young Hasid with an intelligent expression (I'm partial to anyone who looks half blind) welcomed me

in with a handshake and, upon ascertaining that I spoke neither Hebrew nor Yiddish, began to explain to me the concept of a *mitzvah,*
meaning "a good deed." Apparently I was about to perform a very
important *mitzvah.* "I sure hope so, mister," I said in my burgeoning
but imperfect English. "Because pain of dick-cutting must be intol-
erable."

"It's not so bad," my new friend said. "And you're so big, you
won't even notice it!" Upon seeing my still-frightened expression, he
said, "They'll put you under for the surgery, anyway."

"Under?" I said. "Under *where?* Oh, no, mister. I must go back to
my hotel room immediately."

"Come, come, come," said the Hasid, adjusting his thick glasses
with a worn-out index finger. "I've got something I know you're
going to like."

I followed him into the bowels of his house with my head hung
low. After the typical drabness of the one-room Soviet apartment
with the bulbous refrigerator shuddering in the corner like an ICBM
before launch, I found the Hasidic home to be a veritable explosion
of color and light, especially the framed plastic pictures of Jerusalem's
golden Dome of the Rock and the crushed blue pillows embroidered
with cooing doves. (Later, at Accidental College, I was taught to
look down on these things.) Everywhere there were books in Hebrew with beautiful golden spines, which I erroneously imagined to
be translations of Chekhov and Mandelstam. The smell of buckwheat
kasha and used underwear proved homey and inviting. As we progressed from the front of the house to the back, little boys ran between the tree stumps of my legs, and a young chesty woman with
her head wrapped in a handkerchief popped out of a bathroom. I
tried to shake her wet hand, but she ran away screaming. It was all
very interesting, and I almost forgot the painful reason behind my
visit.

Then I heard a low, guttural hum, like the sound of a hundred oc-
togenarians brooding at once. The hum gradually resolved itself into
a chorus of male voices singing what sounded like: "A *humus tov,* a
tsimmus tov, a *mazel tov,* a *tsimmus tov,* a *humus tov,* a *mazel tov,* a
humus tov, a *tsimmus tov,* hey hey, *Yisroel.*" Several terms I recog-

nized: *mazel tov* is a form of congratulation, *tsimmus* is a dish of sugary crushed carrots, and Yisroel is a small, heavily Jewish country on the Mediterranean coast. What all these words were doing together, I couldn't begin to fathom. (Later, in fact, I found out those weren't the words to the song at all.)

Ducking beneath a low frame, we entered the house's back annex, which was filled with young fedora-wearing men hoisting plastic cups along with slices of rye bread and pickles. I was speedily given one such cup, slapped on the back, told *mazel tov!,* then pointed toward an old bathtub reclining in the middle of the room on two sets of clawed feet. "What's this?" I asked my new friend in the thick glasses.

"A *tsimmus tov,* a *mazel tov,*" he sang, urging me forward.

Vodka does not have a smell, but it didn't take long for an eighteen-year-old Russian to register that the bathtub was indeed filled with that substance, along with floating bits of onion. "*Now* do you feel at home?" the happy Hasids shouted to me as I swigged from the plastic cup and chased the drink with a sour pickle. "A *tsimmus tov,* a *humus tov,*" they sang, the men branching their arms and kicking up their feet, their remarkably blue eyes drunkenly ablaze from behind their black getups.

"Your father told us you might need to drink some vodka before the *bris,*" the lead Hasid explained. "So we decided to have a party."

"Party? Where are the girls?" I asked. My first American joke.

The Hasids laughed nervously. "Here's to your *mitzvah!*" one of them shouted. "Today you will enter a covenant with *Hashem.*"

"What is that?" I asked.

"God," they whispered.

I drank several cups' worth, marveling at how the onion helped improve the mixture, and yet the idea of entering into a covenant with God did not go down as easily as the 80-proof swill. What did God have to do with it? I just wanted my father to love me. "Maybe you should take me to hotel, mister," I stammered. "I give you seventeen dollars in my pocket. Please tell my papa I got cut already. He never look down there anymore, because now I am so fat."

The Hasids were not buying my suggestion. "You have to think of us, too," they chanted. "This is a *mitzvah* for us."

"You also getting dick cut?"

"We're redeeming the captive."

"Who is captive?"

"You're a captive of the Soviet Union. We are making a Jew out of you." And with that, they helped me to several more oniony vodkas until the room fairly blared at me with its twirling diorama of top hats and flying sweat.

"To the *mitzvah* mobile!" the youngest shouted in unison, and soon I was enveloped in a dozen velvety coats, snug within the outer layers of my own race, while gently herded out into the Hasidic summer night, where even the yellow-faced moon wore side curls and crickets sang in the deep melodious language of our ancestors.

I was laid out sideways on a soft American van seat, several young men still plying me with vodkas that I dutifully drank, because for a Russian it is impolite to refuse. "Are we driving back to the hotel, mister?" I said as the van careened madly through the populated streets.

"A *humus tov*, a *mazel tov*," my companions sang to me.

"You want to redeem the captive!" I struggled in English, through my tears. "Look at me! I am captive! By you!"

"So now you will be redeemed!" the logic followed, a cup of vodka tipped into my face.

Eventually I was deposited into the overlit waiting room of a poor municipal hospital where Spanish babies cried for milk while my companions pressed themselves against an ad hoc wailing wall, their pale faces red with prayer. "Your father will be so proud," someone whispered into my ear. "Look what a brave man you are!"

"Eighteen is too old for cutting the dick," I whispered back. "Everybody knows this."

"Abraham was ninety-nine when he performed the *bris* with his own hands!"

"But he was biblical hero."

"And so are you! From now on, your Hebrew name will be Moshe, which means Moses."

"I am called Misha. That is the Russian name my beautiful mother call me."

"But you *are* like Moses, because you're helping lead the Soviet Jews out of Egypt." I could almost smell the plastic of the cup pressed to my lips. I drank like the teenage alcoholic I had already become. A piece of rye bread was presented to me, but I spat on it. Then I was on top of a rolling bed wearing a kind of backward dress; then the rolling bed stopped; green smocks billowed all around me; my pants were being roughly lowered by a pair of cold hands. "Papa, make them stop!" I cried in Russian.

A mask was clasped over my face. "Count backward, Moses," an American voice told me.

"Nyet!" I tried to say, but of course no one could hear me. The world broke in pieces and failed to reassemble. When I woke up, the men in black hats were praying over me, and I could feel nothing below the carefully tucked folds of flesh that formed my waistline. I raised my head. I was dressed in a green hospital gown, a round hole cut in its lower region, and there, between the soft pillows of my thighs, a *crushed purple bug* lay motionless, its chitinous shell oozing fluids, the skin-rendering pain of its demise held at bay by anesthesia.

For some reason, my co-religionists thought that my vomiting was a sign of recovery, and they wiped my chin and laughed and said *mazel tov* and *tsimmus tov* and *hey, hey, Yisroel.*

The infection set in that night.

3

Who Killed Beloved Papa?

Who did it? Who murdered the 1,238th-richest man in Russia? Whose hands are stained with a martyr's blood? I'll tell you who: Oleg the Moose and his syphilitic cousin Zhora. How do we know? Because the entire episode was videotaped by Andi Schmid, a nineteen-year-old tourist from Stuttgart, Germany.

On the night in question, Herr Schmid happened to be steaming alongside St. Petersburg's Palace Bridge on a pleasure boat, enjoying the synthetic drug MDMA and tinny house music from the boat's speakers while videotaping a Russian seagull as it attacked an English teenager, a big-eared kipper of a boy, and his pale, lovely mama.

"I have never seen such an angry seagull before," Herr Schmid told me and the police inspectors the next day, resplendent before us in his fuzzy steel-wool pants and PHUCK STUTTGART T-shirt, his boxy Selima Optique glasses casting a penumbra of intelligence around his dull young eyes. "It just kept *biting* the poor kid," Schmid complained. "In Germany the birds are much friendlier."

On Schmid's tape, we see the snow-white seagull snapping its bloody beak as it ascends for another attack on the British family, the Britishers pleading to the gull for mercy, the ship's crew pointing and laughing at the foreigners . . . Now we see the colossal stone piers of the Palace Bridge, followed by its cast-iron lampposts. (Once, in the eighties, during that nice Gorbachev perestroika time, Papa and I went fishing off the Palace Bridge. We caught a perch that looked just like Papa. In five years, when my eyes completely glaze over with Russian life, I will resemble it, too.)

Next Schmid pans 360 degrees to reveal St. Petersburg on a warm summer night, the sky lit up a false cerulean, the thick walls of the Peter and Paul Fortress bathed in gold floodlights, the Winter Palace moored on its embankment like a ship gently undulating in the perpetual twilight, the darkened hulk of St. Isaac's dome officiating over the proceedings . . . Ah! What did Mandelstam write? "Leninsburg! I don't want to die yet!"

And now, as the seagull embarks upon its predatory swoop, making some sort of Slavic bird squawk, we see a Mercedes 300 M-Class jeep—the one that looks like a futuristic, rounded version of the Soviet militia jeeps that used to haul Papa away to the drunk tank— cross the bridge, followed by one of those antic, armor-plated Volga sedans that remind me, for some reason, of the American armadillo. If you look closer, you can almost see Papa's yellow pumpkin head inside the Volga, a squiggle of gray hair forming a childish signature above his otherwise bald pate . . . Oh, my papa, my dead, murdered *papochka*, my mentor, my keeper, my boyhood friend. Remember, Papa, how we used to trap the neighbor's anti-Semitic dog in a milk crate and take turns peeing on it? If only I could believe that you're in a better place now, that "other world" you kept rambling about whenever you woke up at the kitchen table, your elbows swimming in herring juice, but clearly nothing of us survives after death, there's no *other world* except for New York, and the Americans won't give me a visa, Papa. I'm stuck in this horrible country because you killed a businessman from Oklahoma, and all I can do is remember how you once were; to commemorate the life of a near-saint, this is the burden of your only child.

All right, back to the videotape. Here comes the second Mercedes jeep, the last vehicle in Papa's convoy, rumbling over the Palace Bridge, and now we see a motorcycle with two riders passing the jeep, the doughy form of syphilitic Zhora (may he die from his syphilis just like Lenin!) visible behind Oleg the Moose's distinctive fifties pompadour . . . The motorcycle zooms by the Volga, and the land mine, or at least a dark cylinder that must be a land mine—I mean, has anyone actually *seen* a land mine? Ours is not the kind of family that gets sent to fight in Chechnya with the blue-eyed kids—

the land mine is thrown onto the Volga's roof, five more frames, and then *a flash of electric lightning* draws the seagull's attention away from the cowering English folk, and the roof of the Volga is lifted off (along with, we later learn, Papa's head), followed by a plume of cheap smoke . . . *Ba-ba-boom.*

And that, in so many words, is how I became an orphan. May I be comforted among the mourners of Zion and Jerusalem. Amen.

4

Rouenna

When I graduated from Accidental College with all the honors they could bestow on a fat Russian Jew, I decided that, like many young people, I should move to Manhattan. American education aside, I was still a Soviet citizen at heart, afflicted with a kind of Stalinist gigantamania, so that when I looked at the topography of Manhattan, I naturally settled my gaze on the Twin Towers of the World Trade Center, those emblematic honeycombed 110-story giants that glowed white gold in the afternoon sun. They looked to me like the promise of socialist realism fulfilled, boyhood science fiction extended into near-infinity. You could say I was in love with them.

As I soon found out that I couldn't rent an apartment in the actual World Trade Center, I decided to settle for an entire floor in a nearby turn-of-the-century skyscraper. My loft had a startling view of Miss Liberty greening the harbor on one side and the World Trade Center obliterating the rest of the skyline on another. I spent my evenings hopping from one end of my lily pad to the other: as the sun fell on top of the statue, the Twin Towers became a fascinating checkerboard of lit and unlit windows, looking, after several puffs of marijuana, like a Mondrian painting come to life. To complement my sleek art deco apartment, I got an internship at a nearby art foundation run out of a certain munificent bank. The whole thing was set up through the career office at Accidental College, which specialized in finding socially uplifting and highly unpaid internships for young gentlemen and ladies. And so every morning, around ten, my morning gown bedecked with glistening medals from the Accidental College Department of Multicultural Studies (my academic major), I would roll over three blocks to the bank's filigreed skyscraper and perform my filing duties for a few hours.

My colleagues regarded me as something of an oddity, but nothing compared to the young man who dressed up as a hamster during lunch and wept violently in the bathroom for exactly one hour and fifteen minutes (a fellow alumnus of Accidental, needless to say). Whenever the wisdom of having a sleepy Russian Gargantua clattering around the already tight quarters came up, I merely had to say something like "Malevich!" or "Tarkofsky!," letting the reflected sheen of my countrymen's accomplishments glisten off my Multicultural Studies medals.

Eventually the hamster got fired.

Life for young American college graduates is a festive affair. Free of having to support their families, they mostly have gay parties on rooftops where they reflect at length upon their quirky electronic childhoods and sometimes kiss each other on the lips and neck. My own life was similarly sweet and free of complexities, with only one need unaccounted for: I had no girlfriend, no buxom hardworking ethnic girl to urge me off the couch, no exotic Polynesian to fill my monochrome life with her browns and yellows. So every weekend night I would trudge up to these rooftops where Accidental College graduates would huddle together next to groups of students from similar colleges, their conversations forming barbed networks of privileged fact and speculation stretching from the Napa Valley to Gstaad. I basked in this information, making witty observations and absurdist jokes, but my real purpose was more traditional: I was looking for a woman who would accept me for what I was, for every last pound of me, and for the crushed purple insect between my legs.

There weren't any takers, but I was beloved in my own way. "Snack Daddy!" the boys and girls would shout as I ascended the narrow stairways to their rooftops. Back then the girls drank buckets of bitter champagne through straws, and the boys swilled forty-ounce containers of malt liquor, wiping their mouths with the back of their skinny ties. We were trying to be as "urban" as possible without passing into caricature, our eyes briefly skirting the darkened constellations of housing projects pressed menacingly against the distant horizons. I would stand to the side of the snack table, letting my fat settle around me in protective layers as I jabbed a long carrot into a bowl of spinach feta dip. The girls regarded me as a safe confidant, as if my weight had rendered me a beloved uncle. They hoisted buckets of champagne to my lips while complaining of their passing boyfriends, those diffident young *schlemiels* who were also my close friends but whom I would readily betray for just one occidental kiss tasting of spinach and feta.

Filled with champagne, I would return alone to my endless Wall Street loft, take off my clothes, and press myself against the windows, letting the city lights flicker deep inside me. On occasion I would wail this deep-sea arctic wail invented specifically for my exile. I cupped what remained of my *khui* and cried for my papa five thousand miles to the east and north. How could I have abandoned the only person who had ever truly loved me? The Neva River sprang, unprompted, from the Gulf of Finland, the Nile from its Delta, the Hudson from some prosperous American source, and I sprang from my father.

Feeling lonely, I would talk out loud to the Twin Towers of the World Trade Center, which I had nicknamed Lionya and Gavril, begging those two iconic hulks to make me more like them: lean, glassy-eyed, silent, and invincible. Sometimes, when a helicopter passed overhead, I would get on my knees and beg to be rescued—to be hoisted beyond the party-filled rooftops and billowing deck umbrellas onto a secret landscape, an inverted New York whose buildings were dug deep into the ground, the water towers and mansard roofs striking through the center of the earth, much as I wished to strike between the sweaty thighs of my former classmates—those infinitely clever and unflappable girls carved out of soft Californian rock and Roman tufa who breathed more inspiration into my life than all the pale Marxian offerings of the Accidental College Library combined.

And then one day I got lucky. Here's how it happened. During my lunch break, I often liked to take a couple of chicken parmigiana sandwiches and a gallon of caramel fudge into a bar on Nassau Street, which, for those unfamiliar with this part of Manhattan, runs parallel to Lower Broadway into an uncharted fourth dimension, one part Melville, two parts Céline. There, I would round out my meal with a few vodka shots while talking to my lunchtime friend, a spindly middle-aged Jewish stockbroker from Long Island who had long given up on ever encountering human warmth or arousing the love of a woman. His name was Max, of course.

This bar had something of a gimmick, and an effective one at that—its barmaids wore nothing but bikinis. If you bought yourself a specially priced tequila, they would pour lime juice into their considerable cleavage, sprinkle some salt on top of that, and invite you to lick up this mess (after which you downed your shot). Today the "body shot" is an integral part of American courtship, but back then it seemed to me and Max like the height of depravity.

One afternoon we were making merry along with some other Wall Street miscreants, urging two blond barmaids to kiss each other, which they sometimes did for a big tip, when a new staff member came along dragging an artificial palm tree behind her (the theme was tropical). I caught her attention at once. "Holy fucking shit!" she said, dropping the palm and making a cute motion as if rubbing her eyes. "Whoa, daddy!"

"Be nice to Misha," one of the barmaids growled at her.

"Yeah, that's the first rule of the house," another snickered. I was known as a very generous tipper and would occasionally spring for an abortion. Although all the barmaids were from the Bronx, and uneducated, they treated me as something of an innocent child, as opposed to the rooftop girls from Accidental College, who deferred to me as a wise old European. My point is that poor people often have a wisdom and cunning all their own.

"Chill out, bitches," the newcomer said to her colleagues as she slipped out of her jeans to reveal her tightly sheathed mons, packed like a six-shooter in a holster. "I like this guy."

"I think she likes you," Max whispered into my ear, pinpricks of his spit gently tickling my face. He put his palms on the bar and dropped his head into them. He often ended his lunch hour feeling unwell.

"Hi," I said to the young woman.

"Hi yahself, jumbo," she said. "You like these?" She lifted up her breasts with her thumbs, after which they somehow managed to rise on their own, like shy animals peeking out from behind a hedge. "These make you sweat, mister?"

"Very much," I said. "But I've got pretty nice ones myself, miss." I cupped my beauties and rubbed my nipples hard. The other barmaids laughed, as usual. "Get Misha behind the bar!" one of them shouted.

"Dang, mister, you funny!" the new barmaid said. She reached behind me and pulled down on my hair. "But when I'm behind the bar, boy-o, you keep your eyes on *my* titties. I don't need no competition."

"Ouch," I said. She was hurting me. "I was only joking."

She stopped pulling my hair but continued to hold on to it, her palm stroking the preliminary fold of my neck. Her breath was awful— sour milk, rubbing alcohol, cigarettes, post-industrial rot. But she was beautiful in an impoverished kind of way. She reminded me of a lovely olive-colored mannequin I had seen in a store vitrine. The way that mannequin was casually bent over a billiard table, cue in hand, suggested she knew a lot more about the sex act than any woman in Leningrad, even the trollops at the Red October Hotel. My new friend, likewise, looked like she was privy to all kinds of information. She had a large, pretty face set off by small brown mestizo eyes, her pallor a bit gray from sun and vitamin deficiency, and a globe of a belly that looked half pregnant (with processed foods, not with child) in an arousing way. Her breasts were ponderous. "You Jewish?" she asked me.

Max woke up immediately upon hearing "Jewish." "What? What?" he said. "Whad'you say?"

"Yes, I am a secular Jew," I said proudly.

"Knew it," the girl said. "Totally a Jewish face."

"Wait a minute, wait a minute . . ." Max mumbled.

"Look at your pretty face," the girl continued. "I love your little blue eyes, mister, and your big fat smile—oh, *dip!* If you lost some weight, you could be one of those fat movie stars." She brought her hand around to touch my chin, and I bent down to kiss it, in contravention of the bar's unspoken laws.

"My name is Misha," I said.

"Desiree's my bar name," she said, "but I'll tell you my real name." She bent forward, her fast-food breath jolting me out of my antiseptic Accidental College existence and into the world of the living. "It's Rouenna."

"Hi, Rouenna," I said.

She slapped me across the face. "At the bar you call me Desiree," she hissed.

"I'm sorry, Desiree," I said. I did not notice the pain, so taken was I by the prospect of knowing her real name. At that point a customer called her away to lick up salt and lime juice from her cleavage. I have not kept the image of how he squished his acne-covered nose in between her breasts, nor the slurping sounds he made, but I do remember how dignified she looked when she straightened up and wiped the resulting mess with a moist towelette.

"You Jewish boys need a little Manischewitz in between these?" she shouted to me and Max.

"Wait a minute, wait a minute," Max said.

"Oh, relax, pal," Rouenna told Max. "I've been to, like, fifteen bar mitzvahs."

"You're Jewish?" Max said.

"Nah," Rouenna said. "But I've got friends."

"What are you, then?" Max demanded.

"Half Puerto Rican. And half German. And half Mexican and Irish. But I was raised mostly Dominican."

"Catholic, then," said Max, satisfied she wasn't Jewish.

"We *was* Catholic, but then these Methodists came around and gave us food. So we were like—okay, we're Methodists now."

That theological discussion almost made me cry. In fact, I was crying quite readily and happily at that point, my tears dropping with fat thuds on my crotch, where the crushed purple insect was registering its presence. Half Puerto Rican. And half German. And half Mexican and Irish and everything else besides.

• • •

After her shift was over, I took her down the street to visit my outsize loft and, in ridiculous Russian fashion, immediately told her that I loved her.

I don't think she heard me, but she was impressed by my lifestyle.

"Dang, jumbo," Rouenna said, her husky voice bouncing off the hangar-sized living space. "I think I finally made it." She looked around my small collection of artworks. "Why you got all these giant dicks around the house?"

"Those sculptures? Oh, I guess they're all part of a Brancusian motif."

"You a fudge-packer?"

"A what? Oh, no. Although homosexuals do number among my friends."

"What did you just say?"

"Homosexuals—"

"Jesus Christ, man. Who *are* you?" She laughed and punched me full-on in the gut. "Just kidding," she said. "I'm playing hard to get with you, is all."

"Keep playing," I said, smiling and rubbing my stomach. "I like to play."

"Where ya sleep, jumbo? You mind if I keep calling you that?"

"At college they called me Snack Daddy. Here are stairs that go up to my bed."

My bed was a kind of muscular Swedish plank that grudgingly accommodated my bulk à la carte but grunted pathetically when both Rouenna and I tumbled upon it. I wanted to explain to her yet again, though this time in detail, that I loved her, but she was immediately kissing me on the mouth and rubbing my breasts and bellies with both hands. She unbuckled my pants, letting out a gust of stale trapped air. She drew back and looked at me sadly. *Oh, no,* I thought. But all she said was "You sweet."

"I am?" I lay down on the bed completely. I was sweating and jiggling obscenely.

"A heartbreaker," she said.

"No, I'm not," I said. "I've never even really been with a girl before. At college I only got a few hand jobs. And I'm twenty-five, almost."

"You a nice, nice man, that's what you are. You treat me like a queen. I'm gonna be your queen, that all right, Snack Daddy?"

"Uh-huh."

"Show me what you got for mommy." She started to pull hard on the billowing square sail I used as underwear.

"No, please," I said, holding on to my goods with both hands. "I have a problem."

"Your boy too big for me?" Rouenna asked. "It's never too big for mommy." I tried to explain to her about the zealous Hasids and their low-paid proxies at the public hospital, the butchers of Crown Heights. Tell me, please, who in their right mind circumcises a fat eighteen-year-old man-child in an operating room reeking of mildew and fried rice?

I fought with all my mass, but Rouenna overpowered me. My underwear ripped in two. The crushed purple insect shyly drew its head back into its neck.

It would seem to the untrained eye that the *khui*'s knob had been unscrewed from its proper position and then screwed back into place by incompetents so that now it listed at an angle of about thirty degrees to the right, while the knob and the *khui* proper were apparently held in place by nothing more than patches of skin and thread. Purple and red scars had created an entire system of mountain-ridge highways running from the scrotum to the tip, while the bottom had been so eviscerated by post-op infection that instead of being smooth, taut skin, it looked like a series of empty garbage bags fluttering in the wind. I suppose the crushed-insect comparison had worked best when my *khui* was still covered with blood on the operating table. Now my genitalia looked more like an abused iguana.

Rouenna bent forward with the globe of her stomach and rubbed my *khui* with that soft surface. I thought maybe that was the only way she was capable of touching it, but I was wrong. She bent down with her open mouth and breathed on it for a while. My *khui* straightened out and crept toward her waiting orifice. *Stop it!* I told myself. *You're a disgusting creature. You don't deserve this.*

But Rouenna didn't put my *khui* in her mouth. She turned it over, found the most hideous spot on its underbelly—a vivid evocation of the bombing of Dresden—and, for the next 389 seconds (a handy clock helped me count), imparted upon it a single, silent kiss.

My gaze traveled beyond the dark mound of her hair, past the Brancusian dicks lining the walls of my loft, and right out my double-pane windows.

I floated above the city, glancing generously in each direction. The careless hooks and crags of Queens and Brooklyn, slivers of industry, quadrangles of brown-bricked terraced flats; the fanatic middle-class hopes of already half-darkened New Jersey tendering their resignation for the night; the carpeted grid of Manhattan sinking into the flat horizon, the garlands of yellow light—sharp, overreaching—that form the facades of skyscrapers, the garlands of yellow light—diffuse, flickering—that form the sprawl of tenements, the garlands of yellow light—swerving, opportunistic—that form the headlights of taxi caravans: the garlands of yellow light, aye, in their horizontal and vertical arrangements that form a final resting place for the collected hopes of our civilization.

And to my father, I say: *I'm sorry, but this floating feeling, this yellow city at my feet, those full lips around what's left of me, this is my happiness, Papa. This is* my *pierogi.*

And to the generals in charge of the Immigration and Naturalization Service who have been patiently reading this tale of the Bronx mixed-race girl and the overweight Russian, I ask: *In what other country could we have found succor together? In what other country could we have even existed?*

And after getting down on my knobby knees, I say to the INS generals: *Please, sirs.*

I say to them like a child: *Please, please, please . . .*

5

Among the Merry Mourners

On the way home from the Russian Fisherman, my heart broken with news of Papa's death, I squeezed in on the Rover's back bench with Alyosha-Bob and wept into his neck, wiping my nose against his Accidental College sweatshirt. He draped both arms around my head and tickled the willowy hair around my bald spot. From afar it may have looked like an anaconda strangling a rodent, but it was really just my love spilling out over a dear friend. There was even something compassionate about Alyosha's smell that evening—greasy summer sweat, the sharp pungency of fish highlighted by alcohol—and I found myself wanting to kiss his ugly lips. "*Nu, ladno, nu, ladno,*" he kept saying, which could be translated as "It's going to be okay" or "So there it is" or, if you're a less charitable translator, "Enough already."

To be honest, I wept not for my father but for the children. On the way home, we passed by a corner of Bolshoi Prospekt, where last winter I'd had a little breakdown for the stupidest of reasons. I had seen a dozen kindergarten pupils trying to cross the boulevard, each bundled in a jaunty collection of misshapen coats, their *shapkas* falling off their tiny heads, their feet encased in monstrous hand-me-down galoshes. A boy and a girl, one at the front and one in the back, held aloft giant red flags to warn motorists that they were deigning to cross. A young, pretty teacher was on hand to help them ambulate in the right direction. Who knows why—primordial memory, a sudden reprise of my stunted conscience, a big man's evolutionary compassion for anything small—but I wept for the children that day.

Diminutive, cherubic, Slavic, they stood by the teeming Bolshoi Prospekt with those idiotic red flags, their puffy faces producing small steam clouds that looked like little child-thoughts struggling in the monumental cold. The cars kept passing them, the rich man's Audi and the poor man's Lada. No one would pause to let them past. As we waited for the light to change, I opened my window and leaned out, blinking like a great Northern turtle in the chill, trying to read their faces. Were those smiles I saw? Delicate new teeth, wisps of blond hair peering out from the fortress of their hats, and grateful, unmistakable grins accompanied by disciplined Petersburg children's laughter. Only the schoolteacher—silent, straight, proud in the way only a Russian woman who makes US$30 a month could be—seemed cognizant of the collective future that awaited her charges. The light changed, my driver, Mamudov, zoomed ahead with his typical Chechen ferocity, and I looked back at the children, catching the boy with the red flag taking his first careful step onto Bolshoi Prospekt, waving his banner with gusto, as if this were 1971, not 2001, and the flag he held were still the emblem of a superpower. I asked myself, *If I were to give each of them US$100,000, would their lives change? Would they learn to become human beings upon completing their adolescence? Would the virus of our history be kept at bay by a cocktail of dollar-denominated humanism? Would they become, in a sense, Misha's Children?* But even with my largesse, I could see nothing positive befalling them. A temporary respite from alcoholism, harlotry, heart disease, and depression. Misha's Children? Forget it. It would make more sense to have sex with their teacher and then buy her a refrigerator.

And that, to tell you the truth, is why I cried on the drive back from the Fisherman. I cried for the children of some Kindergarten No. 567, and for my own impotence and collusion in everything around me. Eventually, I promised myself, I would cry for dead Papa, too.

After we finally made it home, I started popping Ativans, three milligrams at a time, and chasing them with Johnnie Walker Black. It was a good idea. The two substances worked to bolster each other—

the anti-anxiety meds made me drunker, and the Black robbed me of panic. Actually, what happened was: I fell asleep.

When I woke up, I was lying on top of Rouenna, the only girl I knew who was big enough to absorb my weight. She was snoring peacefully, I could feel her massive vagina rubbing against my tummy. Alyosha-Bob came into the bedroom, trailing the sound of laughter and television from the downstairs parlor.

"Hey, Snack," Alyosha-Bob said. "Microphone check, big buddy." He looked warmly at my naked Rouenna passed out on the bed, or rather, the couch. My favorite room was designed to resemble the office of my New York analyst, Dr. Levine, with two black leather Barcelona chairs facing a matching Mies van der Rohe daybed, the kind I used to lie on five times a week until my fat was branded by its indentations. I managed to find replicas of the colorful Sioux tepee photographs Dr. Levine had hung on his walls, although a copy of the drawing resplendent above his couch—a West African stab at the *Pietà*—has so far proved elusive.

Alyosha-Bob patted my pretty curls. "Captain Belugin wants to talk to you, homey," he said. "Come down to breakfast."

Breakfast? Morning already? The sky out the window was yellow with cheap exhaust and nearby peat fires. It made me hungry for eggs sunny side up served in a Brooklyn diner. I didn't say anything. I imagined I was a hospital patient, and draped myself over my friend. I let Alyosha-Bob lead me into the downstairs parlor, past the six empty upstairs bedrooms with their endless tin-pressed ceilings and salmon-colored walls, past the winding wrought-iron staircase embellished with serpents and apples, which I had recently installed in some bizarre biblical gesture.

Wasn't there a mourning period for dead parents among the Judeans? I distinctly recall Papa made me sit on a box for a week when my mother died, then we covered up every mirror in the apartment. This was according to custom, I suppose, but mostly we were trying to avoid looking at our own fat, teary *punims*. Finally we sold the mirrors, along with my mother's American sewing machine and her two German bras. I can still recall shaky-handed Papa standing in the courtyard of our building, holding aloft the white bra, then the pink one, as the women of our building stepped up to inspect the goods. The Yeltsin era was still ten years away, but already Papa was angling to become an oligarch.

Downstairs, my parlor was lousy with Russians. I suppose that's what you get for living in Russia. My manservant, Timofey, and the junior policemen were making venison pie in the kitchen, singing army songs from their stints in Afghanistan, and propositioning my fat cook, Yevgenia. Andi Schmid, the German boy who had caught my father's last moments, was videotaping himself crawling around the parquet floor, howling fanatically at Lyuba Vainberg's stupid terrier. The widow herself was, by all accounts, still passed out in the downstairs guest room, pumped full of Halcion and our German guest's synthetic drug MDMA.

My appearance stirred no one. The dead man's son might as well have been dead, too. The television was blaring the morning news program, the Minister of Atomic Energy telling his favorite Chernobyl joke, the one about the balding porcupine. Only Captain Belugin got up to shake my hand. "My heart is filled with sorrow," he said. "Your father was a great man."

"He's dead, so he's dead!" one of the policemen yelled from the kitchen.

"Shut your mouth, Nika, or I'll fix you one in the mug!" Belugin shouted. "Forgive Nika," he said to me. "My boys are soccer hooligans in uniform, nothing more." He bowed a little, both hands on his heart. Belugin's manner reminded me of one of Gogol's crafty peasants, the kind of fellow who knew when to flatter his master but also when to copy the ways of educated folk. A far cry from my manservant, Timofey, who thought he was clever if he made off with a block of Dutch cheese or a T-shirt he could pounce at with the Daewoo steam iron I gave him for New Year's.

"Who can forget," said Captain Belugin, "when your dear papa killed that stupid American. Oh, if only we could kill all of them! Now, Germans I like. They're much more civilized. Look at that nice young Andi pretending he's a dog. Keep it up, sonny! What does the doggie say? *Gav, gav!*, he says."

"I'm sorry for interrupting," Alyosha-Bob said. "But why are you here, Captain Belugin? Why don't you leave Misha to his mourning?"

"I am here to settle some business," the captain said. "I am here to talk about the terrible crime that has shaken our world. I am pleased to announce that we have solved the mystery of your father's death, Misha. Your father was killed by Oleg the Moose and his syphilitic cousin Zhora."

"Ah!" I cried, but it was no surprise. Oleg the Moose and my papa were once friends and confederates. They had opened a graveyard for New Russian Jews, famous for its designer tombstones that featured the latest S-model Mercedes superimposed over a kind of ballistic menorah. As a follow-up, they were going to build a chain of American hero-sandwich shops on Nevsky Prospekt. The interiors of several landmark nineteenth-century palaces had been completely wiped out and festooned with inflatable fries and man-sized Pepsi bottles. But then, just at the stage when each investor could smell the sweaty odor of roast beef bathed in oil and vinegar, Papa and the Moose, goaded by their various relations and bookkeepers, went on the path of war.

It was time to say something heartfelt. "The evildoers must be punished," I said quietly and raised a big, squishy fist.

"That's one way to look at it," Captain Belugin said. "Here's another way. Oleg the Moose is a childhood friend of the governor of St. Petersburg. They went to chess academy together. They own adjoining property on Lake Como. Their wives go to the same pedicurist, and their children to the same Swiss boarding school. The Moose will never be prosecuted."

"But there's a tape of him murdering Misha's father," Alyosha-Bob said.

"The tape can disappear," said Captain Belugin, drawing a rectangular outline of the videotape with his index fingers, then making a fluttering motion with his hands.

"What about the German with the camera?" Alyosha-Bob said, pointing to the filmmaker Andi Schmid, who had taken off his PHUCK STUTTGART T-shirt and was thoroughly examining his own nipples. "He's a witness."

"The German can disappear," Captain Belugin said. He drew a slender Teutonic outline with his index fingers and made the fluttering motion again.

"That's ridiculous," Alyosha-Bob said. "You can't just disappear an entire German."

"There are eighty million of them, and they all look fairly alike."

We were pressed into a brief silence by the last remark. "Maybe I should refer this matter to a lawyer," I said at last.

"A *lawyer*!" Captain Belugin laughed. "Where do you think we are, dear boy? Stuttgart? New York? Your father is dead. This is sad for you. But maybe not entirely sad. Everyone knows you don't want your father's business. You're a sophisticate and a melancholic. So here's what we do. We broker a deal with Oleg the Moose. He takes over all of your father's assets for a fair-market value of twenty-five million dollars, plus another three million for killing your papa. Twenty-eight million overall. You and Oleg shake hands. No more blood."

Alyosha-Bob stared into the captain's eyes with an American disgust that I hadn't seen in years. He spat into his own hand in emulation of our lower classes. "How much is Oleg the Moose paying you?" he demanded. "And who approved Boris Vainberg's murder? You or the governor?"

"My commission is fifteen percent," Captain Belugin said, shrugging. "That's the standard commission around the world. As for the second question, why talk about ugly things that will only spoil our friendship?"

Timofey emerged from the kitchen with a plate of mushroom *pelmeni*. I knew Tima was just trying to soothe my nerves with food, but I had no appetite and so, languidly, threw a shoe at my manservant. As the shoe knocked his temple, I saw a clear picture of my death (heart attack, naturally) at age forty-one on a high-speed train approaching Paris, an elegant Euro woman frantically dialing her mobile phone, the remains of a half-eaten train meal lumped on my crotch. Oh, dear me. Oh, dear bear cub. I did not want to die! But what could I do?

"I feel bad for the world around me," I whispered. "Maybe I can start a program for kindergarten children with some of that twenty-eight million. We can call it Misha's Children."

For the first time since I had met him, Captain Belugin surveyed me with genuine pity. He turned to Alyosha-Bob, who was sweating quietly, his bald head glistening, his eyes blinking out a semaphore of useless rage. "Don't worry yourself with ideas," Belugin said to him. "There's no one to turn to. There's only one power structure in Petersburg. Boris Vainberg was a part of it. Then one day, by his own choosing, he was not. The consequences were predictable."

"Go to sleep, Snack Daddy," Alyosha-Bob said to me. "I will talk with the captain some more."

I did as I was told. Back in my bedroom, I hooked my face into Rouenna's fragrant armpit. Half asleep, she leveraged a fatty cut of my shoulder until she was in position to drool on my arm. I kissed her glossy nose with a mad urgency, like a bird plucking worms for her chicks. "Sweeeeeeet," Rouenna exhaled between two complicated snores.

"Love you," I whispered in English.

Meanwhile, on the walnut-trimmed Eames lounge chair where Dr. Levine used to loom behind me on Park Avenue, my manservant had placed my childhood Cheburaskha doll. Cheburashka, a star of Soviet children's television, a cuddly asexual brown creature with his dreams of joining the Young Pioneers and building a House of Friendship for all the lonely animals in town, analyzed me with his enormous liquid eyes. His even larger ears flapped in the summer wind, straining to pick up my lament.

In a week Rouenna would be leaving me to resume her summer studies at New York's Hunter College. And I would be left with nothing.

6

Beloved Papa Is Lowered into the Ground

I don't remember much from the funeral. A lot of Jews came, that's for sure. One of the big *kibbutzniks* from the main synagogue on Lermontov Street told me it was Papa's most fervent wish that I marry a Jewess. He pointed one out to me—tall and skinny, with long wet eyes and a luscious full-lipped mouth—standing by the open grave with a bunch of gardenias pressed to her chest. She was the kind of Russian Jewess who could be sad all year round, who could tell you a thousand different ways in which life was a serious business. "She's looking good," I concurred, "but right now I have my American friend." I bent my head toward Rouenna's shoulder. She had dressed up in her mourning miniskirt, which highlighted her hips and ass, reminding us all of how we came into being. She reached up to fix my blue *blin* of a yarmulke, a likeness of the synagogue's Moorish facade engraved on the back. Papa's favorite.

"When you're ready to be with a real woman, call me at the *shul*," said the Jew. "There's no reason to be all alone in the world."

"Well, I'm not all alone," I said. I put my arm around Rouenna and pressed her close, but he wasn't buying it.

"Act quickly, little son!" he said, apropos of the sad Jewess. "Her name is Sarah, and she has many suitors." He went over to Lyuba, my father's widow, and wiped her tiny nose for her.

Lyuba was a wreck, her usually demonstrative blond hair matted over her delicate skull, her black see-through blouse torn in the traditional Jewish sign of mourning (since when was *she* one of the tribe?), her arms thrown up to the heavens as if begging for the Lord to take her as well. She was howling about how "no one in the world [could] love her like [Beloved Papa]" and falling limp in the arms of fellow mourners.

Papa had wanted to be buried next to my mother, who was interred in an old graveyard in the wretched southeastern section of the city. The graveyard abutted a suburban station, rails littered with the morning's first half-conscious *alkashy,* each trying to suck the last drop out of yesterday's bottle of Golden Barrel beer, the platform stacked with two overturned cylindrical freight cars, one sporting the stenciled legend POLY, the other MERS.

The graves had been vandalized with cunning precision. Even the gold engraving was missing from my mother's tombstone. I could barely make out YULIA ISAKOVNA VAINBERG, 1939–1983, not to mention the golden harp that Papa had added, a reference, I suppose, to her being so cultured. (At least, unlike neighboring gravestones, hers hadn't been crowned with a swastika by the local hooligans.) Oh, my poor *mamochka.* The soft flesh behind her earlobe, perfect for hiding a child's warm nose. Gray sweater torn at the elbow, despite the rat-a-tat of her American sewing machine. Nineteen thirty-nine to 1983. From Stalin to Andropov. What a pathetic time to have been alive.

If only she could have seen me in New York. I would have made her proud. I'd have taken her to a simple clothing shop and bought her a middle-class sweater in some bright new color. That was part of my mother's beauty—she would have had no need for Botox or marabou-covered mules, not like all the visiting New Russian trash. See, when you're cultured, being middle class is enough.

Meanwhile, the haughty Northern sun had assumed its noontime perch and was doing its best to set our skullcaps ablaze. In Russia, even the sun has a distinctly anti-Semitic disposition. Gusts of wind smelling of something Soviet and unkind—polymers?—coated us with empty candy wrappers roused up from the garbage pit of a nearby housing complex, which was, like so many other things, partly collapsed and partly on fire. Gooey with chocolate and spit, the wrappers stuck to us like leeches, turning us into advertisements for such homegrown delicacies as SNEAKERS and TRI MUSHKETEERS.

It was a *shtetl* funeral, in many ways, a kind of impromptu klezmer act minus the musical instruments. Lots of wailing and feigned heart attacks, the pressing of young faces to old bosoms. "Comfort the child!" some putz was screaming in my direction. "The poor orphan! May God watch over him!"

"I'm fine!" I shouted back, waving weakly at the excited mourner, one of my idiot relatives, no doubt. They were all sticking their business cards into my pocket, in hopes of an eventual handout (Papa had left them nothing), and wondering why I was so estranged from the lot of them, why I wasn't friends with my harebrained cousins or slutty young nieces and predatory nephews, who spent their Friday nights tearing down Nevsky in their cheap Russian Niva jeeps, trying to pick up malnourished girls in tight synthetic duds or working-class boys with primitive greaser haircuts. The number of Vainbergs, young and old, still haunting the earth amazed me. During the thirties and forties, Stalin had killed half my family. Arguably the wrong half.

My manservant followed two steps behind me, carrying a leather pouch in which was interred a pair of pork-and-chicken roulettes from the famed Yeliseyev food shop, a bottle of Ativan, and a slug of Johnnie Walker Black, all in case I felt faint and started to teeter over. My only friends, Alyosha-Bob and Rouenna, huddled together in a corner, their relative Western beauty and steady demeanor giving them the air of American movie stars. I spent half the funeral walking toward them but was constantly waylaid by supplicants.

The aforementioned synagogue crew was on hand, old men with shaky hands, moist eyes, and big loose bellies—many mentions of Papa being the moral consciousness of our city by the Neva, a human pillar holding up the Lermontov synagogue like some demented Hebraic Atlas. And, by the way, look at that sad Jewess by the grave! Quiet Sarah! With the gardenias pressed to her heart! *To her very heart!* For no heart beats stronger (or faster) than a Jewish heart! Ah, what a couple we would make! The rebirth of Leninsburg's Jewish community! Why should I be alone for even one more hour? Take this day of sadness, Misha, and make it one of renewal! Listen to your elders! Show the heartless swine who did this to your papa, show them that . . .

Well, the only problem with such a gesture was that the heartless swine in question, Oleg the Moose and his syphilitic cousin Zhora, had actually been *invited* to Beloved Papa's funeral. After Alyosha-Bob had convinced him that I could survive in Europe only with a minimum of thirty-five million dollars, Captain Belugin had dragged them along as a sign of our budding rapprochement. In fact, tall, pale-faced Oleg the Moose and his rosy, horizontal cousin—their shapes roughly approximating Don Quixote and Sancho Panza— were already ambling over to me to share their condolences, my idiot relatives quietly parting before them, cowed by their murderous zeal, the fact that Oleg and Zhora had actually done to Boris Vainberg what each relative had long dreamed of doing.

I backed away, clutching a passing candy wrapper with both of my big, squishy hands, but they were soon upon me. "Your father was a great man," said Oleg the Moose, nervously combing back his pompadour, his trademark single antler. "A righteous man. A leader. He loved his people. I still have that 1989 article about him from the American magazine, the one where he's dancing around with a jug of moonshine. What was it called? '*Shabbat Shalom* in Leningrad.' You know, it wasn't always easy between us, but all our disagreements to the very last were just fights between brothers. I think, in some measure, we're all sort of responsible for his death. So Zhora and I are going to pledge a hundred *shtukas* each to the synagogue. Maybe they'll buy some extra Torahs or something. We're going to call it the Boris Vainberg Judaica Renaissance Fund."

A *shtuka* was a *thing,* or US$1,000, the basic unit of measurement in my dead papa's universe. A hundred *shtukas* was not very much, a week of whoring on the Riviera. I looked down at my pricey German shoes, both covered with a fine iridescent film. What the fuck? Damn polymers floating in from the railroad, likely. I pledged right then and there to donate at least one thousand *shtukas,* US$1,000,000, to Misha's Children.

"You know what, let's make it two hundred *shtukas* each," said syphilitic Zhora, picking violently at a back tooth with his pinkie, looking like the bald Chernobyl porcupine they joked about on television. "The cantor said the synagogue needs a new ark. That's where they stash the Torahs after they're done singing from them."

I stood there listening to my father's killers. Oleg and Zhora were of Papa's generation. All three had been made fatherless by the Great Patriotic War. All three had been raised by the men who had managed to avoid battle, the violent, dour, second-tier men their mothers had brought home with them out of brutal loneliness. Standing before the menfolk of my father's generation, I could do nothing. Before their rough hands and stale cigarette-vodka smells, I could only shudder and feel, along with fright and disgust, appeasement and complicity. These miscreants were our country's rulers. To survive in their world, one has to wear many hats—perpetrator, victim, silent bystander. I could do a little of each.

"How's your health?" I asked syphilitic Zhora.

He made a circular motion around his crotch. "Eh, you know, a little better, a little worse. Every day something new. The key is to catch it at the early stage. There's a new venereal clinic on Moskovsky Prospekt—"

"If you don't want to end up like Zhora, better put a sock on your gherkin," Oleg the Moose said with fatherly solicitude. We laughed quietly. "By the way, how's it going with your visa situation?" he asked. "I think you'll have better luck with the American consulate now that your father is gone. Even the worst tragedies often bring with them something positive."

"Hey, if you go to Washington, tell my son to stop diddling Spanish girls and tend to his studies," said Zhora. "Hold on a minute! I'm going to give you his e-mail address at the university." He handed me a scrap on which he had written, with curly Cyrillic flourishes, Zhora2@georgetown.edu. "And tell him nothing less than Michigan for law school, that little *popka*."

We laughed again, the prickly voltage of fraternity coursing through our triumvirate, leaving me a little shocked. "There's a funny anecdote about three Jews—" I started to say, but was interrupted by a starchy, provincial scream.

"Murderers! Animals! Swine!" Lyuba was shrieking from the open grave. "You took my Boris! You took my prince!"

Before we knew what was what, she made a run for Oleg and his cousin, her skinny arms windmilling past the large patriarchal Vainbergs and all the small fry with their orange perms and leather fanny packs. Tear-streaked and crimson, with a child's delicate pink lips, Lyuba's face looked uncharacteristically young, so young that I instinctively extended a hand to her, because this kind of youth does not survive long in our Leninsburg; it's burned out like those malicious orange freckles that had once ringed her nose.

"Lyuba!" I shouted.

Captain Belugin acted quickly, shoving the poor widow under his blazer and gently herding her away from the funeral party, toward the railroad track with its overturned polymer cars. He was chanting comforting mantras above her cries ("All is normal . . . it's only nerves"), although I could hear her last muffled words: "Help me, Mishen'ka! Help me strangle them with my very hands!"

I turned away from her, looking instead to Sarah, the pretty Jewess, the prize of our people, proffering us a collection of her saddest smiles and also something smooth and pale and blooming in her hands. Gardenias.

Soon it was time to bury Papa.

7

Rouenna in Russia

Ghetto Daze, Part II

"I didn't come all the way to freaking Russia to look at no oily paintings, Snack," Rouenna said. We were in the Hermitage, in front of Pissarro's *Boulevard Montmartre on a Sunny Afternoon*. Rouenna was flying out the next day, and I had thought she might want to check out our city's unequaled cultural patrimony.

"You don't want no oily . . . ?" I stammered. We had spent five years loving each other in New York, and I still had no idea how to respond to the vagaries of Rouenna's mind, which in my imagination resembled a gorgeous ripe sunflower being pummeled in a summer storm. "You don't like late-nineteenth-century impressionism?" I said.

"I came here to be with you, *bobo*," she said.

We kissed: a 325-pounder in a vintage Puma tracksuit and a brown woman in a push-up bra. I could feel the *babushka* guards creaking with racial and aesthetic indignation, but that only made me kiss Rouenna harder as I ran my big, squishy hand along her arched back and into the open crevice of her two-fisted ass.

We heard a cough filled with phlegm and suffering. "Behave yourself in a cultured manner," an old voice instructed.

"What the bitch say?" Rouenna asked.

"The old people will never understand us," I sighed. "No Russian ever can."

"So we outie, Snack?"

"We outie."

"Let's go home and cuddle."

"You got it, shorty." During her two weeks here, I had tried to show Rouenna a picture of life in St. Leninsburg in 2001. I'd bought us a motorboat and a sea captain and taken her around the canals and byways of our Venice of the North. She'd let out a few "ooohs" and "dangs" and "aw, dips" at some of the more spectacular palaces, their fading pastel coloring more appropriate for South Beach than for just south of the Arctic Circle. But, like most poor people, she was less a sightseer at heart than a dedicated economist and anthropologist. "Where the niggaz at?" she'd wanted to know.

I assumed she meant people of modest means. "They're every-where," I said.

"But where the *real* niggaz at?"

I didn't want to take her to the outer suburbs, where I hear people are subsisting practically on rainwater and homegrown potatoes, so I took her to the nether reaches of the Fontanka River, the quasi-industrial area our grandparents called Kolomna. I hasten to paint a picture of this neighborhood for the reader. The windswept Fontanka River, its crooked nineteenth-century skyline interrupted by the post-apocalyptic wedge of the Sovietskaya Hotel, the hotel surrounded by symmetrical rows of yellowing, waterlogged apartment houses; the apartment houses, in turn, surrounded by corrugated shacks featur-ing, in no particular order, a bootleg CD emporium, the ad hoc Mis-sissippi Casino ("America Is Far, but Mississippi Is Near"), a kiosk selling industrial-sized containers of crab salad, and the usual Syrian shawarma hut smelling invariably of spilled vodka, spoiled cabbage, and some kind of vague, free-floating inhumanity.

"This is what I'm talkin' about," Rouenna said, looking around, breathing it all in. "South Bronx. Fort Apache. Morrisania. Fuckin' A, Misha. And you're saying these just average folks?"

"I guess," I said. "I don't talk to the common people much, really. They look at me like I'm some kind of freak. In New York, when I get on the subway and homeys see my size, they give me respect."

"That's 'cause you look like a rap star," Rouenna said, kissing me.

"That's 'cause I *am* a rap star," I said, licking her lips.

"Behave yourself in a cultured manner," a passing *babushka* spat at us.

. . .

Rouenna was no stranger to violent death, so when Papa was blown up on the Palace Bridge, she knew how to be tough and not let me fall into further melancholy. "You gotta 'snap, crackle, pop' out of this," she told me, holding me forcefully by my lower chin and snapping the fingers of her other hand.

"Like the American Rice Krispies cereal," I said, smiling. " 'Snap! Crackle! Pop!' "

"What I just say? Did you call your shrinkie-doodle-doo?"

"He's at a psychiatric conference in Rio all month."

"Now, what do you pay that asshole for? All right, spudster. I'm gonna have to fix you up myself. Take 'em off. Show me what you got for mommy."

I unzipped my Puma tracksuit, letting everything spill out in short order. I got down on the Mies van der Rohe daybed, assuming my analytic position with difficulty. Because my neck is so fatty, I suffer from terrible sleep apnea—impossibly loud snoring, constant shortness of breath. It gets worse when I lie on my back, so when Rouenna sleeps next to me, she instinctively pushes me over on the side with one of her muscular thighs, and I instinctively marshal my fat into an unconscious rollover. A night camera would probably capture something like a postmodern underwater ballet.

"Flip," Rouenna said. I got down on my stomach. "Thatta boy."

She laid her hands on what I call my "toxic hump," a black molten peak of stilled flesh and bad circulation, a monument to inactivity grown during the two years of my Russian exile, the repository of all my anger, a kind of anti-heart on the back of me that keeps the sadness pumping. As Rouenna began to knead and contour the intractable hump with her thick fingers, I began to warble in humility and delight: "Oh, Rowie. Don't leave me. Oh, Rowie. Oh, lovey. Don't go."

The sadness poured out of my toxic hump and flooded the farflung veins buried like transatlantic cables across my body. I recalled my mommy's tear-stained face after she lost me at the Yalta train station one summer and thought the dastardly Gypsies had kidnapped and eaten me. "I would have killed myself if something had happened to you," Mommy said. "I would have thrown myself off the cliff of the Sparrow's Nest." Of course, Mommy lied to me constantly, the way mothers in terrible societies do to keep their children from needlessly suffering. But I knew she was telling the truth just then. She would have killed herself. Her life was contingent upon mine. A nine-year-old child, I briefly foresaw my parents' deaths—cancer ward, a ball of flame—and buried the knowledge deep in my then-tiny gut.

"You're not breathing right, honey," Rouenna said. The idea of my impending loneliness had formed a chicken bone in my throat. I was slowly losing oxygen. "Do like me," Rouenna said. She inhaled slowly, held the air in, then released it all over my left ear. The heavy incidence of sour cream and butter in the Russian diet had added a new dimension to her breath. Her breasts, tied back with a kind of wide summer bandanna, were a reassuring presence against the toxic hump and the warm, sweaty flesh that gathered around it like the foothills of Mount Etna.

"I love you so much," I said. "I love you with everything I have."

"I love you, too," Rouenna said. "You'll get through this all right, baby. You gotta have faith."

Faith was one of Rouenna's specialties. Her family's tiny duplex on Vyse and 173rd in the Bronx fairly burst with olive-skinned ceramic Madonnas nursing sweet baby Jesuses, just as the fifteen reproductive women of the extended household gave sustenance to their newborn Felicias and Romeros and Clydes, everywhere breast milk and obeisance and quiet American devastation. In the late seventies, when Rouenna was a toddler, their apartment building in Morrisania had been torched for insurance purposes. One afternoon a threatening anonymous note was slipped under their door, and by evening "finishers" came to strip their apartment of its electrical wiring and plumbing fixtures. Rouenna's mom draped her with a blanket to protect her from the winter cold, and by nightfall their building joined the parade of torches lighting up the northern bend of the Harlem River. Fortified by the quiet submission of the poor, they trooped over to a homeless shelter that had been recommended to them by other relatives in similar circumstances. Eventually some Methodists won their trust by feeding them. They found her mother a job sweeping city streets, and one of the younger, more mobile grand-mothers was set up selling sweet ices on a street corner (the men of the household had long since fled). The Methodists helped them fill out applications for the new government housing that was then slowly revitalizing the Bronx. By the nineties, Rouenna's family had climbed into the ranks of the lower middle class, their meager but ever-growing worldly goods racing ahead of their obliterated urban psychologies. And then I came along, the "rich Russian uncle sent by God" who had taken such interest in their daughter's development. Little did they know who was saving whom.

"I know you're all heartbroken over your daddy," Rouenna said as she worked the hump, "but I gotta say, he didn't do right by you."

"He didn't love me enough?" I asked.

"He drags your ass to Russia, then he kills the Oklahoma dude, and now you can't leave. My family may be fucked up, but at least we look out for each other. When I told my moms you was Jewish, not Methodist, she was like, 'Long as he treat you good.' "

"It's different in Russia," I said, kissing one of Rouenna's hands, which was cradled beneath my chin. "Here a child is just an extension of his parents. We're not allowed to think or act differently from them. Everything we do is to make them proud and happy."

"Whatever," Rouenna said. "Why don't you just do what makes *you* proud and happy and let your dead father rest already?"

"You know what that would be, sweetie?" I asked.

"You wanna bust a nut in me?"

"I want to do some laundry."

Like all Jewish boys growing up in Russia, I'd had all of my earthly needs (save one) taken care of by my mother, but after Rouenna moved into my gargantuan Financial District loft, she exposed me to a new experience—the Laundromat. At first I insisted that a profes-sional laundress wash our socks and underwear, but Rouenna taught me there was something simple, methodical, and pleasing about doing it yourself. She taught me all about temperatures and deter-gents and how to treat "delicates." After the drying machine stopped spinning, we would roll up our socks together. She would make perfect little balls out of the socks, and when we got home, it was such a pleasure to unroll them and put on a warm fresh pair. I'll always associate self-laundered socks with democracy and the primacy of the middle class.

I took Rouenna down to the cellar. A laundry was already in progress. My manservant, Timofey, was supervising a young new maid as she sorted through my tracksuits and loincloth-style underwear. "Yes, that's how we do it here," Timofey was saying to the maid, nodding sagely. "That's just how the master likes it. What a good girl you are, Lara Ivanovna."

I chased away the servants, threatening to beat them over the head with my shoe (it's a little pantomime I do with the staff; they seem to enjoy it). "Thanks for FedExing me the fabric softener sheets, Rowie," I said. "We don't have the good kind here. I can't get enough of this 'outdoor fresh scent.' "

Rouenna was looking over the control panel of the new washing machine I had airlifted out of Berlin. "How does this work, boy-o?"

"The instructions are in German."

"Duh, I can see they're not in English. Show, don't tell."

"What?"

"Show, don't tell."

"Meaning what?"

"It's something Professor Shteynfarb always says in my fiction class. Like instead of expositing about something, you just gotta come out and say it."

"You're taking a writing class with *Jerry Shteynfarb*?"

"You know him, spuds? He's awesome. He says I have a really authoritarian voice. And you got to have an authoritarian voice to write phat fiction."

"He said *what*?" I dropped a tub of detergent on my sweaty left foot. The toxic hump shot a jolt of despair across my body, filling my mouth with what tasted like bad medicine. I immediately saw Rouenna and Shteynfarb together in bed.

Let me give you an idea of this Jerry Shteynfarb. He had been a schoolmate of mine at Accidental College, a perfectly Americanized

Russian émigré (he came to the States as a seven-year-old) who managed to use his dubious Russian credentials to rise through the ranks of the Accidental creative writing department and to sleep with half the campus in the process. After graduation, he made good on his threat to write a novel, a sad little dirge about his immigrant life, which seems to me the luckiest kind of life imaginable. I think it was called *The Russian Arriviste's Hand Job* or something of the sort. The Americans, naturally, lapped it up.

"You got beefs with Professor Shteynfarb?" Rouenna asked.

"I'm just saying be careful. He's got a reputation in certain New York circles for being very promiscuous. He'll sleep with anybody."

"And I'm 'anybody'?" Rouenna banged shut the washing machine lid.

"You're somebody," I whispered.

"Well, Professor says I got a real story to tell, not like the usual crap about rich whiteys getting divorced in Westchester. I'm writing a story about how they burned down our building in Morrisania."

"I thought you were studying to become a secretary," I said. "A powerful executive secretary."

"I'm broadening my mind, just how you *axed* me to," Rouenna said. "I don't want to just be educated, I want to be smart."

"But Ro—"

"No 'buts,' Snack. I'm sick of you acting like you know what's best for me. You don't know shit." To make her point, she jammed her fist in my mouth. "Now, what the fuck this German thing say?"

I removed her fist and gently cleaned off my saliva with a passing sheet of fabric softener. I wanted to *show*, not *tell*, her how much I loved her, but I found myself impotent and weak, full of words and little else. "*Kalt* means cold, and *heiß* means hot," I explained.

She clicked the dial, and the laundry machine started to rattle in contention. She looked into my blue eyes. "Of course I love you, idiot," she said. And with the effortless bounce of a still-young person, she lifted herself up on her stubby toes, took me by the ears, and slowly showed me how.

8

Only Therapy Can Save Vainberg Now

For two weeks following Rouenna's departure, I lay on my Mies van der Rohe daybed, doing nothing but waiting for Dr. Levine to return from his conference in Rio de Janeiro. One afternoon, as if planning my revenge for Rouenna's possible *amour fou* with the evil Jerry Shteynfarb, I baited a pair of Asiatic university students conducting a census into riding on top of me for about five minutes each. They were from some godforsaken Eskimo province, but they smelled, in a perfectly Russian manner, of dill and sweat. Some multiculturalism! Even our Asians are Russian. The census form was more shocking still. Apparently we now live in a country called "The Russian Federation."

July came around, and I realized that I was looking at the two-year anniversary of my internment in Russia. Two years? How had it come to pass? I had arrived in July 1999, ostensibly to visit my father for the summer, completely unaware that he was about to murder an Oklahoma businessman over a 10 percent stake in a nutria farm. But that's not entirely true. From the moment I bought my ticket, I had a premonition I wasn't returning to New York anytime soon.

You know, this happens a lot to Russians. The Soviet Union is gone, and the borders are as free and passable as they've ever been. And yet, when a Russian moves between the two universes, this feeling of finality persists, the logical impossibility of a place like Russia existing alongside the civilized world, of Ann Arbor, Michigan, sharing the same atmosphere with, say, Vladivostok. It was like those mathematical concepts I could never understand in high school: *if, then*. *If* Russia exists, *then* the West is a mirage; conversely, *if* Russia does not exist, *then* and only *then* is the West real and tangible. No wonder young people talk about "going beyond the cordon" when they talk of emigrating, as if Russia were ringed by a vast cordon sanitaire. Either you stay in the leper colony or you get out into the wider world and maybe try to spread your disease to others.

I remember coming back. A rainy summer day. The Austrian Airlines plane dipped its left wing, and through the porthole I caught first sight of my homeland after close to ten years of living in the States.

Let us be certain: the Cold War was won by one side and lost by another. And the losing side, like any other in history, had its countryside scorched, its gold plundered, its men forced to dig ditches in faraway capital cities, its women conscripted to service the victorious army. From my plane window, I saw defeat on the ground. Windstrewn, deserted suburban fields. The gray shell of a factory sliced in two by some unnameable force, its chimney leaning precariously. A circle of seventies apartment houses, each sinking toward the circular courtyard that separated them, like old men huddled together in conversation.

There was defeat on the faces of the Kalashnikov-toting boys who guarded the dilapidated international terminal, ostensibly from the rich passengers of our Austrian Airlines flight. Defeat at Passport Control. Defeat at Customs. At the curbside line of sad men with battered Ladas begging to ferry us into town for hard currency, defeat. Yet on Beloved Papa's face, prune-dry, oddly sober, infused with a misbegotten familial glow, there was something like incumbent victory. He tickled my stomach and made a manly poke at my *khui*. He pointed proudly at the armada of Mercedeses ready to ferry us to his four-story *kottedzh* on the Gulf of Finland. "Not bad, these new times," he said to me. "Like an Isaac Babel story, but not so funny."

For his dissident Zionist activities in the mid-eighties (particularly for kidnapping and then peeing on our neighbor's anti-Semitic pooch in front of the Leningrad headquarters of the KGB), my father had received a two-year sentence. It was the best gift the authorities could have given him. The months he spent in prison were the most important of Papa's life. Like all Soviet Jews, Papa had been trained as a mechanical engineer in one of the city's second-tier universities, and yet he was a scheming working-class boy at heart, not terribly different from his new criminal cellmates with the greasy necks and unshaven noses. Placed in this element, Papa fronted the gangster talk. He devised all kinds of cigarette-related prison capers. He turned bread crumbs into shoe polish and shoe polish into wine. He smuggled in copies of *Penthouse,* pasted the centerfolds on the back of a willing inmate with girlish hips and rented him out by the hour. By the time Beloved Papa got out, two things had happened: Gorbachev had graciously called off most of that annoying, unprofitable communism with the long lines and detonating television sets, and Beloved Papa had met everyone he would need to know in his reincarnation as a Russian oligarch. All those Georgians and Tatars and Ukrainians with the sweaty-brow entrepreneurial spirit so beloved by the American consulate. All the Ingush and Ossetians and Chechens with the casual attitude toward public violence that would create the fine explosive Russia we know today. These men could throw a punch, strangle a hooker, fake a customs form, hijack a truck, blow up a restaurant, start a shell company, buy a television network, run for parliament. Oh, they were *kapitalists,* all right. As for Papa, he had things to offer as well. He had a good Jewish head on him and the social skills of an alcoholic.

And Mommy was dead. There was no one to knock him over the head with the frying pan. No Mommy, no Soviet power, nothing to fight for—he could do as he pleased. Waiting for him outside the prison gates, he found a chauffeured Volga sedan, the kind that used to ferry around Soviet apparatchiks. And standing in the shadow of the Volga, with his hands in the pockets of his dungarees and fat loving tears in his eyes, was his giant uncircumcised son.

The two-year anniversary of my own Russian imprisonment passed without ceremony. July gained in days; the White Nights were no longer so white, the blanched evening sky gave way to a palette of genuine blue, the seasonal madness of my servants—their lusty cries and frequent couplings—abated. And still I would not leave my bed. I was waiting for my analyst.

On the day Dr. Levine finally returned from Rio, the widowed Mrs. Vainberg called me, begging for an audience, her voice an accordion of unhappiness and dread. "What do I do, Misha?" Lyuba cried. "Teach me how to sit *shiva* for the dead. What are the Jewish customs?"

"Are you sitting down on a cardboard box?" I asked her.

"I'm sitting on a broken toaster."

"Good enough. Now cover up all the mirrors. And maybe don't eat pork salami for a couple of days."

"I'm all alone," she said in a thin, automatic voice. "Your father's gone. I need a man's hand to guide me."

This kind of antediluvian talk made me anxious. A man's hand? Jesus Christ. But then I remembered Lyuba standing up for my Beloved Papa at the funeral, trying to launch herself at Oleg the Moose. I felt sad for her. "Where are you, Lyuba?"

"At the *kottedzh*. The damn mosquitoes are killing me. Ai, Misha, everything reminds me of your father. Like this seven-pronged Jewish candelabra and the little black boxes he used to wrap around his arm. Judaity is so complicated."

"Complicated, yes. I lost half my *khui* over it."

"Would you like to come over?" she asked. "I bought some orange towels."

"I need some rest, *sladkaya*," I said. "Maybe in a week or two." Oh, Lyuba. What would become of her? She was twenty-one. The peak of her beauty had passed. And what did I just call her? *Sladkaya*? My sweet one?

Timofey trudged in, a weak, servile smile hoisted onto his grim physiognomy. "I brought you a fresh bottle of Ativan from the American Clinic, *batyushka*," he said, brandishing a large sack of medications. "You know, Priborkhin's master was also in bed with depression, but then he took a little *Zoloftushka* and some *Prozakchik*, and off he went to run with the bulls in Spain!"

"I don't know about selective serotonin reuptake inhibitors," I said. "I think I should stick just to anti-anxiety meds for now."

"I want only to see *batyushka* smiling and throwing his shoe at me with vigor," Timofey said, bowing as far as his cracked spine allowed.

I dialed Dr. Levine on my *mobilnik*. Our sessions began at five P.M. St. Leninsburg time, which meant morning on Park Avenue, the hearty American grasses swaying over the landscaped median, a procession of dark blue Town Cars ferrying moneymakers downtown, everybody tastefully dressed and with no blood on their hands. Or not too much blood, anyway.

I imagined Dr. Levine—his Semitic face freshly tanned from the beaches of Ipanema, his belly perfectly rounded from a judicious intake of *churrasco* and black beans—looking over the empty leather couch before him, the speakerphone turned on, the room ablaze with photographs of colorful Sioux tepees, perhaps suggesting the pathway to a better self, that tight little wigwam inside my heart.

"I'm mi-se-ra-ble, Doctor," I howled into my *mobilnik*. "Lots of dreams about my papa and me paddling a boat down the Mississippi, which becomes the Volga and then some kind of African river. Or sometimes I'm eating a pierogi and my dead papa's inside. Like I'm a cannibal."

"What else comes to mind about that?" Dr. Levine said.

"I dunno. My manservant says I should start taking reuptake inhibitors."

"Let's wait another week or so before we reconsider your regimen." I listened as Dr. Levine's humane voice crackled across the incomprehensible distance between here and there. I wanted to reach out and hug him across the ether, but that's just the transference talking. In fact, we used to have a strict No Hugs Rule when I saw him in person. "How are the panic attacks?" he asked. "Are you taking Ativan?"

"Yeah, but I've been bad, Doctor! I've been mixing it up with alcohol, which I shouldn't do, right?"

"You shouldn't mix Ativan with alcohol. That's right."

"So I've been bad!"

Silence. I could almost hear him wiping his tender, doughy nose. He gets allergies in the summer, poor guy—his only weakness. Dr. Levine is in his fifties, but, like many Americans of his social class, he has the boxy chest of an athletic twenty-five-year-old and a tight, if slightly feminine, behind. I am not a homosexual by any stretch, and yet I have dreamed many times of making passionate love to his ass, my big body draped over his smaller one, my hands rubbing his sweet gray-bearded muzzle. "Do you want me to say that you're bad?" Dr. Levine said evenly into his speakerphone. "Do you want me to hold you responsible for your father's death?"

"Oh, God, no," I said. "I mean, in some way I've always hoped that he would die . . . Oh, I see what you're saying. Oh, shit, right . . . I'm a bad, bad son."

"You're not a bad son," Dr. Levine said. "I think part of the problem for the past two years is that you don't really do anything with your time. You don't spend it profitably, the way you did in New York. And your father's death obviously doesn't help things."

"Right," I said. "I'm like that Oblomov character who never gets out of bed. How sad for me."

"I know you don't want to be in Russia," Dr. Levine said, "but until you can figure a way out, you have to learn to deal with your situation."

"Uh-huh," I said, fiddling with a fresh Ativan bottle.

"Now, remember when you were in New York, you kept telling me how beautiful Moscow is . . ."

"St. Petersburg, actually."

"Sure," Dr. Levine allowed. "St. Petersburg. Well, why don't you start by going for a walk. Look at some of that beauty you love. Take some time to relax and feel yourself distracted by something other than your problems."

I thought of spending a day at the pleasant Summer Gardens, eating a stick of ice cream beneath a belligerent-looking statue of Minerva. I should have bought many more ice creams when Rouenna was around, although we did enjoy at least five a day. If only I had treated her better, maybe she wouldn't sleep with that bastard Jerry Shteynfarb, maybe she would have stayed with me in Russia. "Yes," I said. "That's what I must do . . . Precisely. I'll put on my walking shorts right away." Then, before I could stop the transference, I blurted out, "I really love you, Doctor . . ."

And then I started to cry.

9

One Day in the Life of Misha Borisovich

I didn't last long in the Summer Gardens. All the shady benches were taken; the heat was abusive; pious grandmothers passing by with their young charges would use me to illustrate four of the seven deadly sins. And my Rouenna, with her zippy bravado and distaste for all things classical ("Some of these statues ain't got no ass, Misha"), was nowhere to be found.

"To the *khui* with this," I said to my Chechen driver, Mamudov, who was keeping me company on a nearby bench. "Let's see if Alyosha is at the Mountain Eagle."

"He can't spend a day without his little mutton kebab," Mamudov opined sourly of my American friend.

We drove over the Troitsky Bridge, the Neva River eager and playful on a summer day, a panorama of gray swells and treacherous seagulls. Alyosha-Bob was indeed parked behind a rickety wooden table at the Mountain Eagle, chasing a vodka bottle with a plate of pickled peppers, cabbage, and garlic. We embraced and kissed three times in the Russian manner. I was introduced to his companions, both employees of ExcessHollywood, his DVD import-export business: Ruslan the Enforcer, a man with a shaved head and a fatalistic expression who handled security for the company, and the young art director and Web designer, Valentin, a recent graduate of the Academy of Fine Arts.

"We're drinking to women," Ruslan said. "Alyosha complains that his Sveta makes fun of his prowess in bed and threatens to leave him if he doesn't move to Boston and give her a comfortable life in the fashionable Back Bay neighborhood."

"Sad but true," Alyosha-Bob said. "Meanwhile, Ruslan tells me that his wife cheats on him with a sergeant in the militia and that he has found stains on her hose and panties."

"Also, when they k-k-k-k-kiss," Valentin stammered shyly, "a suspicious manly scent comes from her mouth."

"And as for our friend Valentin," Ruslan the Enforcer said, gesturing to the artist, "he is not too young to know of heartache, either. He is in love with two prostitutes who work at the Alabama Father strip club on Vasilevsky Island."

"Well, to women, then!" we said, clinking our glasses.

As if drawn by our toast, a pretty Georgian girl with furry arms dropped a fresh bottle of vodka in front of me and threw some charred mutton kebabs on our plates. We chewed on the gristle thoughtfully, slivers of onion crackling between our teeth. The sun sailed westward over the canal running past the ramshackle restaurant, past the disturbing city zoo where the once-proud lions of the Serengeti now live no better than our pensioners, and toward the greener pastures of the European Union.

A typical male Russian sadness descended upon us. "Speaking on the subject of women," I said, "I fear my Bronx girl, Rouenna, may be the quarry of the émigré writer Jerry Shteynfarb."

"I remember that weasel," Alyosha-Bob said. "I saw him in New York once after he wrote that *Russian Arriviste's Hand Job*. He thinks he's the Jewish Nabokov."

Ruslan and Valentin snorted at the idea that such a person could exist. "I don't think they should expose young people to Shteynfarb," I said. "Especially at a school like Hunter College, where the students are poor and impressionable."

We drank to the difficult lives of impressionable poor folk and to the end of American imperialism in the guise of Jerry Shteynfarb. Valentin the artist seemed most roused by such sentiments, knocking his glass over and casting his gaze toward the heavens. He was a lean, sallow fellow with the overearnest expression of the Slavic intellectual. All the distinguishing signs were there: flaxen goatee, bloodshot eyes, porcupine hair, uneven bottom teeth, great big potato nose, thirty-ruble sunglasses from a metro kiosk. "You don't like American imperialism, eh?" I said to him.

"I'm a m-m-monarchist," the fellow stammered.

"Now, there's a popular position for a young man these days," I said, thinking: *Oh, our poor dispossessed intelligentsia, why do we even bother to teach them literature and the plastic arts?* "And who's your favorite czar, then, young man?" I asked.

"Alexander the First. No, wait . . . the Second."

"The great reformer. Well, that's very nice. And who are your whorish friends?"

"They're a mother-daughter act," the artist explained. "Some people derive a thrill from watching a mother and daughter touch. They're from Kursk Province. Very cultured people. Elizaveta Ivanovna plays the accordion, and her daughter, Lyudmila Petrovna, can quote the major philosophers."

His use of their patronymics was strangely touching—I knew immediately what he wanted to do. After all, it is the only path our young Raskolnikovs can follow. "I will save them!" he said, and I knew immediately that he would not.

"Presumably it is the daughter you fancy," I said.

"Both are like family to me," said Valentin. "If you meet them, you see how they cannot live without each other. They are like Naomi and Ruth."

We drank two shots in rapid succession, one to Naomi and one to Ruth. The mood veered toward belligerence and sentimentality. I floated in and out of several conversations.

"Fuck them all," Ruslan the Enforcer was saying at one point, although I was unsure to whom he was referring. "Throw them all under the tram! See if I care!" The Georgian girl came with more mutton and a thick loaf of *khachapuri*, a homey flatbread filled with soft ricottalike cheese. We drank to Georgia, the girl's beautiful, uncontrollable, destitute country, and she nearly threw her arms around our necks and cried out of shame and gratitude.

A new set of vodka bottles came, one for each man.

"It's emasculating," Alyosha-Bob was saying in a dramatic voice that he had started to adopt in Russia. "How can she do this to me? How much more can I give to her? I've given her everything that's in my heart. Why can't she love me for who I am? What does she think is waiting for her in Boston?"

We drank to Alyosha-Bob's heart. We drank to his manhood. We drank to his weak Jewish chin and billiard-ball head. We breathed out the poisonous vapors streaming down our gullets, a rainbow of alcohol floating above our heads, while the setting sun turned the spire of the nearby Peter and Paul Fortress into a flaming exclamation mark. We drank to the setting sun, our silent conspirator. We drank to the golden exclamation mark. We drank to Saints Peter and Paul.

A new set of vodka bottles came, one for each man.

"Why can't my website be called www.ruslan-the-enforcer.com?" Ruslan was saying. "Why does it have to be ruslan-the-punisher.org?"

"Because ruslan-the-enforcer.com is already taken," Valentin gently explained.

"But *I am* the Enforcer. I know Ruslan the Punisher. He lives with his mother by the Avtovo metro station. He is a nothing man. Now people will think that I am him. They won't hire me to do the bloody work. I will be humiliated." We drank to Ruslan's renowned strength and his tough fists. We drank to his bad childhood. We drank to his website.

A new set of vodka bottles came, one for each man.

"I wish Russia were strong," Valentin said, "and America weak. Then we could hold up our heads. Then my Ruth and Naomi could walk down Fifth Avenue and spit on whomever they wanted. No one would dare hit them or make them touch each other." We drank to Russia being powerful again. We drank once more to Naomi and Ruth. We drank to America's eventual comeuppance, which even Alyosha-Bob with his golden American passport thought would happen in due course.

"Speaking of America," Alyosha-Bob said. "Listen, Mishen'ka . . ." But instead of finishing, he hung his head in an alcoholic stupor.

"What is it, Alyosha?" I said, touching his hand. But my friend had drifted off into sleep. His little body could not take as much vodka as my larger one. We waited a few minutes for him to revive, which he did with a start. "Arumph!" he said. "Listen, Mishka. I had a drink with Barry from the American consulate, and I asked the big jerk . . ." His head slumped again. I tickled his nose with parsley. "I asked the big jerk if you could get a visa to the States now that your papa's dead."

My toxic hump throbbed with hope but also with the caveat that life could produce only disappointment. I burped quietly into my hand and prepared to wipe away the tear that would be forthcoming whether the news was good or bad. "And?" I whispered. "What did he say?"

"No go," Alyosha-Bob mumbled. "They won't let in the child of a murderer. The dead Oklahoman was politically connected, too. They love Oklahomans in the new administration. They want to make an example of you."

The tear did not fall. But the anger found its way into my nostrils, from which it came out as a low, sonorous whistle. I picked up the fresh vodka bottle and threw it against a wall. It shattered in a brilliant show of light and clarity. The Mountain Eagle's clientele fell silent, a dozen shaved heads glistening with midsummer sweat, the richer men looking toward their bodyguards with raised eyebrows, the bodyguards looking toward their fists. The Georgian restaurant manager peeked out from his office, took note of who I was, bowed respectfully in my direction, and motioned for the waitress to bring me another bottle.

"Easy, Snack," Alyosha-Bob said.

"If you want to do something useful, throw a bottle at the Americans," Ruslan the Enforcer said. "But make sure to light it first. Let them all burn to death. See if I care!"

"America I want," I said, uncapping the new bottle and, in contravention of all drinking etiquette, pouring it right down my throat. "New York. Rouenna. Take her from behind. Empire State Building. Korean grocery. Salad bar. Laundromat." I managed to stand up. The table spun around me in a fantasia of colors and textures—mutton parts hoisted on spits, egg yolks dripping into cheese pies, stews gurgling with sunflower oil and blood. How could a late-afternoon meal turn so violent? Who were these cretinous people around me? Everywhere I looked, I saw failure and despondency. "They want an example to make?" I said. "I *am* the example. I am the best example for a good, loving, honest person. And I'm going to show them now!" I started staggering toward Mamudov and my Land Rover.

"Don't go!" Alyosha-Bob shouted after me. "Misha! You're not capable of action!"

"Am I not a man?" I shouted Beloved Papa's popular refrain. And to my driver, Mamudov, I said: "Take me to the American consulate."

The generals in charge of the U.S. Immigration and Naturalization Service have surely seen it all. Migrant Mexicans chased by coyotes across the Rio Grande. Pitch-black Africans sealed into shipping containers so that they can sneak into the country, sell sunglasses by Battery Park, and then send food back to their children in Togo. Rafts full of dehydrated, starving, partially naked Hispanics washing up on the beaches of Miami to beg for asylum (I've always wondered why they don't bring along an adequate supply of bottled water and snacks for such a long journey). But have they ever seen a rich and educated person impale himself upon the flagpole bearing the Stars and Stripes? Have they ever seen a person whose wallet contains the U.S. dollar equivalent of a dozen American dreams prostrate himself before them for a chance to see the Brooklyn Promenade once more? Have they ever met a cultured European who would choose the American berserk over the Belgian truffle? Forget the Mexicans and Africans and such. In a sense, my American story is the most compelling of all. It is the ultimate compliment to a nation known more for its belly than for its brain.

As we drove up Furshtatskaya Street, Mamudov told me he would disgorge me at the consulate's entrance and drive around the corner (civilian cars are not allowed to idle near the Americans' sacred space). "You don't look well, excellency," Mamudov said to me. "Why not take a little nap back home? We'll pick up an Asian girl from the brothel and some Ativan from the American clinic. Just as you fancy."

"To the *khui* with the Asian girl," I said, kicking the door open. "Am I not a man, Mamudov?"

Outside I found the prickled atmosphere that occurs whenever a Western consulate is forced to position itself along a dirty third-world street, whenever local neutrons and electrons are not allowed to mix with the West's positive charge. I felt myself repelled by an invisible wind and almost fell backward. The American flag above the consulate's portico, however, gave me a friendly wave of encouragement. I crossed the street and came upon two Russian meatheads, one in a Caesar haircut (to hide a massively receding hairline), the other a flattop, each about two thirds my size, beefed up with buckwheat and cheap sausage, each dressed in uniforms bearing the Stars and Stripes on their shoulders.

"May we help you with something?" the flattop said as I staggered toward the announcement board where the Rules of Humiliation for Russian visa applicants were spelled out in English officialese: *U.S. law places on each nonimmigrant visa applicant a presumption of immigrant intent. The burden of proof is on the applicant to overcome this presumption.* In other words: *You're all whores and bandits, so why bother applying?*

"May we help you with something?" the flattop repeated. His face had a single long crack running from forehead to chin, as if he had been dropped one time too many as a child. "This place isn't for you, fellow. The consulate is closed. Shove off."

"I want to see the chargé d'affaires," I said. "I am Misha Vainberg, son of the famous Boris Vainberg who peed on the dog in front of the KGB headquarters during the Soviet times." I leaned against the wall of the consulate building and spread my arms out, exposing the white of my stomach the way a puppy shows he's defenseless in front of a larger dog. "My father was a very big dissident. Bigger than Sharansky! Once the Americans hear of what he's done for freedom of religion, they'll build a statue to him in Times Square."

The two security guards smiled broadly at each other. It isn't often anymore that you can beat up a Jew in an official capacity in Russia, so when the chance comes, you have to grab it. You have to beat the Jew for church and fatherland or you'll regret it for the rest of your life. The guy with the Caesar cut flexed the rolls of his neck in provocation. "If you don't leave immediately," he said, "you're going to have some problems with us."

"Maybe you should go to the Israeli consulate," the flattop suggested. "You'll have better luck there, I'm sure."

"Suitcase! Train station! Israel!" Caesar chanted the familiar Russian mantra urging Jews to leave the country. Flattop took up the refrain, and they shared an enjoyable moment.

"Just wait until I tell the chargé d'affaires that a pair of anti-Semites is guarding his consulate," I sputtered, alcoholic drool dappling my chin. "You'll be working at the consulate in Yekaterinburg, so dress warm, fuckers."

It took me a while to figure out that they were punching me. I was staring at a woman beating her carpet outside her window, thinking those were the thuds resonating along the quiet street. To be fair to my tormentors, Flattop and Caesar were good strong Russian boys in their late twenties, purposeful and furious. But beating the lard out of me is not an activity to be done casually; it takes hard work and a certain amount of smarts. One can't just keep hitting me in the stomach and tits, hoping that I'll crumple like a cheap pastry.

"Ooooh," I moaned, going through the motions of drunken incomprehension. "What's happening to me?"

"Let's punch him in the liver and kidneys," Caesar suggested, wiping his sweaty brow.

They started aiming for those delicate organs but with few results. The elastic bands surrounding me took each bruise with equanimity. Whenever fist met fat, I merely stumbled to the side, turning to face either Flatty or Caesar. I used each brief occasion to tell them a little about my life.

"I studied multiculturalism at Accidental College . . ."

Left hook to liver.

"My mama named me Misha, but the Hasids called me Moses . . ."

Right jab to left kidney.

"I'm starting a charity for the poorest kids, called Misha's Children . . ."

Hammer blow to liver.

"Rouenna kissed the underside of my *khui* . . ."

Kidneys, one-two punch.

"I am a better American than most native-born Americans . . ."

Roundabout to the spleen.

"I went into analysis to work on my weight issues . . ."

Open-fisted liver poke.

"When I move back to New York, I think I'll live in trendy Williamsburg . . ."

There were curses and panting around me and the plebian stench of heavy exertion. I felt sad for these boys trapped in their stupid Stars and Stripes outfits, guarding the very people they should have hated the most. We would all die together in this stupid fucking city of frozen windowpanes and grotty courtyards. Our gravestones would be vandalized, our names covered with swastikas and bird shit, our mommies with their frying pans rotting away by our side. What was the point of it all? What was keeping us from the inevitable? "You should aim for the throat and spine," I slurred to my assailants. "If you punch my hump, maybe I'll die on the spot. What good is being alive, anyway, when it's always at somebody's mercy?"

The guards slowly lowered themselves to the curb, and I slid down to join them, panting along with them out of camaraderie. They put their hands around my back, so that all three of us were linked. "Why do you want us to hurt you?" Flattop asked. "Do you take us for animals? We don't like hurting people, no matter what you think."

"I have to go to America," I said. "I'm in love with a beautiful girl from the Bronx."

"The famous one with the big ass?" Caesar asked.

"No, her name is Rouenna Sales. She's only famous on her *own* block. I've sent her a dozen electronic mails this week, and she hasn't written back. She's being chased by a poseur who has American citizenship. A writer."

"A good writer?" Caesar asked, taking out a flask and passing it to me.

"No," I said, taking a swig.

"Well, then why are you worried? A smart girl wouldn't go with a bad writer."

Flattop pressed me to him. "Don't despair, brother," he said. "We may have nothing in this country, but our women have kind, beautiful souls. They will love you even if you're lazy or drunk or give them a thrashing now and then."

"Or even if you're fat," Caesar suggested. We took more swigs of the moonshine. As far as my new companions were concerned, I was no longer a parasitic Jew but someone to be trusted. An alcoholic.

"I love Russia in my own way," I blurted out. "If only I could do something for this country without looking like an asshole."

"You said something about Misha's Children," Flatty reminded me.

"How can I mend young hearts when my own is broken? My dear papa was recently taken away from me. They blew him up on the Palace Bridge."

"Very sad," Caesar said. "My father was just run over by a bread truck."

"Mine fell out of a window last year," Flattop said. "It was only the second story, but he fell on his head. Kaput." We each made a deep mourning sound with the combination of our noses, throats, and lips, as if we were tragically sucking noodles out of an iron bowl. The sound traveled slowly down the street, stopping at every door on the way and secretly adding to each household's despair.

"We should get up," I said. "I should leave you be. What if one of your American masters came walking down the street? They would fire you."

"Let them all go to the devil," Caesar said. "We're talking to our brother here. We would die for our brother."

"We're already so ashamed of ourselves to be wearing the American flag on our sleeves," Flattop said. "You remind us of our country's dignity. They can punch Russia over and over again, but she will never fall. Maybe she'll slide down to the pavement as we have . . . you know, for a drink . . . But she will never fall."

"Help me, brothers!" I cried, meaning no more than they should help hoist me to my feet, but they took it in a more spiritual light—they set me upright on my feet, dusted off my Puma tracksuit, rubbed the sore spots where they had hit me, and kissed me three times on my cheeks. "If you have children who need winter boots or anything else," I said, "come by Bolshoi Prospekt on the Petrogradskaya Side, house seventy-four. Ask for Boris Vainberg's son, they all know who I am. I'll give you every one I have."

"If some *mudak* tries to hurt you because of your religion, or laughs at how fat you are, come to us and we will break his head open," Caesar said.

We toasted one last time with the flask, "To our friendship!," and then I zigzagged my way down the street toward my waiting car. A light wind picked me up and guided me forward, cleaning the dust off my neck and wiping a spot of blood from my lower chin. The day was shifting from unbearable humidity to elusive summer pleasure, much as the violence against me had given way to pity and understanding. All I ask is the occasional reprieve.

"Did you talk to the Americans?" Mamudov asked.

"No," I said, massaging the bruised flab around my kidneys. "But I spoke to some Russians, and they made me feel good again. There are wonderful countrymen around us, don't you think so, Mamudov?" My Chechen driver said nothing. "Let's go to the Mountain Eagle," I said. "Maybe Alyosha-Bob and his friends are still there. I want to drink some more!"

Alyosha-Bob and Ruslan the Enforcer had just quit the premises, but the artist Valentin was still dawdling, hungrily finishing up everyone's sour cabbage and cramming several slices of leftover Georgian cheese bread into his broken-down satchel.

"How are you doing, little brother?" I said. "Enjoying the beautiful day?"

"I'm going to see my friends at the Alabama Father strip club," Valentin said sheepishly.

I presumed he meant the mother-daughter whore team. "Hey, why don't I take you and Naomi and Ruth out to dinner!" I said. "We'll go to the Noble's Nest."

The monarchist, although presumably well fed on Alyosha-Bob's ruble, clapped his hands together. "Dinner!" he cried. "How very Christian of you, sir!"

• • •

The Alabama Father strip club was all but empty at this time of day, only four drunk members of the Dutch consulate passed out in the back by the empty roulette table and the imported rum-and-Coke machine. Despite the lack of an audience, Valentin's special friends, Elizaveta Ivanovna and her daughter, Lyudmila Petrovna, were up on the makeshift stage grinding against two poles to the sound of the American super-band Pearl Jam.

The age difference between the artist's friends was not as obvious as I had imagined; in fact, mother and daughter resembled two sisters, one perhaps ten years older than the other, her naked breasts pointing downward, a single crease separating them from the little tummy below. The mother was imparting upon Lyudmila her theory that the pole was like a wild animal that one had to grasp with one's thighs lest it escape. The daughter, like all daughters, was shrugging her off, saying, "*Mamochka,* I know what I'm doing. I watch special movies when you're asleep—"

"You're a dunderhead," the mother said, thrusting to the sound of the ravenous American rock-and-roll band. "Why did I ever give birth to you?"

"Ladies!" Valentin cried out to them. "My dear ones . . . good evening to you!"

"Hi, there, little guy," mother and daughter sang in unison. They each put a hand down their tiny lower garments and writhed with special vigor for the artist's benefit.

"Ladies," Valentin said, "I would like to introduce you to Mikhail Borisovich Vainberg. A very good man. Earlier in the evening we drank to America's downfall. He drives around in a Land Rover."

The ladies appraised my expensive shoes and stopped writhing. They hopped down from their poles and pressed themselves against me. Quickly the air around me was filled with the smell of nail polish and light exertion. "Good evening," I said, brushing my curly mane, for I tend to get a little shy around prostitutes. It was, I confess, nice to feel their warm flesh against me.

"Please come home with us!" cried the daughter, massaging the posterior crease of my pants with one curious finger. "Fifty dollars per hour for both. You can do what you like, front and back, but please no bruises."

"Better yet, we'll go home with *you*!" the mother said. "I imagine you have a beautiful home on the embankment of the River Moika . . . or one of those gorgeous Stalin buildings on Moskovsky Prospekt."

"Misha is the son of Boris Vainberg, a famous and recently deceased businessman," Valentin announced. "He has offered to take us to a restaurant called the Noble's Nest."

"I've never heard of it," said the mother, "but it sounds just grand."

"It's in the teahouse of the Yusupov Mansion," I said with a pedantic air, knowing that the mansion where the loony monk Rasputin was poisoned would not make much of an impression on the ladies. Valentin managed a slight, historic smile and tried to nuzzle up to the daughter, who favored him with a chaste kiss on the forehead.

The Noble's Nest is really quite a place. They normally don't allow whores or low-earning people like Valentin, but because of my fine reputation, the management was quick to relent.

Now, it is no secret that St. Petersburg is a backwater, lost in the shadow of our craven capital, Moscow, which itself is but a third-world megalopolis teetering on the edge of some spectacular extinction. And yet the Noble's Nest has one of the most divine restaurants I have ever seen—dripping with more gold plating than the dome of St. Isaac's, yes; covered with floor-to-ceiling paintings of dead nobles, to be sure. And yet, somehow, against the odds, the place carries off the excesses of the past with the dignified luster of the Winter Palace.

I knew that a fellow like Valentin would rejoice. For people like him, this restaurant is one of the two Russias they can understand. For people like Valentin, it's either the marble and malachite of the Hermitage or a crumbling communal flat in the Kolomna district.

Valentin's tarts wept when they saw the menu. They couldn't even name the dishes, such was their excitement and money lust. They had to refer to them by their prices: "Let's split the sixteen dollars for an appetizer and then I'll have the twenty-eight dollars and you can split the thirty-two . . . Is that all right, Mikhail Borisovich?"

"For God's sake, have what you wish!" I said. "Four dishes, ten dishes, what is money when you're among your brothers and sisters?" And to set the mood for the evening, I ordered a bottle of Rothschild for US$1,150.

"So let's talk some more about your art, little brother," I said to Valentin. I was having some kind of Dostoyevsky moment. I wanted to redeem everyone in sight. They could all be Misha's Children, every last harlot and intellectual with flaxen goatee.

"You see . . . you see . . ." said Valentin to his women friends. "We're talking about art now. Isn't it nice, ladies, to sit in a pretty space and talk like gentlemen about the greater subjects?" A whole slew of emotions, ranging from an innate distrust of kindness to some latent homosexuality, was playing itself out on the artist's red face. He pressed his palm down on my hand and left it there for a good time.

"Valya is doing some nice sketches for us," the mama said to me, "and he's helping us design our Web page. We're going to have a Web page for our services, don't you know?"

"Oh, look, Mama, I believe the two sixteen dollars are here!" Elizaveta Ivanovna cried as the two appetizers of *pelmeni* stuffed with deer and crab arrived, both dishes covered by immense silver domes. The waiters, two gorgeous young kids, a boy and a girl, looked at one another, mouthed *one, two, three,* and then, in tandem, pulled off the lids to reveal the horrid appetizers beneath.

"We're talking about art like gentlemen," Valentin said.

The evening progressed as expected. We drove to my apartment beneath a confusing cross section of the summer sky—the deep blue of the North Sea at the top, followed by the indeterminate gray of the Neva River, and, at the very bottom, a brilliant ribbon of modern orange that hung like a fluorescent mist over the dueling spires of the Admiralty and the Peter and Paul Fortress.

Along the way, we took turns hitting the driver with birch twigs, ostensibly to improve his circulation, but in reality because it is impossible to end an evening in Russia without assaulting someone. "Now I feel as if we're in an old-fashioned hansom cab," said Valentin, "and we're hitting the driver for going too slow . . . Faster, driver! Faster!"

"Please, sir," pleaded Mamudov, "it is already difficult to drive on these roads, even without being whipped."

"No one has ever called me 'sir' before," Valentin spoke in wonderment. "Opa, you scoundrel!" he screamed, flailing the driver once more.

I took them around my apartment, a gorgeous art nouveau lair built in 1913 (generally acknowledged as the last good year in Russia's history), rife with pale ceramic tile and prized oriel windows that captured and teased what remained of the evening light. With each passing room, Valentin and the whores would experience a mild seizure, the young monarchist Web designer whispering, "So this is how it is . . . So this is how they live."

I parked them in my library, the bookshelves creaking with my dead papa's books, the collected texts of the great rabbis, the *Cayman Islands Banking Regulations, Annotated in Three Volumes,* and the ever-popular *A Hundred and One Tax Holidays.* Servants appeared with carafes of vodka. Elizaveta Ivanovna was threatening to play the accordion for us, and Valentin was inciting the daughter to quote at will from the major philosophers, but by the time an accordion was finally produced and a copy of Voltaire cracked open, my guests had fallen asleep on top of each other. Valentin had stuck his big potato nose inside Lyudmila Petrovna's substantial cleavage and placed his arms around her hips as if they were dancing a nocturnal waltz.

I had never seen a man cry in his sleep before.

porkyrussianlover@heartache.com

I left my guests and entered the dimly lit replica of Dr. Levine's office, fished my laptop out from under my Mies van der Rohe daybed, and fired Rouenna an electronic message across the ether:

> *hi pretty baby. its misha. wondering why u haven't written back 2 me 4 so long. tonite chillin with some russian homies (remember how we used to chill?). you'd like 2 of these girlz, they real ghetto. remember how u used to roll up our socks at the laundromat. i miss u.*
> *much luv (4 real)*
> *misha aka snack dad aka porky russian lover*
> *p.s. hope u r doing good in school. anybody special in yr life? lemme know*
> *p.p.s. maybe you can come to p-burg 4 xmas break. maybe u+i can chill?!*

I was about to enjoy my nightly single malt fired up with 2.5 milligrams of Ativan when an incoming message pinged across the screen. I let out a happy little yelp when I saw the overseas sender: rsales@ hunter.cuny.edu. I thought of saving the message until the next day, knowing I wouldn't be able to go to sleep with Rouenna's words lodged like dum-dum bullets in my brain.

Rouenna's missive was as shocking in style as in content. Gone were the hip-hop numeric abbreviations that we used to "conversate" with each other. Rouenna was trying to write like an educated young American woman, although her spelling and grammar were as arbitrary as anything on the corner of 173rd Street and Vyse.

Dear Misha,

First off, I'm really sorry it took me so long to answer your sweet, sweet letters to me. Your a good Boyfriend and I owe you everything, my hunter education, my dentalwork, all my Hopes and Dreams. I want you to know that I love you and I will never take you for granite. Second off, I'm sorry to be writing this letter right after your tragety with your father. I know it really effected you mentally. Who wouldnt feel Sad when someone so close to you gets killed like a dog.

Misha, I've been seeing Proffessor Shteynfarb. Please dont get mad at me. I now you dont like him, but he's been a big help to me, not just "a shoulder to cry on" but an Inspiration. He works so hard, always writing and teaching and going to conferences in miami and holding office hours really late because some students have work in the day or babies. Proffessor Shteynfarb had a hard life being an immigrant so he knows about hard work. All the students like him because he take us serious. And no offense but you never really worked hard or did anything because your so rich and thats ONE BIG DIFERENCE between us.

Proffessor Shteynfarb says I have self as-steam issues because no one in my family ever encouraged me to show my intelligence and all they think about is how to get by and stay out of trouble and take care of there babies. I tell him you did, that you told me to get my GED and go to hunter and that you told my mother and grandmothers and brothers and sisters and cousins and uncles and aunts not to yell at me or talk about all the Mistakes I'd done in the past, like working at that tity bar.

He says yes thats true but that you always veiwed me from the Position of a Colonialist Oppresor. You always secretly look down at me. I tried to talk to you so many times about my Writing when I was in russia but you never seemed to listen. Its always you you you. Your ignoring me just like my family and thats going to hurt my self as-steam. Also Proffessor Shteynfarb said its wrong when you throw

your shoe at your servant (I'm sorry, but I think thats true). Also
he says its wrong when you an your friend alosha try to do your rapping
and pretend your from the ghetto because thats also being a
Colonialist. He gave me a book by Edward Said, which is super hard,
but its worth it.

Proffessor Shteynfarb is making an Anthology of immigrant
writing and he says my story about how they burnt our house down in
morrisania is going to be the pizza resistance of the whole book. I love
you so much, Misha. I dont want to hurt you. I always dream of your
arms around me and your weird kui in my mouth. (I said 'kui' to
Proffessor Shteynfarb and he said that russian women dont ever use
such bad words, and that I was real naughty, ha ha ha!) But lets face
it, your in russia and I'm in America and their never going to let you
out, so for all intensive purposes were not really together. If you want to
stop paying my hunter tuition I would understand, although I would
have to go back to work in the tity bar. But I hope you still love me and
want to do right by me and not hurt my self as-steam anymore.

Loves & Hugs & Big Wet Kisses,
Your Rouenna

P.S. I just want you to know that the thing with Proffessor
Shteynfarb was mutual and that he wasnt trying to kick it to me or to
any of the girls in class. He says he feels bad about being in a position of
authritarity over me but that were equal in a sense because I grew up
impovrished and he's a big immigrant.

I carefully closed the laptop, waited for a beat, then threw it across
the room, shattering a replica of one of Dr. Levine's wigwam photographs. I put a pillow around my face because I didn't want to see
and then covered my ears with the flaps of my arms because I didn't
want to hear. But there was nothing to see or hear—the room was
static and silent except for the whirring of my insulted laptop. I ambulated past the library where the artist Valentin and the hookers
were splayed out over one another, empty vodka carafes lazing by
their feet. "I am the most generous man in the world," I said aloud
as I looked at the sleeping Russians, their stomachs filled with the ex-

pensive food I had bought them. "And anyone who doesn't understand that is a stupid, ungrateful bitch."

I rolled down to the cellar and found my manservant, Timofey, sleeping on a soiled mattress beside my prized German laundry machine. His hands were tucked angelically beneath his big snoring head; the cord of the Daewoo steam iron I had given him for New Year's was tied several times around one leg to prevent another servant from stealing it. I thought about throwing a shoe at him, but instead gently pushed him in the stomach with my foot. "Up, up, up," I growled. "Rise, Timofey. Rise!"

"Please forgive me, *batyushka*," Timofey murmured out of instinct, trying to shake off a deep slumber. "Timofey's just a sinner like the rest of them."

"Make pies," I instructed my manservant, my body leaning precariously over his, so that he held up his arms out of fright. He mumbled incomprehension. I tried to explain: "Meat pies, cabbage pies, venison pies. I don't want you to stop making pies, you hear? Whatever's in the refrigerators, I want to eat it right away. Don't disappoint me, Timofey."

"Yes, *batyushka*!" Timofey cried. "Pies, pies, pies." He sprang up from his mattress and started running around the cavernous cellar, rousing the servants and commandeering them up the stairs. The house shook with commotion. As usual, when crisis struck, the servants began taking their frustrations out on one another. Yevgenia, my fat cook, was hitting her common-law husband, Anton, who in turn was giving it good to Lara Ivanovna, the pretty new servant. I returned to my analytic room and picked up the laptop. The quick-witted Timofey had already furnished my desk with a half-eaten tin of salmon pâté and a tub of artichoke hearts. I began to fill my mouth with two shaking hands as Rouenna's letter came out of the printer.

Shteynfarb. I could see him now: an ugly little man, dry lips, a Mohawk of black hair carved out by teenage alopecia, dark lizard pouches beneath his eyes, everything in his manner filled with artifice, bullshit laughter, and easy bonhomie. He probably impregnated half his writing class, the half that wasn't knocked up already. Rouenna's major accomplishment in life was staying clear of pregnancy by the advanced age of twenty-five. She was the only woman in her family who didn't have kids, for which her *tías* and *abuelas* and *primas* made fun of her mercilessly. Now even that was in danger. And once Shteynfarb gave her one kid, the rest would start coming. Once a girl got "belly" on 173rd Street, she'd be pregnant till menopause.

I reread the letter. It wasn't my Rouenna writing it. The feistiness was gone. The humor and rage. The love, given either unconditionally or with a poor woman's protective reserve. She claimed Shteynfarb was restoring her "self as-steam," but for the first time since I'd met her, Rouenna seemed to me utterly servile and beaten.

Timofey brought in the first steaming meat and cabbage pie, the room suddenly ablaze with heat and sustenance. I licked my lips, locked my feet together, clenched my right hand into a fist, and swallowed the pie in three takes. Then I went back to the letter, circling sentences with my red pen and writing my responses in the margin.

Proffessor Shteynfarb had a hard life being an immigrant so he knows about hard work.

Bullshit, Rouenna. Shteynfarb's an upper-middle-class phony who came to the States as a kid and is now playing the professional immigrant game. He's probably just using you for material. We got so much more in common, the two of us. You said it yourself, Rowie. Russia *is* the ghetto. And I'm just living large in it, that's all. Who wouldn't live large in the ghetto if they could?

You always secretly look down at me.

From the first night I met you, when you kissed my thing so tenderly, there hasn't been another woman in my life. I am so proud of you for being strong and not giving in to peer pressure and trying to make your life better by becoming an executive secretary. You are worth ten thousand Jerry Shteynfarbs on a bad day, and he knows it.

Proffessor Shteynfarb said its wrong when you throw your shoe at your servant

Why don't you ask Professor Shitfarb to explain the term "cultural relativism" to you. When you live in this kind of society, you've got to throw your shoe sometimes.

If you want to stop paying my hunter tuition I would understand, although I would have to go back to work in the tity bar.

Of course I'm not going to stop paying your tuition. I'm the one who got you to stop working at the titty bar, remember? Everything I have is yours, everything to the very last, my heart, my soul, my wallet, my house. [I decided to finish my response with an appeal to Rouenna's favorite imaginary character.] Just remember, Rouenna, that whatever you do, it is between you and God. So if you want to hurt me, go ahead. But you know that He watches every move you make.

I put down my red pen. I was thinking of the homemade sign crayoned on the door of Rouenna's family's apartment by one of her nineteen little nieces: NO SMOKING NO CURSING NO GAMBLING INSIDE THIS HOUSE JESUS LOVES YOU. We used to sit on a creaking bench in a weed-choked yard behind Rouenna's housing complex, doing a bit of what she called "roughhousin'," as beautiful brown children ran around us, engulfed by summertime happiness, yelling to each other: "When I get out, *puta*, I'm gonna break your fucken face, I fucken swear."

What I wouldn't pay for one more July night on the corner of 173rd Street and Vyse, one more chance to kiss Rouenna and cradle her in my big arms. *I always dream of your arms around me and your weird kui in my mouth.*

My laptop beeped demonstratively. I was worried it might be more bad news from Rouenna, but the message was from Lyuba Vainberg, my father's widow.

Respected Mikhail Borisovich,

I have learned to use the Internet because I hear it's how you prefer to communicate. I am lonely. It would be my pleasure to invite you for

tea and zakuski *tomorrow. Please tell me if you can come and if so I will send my servant girl out for meat in the morning. If you refuse me, I won't blame you. But perhaps you will find pity for a lost soul.*
  With respect,
  Lyuba

So that's how it happened between us. We were both lonely and lost.

11

Lyuba Vainberg Invites Me to Tea

Lyuba lived on the English Embankment, a gorgeous pastel crush of mansions anchored by the yellow curve of the old Senate Building. The Neva River does its best to be civil around here, flowing with a majestic resolve and lapping up the granite embankment with a thousand frothy tongues.

Speaking of tongues, Lyuba had prepared one of her celebrated lamb's tongue sandwiches, very tasty and juicy, with extra horseradish and spicy mustard and garnished with a dollop of gooseberry preserve. She even prepared it in the American manner for me, with two pieces of bread instead of one. I quickly asked for seconds, then thirds, to her immeasurable delight. "Ah, but who looks out for your diet at home?" she asked, mistakenly using the polite form of address with me, as if acknowledging the fact that I was thirty.

"Mmmm-hmmm," I said, letting the tender tongue dissolve on my own (*like making out with a sheep,* I thought). "Who cooks for me? Why, Yevgenia, of course. Remember my cook? She's round and rosy."

"Well, I do my *own* cooking now," Lyuba said proudly. "And when he was alive, I always supervised Boris's diet. There are things to consider other than taste, you know. You have to think of your health, Misha! For example, the lamb's tongue is widely known to possess minerals that give you energy and manly power. It's terribly good for you, especially when you alternate it with Canadian bacon, which helps heal the skin. My servant girl gets only the best from the

Yeliseyev store." She paused and looked me up and down, enjoying
my girth, my time-tested ability to expand under pressure. "Perhaps
I should come over and cook for you," she said. "Or else you're always welcome to come here and eat with me."

Death changes people. I had certainly changed since Beloved
Papa's decapitation, but as for Lyuba, she was positively unrecogniz-
able. It's no secret that Papa treated her like his daughter in many
ways—several times she had called him *papochka*, "little father," while
doing an improvised lap dance at the kitchen table or giving him a
supposedly discreet hand job during the Mariinsky Theatre's mind-
numbing performance of *Giselle* (she thought I had dozed off by the
grape harvest scene, but I was not so lucky).

But now that our *papochka* was gone, Lyuba was handling self-
parenting with great aplomb. Her very diction had improved. It was
no longer the sloppy New Russian of her idiot friends, a gangster-
influenced provincial drawl interspersed with borrowed words like
"dragon roll" and "face control," but a more reserved speech, flattened and depressive, the kind favored by our more cultured, penni-
less citizens.

I was also inspired by her choice of dress. Gone was her usual
Leather Lyuba motif; in its place, a blouse and skirt of dark contemporary denim fastened by an oversize red plastic belt with an enormous faux-Texan buckle. It was very Williamsburg, Brooklyn, circa
right now.

"I must wipe your chin," Lyuba said, scrubbing my double grape-
fruit with three of her long mustard-scented fingers.

"Thank you," I said. "I've never learned how to eat properly."
Which is the truth.

"You know, I bought an orange comforter from Stockmann," she
said, and turned away to expel her breath. I smelled the freshness of
a youthful mouth, a strong British breath mint, and the sulfuric under-
current of lamb's tongue. She smiled, her twin cheekbones going off
the scale of Eastern European cheekbones and into lovely Mongolian
territory, while her pinprick nose stretched itself into nonexistence.
Despite the steady drafts of central air-conditioning, your correspon-

dent felt himself becoming warm-faced and a bit untidy beneath the armpits. The denim blouse hugged Lyuba's frame so that when she turned around, one could see an important crease forming between the cheeks of her *zhopa*. Meanwhile, the talk of orange comforters both soothed and intrigued.

"Won't you come and see it?" she said. "It's in the bedroom," she quickly added. "I'm worried it's not the right one."

"I'm sure it's fine," I said, feeling an unexpected jolt of ethical misgiving. This was followed by an image of Jerry Shteynfarb's authorial goatee burrowing into the heat between Rouenna's thighs. The ethical misgivings evaporated. I followed Lyuba.

We passed through the main quarters, a kind of gallery devoted to outrageous Italian furniture, enough glossy mirrored surfaces that I could catch the devastating sight of my own deflated posterior and the halo of my small but growing bald spot. My papa's meter-long oil painting of a wise but grizzled Maimonides with what looked like a ten-ruble note sticking out of his pocket completed the room. Outside the windows, the gracious classical lines of the Twelve Colleges Building suspended over the Neva provided a necessary counterpoint.

"I'm throwing everything out," Lyuba said, sweeping her hand over the ensemble of buffed mahogany monstrosities possibly entitled Neapolitan Sunrise or something of the sort (there are *warehouses* full of this shit in New York's Brighton Beach, in case the intrepid reader is interested). "If you have the time," Lyuba said, "we can drive down to the IKEA in Moscow, maybe get something in paisley."

"What you're doing, Lyubochka, is very healthy," I told her. "We must all strive to be as Western as possible. That old argument between the Westernizers and the Slavophiles . . . It's not much of an argument at all, is it?"

"Not if you say so," Lyuba said. She opened the bedroom door.

I had to look away at first. Lyuba's comforter was the most *orange* thing I have seen this side of the Accidental College library, which was built in 1974, possibly by the American Citrus Growers' Association. It was . . . I couldn't find the right word. An entire sun had exploded in Lyuba's bedroom, leaving behind its afterglow for us to ponder.

"You've become a modern woman," I said, and heaved myself aboard with a few difficult motions.

"Feel the smoothness," Lyuba said as she settled in beside me. "It looks like it's fashionable polyester from the American seventies, but it feels like cotton. I've got to find a good dry cleaner. Otherwise they'll just bleed the orange out."

"That mustn't happen," I said. "You've really got something here." Above her dresser I noticed a framed photograph of Beloved Papa unveiling a tombstone shaped like a giant Nokia mobile phone at his graveyard for New Russian Jews, sacrilegious laughter gathering in his clever eyes.

"But wait, there's more," Lyuba announced. She ran into the bathroom and came out with a pair of orange towels. "This is what you and Svetlana were talking about at the Home of the Russian Fisherman!" she said. "See, I listen to everything you say!"

I squinted at the towels, feeling a spectacular headache gathering steam somewhere in my sinuses. "Maybe you should mix the orange with some other Western color," I suggested. "Lime, maybe."

Lyuba bit her smooth lower lip. "Perhaps," she said. She looked doubtfully at the towels in her hands. "It's hard to know these things, Misha . . . Sometimes I think I'm such a fool . . . Ah, but listen to *this*!" She turned on a little stereo with the flick of one lacquered nail. It didn't take me long to recognize the Humungous G's gorgeous urban love ballad "I'm Busting My Nut Tonight." Lyuba laughed and sang along with the soulful R&B chorus, moving her hands in front of her torso in a sad Russian approximation of slow jamming. "I'm *baaaaasting* my nut tonight / Your *pusseeeee* feels so tight," she sang in a tired but hospitable voice.

"Uhhhh, uhhhh, uhhhh," I grunted along with the chorus. "Uhhhh, shit," I added.

"I know you and Alyosha love this song," she said. "I've been playing it over and over. It's so much better than techno and Russian pop."

"In terms of popular music"—I spoke now with the authority of a former Multicultural Studies major—"you should listen mainly to East Coast hip-hop and ghetto tech from Detroit. We must reject European music categorically. Even so-called progressive house! Do you hear me, Lyuba?"

"Categorically!" Lyuba said. She looked at me with her soft, vacant gray eyes. She pressed both hands into the formidable ridge of her breastbone. "Mikhail," she said, using my formal name, which, for as long as I've lived, usually means some form of punishment is at hand. I looked up expectantly.

"Help me convert to Judaism," she said. She plopped down on the orange comforter, pressed her skinny legs into her tummy, and beamed the inquisitive look of youth in my direction. There was some tenderness there, a warmth in my belly, and I could feel it start spreading below. I looked at her beside me—little Lyuba in her too-tight denim dress, the two firm potato dumplings of her *zhopa* rubbing against my milky outer thigh. I needed to concentrate on the conversation at hand. Now, what was she saying? Jews? Conversion? I had much to say on the matter.

"Turning into a Jew is not a good idea," I told her, my grave tone likening it to turning into a dung beetle. "Whatever you may think of Judaism, Lyuba, in the end it's just a codified system of anxieties. It's a way to keep an already nervous and maligned people in check. It's a losing proposition for everyone involved, the Jew, his friend, even his enemy in the end."

Lyuba was not convinced. "You and your father are the only good people in my life," she said. "And I want to be tied to both of you by something substantial. Think how great it would be if we could pray to the same God"—she turned her matted blond head into her armpit—"and if we could share a life together."

The second part of that sentence I decided to put aside for the moment, because all the lies and evasions in the world were not going to erase her plaintive, impossible plea from my waxy ears. So I wanted to disabuse her of the first part, at least. "Lyuba," I said in my most even (and most detestable) voice, "you must understand that there is no God."

Lyuba turned her pink face to me and smiled gratuitously, favoring me with one of her laminated thirty-one-tooth salutes (a prominent incisor had to be retired last summer after she misjudged the strength of a walnut).

"Of course there is a God," she said.

"No, there is not," I said. "In fact, the part of our soul we reserve for God is a kind of negative space where our worst sentiments reside, our jealousy, our ire, our justification for violence and spite. If you are indeed interested in Judaism, Lyuba, you should carefully read the Old Testament. You should pay particular attention to the character of the Hebrew God and His utter contempt for all things democratic and multicultural. I think the Old Testament makes my point rather forcefully, page by page."

Lyuba laughed at my little tirade. "I think you believe in God in your own way," she said. Then she added, "You're a funny man."

Ah, the impudence of youth! The easy manner of their speech! Who was she, this *Lyuba,* this girl my father had rescued from some Astrakhan collective farm a few years ago, all covered in hog shit and bruises? This sullen teenager he had adopted like the daughter he wished he had fathered instead of me—skinny, loyal, and without a tantalizing purple *khui* he could swipe at. I had always thought of Lyuba as a contemporary version of Fenechka in Turgenev's *Fathers and Sons,* the peasant housekeeper, obtuse and limited, who falls into the arms of the kindly minor noble Kirsanov, to be played in the movie version by Beloved Papa. My capacity for misunderstanding the range of people is truly astonishing. Lyuba was no Fenechka. She was more like a modern-day Anna Karenina or that silly brat Natasha in *War and the Other Thing.*

"Hey," she said. "It's my favorite part of the song. When Humungous G . . . how do you say it? When he *busts.*"

"When Humungous G busts some rhymes," I said.

She stood up on the bed, and with her hands making jabbing urban motions, her hips thrusting like those of a fertile American university student, Lyuba sang:

Seexty-inch plasma screen
Bitch, you never seen
Such mad expensive shit
Poot my fingers on your clit
Uh, sex in the Lex
Check my dzhenuine Rolex
Vaiping cum off your tits
I'm busting phat beats
Right past yo' shoulder
It's over
Now go coook for my kids

"That's very pretty," I said. "Your English is improving."

"And another great thing about Judaism," she said, "is how old it is. Boris told me that by the Jew calendar, we're in the year 5760!"

"It just doesn't stop, does it?" I said. "But what is the past, Lyuba? The past is murky and distant, while the future we can only guess at. The present! Now, that's something to believe in. If you want to know what I worship, Lyuba, it is the sanctity of the present moment."

Words have consequences. For at this point Lyuba jumped up from the bed, unhooked her Texas-style belt, and, in an Olympic moment, catapulted the hem of her long denim dress over her knees, her brown wiry *pizda*, her taut belly, the long pale oval of her face—until, momentarily, she stood there naked before me.

She was staring furtively into some incidental part of me, my abdomen, say, her hands by her sides. After a while, she lowered her gaze still farther, until it fell onto her own breasts, two little white baggies that lay peaceably atop her tanned ribs.

She picked up one breast, squeezed it, and then did likewise with the other.

"Well, that's how it is," she told me with a shrug. "I'm very hot for you inside."

I lay there, half a meter away from this young Russian woman, trying to remember who I was, exactly, and whether sympathy could masquerade for arousal or the other way around. There was reason for both. Lyuba had a lean, athletic body (especially for someone who did nothing all day), interrupted only by a swatch of shiny, hardened skin running along one hip and dipping toward her genitals, where a relative had set fire to her when she was twelve. Beloved Papa had always claimed that this was the part he kissed most gently, but it was hard to tease this simple image—Papa's fish lips puckered atop Lyuba's disfigurement, his everyday rage tempered by compassion—out of my already put-upon imagination.

Events were taking place that made me feel somehow peripheral. Lyuba was lying down on the bed once more, her legs hanging in the air, her *pizda* a cozy brown-fur pelt between them. "I have to prepare myself," she said. She took out a plastic tube and, with a most unpleasant sound, squirted something onto her fingers. She then inserted the fingers inside herself. "This makes it easier for me," she explained.

It was impolite to just sit there and stare. I began to take off my pants so that I could present my purple half-*khui*, my abused iguana, to Lyuba. It is a capital insult in this country not to make love to a naked woman, even if she is related to you. And so I was compelled to act like a man, though in reality I had long ago floated right through the ceiling, past the ocher jumble of Leninsburg roofs, over and around the golden prick of the Admiralty, and onto the dark blue expanse of the Gulf of Finland, where I used to believe my dead mother's essence hovered about in a happy, cultured limbo above the topiary of one of the czars' summer palaces (though, as I've said before, nothing of our personality survives after death).

Meanwhile, in a surprise move, my mercurial genital had already engorged itself and was positioned for love, proof that one doesn't actually have to be present to consummate the sex act. It dawned upon me that Lyuba had set "Busting My Nut Tonight" on repeat play, and that Humungous G's urban missive was helping me focus

on the task at hand. Busting my nut *when?* Why, tonight, of course.
I crawled on my knees along the orange comforter toward Lyuba,
bringing the *khui* toward her.

"My *khui*," I announced sadly.

"Yes, it's your *khuichik*," Lyuba said, tilting her head for a better
view.

"It is possible to touch it now," I whispered, letting Lyuba tug at
my much-maligned *khui*-knob with a cold hand. I turned it sideways
so that she could see the long scar running along its underbelly, the
clumps of skin attached at improvised angles like the fragmented bits
of a car bumper following a head-on collision.

"Ai, what happened?" Lyuba asked.

I took a deep breath and blurted out my story in one long sentence, digressing only to explain the words "*mitzvah* mobile."

She put the purple thing in her mouth to silence me. No matter
how often it happens, it is always surprising to find a woman's wet
mouth drawing tight around my *khui*.

"Mm," she said.

"What?" I said.

She took the *khui* out. "It tastes fine," she said. "You're very
clean."

"Well, I'm not worried about the taste," I said.

"Lie down on me," Lyuba said.

I did as she said. Her body was cold underneath mine, and even
the inside of her *pizda* was barely at room temperature, probably because she had overlubricated with what must have been a very cold
gel. I kept slipping out and getting angry, but I used the anger to
poke her all the harder. We were in the traditional baby-making position, and from my vantage point I could barely make out the con-
tours of her small Slavic breasts. Lyuba's eyes were closed, and she
seemed to be moving her hips from left to right to the sound of Humungous's phat beats, which was not the rhythm I had in mind. "We
should be either dancing or fucking," I complained.

Either dancing or fucking. That was pure Beloved Papa. I even had
that idiotic Odessa gangster accent he used when he thought he was
being suave.

"Sorry," she said, and moved her hips in a more accommodating up-and-down fashion, cupping her breasts to give them more shape. I dutifully tucked into each sturdy nipple with my big American-made teeth, then moved my face up to look into Lyuba's. She was wincing in rhythm to our quiet humping (my weight is an impossible thing to bear), her eyes wet and focused on the ceiling. She squeezed my ass, perhaps to encourage me. She seemed to want me to say something. To commiserate with her. But it's hard to know what to say when you're *khui*-deep inside your father's young wife.

So instead I tried to be gentle. I looked deep into the hollows beside her nose, where a herd of teenage orange freckles once roamed. The surgery that had removed them was not perfect, and I could still see, beneath the initial layer of skin, the afterimage of the burnt-out orange spots. I kissed these blemishes, her childhood's last bequest, drawing a forced smile from Lyuba. I carefully touched the hardened skin where her relative had charred her. It was the consistency of warm cellophane, and it was frightening.

"Ai," she said. "You're tickling me. Will you finish soon?"

"I'm sorry," I whispered. I was sweating all over her. The room was stale and tropical, filled with the odor of an unhealthy male body suddenly pressed into service.

"It's okay," she said. "It's this lubricant—"

"No, it's my fault," I said. "I'm taking all these medications, so it's hard to— Oh! Ah, wait, Lyubochka! Oofa!"

And so it was over. I pulled out of Lyuba and looked at my wet knob. One of my testicles was missing. It had apparently risen up into my abdomen. "Fuck, Lyuba," I said. "I'm missing an egg here. Fuck, fuck, fuck."

"You're not satisfied with me," Lyuba said.

I poked around there for a bit, worried that the nonexistent God was taking His Freudian revenge on me. The testicle descended. My hands were shaking. Humungous G was still singing "I'm Busting My Nut Tonight." Never in my life had I found hip-hop to be so detestable. Plus there was something else to consider. Lyuba. Intercourse. Nature's remorseless path. "Oh, the devil take it," I said. "We didn't use a *prezervatiff*."

"It's Monday," Lyuba said. "I never get pregnant on a Monday."

She was making a fort for herself out of the fringes of the comforter, sinking her whitish body into its orange ramparts with many postcoital sighs, preparing herself for a fine afternoon nap. What did she say? No pregnancies on Mondays. Wonderful. Now, why was Humungous G still rapping? I went over to the stereo and punched it with my big, squishy hand, but the fat urban motherfucker just kept on *bangin'*.

"You're not satisfied with me," Lyuba repeated, clicking off the stereo with a remote control. "Boris usually made a special sound. Like he was happy."

"No, it was very nice," I said. I tried to think from a goal-oriented perspective, just as they taught us at Accidental College. "I finished inside you."

I looked up at the photograph of my father happily unveiling the Nokia-phone tombstone, three Soviet-era gold teeth glinting in the sun, a combed-over black curl forming a Spanish ¿ across his forehead. I felt myself losing my precarious hold on consciousness and set myself down on the bed. Lyuba yawned widely, and I smelled her lamb-tongue breath once more, which reminded me quickly of every Russian person I had ever known—from my dead grandmothers, who took me for stroller rides along the English embankment, to Timofey, my loyal manservant, who was presently waiting for me with the Land Rover on the very spot where I was once strolled. All of us had enjoyed a lamb's tongue in our lifetime. How droll!

"Let's get some sleep, then," Lyuba said. "Our bed is very comfortable. It's like staying at the Marriott in Moscow."

Our bed, indeed, was very comfortable. Her *zhopa* rubbed at me from behind, the way Rouenna's used to rub me when I couldn't fall asleep during anxious nights. Lyuba seemed to want me to put my arms around her little body. Her hair smelled musty and yet artificial, like nothing I had encountered before. I imagined Lyuba as a woman in her thirties, her hair hennaed a popular aquamarine color, her posture stooped like that of so many of our premature *babushkas*. Would she even be alive then?

"I hope we make lots of love together, little father," she whispered.

I tried to go to sleep, but there was nothing to dream about, except the usual Eastern European nonsense about a man sailing an inflatable Fanta bottle around the world looking for happiness. But one thought remained and would not be extinguished.

That wasn't too bright, Misha.

The curtains of consciousness were being lowered around me, gray and gold-sequined like a fading summer day here in our crappy Venice of the North.

Not too bright, you stepmother-fucking, father-hating joke of a man.

12

Everything Has Its Limits

Two hours later, outside her bedroom door, Lyuba's servants had fallen asleep, much like their mistress. Their ears were pressed to the door; even in their evening stupor, they were listening for sounds of our bed creaking. "Scoundrels," I hissed at the mess of bleary-eyed bodies. "You like to hear your mistress fucking hard, eh? May the devil take you! Well, enough! Everything has its limits, don't you know!"

Out on the English Embankment, Timofey and my driver, Mamudov, were sitting on the hood of the Land Rover drinking shots of vodka, blasting the Spartak-Zenit football match on the speakers, and hugging each other in a warm drunken embrace. "Hullo, gentlemen!" I shouted to them in English. "Do you want to hear something? I'll tell you, then! Everything has its limits!"

And I walked off down the embankment like a supercilious transvestite bitch, swinging my hands in the air and my hips below. I passed by the Bronze Horseman, the statue of the curly-haired asshole Peter the Great charging up a steep rock, galloping northward, abandoning the ruined city he founded for the fair shores of Finland, leaving those of us without an EU visa nothing but the tail end of his fat bronze mare.

"Everything has its limits!" I shouted to a wedding party posing beneath Peter, skinny-ass twenty-year-olds who could not grasp the empty terror of the rest of their lives.

"Hurrah, strange one!" they shouted at me, vodka bottles raised, drunk as all get-out.

One of their grandmothers stood guard over their wedding car, a crushed Lada micro-sedan festooned with blue and white ribbons. "That's what I thought, too," she happily told me through her two teeth. "That everything has its limits. But each year I'm proven wrong!"

"Rejoice, *babushka*!" I shouted. "Soon things will change. There will be limits! To everything!"

"Yes, limits or labor camps," the grandmother said. "Either way, I'm happy."

By this point Timofey and Mamudov were following behind me in the Land Rover, Timofey leaning out his window, yelling, "Come back, young master! All will be well! We'll go to the American Clinic. Dr. Yegorov, your favorite, has walk-in appointments today. A new supply of Celexa just came in."

I turned around, one hand on my hip, one giant fist in the air. "Won't you acknowledge, dear Timofey, that everything has its limits?" I shouted. "That I am not just some educated, Westernized animal you can kick in the mug?"

"I acknowledge!" Timofey yelled. "I acknowledge! What more do you want?"

But I wanted more. Oh, did I ever want more. I took off down the embankment, my buttery thighs slapping against each other, until I hit the green confectionery of the Winter Palace, one of its lesser buildings draped with the sign THIS YEAR'S WHITE NIGHTS BROUGHT TO YOU BY DAEWOO. I stopped and breathed in the cheap diesel fuel and burning tar, the heavy air of a third-world metropolis misplaced five thousand kilometers to the north, but lacking the rich scent of burning goat and honey cakes.

Even the evocative stench of poverty we couldn't get right.

Turning on the Palace Bridge, I counted three of the cast-iron lampposts, until I reached the stretch of asphalt where my father was executed. There was nothing there. Just a traffic jam of old Ladas, with one lone Land Rover bringing up the rear. "*Batyushka,* come back," I could hear Timofey screaming in the distance. "There's no need to panic! We have Ativan in the car. Ativan!"

I sat down by the third lamppost. The city's horizons were crowding me in; the fortresses and domes and spires were meant for either a smaller person than me or a greater one. But understand me: I was looking for something in the middle. I was looking for a normal life. "Everything has its limits," I said to the crush of passing Ladas and their haggard occupants. "Everything has its limits," I whispered to a teenage boy writhing in a Polish hatchback rigged up as a municipal ambulance, its broken siren emitting the wrong squawk, more a dirge than a warning.

Timofey had quit the Land Rover and was running toward me with two bottles of meds in each hand. I took out my *mobilnik* and dialed Alyosha-Bob. It was Monday evening, and I knew I would hear the motley sounds of Club 69 on the other end.

"Yo!" Alyosha shouted past the din.

Club 69 is a gay club, but anyone who can afford the three-dollar cover charge—in other words, the richest 1 percent of our city—shows up there at some point during the week. Homosexuality aside, this is without a doubt the most normal place in Russia, no low-level thugs in leather parkas, no skinheads in jackboots, just friendly gay guys and the rich housewives who love them. It brings to mind that popular phrase bandied about by expatriate Americans over their bagels and cream cheese: *civil society.*

Alyosha-Bob and his Svetlana were sitting beneath a statue of Adonis, watching a submarine captain trying to sell his young crew to a gay German tour group. The seventeen-year-old boys were awkwardly trying to cover their nakedness, while their drunken captain barked at them to let go of their precious goods and "shake them around like a wet dog." I suppose civil society has its limits, too.

"I've got to get out of Russia," I said to Alyosha-Bob. "Everything has its limits."

"Yes, fine," Alyosha-Bob said. "But why now, exactly?"

I saw my future with Lyuba. Picking out paisley furniture in Moscow's IKEA. Being called little father as I mounted her. Supper beneath the meter-long oil painting of Maimonides; dinner next to Papa's censorious black-and-white gaze. Eventually two rich, unhappy children: a five-year-old boy in a Dolce & Gabbana gangster suit, his younger sister lost beneath an alligator's worth of leather accessories. Everywhere around us snickering servants, collapsed infrastructure, sniveling grandmothers . . . Russia, Russia, Russia . . .

But how could I explain all this to Alyosha-Bob? St. Leninsburg was his playground. His drunken dream come true.

"Are you running away because you fucked Lyuba today?" Svetlana asked.

"Is it true?" Alyosha-Bob asked. "You gave it to Boris Vainberg's old lady?"

"Do you see what kind of a city we live in?" I said. "I gave it to her just three hours ago. We should never hand out *mobilniki* to the servants. It's probably the talk of the Internet by now."

"I agree with you, Misha," Svetlana said. "You *should* leave. I keep telling this idiot"—she pointed to Alyosha-Bob—"that we have to get out of here, too. There's a one-year master's in public relations program at Boston University. They have this practice lab where you can work as an account executive for local nonprofits. I could work for the Boston Ballet! I could be cultured and clever and earn a respectable living. I'd show the Americans that not every Russian woman is a whore."

"Listen to her," Alyosha-Bob said. "The Boston Ballet. And what's wrong with our Kirov? It was good enough for Baryshnikov, no?"

"You just want to spend your whole life here, Alyosha," Sveta said, "because back in America you're a nothing man."

"Shh! Look who's here," Alyosha-Bob said. "The murderer."

Captain Belugin, wiping his hoary face with the sleeve of his green Armani shirt, ambled over to our table. He looked older than when I'd seen him at Papa's funeral, his ears drooping down like cabbage leaves. "*Allo,* brothers," he said, crashing down on a stool. "Sveta. How are you, pretty one? *Nu,* we're all aficionados of Club 69, I see. And what of it? It's a good business to be queer. Sometimes I like a little boy beside me. They're more hairless than my wife. More feminine, too. Hey, Seryozha." He waved to a cherubic young fellow in a thong, dishing out vodka from a slop pail. "Give it here, good lad."

"Well, my Alyosha's not a pederast," Svetlana said. "He merely comes to Club 69 for the atmosphere. And to make connections."

"Hi, Seryozha," I said to the friendly boy. "How's life, cucumber?"

"Seryozha number one, true love forever, I am only just for you," Seryozha said in English, blowing me a professional kiss.

"Seryozha's going to Thailand with a rich Swede," Captain Belugin announced as Seryozha smiled at us like a shy albino marmoset. He scooped the vodka out with a beaker, pouring us a hundred grams a head. "Better watch out for the cockroaches there," said Belugin. "They're like this . . ." He spread out his arms, favoring us with his briny armpits.

"Cirrus, Europay, ATM, one-stop banking . . . Super Dollar, why you lonely?" Seryozha said. He wiggled his tush for us and left.

"Good boy," Belugin said. "We could use him on the force. They're so clean here. Hygiene. Morality starts with hygiene. Just look at the Germans." We glanced over to the middle-aged members of the German tour group throwing deutsche marks at our teenage countrymen, bringing us tidings of an advanced civilization. We heard an enormous cheer from downstairs. The floor show was about to start— the pioneer songs of our youth bellowed out by muscular drag queens in full Soviet regalia. I found it very nostalgic.

"I wish I could leave this stupid country just like Seryozha," I said.

"And why can't you?" Belugin asked.

"The Americans won't give me a visa because they say my papa killed that Oklahoman fellow. And the European Union won't let any Vainbergs in, either."

"Ach," Belugin said to me. "Why do you want to move to the West, young man? Things will improve for our people, just you wait. In a mere fifty years, I predict, life here will be brighter than even in Yugoslavia. You know, Misha, I've been to Europe. The streets are cleaner, but there's no Russian *soul*. Do you know what I'm talking about here? You can't just sit down with a man in Copenhagen and look him in the eye over a shot glass and then—*boof!*—you are brothers forever."

"Please . . ." I said. "I want to . . . I want—"

"Well, of course you *want*," said the captain. "What kind of a young man would you be if you didn't *want*? I understand you implicitly. We old men were once young, too, don't forget!"

"Yes," I said, following his logic. "I'm young. So I want."

"Then let me help you, Misha. You see, I am originally from the Republic of Absurdsvanï, land of oil and grapes. Absurdistan, as we like to call it. I'm a Russian by blood, but I also know the way of the infamous Svanï people, those lusty Southern black-asses, those Cretins of the Caucasus. Now, one of my friends in Svanï City is a counselor at the Belgian embassy. A European of great learning and propriety. I wonder if, for a small sum, he could arrange for your citizenship in the Flemish kingdom . . ."

"That sounds like a sensible idea," Alyosha-Bob said. "What about it, Misha? If you get a Belgian passport, you can travel all over the continent."

"Maybe Rouenna will come live with me," I said. "Maybe I can tempt her away from Jerry Shteynfarb. Belgium is full of chocolate and fries, right?"

"We could fly down to Absurdistan next week," Alyosha-Bob said. "I own a branch of ExcessHollywood there. There's a direct Aeroflot flight on Monday."

"I'm *not* flying Aeroflot," I told my friend. "I don't want to die just yet. We'll take Austrian Airlines through Vienna. I'll pay for everything."

I pictured myself sitting at a zippy Belgian café watching a multicultural woman in a thong eating a frankfurter. Did such things happen in Brussels? In New York they happened all the time.

"So, Belugin," Alyosha-Bob said to the captain. "What's it going to cost for Misha to get his Belgian passport?"

"What will it cost? Nothing, nothing." Captain Belugin waved it off. "Well, almost nothing. A hundred thousand U.S. for my Belgian friend, and a hundred thousand for me as an introduction fee."

"I want my manservant to come with me," I said. "I need a Belgian work visa for my Timofey."

"You're bringing your manservant?" Alyosha-Bob said. "You're quite a Westerner, Count Vainberg."

"Go to the *khui*," I said. "I'd like to see you wash your own socks the way I once washed mine with my working-class girlfriend in New York."

"Boys." Captain Belugin put a hand between us. "A work visa is the height of simplicity. Another twenty thousand for me, and twenty thousand for Monsieur Lefèvre of the Belgian embassy. You'll be fast friends with Jean-Michel. He likes to run over the locals with his Peugeot."

"Has Oleg the Moose's money been moved to Misha's offshore accounts?" Alyosha-Bob asked.

"Misha's got about thirty-five million dollars in Cyprus," Belugin said, looking over his yellow fingernails, obviously not too impressed by the remainder of Beloved Papa's carefully hoarded fortune, a long trail of wrecked factories, misappropriated natural gas concessions, the much-talked-about VainBergAir (an airline without any airplanes but with plenty of stewardesses), and, of course, the infamous grave-yard for New Russian Jews.

It didn't sound like much money to me, either, to be honest. Let's do the math. I was thirty, and the official life expectancy for a Russian male is fifty-six, so I probably had another twenty-six or so years to live. Thirty-five million divided by twenty-six years equals about US$1,350,000 a year. That wasn't much for Europe, but I could survive. Hell, I got by on a mere US$200,000 a year in New York when I was young, though I didn't have a manservant to support, and I often denied myself certain pleasures (never have I owned a hot-air balloon or a Long Island bungalow).

But who cares about my poverty! For the first time in an eternity, I felt a current of pure pleasure wend itself around my beleaguered liver and up my bloated lungs. Freedom was upon me.

I remembered my childhood escapes from Leningrad, the annual summer train trip to the Crimea. Blessed memories of little Misha leaning out the carriage window, the Russian countryside crawling up to the train tracks, an occasional aspen whipping Misha's curious face. I always knew that summer was drawing near when my mother came over with my crumpled Panama hat and sang an improvised tune for me:

Misha the Bear
Is leaving his lair
He's had enough
Of winter's despair

Yes, I've had enough of it, *mamochka*! I smiled and hiccuped into my shot glass. There was something oddly fetching about the prospect of being alive today, knowing that next week I would follow Peter the Great's bronze steed. I would fulfill every educated young Russian's dream. I would go *beyond the cordon*.

"Here's what I want you to do," Captain Belugin said. "As soon as you land in Absurdistan, go to the Park Hyatt Svanï City and talk to Larry Zartarian, the manager. He'll make all the necessary arrangements. You'll be a Belgian in no time."

"Belgium," Sveta said wistfully. "You're a very lucky man."

"You're a great big cosmopolitan whore," Alyosha-Bob said, "but I love you."

"You're a traitor to your country, but what can be done?" Captain Belugin said.

I reflected upon their words and raised a toast to myself. "Yes, what can be done?" I said. "Everything has its limits."

The glasses clinked. My future was set. I drank vodka and felt ennobled. Of course, with the benefit of hindsight, I can tell you now: I was wrong about everything. Family, friendship, coitus, the future, the past, even the present, my mainstay . . . even that I managed to get wrong.

13

Misha the Bear Takes to the Air

I assembled my household staff and told them they were free of my service. They immediately started crying into their aprons and tearing at their hair. "Don't you have some province you can go to?" I asked them. "Aren't you tired of city life? Be free!" The problem, it turned out, was that they had no money, and their provincial relatives had all but forsaken them; soon enough they would face homelessness and starvation, then the onset of the terrible Russian winter. So I gave each US$5,000, and they all threw themselves around my neck and wept.

Moved by my own largesse, I summoned Svetlana and the artist Valentin, who was still camped out in my library along with his Naomi and Ruth. "I'm starting a charity called Misha's Children," I said. "I have allocated US$2,000,000 to benefit the children of the city I was born in."

They looked at me sideways.

"That's St. Petersburg," I clarified.

Still no reaction.

"Sveta," I said, "you've mentioned how you want to work for a nonprofit agency. This is your chance. You will be the executive director. You will airlift twenty progressive social workers from Park Slope, Brooklyn, and set them to work on the most incorrigible of our children. Valentin, you will be the artistic director, teaching the young ones that redemption lies in Web design as well as clinical social work. Your salaries will be US$80,000 per annum." (To give the reader a sense of scale, the average Petersburg annual salary is US$1,800.)

Sveta asked to see me in private. "I am most honored," she said, "but I think it is foolish to entrust Valentin with such responsibility. I know he works for Alyosha and is designing a website for him, but he's also quite a superfluous man, wouldn't you say?"

"We're all fairly superfluous men," I said, pace Turgenev. I shook her hand, kissed the weeping Valentin three times on the cheeks, bade farewell to his whores, then summoned my driver for the last time. It was early Monday morning, the population still working through a collective hangover, but Petersburg, when free of the human element, looks especially fine. The palaces on Nevsky Prospekt, wishing to properly say goodbye to me, dusted themselves off and bowed their chipped baldachinos in my direction; the canals flowed most romantically, hoping to outdo one another; the moon fell and the sun rose to demonstrate the nocturnal and diurnal lay of the land; but I would not be moved. "Forward, not a step backward," I said, washing my hands clean of Peter the Great's creation. We pulled into the ridiculous airport, a monstrous beige fort where Western tourists were abused in a hundred different ways, a tiny shat-upon redoubt more suited to Montgomery, Alabama, than a city of five million souls. At Customs there was a sad scene as Timofey's son, Slava, wept on his father's neck. "I'll send for you, sonny," my manservant said, patting the young man's balding head. "You'll join me in Brussels, and we'll be merry together. Take my Daewoo steam iron."

"I don't need any Brussels," Slava said, spitting into his own hand. From the way he pronounced the name of the Belgian capital, it was clear he had never heard of it. "I need my papa."

I could commiserate with him—I needed my papa, too.

The Austrian Airlines plane timidly pulled up to the gate. By a quirk of geography, Petersburg is only a forty-minute flight from the ultra-modern city of Helsinki, Finland, the northeastern bastion of the European Union. After we'd boarded and the plane had hobbled down the rutted runway and ascended, we looked down at the country beneath us, at the strange shapes of superannuated factories squatting below. I considered composing a proper fare-thee-well to the nation that had nursed me with sour milk and a cold nipple, then held me in her thick, freckled arms for too long. But before we knew it, Russia was gone.

Timofey was sent to economy, while Alyosha-Bob and I enjoyed the first-class cabin. It was still morning, so we limited ourselves to Irish coffees and a light snack of Scottish salmon and crepes. Grabbing my stomach in two hands, I rolled the toxic hump against the wide lumbar-supporting seat, gasping with pleasure. I don't think any man has ever been as excited to fly over Poland in an Airbus jet. I grabbed a butter knife and challenged Alyosha-Bob to a mock duel; we clanged utensils for a while, my friend clearly sharing in my joy, but it seemed the other first-class passengers were not amused by our exuberance. Even this early in the day, the multinational businessmen were clacking away on their laptops with one hand and spreading Nutella over their crepes with the other, whispering to their companions on how best to carve up Russia's dwindling industry and win favor with some American mutual fund.

Then I noticed the Hasid.

Be good, I told myself, knowing that in the end, it would not be possible to hold my tongue. He was in his thirties, scraggly-bearded and pimpled, as are they all, with red eyes round as coins. He did not wear the usual top hat, just a jaunty fedora, beneath which peeked out the half-moon of his yarmulke. I doubted he had actually bought a first-class ticket, this citizen of the Eternal *Shtetl,* so perhaps some kind of upgrade scheme was in effect. You never know with these people.

A stewardess was bent over the Hasid, trying to coax him into accepting a kosher meal of chicken livers on toast points that they had prepared especially for him. The Hasid blinked repeatedly at the hostess's young Austrian bosom, but on the subject of the livers, he would not yield. "It has to be certified," he kept saying, nasally and dourly. "There are many ginds of gosher. Where's the certifigation?"

"No, this is kosher, sir," the stewardess insisted. "Many Jews have eaten it. I've seen them eat it."

"I need proof," the Hasid whined. "Where's my proof? Where's the certifigate? I need the rabbinigal supervision. Show me the proof and I'll eat it." Eventually the stewardess left, and when she did, the Hasidic cretin reached into a velvety black pouch to produce a can of tuna, some mayo, and a slice of matzoh. Licking his fat lips, he hunched his shoulders and, with some effort, pried the lid off the tuna can. Then, as if lost in one of his interminable *Baruch, Baruch* prayers, the Hasid began to thoughtfully mix the mayonnaise and the tuna together, rocking slowly as he did so. I watched him for about four hundred kilometers of airspace, mixing his mayo and tuna, then spreading it carefully on the brittle matzoh. Each time the stewardess passed, he would shield his creation from the gentile passage of her Teutonic behind. "A firm Austrian ass," he seemed to be saying to himself, "does not mix with my kosher tuna fish."

Would it be eliminationist of me to say that I wanted to kill him? Are there certain feelings that, as a Jew, I may safely harbor in my fat heart that a non-Jew may not? Would it really be self-hatred to despise this man with whom I shared nothing more than a squirrelly strand of DNA?

The Hasid lowered his mouth into his beard to murmur a few words of thanks to his god for this pathetic bounty, then, with a crackle, bit into his store-bought tuna and glorified cracker. Thinking about the cheap fish combined with the foul inner lining of his mouth nearly turned my stomach. Since I was four rows away, it would not have been possible to smell the pungent Hasid, but the mind creates its own scents. I could no longer keep silent.

"Fräulein," I called to the stewardess, who ambled over and gave me, at best, a business-class smile, front teeth only. "I am horribly offended by the gentleman Hasid," I said, "and I would like you to ask him to put away his awful food. This is first class. I expect a civilized ambience, not a trip to Galicia circa 1870."

The stewardess fully opened her mouth. She held her hands before her in some kind of protective gesture. I noticed the little poky hips stretching her uniform: sexy, in a childbearing way. "Sir," she whispered, "we allow our passengers to bring their meals on the plane. It is to accommodate their religion, yes?"

"I am a Hebrew," I said, showing her my big, squishy hands. "I share the same faith as that man. But I would never eat such a meal in first class. This is barbarity!" I was raising my voice, and the Hasid craned his neck to look at me. He was a sweaty sight, eyes moist, as if he had just emerged from his prayer house.

"Easy, Snack Daddy," Alyosha-Bob said. "Chill."

"No, I will not chill," I said to my homey. And then to the stewardess: "I am a patron of multiculturalism more than anyone on this plane. By turning away your chicken livers, this man is practicing a most sanctimonious form of racism. He is spitting in all our faces! Chiefly mine."

"Here we go," Alyosha-Bob murmured. "Put our Misha in a Western setting, and he starts acting out."

"This is not acting out," I hissed. "You'll know when I *act out*."

The stewardess apologized for my distress and told me she would bring around a higher authority. A tall, homosexual Austrian man soon appeared and told me he was the chief purser, or something of the sort. I explained my predicament. "This is a very awkward situation," the purser began, staring at his feet. "We are—"

"Austrian," I said. "I know. It's fine. I absolve you of your terrible guilt. But this is not about you, it's about us. It's good Jew versus bad Jew. It's mainstream versus intolerance, and by supporting the Hasid, you're perpetuating your own hate crime."

"Eggs-cuse me," the Hasid was saying as he stood on his hind legs to a tremendous Hasidic length of almost seven feet. "I goudln't help overhearing—"

"Please, sir, sit down," the purser said. "We're taking care of this."

"Yes, sure, coddle the Hasid," I said, and then rose myself, smacking the purser lightly with my stomach. "If this is how you run your first class, then I will go to economy to sit with my manservant."

"Your seat is *here*, sir," said the stewardess. "You have paid for it." The purser, meanwhile, fluttered his dainty hands to indicate that I should keep walking right out of his gilded realm. Alyosha-Bob was laughing at my foolishness, tapping his head with his fist to indicate that I was not all well.

And he was right: I wasn't all well.

"Because of you, I am not a man," I spat at the Hasid as I walked past his row. "You took the best part of me. You took what mattered." Before leaving, I turned around to address the first-class passengers: "Beware of their *mitzvah* mobiles, fellow Jews among you. Beware of circumcisions late in life. Beware of easy faith. The Hasids are not like us. Don't even think it." With those words, I pulled back the curtain into steerage. I will not risk humanizing the first-class Hasid by writing down in detail the medieval horror upon his pale face, the cyclical, never-ending fright that so distorts our people.

In the cramped economical quarters, by a reeking bathroom, in the midst of a wildly discordant color scheme drawn to make poor folk feel better about their travel, I found a seat next to my Timofey. "What are you doing, *batyushka?*" he whispered. "Why are you here? This place is not for you!" Indeed, it was difficult to reach a rapprochement between my girth and the Austrian concept of an economy seat; I ended up with my ass where my back should have been, palms pressed into the seat in front of me.

"I am here out of principle," I told my manservant, reaching over to pat his spongy old head with its thick womanlike hairs. "I am here because a Yid tried to take my honor."

"There are Jews and there are Yids," Timofey said. "Everyone knows this."

"It's not easy to be a cultured man nowadays," I told him. "But I'll be fine. Look out the window, Tima. Those mountains could be the Alps. Would you like to see the Alps someday? You could go with your son and have a little picnic."

A look of such transcendent disbelief came over Timofey that I could only feel grief for him. And grief for me, too. There was enough grief on the plane for both of us.

Good grief, as the Americans say.

14

The Norway of the Caspian

We landed at the Viennese airport, taxiing past the glassed-in main terminal where the planes always ran on time, to a problematic side-show of a building reserved for flights to the not-quite-ready-for-Europe places like Kosovo, Tirana, Belgrade, Sarajevo, and my native St. Leninsburg. There were no jetways at this diminished building; two buses came to pick us up, one for the first- and business-class passengers, another for the rest of us. I watched from my window as the wily Hasid maneuvered to be the first aboard the first-class bus, clutching his velvety tuna pouch as if it contained the diamonds he surely sold for a living. Shame, shame.

Walking down the stairs, I made sure to breathe in the fine European Union air before being bused to the cigarette-smoke-filled terminal where the rest of my YugoSovietMongol brethren waited unhappily for their flights back to Tartary. I tried to make my way to the main terminal, but you had to pass an immigration counter with a normal Western passport before you could buy cigarettes duty-free or move your bowels astride the latest model of Austrian toilet. Soon, very soon, I would have my Belgian passport. Not soon enough, let me tell you.

Alyosha-Bob whiled away the hours before our next flight laughing at my anti-Hasid campaign, making side curls out of the shaggier portions of my hair. He would run up and, like a child, throw himself on the loose hams hanging off my back. I tried to walk away from him, but he's the faster of the two of us. By the time they started boarding our flight to Svanï City, he had curled me a nice set of *payess*.

As the flight was announced, the most olive-skinned people in the terminal rushed the gate, and soon a jostling mass of mustached men and their pretty dark wives, each wielding bags from Century 21, the famed New York discount emporium, had laid siege to the poor Austrian Airlines personnel. This was my first introduction to the Absurdistan mob—a faithful re-creation of the Soviet line for sausages, fueled by the natural instincts of the Oriental bazaar. "Calm down, ladies and gentlemen!" I shouted as young, hairy men bounced off me, seemingly using my mass to ricochet to the front of the line. "Do you think they'll run out of seats on the plane? We're in Austria, for God's sake!"

Once aboard, the Absurdis began unwrapping their many purchases, modeling designer ties for their wives, and exchanging footwear across the aisles. Their first-class shenanigans did not manage to offend me as much as the Hasid's had on the last flight, perhaps because the Hasid was one of my own, while the only occasion one has to meet an Absurdi in St. Petersburg is at the market, when one is searching for a gorgeous flower in the middle of winter or wants to make a pet of some exotic mongoose. I don't mean to denigrate the Absurdis, or whatever they call themselves. They are the resourceful and clever representatives of an ancient trading culture, which, along with the massive quantities of oil lapping at their shores, helps explain why their country is the most successful of our formerly Soviet republics, the so-called Norway of the Caspian.

I turned to the window to watch our plane follow the curves of the Danube as the orderly Austrian houses with their peaked roofs and backyard swimming pools turned into the housing projects surrounding the stumpy castle of Bratislava, Slovakia, which in turn gave way to the melancholy buildup of Budapest (I could even make out the fin de siècle Parliament building on the Pest side and the old Austro-Hungarian seat of power on the Buda), which eventually surrendered to some sort of war-torn Balkan landscape, cities shelled into random organic forms, gaping bridges, the jumble of wrecked orange-tiled houses clustered together like coral reefs. "I'm taking one step backward so that I can jump clear across the board," I consoled myself. As the West receded into another time zone, the stewardesses compensated by serving us a crispy quail salad of the first order; the drinks menu offered up some pleasant surprises as well, especially in the port category.

"I'm going to miss you, Snack," Alyosha-Bob said as he drank a glass of forty-year-old Fonseca. "You're my best friend."

"I'm sentimental already," I sighed.

"Belgium's going to be good for you," my friend said in English, the language we spoke when we were alone, our fooling-around language. "There's nothing to do there. There's no one to fight against. You won't be such a nut job. You'll cut back on the emotions. I can't *believe* you actually started that Misha's Children thing and hired Valentin and Svetlana to run it."

"Remember the motto of Accidental College? 'Think one person can change the world? So do we.' "

"Didn't we used to make fun of that motto, like, *every single day,* Snack?"

"I guess I'm growing up," I said smugly. "Maybe I'll get a doctorate in Multicultural Studies in Brussels. Maybe that will make me look good to the generals in charge of the INS."

"What the hell are you talking about?"

"They love multi—"

"Shhhh," Alyosha-Bob said, putting a finger to his lips. "It's quiet time now, Misha."

Our plane began its approach to Svani City. The light of early evening revealed a green mountainous terrain skirted by pockets of desert, which were, in turn, filled in with pockets of something partially liquid resembling a sick man's gastric misadventures. The farther we descended, the more pronounced became the battle between mountain and desert, the latter pockmarked by lakes iridescent with industry and on occasion surrounded by blue domes that could have been either giant mosques or small oil refineries.

It took me some time to realize that we had reached the shores of a major body of water, that the brown, alkaline vistas of the corroded desert now brushed up against a dull band of gray that was, in fact, the Caspian Sea. A circuit board of oil derricks strung together the coastline and desert, while farther out to sea, massive oil platforms were connected to one another by slivers of pipeline and, in some places, maritime roads upon which tanker-trucks left vapor trails of yellow exhaust.

We descended rapidly into this apocalypse. Apparently I had misjudged not only the borders of the sea but the depth of the local sky, which collapsed before our advance, as if estimating correctly that another planeload of money had arrived from Europe and that dollar bills and euros would soon fall like snowflakes upon the ruling class.

As the plane touched down, the yokels in economy clapped in typical third-world fashion, cheering our safe arrival, while we in first chose to keep our hands in our laps. We taxied past a billboard. Three stylish teenagers, a redheaded beauty, an Asian beauty, and a young black man in dreadlocks (a feminine beauty in his own right), critically regarded us with their handsome, expressionless eyes. THE UNITED COLORS OF BENETTON WELCOME YOU TO SVANÏ CITY, the billboard read.

In keeping with the progressive theme, the arrivals terminal was newly built to resemble a post-Mongolian yurt made of tinted glass, corrugated steel, and the occasional exposed pipe—the kind of generic design favored by mineral-rich nations teetering between Eastern exotica and Western anonymity. Inside, we found a cool, open metallic shed layered with the smells of perfume counters and stores dispensing freshly baked baguettes along with the most cultured of yogurts, the small flags of the world's countries and the oversize flag of Microsoft Windows NT limply hanging from the rafters to remind us that we were all global citizens who loved to travel and compute.

But the Absurdi citizens were not yet accustomed to the new world order. Despite the trappings of modernity around them, they rushed toward Passport Control, shouting in their incomprehensible local tongue and hitting one another with their Century 21 bags. Alyosha-Bob had a multiple-entry Absurdi visa that entitled him to join an expedited lane, while Timofey and I stood in an endless queue for foreigners, waiting to get our visa photos taken.

Help was on the way. A group of fat men in blue shirts and brick-sized epaulets on their shoulders were soon circling around me, eyeing my bulk with warm Southern eyes. Just so you know, I'm an *attractive* kind of obese person, with a head that is proportionally sized to my torso and the rest of my fat distributed evenly (save for my deflated ass). On the other hand, these Absurdi fellows, like most overweight people, resembled huge moving tents, tiny heads wedded to larger and still-larger girth. One of them had a camera tied around his chest. "Excuse me," he said in Russian, the lingua franca of the former Soviet empire, "who are you by nationality?"

I sadly held up my Russian passport. "No, no," the fatty laughed. "I mean by *nationality*."

I saw what he was after. "Jew," I said, patting my nose.

The photographer put his hand to his heart. "I am very honored," he said. "The Jewish people have a long and peaceful history in our land. They are our brothers, and whoever is their enemy is our enemy also. When you are in Absurdsvanï, my mother will be your mother, my wife your sister, and you will always find water in my well to drink."

"Oh, thanks," I said.

"A Jew shouldn't have to wait in line to have his picture taken. Let me do it for you right away. Smile, mister!"

"Please get my manservant, too," I said.

"Smile, manservant!"

Timofey sighed and crossed himself. I was handed two small photos. "Remember what I said about my mother being your mother?" the photographer asked. "Well, sadly, *our* mother is in the hospital with a collapsed liver and a keloid scar on the left ear. Would it be possible—"

I had already prepared several US$100 bills for this kind of eventuality, one of which I handed to the photographer. "Now we must go to the line for the visa application blank," the photographer said. "Oh, look! A colleague of mine wants to speak to you."

An even larger man with a frilly mustache and a riot of bad teeth waddled over to me. "We must be related," he said, patting my belly. "Tell me, who are you by nationality?"

I explained. He put his hand to his heart and told me that the Jewish people had a long and peaceful history in Absurdistan and that any enemy of mine was also an enemy of his, while his mother was my mother and his wife my sister. There was also water from his well to drink. "Why should a Jew have to wait in line for a visa application blank?" he wondered. "Here! Take one!"

"You are very kind," I said.

"You are very Jewish. In the best possible sense." Then I was told that my sister (his wife, that is) suffered from gastritis and an engorged pudendum. The US$200 I gave him would go a long way toward her medical care. "And now you must go to the processing line. But look! A colleague of mine would like to help you out."

An older fat man, the skin around his eyes turned into pure leather from a lifetime's sleep apnea, came over to me and made the sounds of a steam engine. It took me a while to figure out that he was trying to communicate with me in the Russian tongue. I caught on to the part about water from his well to drink and that a Jew shouldn't have to wait in the processing line. "Let me help you fill this out," the man puffed, taking out a pen and unfurling the fearsome four-page visa application. "Last name."

"Vainberg," I said. "Written just like it sounds. Veh . . . ah . . . eee . . ."

"I know how to write," the older man said. "Given name."

I told him. He wrote it down, then looked over his handiwork. He squinted carefully at the combination of "Vainberg" and "Mikhail." He looked at my body type and my soft red lips. "Are you the son of Boris Vainberg?" he asked.

"Boris Vainberg, deceased," I said, my eyes watering dutifully. "He was blown up by a land mine on the Palace Bridge. We have a videotape and everything."

The old man whistled to his colleagues. "It's Boris Vainberg's son!" he shouted. "It's Little Misha!"

"Little Misha!" his colleagues shouted back. "Hurrah!" They stopped extracting money from dazed foreigners and waddled over to me, sandals slapping against fake marble. One of them kissed my hand and pressed it to his own heart.

"He has his father's face."

"Definitely has those big lips."

"Massive forehead, too. Thinks about everything, this one."

"Typical Vainberg."

"What are you doing here, Little Misha?" I was asked. "Did you come for the oil?"

"Why else would he come here? For the scenery?"

"To be honest—" I started to say.

"You know, Little Misha, your father once sold an eight-hundred-kilogram screw to KBR! He was some sort of subcontractor. He took them for five million! Ha ha."

"What's KBR?" I asked.

"Kellogg, Brown and Root," my new companions said in unison, shocked that I wasn't aware of such an institution. "The subsidiary of Halliburton."

"Oh," I said. But my curled upper lip betrayed my ignorance.

"The American oil-services company," I was told. "Halliburton's KBR unit runs half the country."

"And my father cheated them?" I asked brightly.

"And how! He really Jewed them up!"

"My father was a great man," I half said and half sighed. "But I'm not here for the oil."

"Little Misha doesn't want his father's business."

"He's a sophisticate and a melancholic."

"That's right," I said. "How do you guys know that?"

"We're people of the Orient. We know everything. And what we don't know, we can sense."

"Are you going to buy Belgian citizenship from Jean-Michel Lefèvre at the Belgian consulate? Are you going to be a Belgian, Little Misha?"

I looked around apprehensively, wishing Alyosha-Bob were around to guide me. "Maybe," I said.

"Smart man. It's no fun to have a Russian passport."

"Did your father ever mention our little gang at the airport?" the older man inquired.

The others looked up at me expectantly, their stomachs leaning toward mine as if trying to make its acquaintance. My instinct is to try to make everyone around me happy, so I obliged them. "He said a bunch of fat crooks were robbing Westerners at Immigration," I said.

"That's us!" they cried. "Hurrah! Boris Vainberg remembered us!" The older man commanded his colleagues to give me back the money they had inveigled from me. Timofey and I immediately had our passport stamped with a dozen bizarre shapes and patterns, and we were ushered past the Immigration and Customs points and into the sunshine, where Alyosha-Bob awaited with his driver.

The Absurdi heat surrounded me as if I had entered a lit stove. It wiped out the remaining moisture in my mouth, invisible flames working their way into the crevice between my tits, searing away the sweat and damp. My sweat glands started pumping, but they could not keep up with the requirements of a 325-pound body. I was on fire. I almost passed out before Timofey had stuffed me into the waiting German sedan. *Lord help me!* I thought as the air-conditioning kicked in. *Help me survive this Southern inferno.*

From the start, I was supremely uninterested in the country around me, which looked pretty much the way I felt. Tired. The landscape consisted of gray-brown lakes surrounded by the skeletons of oil derricks and the modern spheres of refineries. There was barbed wire everywhere, along with signs promising death to anyone who veered off the highway. Trailer-trucks bearing the logo of Kellogg, Brown & Root swerved ahead of our car, the drivers honking at us maniacally. Even with the car windows up, Absurdistan smelled like the moist armpit of an orangutan.

I snoozed for a bit, the leather seats doing right by my hump. We passed a church of charming Eastern simplicity, square and compact, as if carved out of a single piece of stone. "I thought this was a Moslem country," I said to Alyosha-Bob.

"Orthodox Christian," Alyosha-Bob explained.

"No kidding. I always pictured them on their knees before Allah."

"Two ethnic groups, the Sevo and the Svani. Both Christian. That's a Svani church right there."

"How can you tell, Professor?"

"You know what a standard Orthodox cross looks like." He drew a cross in the air: ☦. "Well, that's the Svani cross. But the Sevo cross has the footrest reversed. Like this." He drew a different cross in the air: ☦.

"That's pretty stupid," I said.

"You're pretty stupid," Alyosha-Bob said. We horsed around for a bit, Alyosha-Bob painfully pinning one of my thigh flaps between his two sharp elbows. "The master suffers from thigh pains," Timofey cautioned my friend as he gently pulled him off me.

"The master suffers from a lot of things," Alyosha-Bob said.

I looked out the window, taking note of a billboard advertising a housing development called STONEPAY. An Aston Martin idled in the circular driveway of a mortar-and-glass insta-mansion. A Canadian flag flew from the mansion's portico to denote stability.

This was followed by a billboard featuring three near-naked brown women dripping with gold and filled with silicone leaning over the crotch of a black man in prison stripes. 718 PERFUMERY: THE ODOUR OF THE BRONX IN SVANI CITY.

I sighed loudly and looked away, snuggling my head into the crux of my arm.

"What now?" Alyosha-Bob asked.

"Nuthin'."

"Is this about the 718 Perfumery?" Alyosha-Bob said. "You're still thinking about Rouenna and Jerry Shteynfarb, aren't you?"

We sat in the car quietly, watching the iridescent landscape bubble and stew before us. Feeling my pain, Timofey sang a song he had made up to celebrate my new nationality. Here's the only stanza I remember:

My sweet batyushka, *kind* batyushka,
Off to Belgium he will go . . .

My sweet batyushka, *bright* batyushka,
He likes to play in Belgian snow . . .

Svaní City clung wearily to a small mountain range. We took an ascending road away from the gray curve of the Caspian Sea until we reached something called the Boulevard of National Unity. We found ourselves, in a manner of speaking, on the primary thoroughfare of Portland, Oregon, U.S.A., where I had once misspent a couple of weeks in my youth. We passed shops of unmistakable wealth, if somewhat curious provenance—an outlet that sold the nightmare products of the American conglomerate Disney, an espresso emporium named Caspian Joe's (a bright green rip-off of a famous American chain), a side-by-side presentation of the popular American stores the Gap and the Banana Republic, the above-mentioned 718 Perfumery, rife with the odors of the Bronx, and an Irish theme pub named Molly Malloy's crouching drunkenly behind imported ivy and a giant shamrock.

After Molly's, the boulevard turned into a canyon of recently built glass skyscrapers bearing the corporate logos of ExxonMobil, BP, ChevronTexaco, Kellogg, Brown & Root, Bechtel, and Daewoo Heavy Industries (Timofey grunted happily at the makers of his beloved steam iron), and finally the identical Radisson and Hyatt skyscrapers staring each other down from the opposite ends of a windswept plaza.

The Hyatt lobby was an endless skylit atrium where multinational men buzzed from one corner to another with the hungry, last-ditch exasperation of late-summer flies. Everywhere I looked, there seemed to be little corners of ad hoc commerce, plastic tables and chairs clumped together under signs with strange legends such as HAIL, HAIL BRITANNIA—THE PUB. One of these hives was a golden-lit affair called RECEPTION. There a smiling boy of seemingly Scandinavian origin spoke to us in smooth business-school English. "Welcome to the Park Hyatt Svaní City," he said, beaming. "My name is Aburkharkhar. How can I help you gentlemen today?"

Alyosha-Bob ordered a penthouse suite for the two of us and a little shed behind the pool for Timofey. A glassed-in elevator hoisted us forty stories through the sunny atrium, so the next thing I knew, I was looking at a happy Western parody of a modern home, with marble countertop on everything from the desks to the nightstand to the bathroom sink to the coffee table. For a second I thought I had actually arrived in Europe, so I muttered the word "Belgium," fell to my knees, doubled over, enjoyed immensely the feeling of plush carpeting enveloping my breasts and cradling my stomach, and bade the waking world goodbye.

15

Golly Burton, Golly Burton

Rouenna came to me in a dream. She stood in a field of autumnal grass, backlit by a nearly extinguished sun, the locks of her scrappy dark hair alternating yellow and brown. Instead of her usual celebration of everything tight and pushed up, she wore simple blue coveralls that made her body hard to fathom. Her skin had a pink, childlike quality that made me think she was already pregnant by Shteynfarb. In the distance, a neon sign hoisted between a pair of birch trees flickered with different words. EVROPA. Then AMERIKA. Then RASHA.

Rouenna held out a shiny green apple to me. "It's eight dollars," she said.

"I'm not paying eight dollars for an apple," I said. "You're not doing right by me, Rouenna."

"This is the best apple in the world," she said. "It tastes like a pear." She spoke in an educated Mid-Atlantic accent, her face radiant but impassive, as if she were suddenly rich. She brought the apple close to my chest, where it floated out of her hand. Dry air-conditioned air swept into my face, making my teeth chatter. I looked around, trying to pinpoint the source of the cold, but all I saw was an eternity of matted yellow grass.

"I'm trying to cut out the trans fats," I said. "No more partially hydrogenated oils. I'm going to eat only slow food from now on. I'll lose weight. You'll see."

"Eight dollars," Rouenna insisted.

I stuck my hand inside my heart and took out precisely eight U.S.

dollars, which I handed to her. Our hands barely touched. "What's going to make you love me again?" I asked.

"Take a bite," she said.

The apple flooded my mouth with freshness, as if I were biting the color green. I tasted pear, as promised, but also rosewater and white wine and my beautiful mother's sweet cheek. The roof of my mouth froze in wonder, as if stroked by an invisible ice cube. I tried to speak but only gurgling came out. I wanted to hug Rouenna, but she lifted up her hand to stop me.

"Be a man," she said.

I gurgled some more, flapping my arms in front of me.

"Make me proud," she said.

I woke up with puddles of drool flowing down both cheeks. I was still on the floor of our Hyatt penthouse, my arms spread out as if I were Jesus at the end of his life. "I flipped you over on your back," Alyosha-Bob said. "You were gagging."

Apparently it was morning the next day, our wood-and-marble suite flooded with light as if we were living inside a golden humidor. Timofey was in my bedroom, sorting out my vintage Puma tracksuits and my collection of anxiety medication. Alyosha-Bob had already unpacked his own things on top of a dresser in a careful American manner, underwear folded into quarters, T-shirts neatly squared. "You've got a message from Zartarian, the hotel manager," he said. "This is the guy Captain Belugin told you to look up."

Dear The Respectable Misha Vainberg,

We are dripping with delight now that you have choosen to stay with us at Park Hyatt Svani City. Your father was big lover for us. Now he is dead, our ship has run aground. Kindly visit the lobby when you are convenient and ask for Your Faithful Servant, Larry Sarkisovich Zartarian.

I read the note aloud to Alyosha-Bob, imitating the hotel manager's no doubt thick accent with a hint of childish cruelty. "When am I going to become a Belgian, already?" I asked.

"Go talk to Zartarian," Alyosha-Bob said, waving me out the door.

As I stepped into the corridor, I was waylaid by a tall, tanned beauty with electric lips, a clingy camisole reaching down to her hot pants. "Golly Burton, Golly Burton!" she said. "You Golly Burton?" She poked at me with an audacious finger. Her face was as powdered as an American doughnut.

"Eh?" I said.

"Golly Burton? KBR? Thirty percent discount for you." She grabbed my hand and pressed it to her wet forehead. "Ooofa, I have such hot temperature for Golly Burton. Thirty percent discount. You so aroused, mister. You bust a nut right now, maybe."

"I don't understand this 'Golly Burton,' " I said in Russian. "Do you mean Halliburton? Thirty percent discount for Halliburton?"

The woman spat on the floor. "You're a Russian?" she hissed. "Fat, dirty Russian! Don't touch me! Disgusting Russian!" She stomped away on her impossible high heels.

"That's racism, miss!" I yelled after her. "Come back and apologize, you stupid black-ass . . ."

In my golden, glassed-in elevator, I fell like Icarus from my lofty penthouse to the busy hotel lobby, where the local merchants promptly sold me a Gillette Mach3 razor, a bottle of Turkish Efes beer, and a box of Korean condoms. Upon hearing the name Misha Vainberg, reception steered me to Larry Zartarian's office. Zartarian sprinted from behind his desk and gave one of my big, squishy hands a sweaty workout with both of his. "Now our humble hotel has a guest worthy of the name Hyatt," he said in accented but presentable Russian.

The Armenian (as I deduced from his last name) manager reminded me of my old college friend Vladimir Girshkin. Girshkin was a fellow Russian Jew who emigrated to the States at age twelve and became perhaps the least remarkable Russian émigré at Accidental College, a quiet foil for that bastard Jerry Shteynfarb. Like Girshkin, Zartarian was a short, unattractive man with a sporty, receding hairline compensated for by an outrageously thick goatee. Given all his nervous pleasantness, one got the sense that his endlessly aggrieved mother lived beneath his desk, shining his shoes and tying the laces into double knots. These kinds of lost, overeducated mama's boys were perpetually stumbling down a corridor with two distant exits, one marked HESITANT INTELLECTUAL and the other SHYSTER. The last time I read about Vladimir Girshkin in the Accidental College alumni magazine, he was running a pyramid scheme somewhere in Eastern Europe. Managing the Park Hyatt Svanï City was probably not a dissimilar calling.

"Sit, Mr. Vainberg, sit." The Armenian pushed me into a sumptuous leather container. "Is there enough room for you in there? Should my girl fetch you an ottoman?"

I grunted approval and looked around. The manager's office was dominated by an oil portrait of a dapper white-haired gentleman handing an oddly shaped cake to what looked like his porky, mustached son. Both men were smiling slyly at the viewer, as if inviting the beholder to share in their cake. Two Orthodox crosses loomed in the background, their footrests tilted in different directions, the Kellogg, Brown & Root logo floating between them in a blurry supernatural haze. I had to moo in bewilderment.

"The old guy's the local dictator," Larry Zartarian explained. "His name is Georgi Kanuk. He's giving Absurdistan to his son Debil for his upcoming thirtieth birthday. KBR completes the trinity. The Father, the Son, and the Holy Halliburton."

"So the cake represents the country," I said. The misshapen torte was indeed studded with candles shaped like miniature oil derricks. To judge from the evidence presented, the Absurdsvanï Republic resembled a fierce bird dipping its tail into the Caspian Sea. "What does it all mean?" I asked.

"Georgi Kanuk, the dictator, is about to croak," Larry Zartarian informed me. "They're gearing the people up for a family dynasty. Kanuk and his son Debil are of the Svanï persuasion, so the Sevo aren't too happy with that."

"Enlighten me," I said. "The Sevo are the ones who have Christ's footrest going in the wrong direction, right?"

"Sevo, Svanï, they're all identical half-witted ignoramuses," the manager said, switching to perfect American English. "These people aren't called the Cretins of the Caucasus for nothing."

"Aren't you going to ask me who I am by nationality?"

"It is clear to both of us who we are," Zartarian said, bowing his muscular nose toward my equally prominent proboscis.

I offered Zartarian my Turkish beer, but he politely refused, tapping at his watch to indicate that a Western man did not imbibe in the daytime. "How did you perfect your English?" I asked him.

"I got lucky," the manager said. "I was born in California. Grew up in Glendale."

"So you're an American!" I said. "An Armenian-American. And a Valley boy, too. How blessed your life must be. But how did you end up *here*?"

Zartarian sighed and put his head in his hands. "I went to the Cornell School of Hotel Administration," he said. "It was the only Ivy League school I could get into. My mother forced me to go. I just wanted to work in film, like everyone else."

Zartarian's tale was interrupted by the sound of breaking china outside his window, accompanied by female yelps in some local language. "Ugh, I hate the hospitality industry," he said. "The work never stops, and all the Hyatt guests are major assholes, present company excepted. They freaking pigeonholed me because my parents were from this part of the world and I took Russian in school. They made me the youngest Hyatt manager in the world. Tell me, why did all this history have to happen to me?"

"I commiserate with you entirely," I said, popping open the Turkish beer to water my dry, filthy mouth. "I, too, am cursed by my upbringing. But at least your mother must be proud."

"Proud?" Zartarian massaged his bare temples. "She lives in the suite below mine. She won't let me out of her sight. I'm a nervous wreck."

I recommended psychoanalysis to the hotel manager, but we both agreed Absurdistan was not the best place to find a good Lacanian. "I really miss L.A.," Zartarian said. "I got a drop-top Z4 Beamer in the garage downstairs, but where the hell am I going to drive it? Into the Caspian?"

I remembered a piece of unsettled business that was bothering me, an insult against my person. "Larry, why won't the hookers in your hotel sleep with Russians?"

"They've got an unofficial service provider's contract with KBR, Misha. There's so much business on that end, my girls all got big heads now. 'No more dirty Russians,' they tell me. 'No Chinese, no Indians. Golly Burton or we go home to our villages.' "

"Doesn't Hyatt HQ mind the prostitution? The whores are chilling right by the penthouse suites."

"My hands are tied," Larry Zartarian said. "Look at what I'm up against. An ancient trading culture. Halliburton. It's cultural relativism, Misha. It's Chinatown."

"I'm just a little offended, is all," I said. "I like to think of the Hyatt as a multicultural space. And then some whore calls me a dirty Russian. Where's the respect?"

"Listen, Misha, we're becoming friends. Do you mind if I ask you something personal? Why did you sleep with Lyuba Vainberg? Everyone knows you're a sophisticate and a melancholic. But *popping* Boris Vainberg's wife? Why'd you do it?"

"How do you know about that?" I shouted, grabbing an Ativan bottle out of my fanny pack. "Christ almighty!"

"Everyone knows everything about you, Misha," Zartarian said. "Your father was legendary here. He sold the eight-hundred-kilogram screw to KBR, remember?"

I uncapped the Ativan and let two pills roll down my throat, chasing them with the Efes beer. "This really isn't my year," I muttered. "I hope the whole world goes to hell, to be honest."

Larry reached over and stroked my hand below the elbow. "Your luck's about to change," he said. "I spoke to Captain Belugin. We'll get you your Belgian citizenship today. Maybe Rouenna will move with you to Brussels if you treat her right. Take her writing seriously, for God's sake. You know how we Americans are about self-expression."

"Good point," I said.

"Go down to the Beluga Bar," Zartarian said. "Your friend Alyosha-Bob will be dining with Josh Weiner from the American embassy."

"That name sounds familiar," I said.

"In a few minutes, this little native guy is going to show up. We call him Sakha the Democrat. He works for some local human rights agency. Buy him a turkey burger with fries, and he'll take you to meet Jean-Michel Lefèvre of the Belgian consulate. Just follow him out of the hotel after lunch, and I guarantee you you'll be a Belgian by sundown."

I shook Larry Zartarian's hand. "You're a nice man," I said. "I won't forget your kindness."

"Please drop me an e-mail when you're in Brussels," Zartarian said. He swept his hands around the perimeter of his office with its bleeping computer monitors and stacks of yellowing official documents, each likely an Absurdi request for a handout.

"You have no idea how fucking miserable I am," he said.

16

Gimme Freedom!

The poolside Beluga Bar was sweltering. Hyatt boys had been conscripted to throw ice cubes into the pool, and gigantic portable fans had been brought in to tickle our sweaty bodies with rotating gusts of salvation. On one side of the pool, the hotel's male and balding guests were gorging themselves on plates of sturgeon and freshly grilled hamburgers. On the other side of the pool, the Hyatt's hookers had arranged themselves on green chaise longues and were fanning each other with abandoned copies of the *Financial Times,* occasionally ululating the name of their favorite American company, Golly Burton, to the oilmen dining across the pool. The oil workers, many of whom sported thick Scottish accents, shouted back incomprehensible British terms of endearment. Even with my perfect knowledge of English, I could not understand why a woman might be flattered to be called a "bird."

Alyosha-Bob was sitting next to a young man in khakis and a striped polo shirt who was minding a large Hyatt menu with skeptical eyes, his finger running down the price column. He had a familiar-looking cold sore that reminded me for some reason of an ice age crevice that snagged across the arboretum of Accidental College. As I approached the table, I tried to remember his name but kept coming up short. There is a class of Americans, a cheap pansy upper class, whose members are utterly indistinguishable to me. "Josh?" I said. "Josh Weiner?"

Weiner looked up to my encroaching shadow. "Snack Daddy?" he said. "Holy shit! Bob just told me you were down here. What's the word, Big Bird?"

"Class of '94, right?" I said. "You had the six-foot bong on College Street. What was your house called again?"

"Ghetto Fabulous House," Weiner said. We gave each other an urban smack of the palm, knocked our fists together, and shot an imaginary finger gun at each other.

"Remember how the freshmen used to rub your belly for good luck before midterms?" Weiner said. "Mind if I give it a rub now, Snack?"

Actually I remembered this belly-rubbing ceremony all too well. The humiliations of so many little white hands casually stroking my love pouch in the dining hall. How I begged all those Noahs and Joshes and Johnnys to stop. "I'd prefer it if you didn't," I said. "My analyst says it reinforces certain behavioral patterns. Child-rearing issues and such. It makes me feel violated."

"Uh-huh," Weiner said. "Hey, Snack, I was just asking Bob if you guys still keep in touch with Jerry Shteynfarb. I'm totally into that *Russian Arriviste's Hand Job*. It's so funny. And full of pathos, too. Just how I like it. Homeboy made good!"

Mention of my competitor, together with the belly rubbing, dispelled my generous mood. "I hear you're with the *State Department*," I spat at Weiner. The young diplomat's chair practically slipped out from beneath his slender East Coast frame. The foreign service was not an acceptable career choice at Accidental College, where a surprising number of graduates went on to raise organic asparagus along the Oregonian coast. Even during his college years, Weiner had exhibited unhealthy tendencies, such as writing the sports column for the *Accidental Herald*, the school newspaper, the kind of job only a clueless and entirely ambitious immigrant would take.

"Hey, easy, dog." Weiner laughed, scratching at his thinning cowlick. "If you think I sold out, like, check out my paycheck. Shit."

I continued looking at him with my meanest, bluest eyes.

"So, let's talk politics, dog," Alyosha-Bob said, changing the subject. "Word on the Absurdi street is that the Sevo are gonna go apeshit if Georgi Kanuk's idiot son takes over. What's the official U.S. position on this one?"

"We're not really sure," Josh Weiner admitted as he pillaged a bowl of complimentary smoked almonds. "We've got a little problem. See, none of our staff actually speak any of the local languages. I mean, there's one guy who *sort* of speaks Russian, but he's still trying to learn the future tense. You dogs are both from this part of the world. Do you know what's gonna happen after Georgi Kanuk dies? More democracy? Less?"

"Whenever there's any kind of upheaval in this country, the pistols come out," Alyosha-Bob said. "Think of the Ottoman rebellion of 1756 or the Persian succession of 1550."

"Oh, I can't think that far back," Josh Weiner said. "That was then, and this is now. We're in a global economy. It's in no one's interests to rock the boat. Look at the stats, homeboys. The Absurdi GNP went up by nine percent last year. The Figa-6 Chevron/BP oil fields are coming online in mid-September. That's, like, a hundred and eighty thousand barrels a day! And it's not just oil. The service sector's booming, too. Did you see the new Tuscan Steak and Bean Company on the Boulevard of National Unity? Did you try the *ribollita* soup and the *crostini misti*? This place has serious primary and reinvestment capital, dogs."

"What about this Sevo-Svanï thing?" I asked. "Larry Zartarian said—"

"Oh, to hell with Christ's footrest. These people are pragmatists. 'Fuck you, pay me,' that's their attitude. And speaking of pragmatism, here comes my democratic friend."

A small, hook-nosed man was running our way. For a second I thought I was looking at an exact copy of my dead papa in his lackluster pre-oligarch days. Intelligent brown eyes, pet-goat beard, miniature yellow teeth. He was probably a poor ex-Soviet academic in his forties, married to a wife who suffered from a heart murmur, the father of two brilliant, inquisitive children with flat feet. "Gentlemen, meet Sakha the Democrat," Josh Weiner said. "He edits the glossy journal *Gimme Freedom!* It's one of our little projects here."

"Forgive me for being late, Mr. Weiner," Sakha panted, clutching at a bright orange tie. "I hope you have not already eaten. I am so very hungry."

"We're just about to order," Alyosha-Bob said. "Mr. Sakha, this is my college buddy Misha Vainberg."

"The Jewish people have a long and peaceful history in our land," Sakha said, putting a shaking hand to his heart. "They are our brothers, and whoever is their enemy is our enemy also. When you are in Absurdsvanï, my mother will be your mother, my wife your sister, and you will always find water in my well to drink."

"Thank you," I said. "I wish I could reciprocate, but my dear mother's dead, and my girl just ran off with some schmuck."

"That's just the way they speak here," Josh Weiner explained to me. "It doesn't really mean anything." The look I gave him indicated that he was not worthy of sharing the same planet with me.

We summoned the waiter, and I ordered three sturgeon omelets and a Bloody Mary pitcher. "May I have the chicken cordon bleu on a roll with tomato, pickle, and french fries, Mr. Weiner?" Sakha the Democrat asked. He brought his menu closer to the young diplomat. "It's the deluxe platter . . . right here . . . under 'Fresh from the Henhouse.' "

"Just get the chicken cordon bleu on a roll," Weiner said wearily. "They're cutting back our democracy budget. We can't afford deluxe platters anymore."

"I'll pay for your french fries, Mr. Sakha," I said.

"Oh, thank you, Mr. Vainberg!" Sakha the Democrat cried. "It's so good to see a young man interested in pluralism."

"How can you do your important work on an empty stomach?" I said to him. I watched Josh Weiner unfurl his lower lip my way, menacing me with his active cold sore.

"And who are you by profession?" Sakha asked me.

"I'm a philanthropist," I said. "I run a charity in Petersburg called Misha's Children. It's my gift to the world."

"You have an open heart," said my new friend. "That is so rare these days."

"Sakha just came back from a democracy forum in New York," Josh Weiner said, "where he bought himself that nice orange tie. We provided airfare and five nights' accommodation in a four-star hotel. I'm assuming he paid for the tie himself. There certainly wasn't a budget line for it."

"It *is* a very nice tie," Alyosha-Bob said. "What is it? A Zegna?"

"I bought it in Century 21," Sakha said, nodding happily. "The actual color is called Dark Orange Equestrian. Some say the Svanï people were originally horse cultivators. Did you know that our archaeologists found a clay pot in the Grghangxa region, dating to 850 B.C., which shows a local man wrestling a pony? Now I can also claim to be an equestrian with my tie! Of course, I am only joking, gentlemen. Ha ha."

"You are Svanï by nationality?" I said.

"I am Sevo," Sakha the Democrat told me. "But it makes no difference. Svanï, Sevo, we are the same people. The distinctions are only useful for the ruling class . . ."

"How so, Mr. Sakha?" I asked.

"So that they can better oppress us!" he cried. But instead of elaborating, the democrat spent the next fifteen minutes looking expectantly in the direction of the kitchen. The food finally arrived. After putting half the fries into his briefcase "for my three little girls," Sakha dispatched the chicken cordon bleu faster than I could lay to rest the first of my three sturgeon omelets. The pickle he saved for last, savoring every wet crunch, his eyes likewise moist with pleasure. "The most delicious food in the world," he said. "Like in the American restaurant Arby's. It's not every day one gets to enjoy french-fried potatoes like these."

I looked triumphantly at Josh Weiner. "My pleasure," I said.

"Tell you what, Sakha, old worm, why don't we split the New York–style cheesecake," Josh Weiner suggested. "And we'll get the pot of coffee for two."

"I got a much better idea," I said. "Sakha, why don't you go to the sundae bar inside and help yourself to all the trimmings. Just tell them to put it on my tab. Misha Vainberg, penthouse suite."

"If only my little girls could see me now," Sakha whispered to himself as he took off for his tasty treat.

"Misha's Children," Josh Weiner said, looking up at the heavy atmosphere hanging above us like a dollop of clotted cream. "Un-*fucking*-believable. You just make it up as you go along, don't you, Vainberg? You just opt out of reality every day, don't you, dog? And when it catches up with you, you just sign a check."

I foraged through my last omelet, lapping up chunks of delicious hormone-free Absurdi egg, and breathing in the salty freshness of the sturgeon. "At least I'm helping people," I whispered.

We sat there without uttering a word until Sakha returned with a concoction that resembled a frigate parked on top of an aircraft carrier. "The banana I skipped," he said, giving me an accounting. "I can get a banana anywhere. These here are Oreo-cookie clusters."

"Eat, eat," I said, patting him on the sleeve. "I want you to be happy." After the sundae was finished and its various juices slurped up, our group made haste to disband. Josh Weiner and I barely looked at each other as we committed the standard urban smack of the palm ("high-five") and knock of the fist. We even failed to shoot an imaginary finger gun at each other in parting, unthinkable for a Multicultural Studies major and a former resident of Ghetto Fabulous House. All in all, it was not a proud day for Accidental College.

"Walk behind me," Sakha the Democrat told me when my fellow alumni had gone. "I've roused your manservant from his shed behind the pool. Monsieur Lefèvre is waiting for us behind the McDonald's on the Svanï Terrace."

"Where's that?" I asked, but Sakha was already headed for the lobby.

17

King Leopold's Belgian Congo

We had driven off the Boulevard of National Unity, with its multinational skyscrapers and chain stores, and onto a broad natural platform overlooking the city. Sakha the Democrat, glowing with the pride of a know-it-all intellectual, had asked me to come out of the car and survey the landscape with him. As we left the American SUV embellished with the Hyatt logo, my manservant, Timofey, rushed up to me and unfurled a beach umbrella above my tall frame as if I were some African ruler arriving at the airport. The umbrella didn't help. Sweat fell from me in sheets of water and steam until I smelled like a hamburger.

We looked down upon the city. "Look, Mr. Vainberg!" Sakha said. "Have you ever seen such loveliness? Perhaps it does not match your native Petersburg, or, being a Jew, your beloved Jerusalem, but all the same—the hills, the sea, the architectural ensemble wrought over the centuries . . . Doesn't your heart tremble?"

But it wasn't trembling. The Absurdi capital looked like a miniature Cairo after it had crashed into a rocky mountain. There were three populated terraces jutting out from this mountain, little serving platters of humanity clinging to the inhospitable rock and connected by a winding road. At the top, the International Terrace was home to the multinational skyscrapers, the embassies, and the major retailers (for example, Staples, Hugo Boss, the 718 Perfumery, Ferragamo, the Toys "R" Us superstore). Farther down, the Svanï Terrace, the traditional home of the majority Svanï people, had a famous used-remote-control market, along with a part of the minaret-studded

Moslem quarter snug behind an ancient fortifying wall. "I knew there were Moslems here!" I exclaimed to Sakha. "Moslems live in the Orient. It's a fact." Finally, the Sevo Terrace, the traditional home of the minority Sevo people, was composed of art nouveau mansions built for turn-of-the-century oil barons forming a precise grid around what I later learned was called the Sevo Vatican—"Oooh, that thing looks like an octopus!" I cried to Sakha—a vast white dome with an octet of arches spreading in each direction, which, at least in my mind, resembled a pale tentacled sea creature washed up on the beach. A six-meter Sevo cross gleamed from the octopus's head, its footrest facing in the wrong direction.

Next to the Sevo Vatican, an esplanade ran toward a small container port that quickly gave way to the real business of the city. And here it became obvious that the city formed no more than a footnote to what actually had rendered these Sevos and Svanïs first into a Soviet republic and then into a cantankerous modern state. *Absurdistan was the Caspian Sea, and the Caspian was the oil it held in abundance.* The oil derricks began as soon as the last speck of humanity ended. The oil refused to give the city even the briefest of respites; it denied its inhabitants the chance to look into the waters and see their own reflection. The humble derricks of Soviet construction, cheap yellow rust buckets in the ruined sea, quickly surrendered to behemoth Western oil platforms, their warning lights flashing from thirty-story rigs, their floating enormity forming a second skyline that rivaled the skyscrapers of the International Terrace. With its three descending terraces, Svanï City rushed out to meet the Caspian, and the Caspian turned it back with an oily slap of the waves.

"Don't look at the oil industry so much," Sakha said, following my gaze. "Look at the city. Try to imagine the sea completely free of petrol and the city standing proudly above it."

I shifted my gaze from the oil rigs to the Sevo and Svanï terraces beneath me. I hummed John Lennon's useful ditty "Imagine." I *imagined* flying over the city in a helicopter, absorbing its many architectural flourishes and dramatic natural features, but the chopper just kept flying in a northwesterly direction until it reached the southern tip of Manhattan island, spread its helicopter shadow over the asphalt conglomerations of downtown and midtown, then streaked past the gables and dormers of the Dakota Apartments on New York's Central Park, where Mr. Lennon once lived and died.

And then I was on an IRT train headed north to East Tremont Avenue in the Bronx. It was wintertime, the heat had been turned up, and in my rabbit-lined coat, I could feel the sweat gathering between the second and third folds of my neck, which, taken together, formed a fleshy sieve. I could feel the cool water dribbling down to my breastbone and irrigating the curly hairs of my groin. I was hot and cold, anxious and in love. The citizens on the trains bound for New York's outer boroughs far exceeded the dimensions of the white people lounging around downtown. My fellow fatties were stoic, multicultural, dressed in billowing down jackets that could save an astronaut from the asphyxiation of space. They leaned against the doors for balance as they pried apart chicken wings and fried oxtails with their teeth, spitting bones and gristle into waiting plastic bags. Who were these Amsterdam Avenue Atlases? These Cypress Hills Caligulas? If I weren't such a priss about getting my hands greasy, I would have joined them in consuming a small Saran-wrapped mammal here amid the bright deoxygenated glare of the 5 train.

And the girls! Oh, how they disturbed me. Each with a little bit of my Rouenna in her—a plushy nose, a gangsta-shaved eyebrow, a plump lower lip glistening beneath a mound of gloss—each yelling and laughing at her school friends in the Bronxian patois I was just beginning to understand. It was February, and the young ladies may have been clad in heavy down jackets, but somehow, with a warm Southern flair, they managed to be half naked at the same time, flashing me their pubic bones, the Y-shaped pre-crease of their deep posteriors. And every once in a while, in an answer to most of my dreams, their thick, fleshy armpits came into view and I squinted to discern a trail of shaved crinkly hair, the phantom of a formerly rich tuft, for I belong to the school that equates armpit hair with untrammeled sexuality.

By the Third Avenue–149th Street stop, I could already glimpse the light-handed winter sun slipping its rays down the station's stairways. A second later, we were free of the subway tunnel and the Bronx was around us, the subway car flooded with so much brightness it seemed a second sun had been pressed into service.

I gasped at the rectangular chimneys crowned with round water tankers (lowercase i's); at the tall housing projects forming stout consonants (uppercase L's and T's); at the strange Tudor-style row houses that must have wandered in from some quaint English suburb; at the faraway Gothic tower denoting several lifetimes of failed public education; at the sharp, poignant smell of cherry bubble gum and cheap shampoo; at the old man in sunglasses and earphones who boarded at Freeman Street and who sang (mostly) for his own pleasure "Ain't no use / Cain't help myself"; at the Moslem girls in fluorescent yellow skirts and clashing gray head scarves, huddled together for safety near the conductor's booth; at the lives of thousands whose flats lay eye level with the elevated train like some updated Edward Hopper painting; at the budding Latina social worker who cheerlessly highlighted a textbook called *But They All Come Back: Facing the Challenges of Prisoner Reentry;* at the freshly painted azure fire escapes stirring to life the faded art deco brickwork beneath; at the urban catastrophe that is the Cross Bronx Expressway (and at the trash-strewn lots that bracket it); at the 350-pound woman (my long-lost fellow traveler) who got on at 174th Street, and especially at the tube top beneath the bulletproof shell of her down jacket with the rhinestone-studded words HOT 'N' SEXXXY; at the inquisitive child (all eyebrows and stunted teeth) who couldn't take his eyes off the book in my lap (William Dean Howells's *A Hazard of New Fortunes*) and who asked me, "Whatchoo be readin', *papi*?"

I fell out of my New York reverie as quickly as I had once fallen into my Beloved Papa's hazardous "new fortunes." Sakha was still speaking and gesturing at length. I made an attempt to follow him, to return to the country around me, to make a connection with the world I now inhabited and couldn't wait to leave. I felt the need to say something intelligent, as one frequently does around intellectuals. "So do the Sevo live on the Sevo Terrace and the Svanï on their own terrace?" I asked.

"Originally, yes. The city's geography kept us apart during the Three Hundred Year War of the Footrest Secession, and it hindered the Ottoman, Persian, and Russian conquerors. But in the last two centuries, people have generally lived anywhere they want. In Soviet times, half the population married outside their group. The distinctions between us are all but meaningless now."

"Do *you* live on the Sevo Terrace?" I asked. I could barely pay attention to what I was saying. Part of me was still on the 5 train with the HOT 'N' SEXXXY woman, but I willed that part to disappear.

"Oh, no." Sakha laughed. "I am a very poor democrat. I can't afford to live on the terraces. I live in Gorbigrad." He gestured toward a distant mound of (what I thought was) an unpopulated orange rock jutting out into the bay, its coloring reminding me of the much-celebrated Grand Canyon in Arizona.

"You live alone on a barren rock?" I said.

"Look closer," Sakha said. As I squinted and shielded my face against the sun, I made out a stacked anthill of thousands of yellowing Khrushchev-era apartment buildings, along with what looked like vast quantities of housing possibly made out of burlap and tarp. "The Gorbigrad *favelas*," Sakha said. "Home to over half of the city's population. Named after Gorbachev, the man the locals *still* blame for everything that happened."

"Wait, so this is *not* a rich country?" I said. "What about all the oil?"

"The UN Human Development Index ranks us slightly below Bangladesh. In terms of infant mortality—"

"Oh, you poor people," I said. "I had no idea."

"Welcome to the Norway of the Caspian."

"I wish I could open an outpost of Misha's Children here, Mr. Sakha. I wish I had more money and time to spare."

"You're a very kind man," Sakha said. "They really gave you and Josh Weiner a priceless education at that Accidental College."

" 'Think one person can change the world?' " I said in English. " 'So do we.' "

"What's that?"

"The motto of Misha's Children."

"I wish it were my motto as well," Sakha said. He sighed and put his hands on his hips, an unacademic and frankly surprising gesture. "I can't complain, Mr. Vainberg," he said. "The Americans have really been helping us out. Xerox machines, free use of the fax lines after nine P.M., discounted Hellmann's mayonnaise from the commissary, five thousand free copies of *An American Life* by Ronald Reagan. We know what democracy looks like. We've read about it. We've been to Century 21. But how do we make it happen *here*? Because frankly, Mr. Vainberg, once the oil runs dry, who in the world is going to know we even exist?"

I considered telling him that no one knew they existed anyway but thought it might be tactless.

"Maybe you should move your daughters to Belgium," I said. "I'll pay for their plane tickets."

"You are thoughtful and sincere," Sakha said, and then, in all contravention of the rules of the manly Caucasus, he turned away and made a tearful gurgle with his sickle-shaped nose.

"You can't choose where you're born," I said, and immediately felt like an asshole for saying it.

Sakha looked back from the derrick-studded horizon to my own sweltering frame. "Are you hot, Mr. Vainberg?" he said, laying his hand on one of my wet shoulders. "Let's get back in the car. Monsieur Lefèvre is waiting for us by the McDonald's dumpster."

I nodded in agreement. But as we turned toward the car, Sakha looked back once more at the city beneath us. "Did I mention," he said, "that the Sevo Vatican was originally covered by hexagonal tiles made of gold leaf that were given to us as a tribute by the khan of Bukhara and that the hexagonal motif represents the six great cities of Sevo antiquity?"

"I think you did mention that, yes," I said.

"And I told you the names of all six cities?" Sakha said. "Maybe I forgot to mention them."

"Yes, you told me, Mr. Sakha," I said. "Your country has a proud history. I understand that."

Sakha nodded and pulled at his orange Zegna tie. "All right, let's go," he said.

• • •

Journeying from the International Terrace to the Svanï one, we had left a fledgling Portland, Oregon, and arrived in Kabul. Gone were the Hyatts and fake Irish bars. Here the local business scene consisted of middle-aged men smoking cigarettes and gossiping around idled taxis. Rounding out the economy, younger men and boys ran around with buckets of sunflower seeds that they would wrap in a paper cone and sell for five thousand absurdis a portion (about US$.05, I later found out).

The McDonald's was situated behind a prominent square that, during the Soviet era, must have hosted its share of May Day parades but had been turned into an ad hoc market for used remote controls. We walked past hordes of potential buyers aiming the orphaned devices at the sky, as if trying to turn off the scorching sun. Above the gleaming pile of remotes stretched an enormous mural of Georgi Kanuk and his son Debil, dancing with each other on the helicopter deck of a Chevron offshore oil platform. A large man in a bow tie and tails stood off to the side of the deck, writing something with a quill upon an ancient scroll. He was as neatly mustached as the dictator and his son, and boasted an incongruous poof of African-looking hair. "Who's that?" I asked.

"Alexandre Dumas," an old remote seller told me. "He came to our country in 1858. He called the Svanï people 'the Pearls of the Caspian.' He loved our dried beef and wet women. When he came down to the *Sevo* Terrace, he was robbed by ruffians and cheated by the local merchants. He hated it there."

I looked to Sakha, who merely shrugged. "It's an old Svanï story," he said.

"And who are you by nationality?" the remote seller started to ask, but Sakha whisked me away to our destination.

We strode into the all-beef smell of McDonald's, where I was regarded by the hungry customers as a kind of living embodiment of the fast-food lifestyle. "Personally I favor the slow-food movement," I loudly announced to a family splitting the smallest McDonald's hamburger into six parts so that each family member could savor a little taste. Poor souls. Here they were living by the Caspian Sea, surrounded by delicious fresh sturgeon and wild tomatoes, and nonetheless they came to McDonald's. I made a mental note to check up on the diets of Misha's Children. Hopefully the progressive Park Slope social workers had already made their way to St. Petersburg and had set to work on the little ones.

"Hey, it's that democrat!" someone shouted at Sakha. "Hey, democrat, buy me a shake, will you? I'll believe in anything you say."

A tall Slavic man in his late teens approached, stiff and official in his disposable McDonald's uniform, but with enough of a homosexual smile to make a name for himself in Petersburg's Club 69. His Cyrillic tag labeled him a *Dzhunior Manadzher.* "Sir," he said. "Are you here to see Monsieur Lefèvre?"

"Certainly I am not here to eat your criminal food," I replied.

"Please come with me," said the junior manager. "In the meantime, Mr. Sakha and your manservant can enjoy a free cheeseburger. No, Mr. Sakha, you may *split* one cheeseburger, that's all."

He took me past the bathrooms reeking awfully of industrial detergent, past a framed print of California's Pacific Coast Highway, and to a door that opened to a small cul-de-sac where the McDonald's garbage was stored in vast plastic containers. It took me a while to pinpoint Jean-Michel Lefèvre of the Belgian consulate, lying atop a soiled mattress, with both hands grasping the edges, as if he were Jonah just spat out of the whale.

"Monsieur Lefèvre isn't feeling well," the slender Russian boy told me. "I'm going to get him something to drink."

"Misha," the Belgian bellowed into the mattress. "Bring vodka," he said in Russian.

"Are you talking to me?" I said.

"I am also called Misha," said the boy, leaving us alone.

The Belgian used his elbows to flip over onto his back, where he could get a proper look at me. "Mother of God," he said in English. "You're big. You're bigger than in Captain Belugin's photograph. You're the biggest thing ever."

"I am a big man, yes," I said. Lefèvre was himself a blond, emaciated fellow likely in early middle age, stubbly, red-eyed, and nicely browned by the Absurdi arrangement of sun, water, and sand. What-ever awful thing that had happened to him must have happened quickly and irrevocably.

"So," said Lefèvre with a smirk. "Who wants to be a Belgian?"

"I do," I said. Was he trying to make some kind of joke? "I have paid US$240,000 to Captain Belugin. That should buy citizenship for me and a work visa for my manservant. Everything should be in order."

"Mm-hump," said the Belgian, throwing up a hand and letting it hang in front of him limply. "Everyone wants to be a Belgian. Well, I don't want to be a Belgian, no, sir. I want to be a Mexican Zapatista or a Montenegrin. Something fierce." He yawned and scratched the perfectly white bridge of his nose. I noticed his sunglasses lying bro-ken at his feet.

Misha the McDonald's junior manager returned with a bottle of Flagman vodka and a McDonald's paper cup. He emptied the vodka into the cup, gently tilted Lefèvre's head, and poured the vodka into the diplomat's mouth. There was some gagging, but mostly the alco-hol found its way into the Belgian's bloodstream, where it quickly reddened his tan.

"What are you?" Lefèvre asked me as he let Misha wipe his face with a McDonald's paper hat. "What do you do?"

"I'm a philanthropist," I said. "I run a charity called Misha's Chil-dren."

"Are you some kind of pedophile?"

"What?" I fairly shrieked. "How can you? How awful! All my life I've wanted to help children."

"I just thought because you're so fat and puffy—"

"Stop insulting me. I know my rights."

"You're not a Belgian yet, friend," he said. "I'm just joking. We have a problem in Belgium with pedophilia. Big scandal. Even the government and police people are implied."

"Implicated," I corrected him.

"I thought you should know more about your new nation before you signed on. Anything else you wanted to know?"

I considered all the things I wanted to know about Belgium. There weren't many. "You have this queen Beatrix, no?" I asked.

"That would be Holland."

"And you have a shameful history in the Congo. Your Leopold was a monster."

"He's your Leopold now, Vainberg. *Our* Leopold. Our Leopold of the Black Sorrows." Lefèvre reached under the mattress and took out a business envelope that he tried to throw my way, but it landed in exactly the opposite direction, atop a plastics recycling bin. The other Misha picked it up and brought it to me.

I tried to stick my big, squishy hand inside, but to no avail. After tearing the envelope to bloody pieces, I withdrew a purple Belgian passport.

I opened it. Beneath a faint hologram of what I imagined was the Belgian Royal Palace, I saw a grainy duplicate of my Accidental College yearbook photograph, the travails of a grossly overweight twenty-two-year-old already hanging from my chin.

"For more information on Belgium, visit www.belgium.be," Lefèvre said. "They have some information in English, too. You should at least know the name of the current prime minister. They sometimes ask that at Immigration."

"This looks so real," I said.

"It is real," the diplomat told me. "According to official records, you became a citizen of Belgium in Charleroi last summer. You were granted political asylum from Russia. You're a Chechen sympathizer or something. A Jewish Chechen sympathizer, that's you."

I pressed the passport to my nose, hoping to smell Europe—wine, cheese, chocolates, mussels, Belgian as opposed to McDonald's fries. All I smelled were my own odors reflected back—a hot day, a tired man, hope tempered with sturgeon. "This is very good," I said.

"No, it's not very good," said Lefèvre.

"Well, it's very good for me," I said. I was trying to stay positive, as they do in the States all the time.

The diplomat smiled. He gestured for the other Misha to tilt his head and administer the vodka inside the McDonald's paper cup. In between swallows, he started singing the anthem of my new homeland:

O Belgique, ô mère chérie,
A toi nos coeurs, à toi nos bras,
A toi notre sang, ô patrie!
Nous le jurons tous, tu vivras!
Tu vivras toujours grande et belle
Et ton invincible unité
Aura pour devise immortelle:
Le roi, la loi, la liberté!

With each French word, he stared farther into the blue void of my pretty eyes, grimacing, guffawing, and willing upon me every failure of which I knew myself capable. I stood there and listened. Then I said, "You know something, Mr. Lefèvre . . ."

"Hmm?" he said. "What do I know?"

"Everybody hurts," I said.

The diplomat curled his fine lips, seeming surprised for the first time. "Who hurts?" he asked. "What are you talking about?"

"Everybody hurts," I said once more. Despite the logistical problems posed by my weight, I lowered myself to the ground and extended my hand to take the vodka cup from his hand. Lefèvre reached over, and our hands met briefly, his as wet and vulgar as my own. I took the cup and spilled some vodka on my new passport.

"What are you doing?" shouted the diplomat. "That's an EU passport!"

"In Russia, when one graduates from a university, he spills vodka on his diploma for good luck."

"Yes, but that's an EU passport!" the diplomat repeated, scrambling backward on his mattress. "You paid hundreds of thousands of dollars for it. You don't want it smelling like vodka."

"I can do as I please!" I began to shout, my anger suddenly matched by the sound of crashing china and cutlery behind me. We looked to McDonald's, aware that the restaurant offered only plastic and paper service.

"What are these idiots doing now?" Lefèvre said.

Several middle-aged women with very full lungs were screaming inside the McDonald's. Almost immediately, the women's roar was joined by a distant counterpart, issuing presumably from the Sevo Terrace below. A strange sonic displacement seemed to be taking place all around us, as if the summer heat with its layers of shimmering, highly sulfuric air were taking on an acoustic quality. "Shit," Lefèvre said as the recycling bins started to shake violently, which I surmised could not have been the result of the female screaming alone. "Oh, fuck me," he said.

Sakha ran out of McDonald's, his hands trembling with the yellow remains of a cheeseburger, his Zegna tie stained with a trail of ketchup. He tried to speak but could only sputter and whinny in an impotent intellectual way. It took the McDonald's junior manager, Misha, to make the situation clear for us.

"Georgi Kanuk's plane has just been shot down by Sevo rebels," he said.

18

To the Hyatt Station

"I predict," said Lefèvre, "that we're all going to die here in Absurdistan."

A lone MiG-29 punched a hole through the stratosphere above us and swooped alarmingly over the gray bowl of the Caspian. The Svanï Terrace rumbled in its wake.

"We're Belgians," I shouted at the diplomat, brandishing my new passport at him. "Who would want to hurt us?"

"I predict that before this ends, we will all be dead," repeated Lefèvre.

"What the hell, Jean-Michel?" Misha the junior manager said. "You told me there wasn't going to be a civil war until August. You said everything would be quiet through July. We would get the Vainberg money and leave. We were going to be on a plane to Brussels next week."

"We're not going anywhere," the diplomat said. "They've shut down the airport by now. That's for certain."

"How could this have happened?" the junior manager shouted, one hand raised in anger, the other draped passionately over his hip. "And what about that luxury American Express train that runs across the border? The one that costs five thousand dollars a ride. How could they cancel that?"

"I'm sure it's all finished," Lefèvre said. "They lied to me."

"Who lied to you?" the junior manager said.

"Everyone," Lefèvre said. "Sevo, Svanï, Golly Burton . . ."

I turned to Sakha, who looked as discarded as a burger wrapper.

"Sakha, what's happening?" I said. "They don't shoot Belgians, do they?"

"Vainberg," Lefèvre said, "you have to do something important."

"I'm always ready to do something important!" I cried, scrambling over a recycling bin to get to my feet.

"You have to get the democrat to the Hyatt immediately. Put him under Larry Zartarian's protection. It's not safe for him out here."

My heart beat like that of a young girl in love. I was blissful and manic at the same time. *Think one person can save a democrat? So do I.* "We have a Hyatt jeep out front," I said. "But are you going to be okay, Monsieur Lefèvre? Is there anything I can do for you?"

"Just get the fuck out of here," Lefèvre said. "Everybody hurts, Misha. But some hurt more than others."

"What?"

"Godspeed, Gargantua! Go!"

The starchy McDonald's was filled with the sounds of women and children whimpering, the men contributing an undignified stream of curses revolving around the all-purpose Russian swear word *blyad,* or "whore." The people had hidden beneath the greasy square tables and behind the counter, as if a robbery were in progress. Cardboard versions of the McDonald's mascots, a scary American clown and some kind of purple blob, had been commandeered as "human" shields by several armed customers.

"They think this is a multinational space," Sakha said. "They think they'll be safe here. The only safe places are the embassies, the Hyatt, and the Radisson."

"Yes, yes!" I said, not knowing what I was agreeing to but thoroughly enjoying every second of it. "We'll get you to the Hyatt, Mr. Sakha. You have my word as a Vainberg."

Outside, we became aware of what had accounted for the initial noise of crashing china and cutlery. The used-remote-control market was being pulverized beneath the tread of the advancing heavy infantry. I was looking at a convoy of stubby caterpillars outfitted with battering rams, which I realized were Soviet T-62 tanks, followed by a ring of equally obsolete BTR-152 armored personnel carriers, forests of anti-aircraft cannon poking out of the roof hatches. (When

I was a child, the Red Army was one of my main pre-masturbatory obsessions.)

Circuit boards, batteries, and infrared bulbs rained down on us in batches of crushed civilization. The remote sellers tried to salvage their wares, dumping the choicest models into their burlap sacks and then slaloming between the slow-moving vehicles to the relative safety of the Moorish-style opera house adjoining McDonald's. Alexandre Dumas looked down upon them silently from his mural, recording everything on his scroll.

The sound of heavy machine-gun fire reverberated throughout the city. I searched excitedly for the telltale plumes of smoke that to me define a war zone, but the sky was given over entirely to the treacherous sun. It was time to do something manly and American. "Go, go, go, motherfuckers!" I yelled to Sakha and Timofey, pushing them toward our car. The jeep's alarm was blaring and a rear window had been partly smashed, but the imperious Hyatt logo had apparently scared off the thieving locals. "You have to drive this thing," I said to Sakha, goading him into the driver's seat. "I have no idea how to do it, and my manservant's no better."

Sakha was hyperventilating. He kept pointing at his *mobilnik* and gesturing toward Gorbigrad, meaning, I suppose, that he wanted to call his family. I reached for my fanny pack and took out a bottle of Ativan. "What is that?" Sakha wheezed. "Valerian root?"

"Hardly," I said. I crammed a handful of Ativan into his mouth and flooded that orifice with forty ounces of Coca-Cola from the cup holder. "This is going to take effect immediately," I lied. "Breathe, Mr. Sakha, breathe. Would you like me to sing a calming Western song? 'My name is Luka,' " I sang. " 'I live on the second floor.' "

"Stop," Sakha said. "Stop singing, please. I need to think positive thoughts. I want to see my girls again."

A passing T-62 had begun to rotate its barrel our way, like a slow child trying to make friends. "Drive!" I shouted to Sakha.

We careened through the McDonald's parking lot and toward a half-assed side street. Wretched balconies groaned beneath laundry lines, terrified occupants peered out their windows, from every direction televisions cackled in the local tongue announcing imminent disaster. The radio station was playing Tchaikovsky's *Swan Lake,* a sure sign that things were much worse than they appeared. We ran through a gauntlet of terrified city cats and swerved onto yet another narrow street, this one dominated by the stone face of a Svanï church.

Soldiers had formed a checkpoint by the road leading up to the International Terrace. We found ourselves at the end of a long queue of stalled Zhigulis and Ladas. The cars ahead of us were being searched by short, skinny youths wearing dark mustaches in full bloom and fatigues stitched only with the Russian word *soldat* ("soldier"). Grenades hung from their belts. Some of them were flopping about in pink beach sandals.

"If they see that I'm a big democrat, they'll shoot me," Sakha said. "Georgi Kanuk's son is worse than his father. He ran the special forces. His hands are covered with blood. He'll want revenge for his father's death."

"You're with me," I said. "I'm a Vainberg. A Belgian. A Jew. A rich man. You're taking me to the Hyatt. We're important people, Sakha. Have faith in yourself."

"I'm calling my family," Sakha said, unholstering his phone. He started to cry as soon as the connection was made. He spoke in the local tongue and partly in Russian. "Did you take the girls to ExcessHollywood?" I heard him sob. "Did they have *Toy Story 2?* Tell them I'll be home tomorrow and we can watch it together. Or maybe they can come to the Hyatt and we'll watch it on Larry Zartarian's big screen. Would they like that? Oh, my sweet little monkeys. Never let them go. Never let them out of your sight. I should have known this would happen. I should have applied for that fellowship at Harvard. I've been listening to Josh Weiner for too long."

"That's enough!" I commanded. "Wipe your eyes and turn off the phone. It's almost our turn. Be strong!"

A barely pubescent soldier tapped on our window. He stared at my heavy tits and then at the shaking Sakha and my benighted Timofey, trying to comprehend our menagerie. "Who are you by nationality?" he barked at the democrat, filling our car with the stench of garlic and alcohol, along with the familiar scent of something pubic and male. Sakha started mooing to him hopelessly. The soldier ignored him and, with one dark long paw, reached into his shirt and took out a small golden cross hanging from a chain. He examined the Sevo footrest, then threw the cross back into Sakha's face. "Get out of the car, *blyad*," he said to Sakha.

"I'm Belgian," I shouted, waving my passport. "I'm a Belgian citizen. We're going to the Hyatt. We're in a Hyatt car. This is my driver. I'm a very important man, a Jew."

The soldier sighed. "The Jewish people have a long and peaceful history in our land," he recited. "My mother will be your mother—"

"Forget my mother for a second," I said. "Do you know who my father was? He was Boris Vainberg."

"I'm supposed to know every Jew in the country?" the soldier asked. He raised his Kalashnikov and skillfully placed it directly inside the knot of Sakha's Zegna tie. A familiar liquid was dribbling along the inseam of the poor man's trousers and onto his shoe. His body glowed red from within his crisp cotton outfit. It was possible he was having a heart attack.

I, on the other hand, had never felt more in control.

"You don't know who Boris Vainberg was?" I shouted at the soldier. "He sold the eight-hundred-kilogram screw to KBR."

"You're with KBR?" the soldier asked.

"Golly Burton, Golly Burton," Timofey brayed from the backseat.

The soldier lowered his gun. "Why didn't you say so from the start?" he said. He looked at us with sad, childish eyes, resigned to the prospect of one less beating. "Move along, sirs," he said, throwing us a lazy salute.

Sakha managed to throw the car into gear, and we slowly proceeded up to the International Terrace, behind the rump of an armored personnel carrier. The democrat had stopped crying and now produced only short bursts of urine, his hands dug into the steering wheel, his eyes following the anti-aircraft gun bouncing directly in front of us.

"Wow," I said in English. I turned around to look at my manservant. "Did you see that, Timofey? We did it. We saved a life. What does it say in the Talmud? 'He who has saved a life has saved an entire world.' I'm not religious, but my God! What an accomplishment. How do you feel, Sakha?"

But Sakha could not supply the words of gratitude I deserved. He merely breathed and drove. I decided to give him some time. I was already composing an electronic message to Rouenna about the day's exploits. What had she told me in that dream about the eight-dollar apple? *Be a man. Make me proud.* Done and done.

The Boulevard of National Unity was choked with eight-wheel BTR-70 armored personnel carriers, whose sloping, boatlike hulls would be familiar to anyone who watches BBC World. Tanks guarded the strategically important Benetton store and the 718 Perfumery. Slender Absurdi men in black jeans and tucked-in dress shirts, armed only with their holstered *mobilniki,* darted along the boulevard, minding the drunken soldiers who would hurl abuse at them on occasion, promising to inflict anal sex upon them and whatnot.

Nearing the Hyatt and Radisson skyscrapers, we were caught in a mass of screaming and shoving pedestrians bent on the same destination. Soldiers had surrounded them and were tearing through their documents and pulling at their crosses. They slapped people across the head or fondled young girls with giggly pleasure. At the heart of the action, a young soldier was trying to tug a chain off a matronly neck while punching her in the mouth. "Robbery!" the woman was yelling. "Save me, citizens! Robbery!" For some reason, Timofey and I both laughed nervously at the large woman's strife. We were reminded of something deeply Soviet—a person's dignity being slowly dismembered in front of others.

Respectful of the Hyatt sign on our jeep, the soldiers waved us through, the locals banging on the sides of our vehicle, hoping we could enable their safe passage to the hotel. "Unfortunately we have to save our own hides first," I said to Sakha.

The democrat nodded and said nothing. As we maneuvered into the Hyatt's circular driveway, he shouted two words that made no sense, turned the wheel sharply to the left, and slowly drove us into the camouflaged side of a BTR-70. The air bags inflated before us. Smothered with white, my fat cheeks scratched by the billowing nylon, I stumbled out of the jeep. An officer was running up to us, followed by a line of soldiers. At last I understood what Sakha was screaming behind me. Two words. "Colonel Svyokla."

In a novel written during the golden age of Russian literature, a man named Svyokla would look like a *svyokla*, that is to say, he would be red as a beet. But in the era of modern produce, Colonel Svyokla's head resembled a giant genetically modified peach, fraudulently spherical and ripe, the skin dry and crisp. He wore neither the democratic goatee favored by Sakha nor the Middle Eastern mustache sprouting from his soldiers' lips. He looked like one of the dignified older men from the Caucasus whom one often finds in the back of St. Petersburg casinos, sipping Armenian cognac with some beauty, ignoring the hurly-burly provincialism at the roulette wheel and the so-called dance floor.

"Misha Vainberg," Colonel Svyokla said, shaking my hand. "What a pleasure. My mother will be your mother . . ."

While he addressed me, the soldiers were dragging Sakha out of the Hyatt jeep. Sakha was not resisting them; he was merely being carried along by their collective force, his dark head bobbing in a sea of camouflage. "I used to work for your father, Boris, as his local oil consultant," Colonel Svyokla said, gamely ruffling my hair. "His death was a terrible tragedy. A major light was snuffed out for the Jewish people. My condolences."

At the far edge of the driveway, beneath a sign reading DANGER: LOW OVERHEAD CLEARANCE, a group of men had been assembled at gunpoint. They stood there with a terrible resignation, their ties hanging limply around their necks, arm hair glistening beneath their short sleeves, some of their eyes already swollen shut, presumably from rifle blows.

"There has been an attempted Sevo putsch," the colonel explained to me. "We'll take care of it in a few minutes. Go back to the hotel, Misha."

I ran as quickly as my weight allowed and burst headlong into the chilled Hyatt lobby. Alyosha-Bob and Larry Zartarian caught me in an embrace, and we all fell to the marble floor.

"You have to . . . You have to . . ." I said, scrambling all over them, my hands flopping up and down as if I were swimming toward a distant lighthouse.

"There's nothing . . . There's nothing . . ." both of them were saying in answer. "There's nothing we can do."

I spotted Josh Weiner among a clutch of oil workers, their hands filled with afternoon beer mugs. "Josh," I cried. "Josh, help me. They've got Sakha."

The diplomat was looking deep into his palms, which he had stuck out in front of him. He turned his hands over carefully, never shifting his downward gaze.

"Josh!" I said. Timofey leveraged my weight with his and brought me to my feet.

I hobbled over to Weiner, but he silently turned away from me.

"We've already filed a protest," I heard him say.

"The people they're going to shoot . . . they're not rebels. They're all democrats!"

"Did you hear what I just said, Vainberg?" Weiner grated through his teeth. "We've filed a protest."

I turned around and made for the sunlight. "Misha, no!" Alyosha-Bob shouted, throwing himself upon me, but I knocked him out of my way with one enormous squishy fist.

I emerged onto the driveway to the sound of angry male voices. "On the ground!" the soldiers were yelling to Sakha and his cohorts. I *felt* them. I felt the soldiers with their warm ethnic blood and clan loyalties, their adolescent swagger and inbred psychoses, their made-up heraldry of lamb pie, plum brandy, and a hairy virgin for the wedding feast.

"On your knees!" the soldiers shouted.

The men, some of them heavy, others bestowed with an academic's lack of physical grace, found it difficult to arrange themselves in this tenuous position. Several were tipping over and had to be dragged up by their collars. The soldiers had fallen in line behind them, one soldier to a man, a ratio that did not bode well.

Sakha's eyes fixed on me. There were tears on his face; I couldn't see them, but I knew they were there. "Misha," he shouted to me.

"Mishen'ka, please. Tell them to stop. They will listen to a man like you. Please. Say something."

I felt Alyosha-Bob's hand tugging on my sleeve, his little body pressing into mine. "Golly Burton!" I yelled. "KBR!"

The soldiers looked to Colonel Svyokla, who nodded. They shot the men through the back of the head, the bodies of their victims jerking up in unison with the discharge, then hitting the driveway with tremendous speed, a cloud of loose gravel swirling around them.

The spent bullet casings rolled down the driveway to my feet. A dozen bodies lay on the ground.

19

My Gray Reptile Heart

Forty stories above the war, civilization à la Hyatt enclosed us.

Generators hummed deeply within the skyscraper, allowing the illusion that we were on an American spaceship floating past the tanks and armored personnel carriers, the fake Irish bars and Royal Dutch Shell oil platforms, toward some remarkable and disingenuous Hollywood conclusion. "Everybody into the pool! It's party time!"

I dialed, and misdialed, and dialed again Dr. Levine's number. Finally the good doctor came on the line, coughed, sneezed (seasonal allergies again), hacked, and wished me a good day. "Dr. Levine, emergency," I said. "I'm in Absurdsvanï Republic. I'm in great danger. Terrible things. Please advise me—"

With great patience and analytic equipoise, Dr. Levine beseeched me to calm the fuck down. "Now, where is this place?" he asked.

"Have you been watching the news?"

"I saw the news last night."

"So you heard about the civil war."

"What civil war?"

"In Absurdsvanï. In the capital. They've sealed off the airport. And they shot my friend in the back of the head."

"Okay, let's start from the beginning." Dr. Levine sighed. "What is this Absurdsvanï?"

"Absurdsvanï is on the Caspian Sea."

"Which is where, exactly? My geography's a little off."

"The Caspian Sea? It's, you know, south of Russia, near Turkmenistan—"

"Where?"

"Near Iran."

"Near Iran? I thought you were still in Moscow last time you called."

"St. Petersburg."

"Still, Iran must be a great deal farther off than Moscow. What are you doing there?"

I explained in so many words that I had traveled to Absurdistan to buy European citizenship off a crooked Belgian consular official after nailing my dead father's young wife. A reproachful silence followed. "Is this a legal way to get citizenship?" Dr. Levine asked.

"Well," I said. " 'Legal' is a relative word . . ."

You son of a bitch, I thought. *How dare you suggest that I shouldn't avail myself of every last chance to get out of Russia when your own great-grandparents probably bribed half the czar's men in the Pale of Settlement and then sneaked out in a mail bag, just to make sure their descendants could lounge on a fine walnut-trimmed Eames chair on the corner of Park Avenue and Eighty-fifth Street, issuing half-baked censorious statements to the insulted and injured and collecting US$350 an hour for the privilege?* But instead of saying this, I started to cry.

"Let's go through the important questions first," Dr. Levine said. "There seem to be a lot of people being shot to death or blown up by land mines in your recent past. So let me ask you: Are you in a safe place? Is your life in any immediate danger? And, given the possibility that you may now experience symptoms of post-traumatic stress such as feelings of detachment, anger, and helplessness, do you think you can make rational decisions that will keep you safe in the future?"

"I'm not sure," I said, choking off my sobs to concentrate. "My friend Alyosha-Bob is trying to get us out of here. He's very smart, you know."

"Well, that's positive," Dr. Levine said. "In the meantime, you should spend your time constructively. Try to occupy yourself as you did in Moscow. If it's safe to do so, go for a walk or do some exercise. This type of activity, combined with three milligrams of Ativan a day, should lower your anxiety level."

"Do you think I can really—"

"Look, why don't you just try to relax?" Dr. Levine said. I could hear him slurping on his beloved citrus shake with vitamin boost, the modern equivalent of the analyst's cigar. "Just don't get so worked up," he said.

"*Try* to relax? How do I do that? That's like trying to drink my way to sobriety."

"You know what helps another patient of mine when he gets all worked up? He goes out and buys a suit. Why don't you go out and buy a suit, Misha?"

"I'm too sad to buy a suit," I whispered.

"What else comes to mind about that? About your sadness."

"No one cares about me, not even you, Doctor," I said. "I saw a nice democrat killed in front of me, and I try to grieve the best I can for him, but I can't. And I try to grieve for my papa, but nothing, as you say, 'comes to mind about that.' And I try to be good, I try to help people, but there's no way to be good here, or if there is, I don't know it. And I'm scared, and I'm lonely, and I'm unhappy, and I'm chastising myself for being scared, and lonely, and unhappy, and for being alive for thirty years and having nobody, not one soul save for Alyosha, who would care for me. I know there are people in New York and Paris and London who have the same problems, and that I shouldn't feel exceptional by comparison, but everything I do and everywhere I go, it's all wrong, wrong, wrong. And it can't just be me. I need to know that it's not just me. I need to hear that I'm better than this. I wake up in an empty bed and I look at my heart and it's gray. Literally. I take off my shirt, I pick up my breast, and my heart's all leathery and gray like a reptile's."

I heard several bouts of strained nasal breathing. I grasped the receiver, waiting to hear that it wasn't just me, that I was better than this, and that there was no such thing as a gray reptilian heart. "Say it!" I whispered, barely audibly, and in Russian. "Do your job! Make it work! Give me some happiness!"

More analytic silence followed.

"It is true," Dr. Levine grudgingly allowed, "that the circumstances in which you live present a unique set of problems."

"Yes," I said. It was true. Bad circumstances made for unique problems. I waited for more. I waited for one minute, then for another, but in vain. *Oh, come on, Doctor. Throw a dog a bone. Tell me I'm better than this. Talk about my heart.* I put my face in one of my big, squishy hands and I cried, exaggerating my wails in the hope that the doctor would take pity and absolve me of my sins.

But he wouldn't do it. Not for US$350 an hour. Not for all the money on the Cayman Islands. Not for all the money in this gray-hearted world of mine.

As depressed and immobile as a twenty-first-century Oblomov, I lay on my bed scrolling through the darkest corners of the Internet, the laptop whizzing and bleating atop the mound of my stomach. I watched all kinds of unfortunate women being degraded and humiliated, tied up, spat upon, forced to swallow gigantic penises, and I wished I could wipe off their dripping faces, whisk them away to some Minneapolis or Toronto, and teach them to take pleasure in a simple linear life far from their big-dicked tormentors.

I decided to write Rouenna an electronic letter.

Dear Rouenna,

I am in a small country called Absurdsvaní, to the south of Russia, near Iran. A civil war has broken out and innocent democrats are being shot in the street. I am trying to save as many people as I can. The Belgian government has awarded me citizenship in recognition of my services, but it may be too late to save my own life. Pray for me, Rouenna. Go to mass with your abuela *Maria and pray for my soul.*

I don't know if your new boyfriend has taught you to read Freud yet, but I want to tell you about a dream I had in which you sold me an apple for eight dollars. My analyst says it means that everything you ever did for me was conditional upon my money. From the very beginning when you saw my loft and said, "Dang, jumbo, I think I finally made it," you were using me. (See, I don't forget a thing!) My analyst, who is a medical doctor, says you better change, Rouenna, because what you're doing to me is going to destroy you inside. You're

*the one who's going to be hurt by your actions and that's a medical
opinion. Think about it!*

*If I make it out of here alive I'll still be yours forever, because you're
the only thing that makes my life worth living.*

Your Loving Russian Bear, Misha

Actually, I hadn't gotten around to mentioning the apple dream to
Dr. Levine, but it was always useful to bring up an authority figure
with Rouenna. As soon as I sent the message, an auto response
popped up on my screen.

*Hey there cowboys and cowgirls! I cant answer your message right
now because me and my man are going up to CAPE COD for a week
just to chill out from all the stress thats been killing us!!!! While y'all
steaming like chinese dumplings in NYC we'll be staying at a famous
film director's house in hiyanissport (cant say who it is or Proffessor
Shteynfarb will kill me!). Ha ha. Just kidding. I'll be back next
Wednesday so dont miss me too much. Kisses, R.*

*Thought of the Day: "The earth swarms with people who are not
worth talking to." —Voltaire, French Philospher. Totally true!!!!!*

I reread the message, the laptop pneumatically rising and falling
on my belly with each breath. There was a phrase that had stuck in
my mind. It wasn't the Voltaire. I reread Rouenna's message. "Film
director." That was it. Not a movie director, but a *film* director.
Christ. I tapped at the keyboard with a numb forefinger, winding
my computer back to the stream of pornography, the clean-shaven
vaginas confronted with twirling batons. I fell asleep in a whirlpool
of rage, a woman's false moaning registering thinly on the laptop's
speakers.

A hand was rubbing my shoulder, but I couldn't connect it to the familiar voice telling me to "Wake up, Misha." The hand continued to
massage me, infusing my shoulder with the smell of alcohol and man
sweat.

"Don't touch me!" I cried, jolting awake and smacking hard at the hand on my shoulder. For an odd second, I was surprised to find Alyosha-Bob standing beside me and not my father.

"What the fuck, Misha?" Alyosha-Bob said, rubbing at his hurt. "What's wrong with you?"

"I don't know," I whispered. "I'm sorry."

The globe of Alyosha-Bob's head hovered over me, blue veins forming rivers of concern, his nose a living, breathing subcontinent. He was wearing nothing but sweatpants, his naked chest sporting a standard Orthodox cross and a Jewish c'hai. Recently my friend had been flapping his fish lips about adding some religious meaning to his life. I wanted to ask him: why are Americans always searching for something when clearly there is nothing to be found?

He picked up the laptop from my belly. "Oh, that's nice, Snack," he said. "Stuffherass.com. Is that your new girlfriend in the dog collar?"

"I'm sorry I hit you," I said. "I just don't want to be touched right now."

"What did your analyst say?"

"Post-traumatic stress. Blah, blah, blah."

"What else did he say?"

"He told me to go for a walk. You know, get some exercise. Buy a suit."

"Brilliant as ever." Alyosha-Bob laughed. "I ordered buffalo wings from room service. They're in the living room. There's Black Label in the minibar."

The buffalo wings were dry and inauthentic, and it took four buckets, or forty-eight wings, to satisfy me. I sucked on the brittle bones as if I were a pornographic understudy myself, savoring the mild tomato-based "hot sauce" dribbling past my chin and onto my Hyatt bathrobe. I let the invisible central-air currents stroke my stubbly face. Hot sauce and air-conditioning: when I put them together, I almost felt safe.

Alyosha-Bob was typing on his laptop with one hand while the other was switching television channels with a hefty zapper. He was trolling for news about Absurdistan. "CNN nothing, MSNBC nothing, BBC almost nothing, France 2 something, but *je ne comprends pas* what it is . . . Looks like we're stuck with ORT."

He turned on one of the Kremlin-controlled Russian networks, all Putin, all the time. True enough, the Russian president was giving a press conference. He looked the way he always did, like a mildly unhappy horse dipping his mouth into a bowl of oats. "Absurdsvanï is an important partner for Russia, strategically, economically, and culturally," Putin sadly imparted into the microphone. "We hope for a cessation to the violence. We implore the Sevo leadership to respect international norms."

Alyosha-Bob switched to another Russian government channel. Come to think of it, they were all government channels. A young Western-looking reporter stood in front of a marble slab etched with the words PARK HYATT SVANÏ CITY.

"Hey, that's our hotel," I said.

"So far, a modest death toll," the reporter was saying. "Sixty-five people killed in the conflict, twelve of them armed Sevo coup plotters shot by security forces in front of the Hyatt Hotel."

"Sevo *coup* plotters?" I said. "*Armed*? They were just democrats with expensive ties."

The reporter continued, "As a result of the personal mediation of President Putin, a temporary cease-fire was signed today in Svanï City."

"That's a good sign!" Alyosha-Bob said. "They might reopen the airport."

I made a halfhearted snort of affirmation. To be honest, the idea of moving from the Hyatt seemed fantastical to me. I wanted to go back to my room and look at the poor girls on the Internet some more. I wanted to tear their tormentors apart with both hands.

The reporter went on, "Today the new president of the republic, Debil Kanuk, son of the murdered state leader Georgi Kanuk, met with the leaders of the Sevo rebellion, who are calling themselves the State Committee for the Restoration of Order and Democracy, or SCROD, according to the English acronym."

"That's a fish, isn't it?" I said. "They named themselves after a fish."

"Not even a good fish," Alyosha-Bob said.

The Svanï leader shook hands with his older but better-dressed Sevo counterparts. They all smiled as if they had just returned from a triumphant duck hunt.

"Who do you like more, Svanï or Sevo?" I asked my friend.

"They all suck," Alyosha-Bob said. "Larry Zartarian said this whole war is about an oil pipeline KBR is building from the Caspian through Turkey. Everyone wants it to go through their territory so they can profit from the kickbacks."

Watching the proud, well-tailored Sevos shake hands with the distasteful Debil Kanuk, his oily forehead dripping pancake makeup beneath the klieg lights, I decided to root firmly for the Sevo people. If only in Sakha's memory.

And then I recognized one of the men standing next to Debil Kanuk. Crisp olive uniform, dim eyes perpetually scanning the horizon, red fists hanging like pomegranates above his hips. It seemed Colonel Svyokla was smirking directly at me, daring me to save Sakha's life.

He spoke calmly into the microphone. After the hoglike bursts of language coming out of Debil Kanuk, the colonel seemed positively an orator. "Until the murderous Sevo plotters responsible for downing President Georgi Kanuk's plane are apprehended," he said, "the republic's borders will remain sealed and closed to all air traffic. There will be justice for the Svanï people."

"Damn!" Alyosha-Bob said. "What the hell, Misha? They're not going to let the foreigners leave? What do they want from us? This is bullshit!" He stopped to look at me. "Are you crying, Snack?"

I touched my face. It was true. My cheeks were soaked, and my nostrils were filled with the sea breeze of my own body salt; meanwhile, in back of me, the toxic hump was hitting all the familiar bass notes: "DES-pair, DES-pair, des-PAIR." It was all happening again. The driveway. The spent bullet casings. The rising cloud of gravel. The bodies jerking upward. Sakha's last words to me: *Mishen'ka, please. Tell them to stop. They will listen to a man like you.*

Alyosha-Bob switched off the television and walked over to me.

"Come on, Snacky," he said. He made an open-armed gesture toward my body.

"Go ahead," I sobbed, leaning toward him. He sat down and put my head on his warm, naked shoulder. The tears kept coming, easily, aimlessly, with regard for nothing but the salty streams they forged across my friend's body, eventually pooling inside his cavernous belly button.

"Let's rap a little," he said. "Would you like to rap a little, Misha? Remember who we are? We're the Gentlemen Who Like to Rap!"

"I remember," I said. I smiled just enough to reassure Alyosha-Bob that I was still salvageable.

"Then how about some ghetto tech? How about a little 'Dick Work'?"

"Okay," I said, glancing shyly between my legs.

" 'Lemme see yoah dick work, / Lemme see yoah dick work,' " Alyosha-Bob sang into an imaginary microphone, mimicking the tone of a young promiscuous woman from the Detroit ghetto. " 'Lemme see yoah dick work . . .' "

He leaned the microphone over to me. Pretending to be this imaginary ghetto woman's paramour, I sang in a false ghetto-pimp baritone: " 'Let me see dat *pussy* work.' "

We both laughed. "Good boy," Alyosha-Bob said. "That's how we do it. That's how we *hit it*. Straight-up Detroit shit. Call-and-response. You're my nigga."

"And you are mine," I said, kissing him on the cheek. I felt something bright and piercing at the tip of my belly. Could rap be any more empowering? Was it true that the people who had nothing were the most fortunate people of all?

Our embrace was interrupted by the dull but steadily appreciating roar of an aircraft. Alyosha-Bob sprang to the window and pulled open the blinds.

"Get over here, Misha!" he said.

"Do I have to?"

"Look!"

A Chinook helicopter, a kind of mechanized air cow, bulky and graceless beneath its two rotors, was flying over the oil fields, headed for the International Terrace. I made out the inscription on its side, white English letters on camouflage.

"Get your manservant and your laptop. And your Belgian passport, too."

"Why?"

"Fall of Saigon, '75."

"Je ne comprends pas."

"Shake a limb, Snack. We're gonna make a run for the embassy."

The U.S. ARMY had arrived in Svanï City.

20

The American Gambit

The American embassy was situated in the shadows of the Exxon-Mobil skyscraper, a freshly built rectangle of salmon-hued glass with art deco bands of chrome meant to evoke permanence and easy history. The embassy itself was housed in an old pastel academy once used to educate the sons of local czarist nobility. In the wake of the attacks on American embassies in Africa, a moat of trenches and razor wire surrounded the American outpost in Absurdistan. The gathering crowds, however, were well equipped with wire cutters and the like, and they charged the compound with bravado, as if the incoming helicopters had convinced them they were extras in a Hollywood historical drama.

Some were older, but the majority seemed to be of college age, dressed to look as nonthreatening and American as possible. They carried signs that listed the reasons for being accepted aboard the hovering Chinooks, among other things: 21 YR. OLD GIRL, <u>NOT</u> PROSTITUTKA, HAVE STUDENT VISA TO CALIFORNIAN UNIVERSITY AT THE NORTHBRIDGE + MINE FAMILY HAS GAS. And: PLEASE LET ME GO WITH YOU—SECRET POLICE WILL DIE ME, BECAUSE I POLITICAL AGAINST DEBIL KANUK DICTATOR. And: WE ♥ HALLIBURTON, KBR #1, GO HOUSTON ROCKETS! And: AMERICA: IF YOU DON'T CARE ANYTHING ABOUT US, $AVE OUR OIL. My favorite, hoisted by a grizzly old pensioner, a simple retired laborer by the looks of him, whose sign was nonetheless written in perfectly correct English: WE ARE NO WORSE THAN YOU ARE. WE ARE ONLY POORER.

"American and EU citizens coming through," Alyosha-Bob

shouted, pushing aside the little brown Absurdis around us. I picked up his war cry, and even Timofey started shouting: "American and yoo-yoo, commie fru!"

Our U.S. and Belgian passports held aloft, we were quickly diverted toward a VIP line, where the potential aspirants were taller and whiter and fatter—more my speed all around. The only dark standout was Larry Zartarian, the Hyatt manager, who was trying to shove his mother into the arms of a consular officer, shouting, "Cysts! Deadly cysts! She needs emergency medical care at Cedars-Sinai. My mother will be your mother! Take her away from me!" The black-clad mama (a near-double of her son, only with her whiskers more expertly cropped) shouted back, "No, no, I won't go! He won't live without me! He doesn't know how to live. He's an idiot."

We spotted Josh Weiner scurrying around behind several marine guards, dribbling saliva into his cellular phone and waving around a clipboard. "Weiner!" Alyosha-Bob shouted. "Class of '94!"

Weiner flashed us a bullshit grin and waved the clipboard, then pointed to his watch to indicate he was busy. "Oh, come on!" Alyosha-Bob shouted. "Don't make me write to the alumni newsletter!"

The diplomat sighed, slammed shut his phone, and came over to us. "Say, what's the deal here, Joshie?" Alyosha-Bob said, putting a friendly hand into the crook of Weiner's arm. "Think we can get our asses on that whirlybird?"

"What kind of citizenship does he have?" Weiner said, gesturing my way but not looking me in the face. The State Department always deals with me in the third person.

"Misha's an EU citizen," Alyosha-Bob said. "He's a Belgian."

"For right now, they're just letting Americans go up," Weiner said.

"That's fine," I said. "Don't worry about it, Joshie. I'll just die here like your friend Sakha."

"Take it easy, Misha," Alyosha-Bob said.

"That's not fair," Weiner said.

"Hey, Joshie, did you file the protest?" I said.

"What protest?"

"You told me you were going to file a protest. Remember? Right before they shot Sakha. How's that protest going for you? Any word yet?"

"Oh, *whatever,* Snack Daddy," Weiner said. "Keep thinking it's all my fault. I'm just a low-level State Department employee. You think I actually save people's lives? You think I'm Oskar *fucking* Schindler? I did everything I could for Sakha. He ripped us off left and right, too. That Zegna tie was just the tip of it. He 'borrowed' baby formula from the commissary, and he used improper channels to get his niece a scholarship at Penn State. And that's just what we *know* about. These people are operators. Don't kid yourself."

I took a step toward Weiner, an aggressive step, but Alyosha-Bob's body was already between us. "You know something, Snack?" Weiner said, backing away from me quickly. "Go ahead. Get the fuck out of here. I really don't care anymore. Go eat Cheetos by the ton and have your belly rubbed by freshmen. Just don't consider me your friend, all right? Because you never were."

He waved us through toward the line of fully accredited Americans queuing at the foot of the ExxonMobil Building, bewildered-looking embassy families toting precious duffel bags, oilmen garrulously sharing in the fun of evacuation, slapping one another on the back and fondly recalling the Hyatt's full-tilt prostitutes.

"Hey, big boy," one of these specimens shouted at me. "Hey, scumbag."

Big boy? Scumbag? I put both hands between my chests to indicate having taken affront. Before me stood a bowlegged orangutan in drawstring shorts and a U.S.S. *Nimitz* cap.

"Roger Daltrey," he spat at me.

"Who?" I said. The name reminded me of a band member of some famous U.S. or British rock-and-roll band, but all my musical references were modern and focused on hip-hop and multiculturalism. "Who's Roger Daltrey?"

"You don't even know, do you?" said my antagonist, doffing his cap so that a halo of deeply receding red hair floated above him to match his angry words. "You fucking Russians don't even remember who you kill. Fucking animals."

"Oh, shit," Alyosha-Bob said, once again thrusting his small frame between me and my tormentor.

"What?" I said.

"Oh, shit," Alyosha-Bob said again, the repetition dull yet meaningful in my ears.

"Your father killed my uncle," the American explained. "Over nothing. Over a rat farm."

"Huh?" I was dizzy with confusion and low blood sugar. What was he talking about? The Oklahoma businessman? The one Papa allegedly had executed in Petersburg? "But you're not from Oklahoma," I said. "You sound like you're working-class New Jersey. Are you sure you're related? The Oklahoma guy was supposed to be educated."

"What did you say, asshole?" the putative relative of the dead Oklahoman Roger Daltrey shouted at me. "What did you say to my face? I'm *uneducated*?"

"Shut up, Misha," Alyosha-Bob growled at me. "Shut up and stay calm."

"You know, I Googled your father," the Daltrey relative said, "and he was just a total prick. Assholes like him ruined your country and ruined this one, too. They should send all of you to the Hague, stand you up on war-crimes charges."

A cry dislodged itself from somewhere between my sternum and my groin, from someplace wet and lonely and orphaned. I found myself lapsing into the heavily accented English of my first years in the States as I shouted, "BELOVED PAPA WAS NO TOTAL PRICK!"

And with those words, I reached past Alyosha-Bob and clipped the American on the side of the head, one ferocious squishy bear paw striking him someplace relatively soft and unbreakable, not far removed from the small clump of brain that kept his vitals going.

My antagonist collapsed immediately and started roaring with shame and pain. Momentarily, Josh Weiner and his superiors were on the scene, men in pressed shirts and sober ties who held me back from the violence that had instantaneously gone out of me. "Beloved Papa was no total prick," I said quietly, nodding in affirmation. "He was a Jewish dissident. A man of conscience."

"My uncle has three children," the American groaned. "Three orphaned children, you fat useless fuck."

"We're sorry about all this," Alyosha-Bob beseeched the diplomatic staff and the arriving marines. "My friend lost his temper. He's a Belgian, that's all."

"Sir," the tallest and grayest of the diplomats told me, "we have to ask you to leave the embassy grounds."

I looked into his officious face, smooth and hard like an actor's or a politician's. "These are *Exxon* grounds," I said miserably.

"You're the son of Boris Vainberg," the older diplomat said. "I know all about you. There's no way I'm letting you board a United States aircraft."

"He's nothing like his father," Alyosha-Bob said. "He's not a killer. He studied multiculturalism at Accidental College. Weiner, tell them." He looked around for our classmate, but Josh Weiner was nowhere to be found.

"You go on without me," I told Alyosha-Bob. "There's no reason for you to stay here. Go. I'll find a way out of here myself."

"You'll die here," Alyosha-Bob said. "You don't understand anything."

I looked at him, trying to decide if I should be angered by his remark. Did I understand anything? My understanding had limits, that was certain, but my friendship with Alyosha-Bob had none. My friend stood before me, pained and small—a thirty-one-year-old man who seemed older by twenty years, as if each year spent in Russia had cost him three years more. Why had he come here? Why had he decided to become my brother and safekeeper?

"I miss Svetlana," Alyosha-Bob said. "You never understood just how much I love her. You think it's all just political economy in the end, but it's not. You think she's a passport whore, but she loves me more than you can know, more than any woman's ever loved you."

"Sir." A marine was laying his hands upon me, as if inducting me into some sacred ritual with violent overtones.

"Go," I said. "I'm not as helpless as you think. Go to your Svetlana. You're right in everything you say. We'll meet up in Brussels someday."

Alyosha-Bob stretched out his arm to embrace me, thought better of it, turned around so that I wouldn't see his tears, and walked toward the sheets of ExxonMobil glass vibrating beneath the arrival of another mighty Chinook. I went partly limp, nearly tipping over the marine beneath me (such pretty eyelashes he had, this Latino-American trooper), as other American hands picked up the slack and guided me toward an exit, toward a hole in the razor wire big enough to fit me.

21

The School of Gentle Persuasion

I met Alyosha-Bob on the last day of our first semester at Accidental. I could hardly believe that I had emerged from one hundred days of American college instruction with remarkably good grades (an average of 3.94 out of a possible 4.0 points) and as the recipient of a furtive (albeit monocultural) hand job given behind a beer truck by a white girl with greasy mitts and a stutter.

It was the middle of December, and the midwestern campus was not so much blanketed by snow as encased in it. Most of the student body had already left for the East Coast or Chicagoland to join their families for the Kwanzaa vacation; the few of us who remained were knocking about the campus drunk and stoned and in search of fellow humanity. Back then my coat pockets were always stuffed with ham sandwiches (heavy on the mayonnaise) and bags of corn chips, while my freezing fingers were clasped around a marijuana roach from which I sucked with tremendous force and greed. That year had been my first encounter with marijuana, and I was seriously addicted.

It was nighttime. Two in the morning. A comfortable American bed awaited me somewhere, but I was not ready to go home. The pride of the campus was a truly magnificent chapel built in a naive Moorish style in front of which I would stand at night, smoking joint after joint and imagining that maybe a better life awaited us after death (the year was 1990, the time of perestroika, and many thoughtful Russians were hopeful that God existed). But on that night the chapel refused to reveal to me its closely held Presbyterian secrets, the proportion of good works and industry that would win me a place in the part of paradise reserved for American passport holders. On that night I was left with only the truth that nothing of our personality survives after death, that in the end all that was Misha Vainberg would evaporate along with the styles and delusions of his epoch, leaving behind not one flutter of his sad heavy brilliance, not one damp spot around which his successors could congregate to appreciate his life and times.

I started to shake in both anger and fear, wrapping my arms around me in a sorrowful embrace, for I so loved my personality that I would kill everyone in my path to assure its survival. *Very well,* I thought, *if faith will not comfort me, then I will turn to progress.* I stalked off to the other side of the campus and found myself in a newly built quadrangle, where the modern festive greens and yellows of the dormitories shivered astride windowpanes encrusted with snow. I sat down in a snowdrift, opened a bag of corn chips, and swallowed them all in one go. Then I lit the remainder of a joint and realized that I should have smoked the marijuana first and eaten the corn chips second. When would I learn already?

Laughter and a flash of light from somewhere above as a square black solid, a burial casket, it would seem, flew through the air and landed softly on a neighboring mound of snow, where it lodged at an angle like a gravestone. Frightened, I backed my ass farther into the snowdrift, peeled the cellophane off a frozen ham sandwich, and nervously started eating. Death was everywhere around me. Cold American death.

A second casket was launched. It somersaulted briefly in the frozen air, then fell squarely before my feet. The laughter increased, and I covered my head with my hands and howled in terror. Who could be doing this to me? Who could be so cruel as to bait a foreign man under the influence? I opened another sandwich and swallowed most of it strictly out of fear.

And then a third object, a piece of serrated cardboard, fell by my feet. I put down my food and took a better look. It was part of a Scrabble game board, a curious American game that rewards a player's knowledge of English lexicography and orthography. I crawled toward one of the burial caskets, my monstrous Soviet mittens filling with snow, until I made out the word BOSE glittering at the base. Like most Russian children, I had spent my youth lusting after Western technology, so I knew immediately that the object before me was a pricey stereo speaker. Now, why would someone be flinging such a treasure from a dormitory window? I elected to find out.

Inside the dormitory, one got the impression of a hastily assembled submarine with small porthole-shaped windows and exposed piping overhead, along with the steady hum of distant propulsion, as if we were burrowing our way beneath the midwestern tundra, hoping to emerge either in the California sun or on the elevated B line rumbling toward Grand Street. The moodily lit lobby was given over to a long row of vending machines from which I procured a dozen delicious MoonPies, their chocolate crust breaking beneath my tongue, bathing it in soft white artificial marshmallow.

"Ho-kay," I said to the empty hallways, on which corkboards were lined with notices demanding swift lesbian action against fat men who got hand jobs from oppressed sisters behind beer trucks. "Bery vell," I said, flexing my stuffed nose. "Such a voman must be prodected."

Savoring my MoonPies, I crossed the lifeless hallways, my ears pricked for the sound of Rastafarian music, my stuffed nose trying to follow the telltale trail of purple haze sneaking out from beneath some yellow-lit doorjamb. Finally, on the topmost floor, such a place was found, absent the Bob Marley but filled to the brim with loud male voices trying to outdo one another, as if to impress a woman.

I produced one of my big, squishy hands and knocked.

"Fuck you!" yelled a familiar Russian-tinged voice. I put my hand down and felt insulted. Why didn't anyone like me? But as I backed away from the door, the same voice shouted, "Oh, whatever. Come in."

Delighted by the change of heart, I opened the door to face that little runt, the Russian émigré Vladimir Girshkin, a sophomore of no great distinction who nonetheless condescended to me because of his nine-year American tenure and his fine American accent. Girshkin was drunk and high, more so than me, and his whole florid, goateed being repulsed me. Next to Girshkin was Jerry Shteynfarb the future novelist, ensconced in some hippie Salvadoran poncho with a GIVE PEACE A CHANCE button pinned to his heart.

A man-sized industrial fan twirled its mighty propeller by the window, creating an unnatural breeze that tempered the suffocating dormitory heat. Pieces of paper and cardboard were being sprayed out of the fan, like the bits of potato salad trying to escape my mouth at a Women's Studies picnic. Alyosha-Bob, naked save for a pair of cotton boxers, was feeding a hardcover book into the giant fan, its remainders flying out the window and onto the snow-covered quadrangle.

"Die, Pasternak, die!" he was shouting.

"Hey, Bob," Jerry Shteynfarb casually said, "what do I do with the toaster oven?"

"Toss it!" Alyosha-Bob shouted. "The fuck I gonna use it for? I'm never eating again. Hey, look at this, guys. Fucking *Ada*. Take that, Nabokov! You sixteen-karat bore!"

"Right on," said Shteynfarb and, without any compunction, hurled the toaster oven out the window, his weak literary arm straining under the metallic load.

"Hey, guys," I said. I blew my nose against my coat sleeve. "Hey. Why you throwing everything out the window?"

"Because every *sing*," Shteynfarb said, mimicking my accent, "must go. That's *vai*."

"We've each taken three tabs of acid," Vladimir Girshkin explained, his eyes dark and blank beneath his tortoiseshell granny glasses. "And now Bob is getting rid of all his worldly belongings."

"Oh," I said. "Maybe he's a Buddhist."

"Oh," said Shteynfarb. "Maybe he's not. Maybe he just wants to say fuck-all to everything for no reason. Does everything have to be systematized for you, Misha?"

Alyosha-Bob had turned his dilated pupils my way and challenged me with a skinny red index finger. "You're Snack Daddy," he said, using the nickname I had managed to acquire through my dining hall exploits. I stood in awe of his near-naked splendor, the way he appeared perfectly sane and competent even as he presided over the demise of all the beautiful things his parents must have bought him.

This was a new kind of Jew, a super Jew, one divorced from the material world.

"You're Queasy Bob," I said. "I've seen you around the Honor Scholars' Library."

"I know about you," Alyosha-Bob said. "You're the son of that refusenik Boris Vainberg. You're the real deal. You're like a part of history."

I smiled at all three designations. "No, I'm not so big a person as you think," I said. "I am just . . ." I stopped to pick through my vocabulary. "I am just . . . I am just . . ."

"You heard him, he is just," Vladimir Girshkin said.

"Misha the Just," Jerry Shteynfarb said.

"Snack Daddy the Magnificent," Girshkin picked up.

I looked sadly at my compatriots. Three Russians from Leningrad. Striving for the attention of a solitary American Jew. Why couldn't we do better by each other? Why couldn't we form a team to assuage our loneliness? One day I had offered Girshkin and Shteynfarb some homemade beet salad and a loaf of authentic rye bread from the local Lithuanian-owned bakery, but they had only laughed at my nostalgia.

"I am just a student of history," I told Alyosha-Bob.

"Say, Bob, whaddaya want to do with this?" Vladimir Girshkin said as he picked up a framed photograph of a sweet, dimple-faced Alyosha-Bob huddled beneath his impossibly beautiful mother, an Assyrian princess in hoop earrings, her lustrous hair held back by chopsticks, and his father, a Yankee professor adrift in a corduroy suit one size too large. Later, I would spend my summers with the Lipshitzes at their upstate New York farm, watching them administer their stunningly profitable business, Local Color. They catered to wealthy New Yorkers and Bostonians who would rent out their spread for weddings. During the ceremony, they would be joined by the local townspeople, the local color, as it were—articulate, poor black and white families who would show up and pretend to be longtime friends of the bride or groom, talking in their catchy, bebop dialects about failed crop cycles and the demise of the rust belt. I learned

much about the unhappy state of the American family from my summers with the Lipshitzes, especially about the use of silence as a cor-
rective tool.

"Break the glass," Alyosha-Bob said of the framed photo, "then
shred the picture in the fan and throw the frame out the window."

"Aye-aye, Captain," said Vladimir Girshkin. He picked up a paper-
weight of St. Basil's Cathedral that had been sitting peaceably amid
the junkscape of Alyosha-Bob's desk and started smashing the family
portrait, the jarring noises drowned out by the twirl of the industrial
fan.

"Should I shred your clothes before throwing them out?" Jerry
Shteynfarb asked, rustling through a huge pile of rugged outerwear.

"Give me my coat," Alyosha-Bob said.

He put on a pair of baggy denims and a hoodie, a prescient evocation of the gangsta-rap phenomenon that was just starting to spill out
of South Central, while Shteynfarb fixed him with his snide authorial
gaze. I wondered if Shteynfarb had taken the acid at all; possibly he
was here only to observe Alyosha-Bob, to gather material for his un-
funny short stories chronicling the differences between Russians and
Americans. "Your coat?" Shteynfarb said. "What the hell for?"

"I want to go for a walk with Misha."

"But we're throwing all your stuff out!" Girshkin shouted. "You
promised us."

"Carry on without us, boys," Alyosha-Bob said. "We'll be back
before sunup. And then we'll all go to the Pen and Pencil for breakfast. How 'bout that?"

Before the disappointed Russians could answer, Alyosha-Bob had
escorted me out onto the quadrangle, which was now covered with
a pile of his shredded books and broken records, forming a collage
around the twisted form of his rowing machine and the dark remains of his stereo. Girshkin and Shteynfarb were still following orders, dutifully tossing out the smashed carcass of an Apple Macintosh
computer and a lovingly slashed beanbag.

Alyosha-Bob and I trundled rhythmically through the snow, walking in no prescribed direction but stealing occasional happy looks
at each other. "Queasy Bob," I said. "Why, if I may ask, are you dis-

pensing with all of your personal effects? Are you indeed a Buddhist?"

"I'm not anything," he said, breathing hard against the cold. "But I want to be a Russian. A real Russian. Not like Shteynfarb or Girshkin."

I sighed with pleasure at the unspoken compliment. "But real Russians love all the things you have thrown out," I said. "For example, I am now asking my father to send money so that I may buy an Apple Macintosh computer. Also I would like Bose speakers and a Harman Kardon subwoofer."

"You really want all that shit?" Alyosha-Bob asked. He stopped walking and looked at me. In the wintry light, I could see his chilled face, slightly cratered with the aftereffects of late chicken pox, so that his physiognomy mirrored the moon that hung above us, the rich, industrialized American moon.

"Oh, yes," I said.

"That's interesting," he said. "I've been associating Russian life with spirituality."

"Well, some of us are believers," I said. "But mostly we just want things."

"Oh," he said. "Wow. I think Girshkin and Shteynfarb have really led me astray."

We walked on, compacting the snow beneath us into tiny abstract monuments to our future friendship, following in the wake of the lamp-lit beacons of our own breath. "Let's talk in Russian from now on," he said. "I know only a few words. *Shto eto?*" He pointed at a contorted insect of a building, its chimney pumping effluent into the night. What is it?

"Waste incineration plant," I said in Russian.

"Hmm." I noticed his boots were untied but decided not to say anything, to preserve the sanctity of the moment. The landscape of the empty campus unfolded before us, as ominously still as a desert ruin. On most days I felt that the imposing neo-Gothic collegiate architecture was challenging me to excellence, but that night I felt the deep wooden hollowness of an Accidental College education, as if everything I had needed to know lay in some puddle of blood on a

street in Vilnius or Tbilisi. Perhaps the most important part of my
college days would consist of instructing Alyosha-Bob, of forging his
peculiar Russian-bound destiny. *"A shto eto?"* Alyosha-Bob asked,
pointing at what looked like a broken spaceship.

"Student psychiatric clinic," I said in Russian.

"A shto eto?"

"Gay and Lesbian Liberation Center."

"A shto eto?"

"Nicaraguan Sister Co-op."

"A shto eto?"

"The Amazon Rain Forest Experience." The words in Russian
were becoming progressively harder and inane-sounding, so I was
particularly happy when the college campus exhausted itself and we
found ourselves deep in the impoverished countryside that ringed
Accidental. "Cornfield," I said. "Cow barn. Mechanized tractor. Grain
depository. Poultry shed. Pig corral."

We wandered through several kilometers of agriculture, onto the
highway that led into the nearest big city. The sun was rising over a
nearby strip mall when we decided to stop and turn back. A phalanx
of local police cars, sirens ablaze, streamed past us on the way to
campus. We assumed, correctly, that the officers were heading for
Alyosha-Bob's dormitory to arrest Girshkin and Shtenyfarb for van-
dalism and defilement of college property. Excited by this knowledge, we laughed and shouted into the subzero morning air until our
frozen throats failed us. I hugged Alyosha-Bob's shivering body,
wedging him within my folds to show him what real friendship meant
in Russian.

I thought we would never be apart.

22

My Nana

I was wrong.

Back in Absurdistan, scared and all alone, I crawled under my bed and wept.

When Beloved Papa found out that his own father had been killed fighting the Germans in a battlefield near Leningrad, he reportedly hid under his bed and cried for four days, refusing bread and kasha, nourished only by his own tears and the memories of his dead father's caress. I resolved to do the same, although there were some obvious differences between our situations. Papa had been three years old, while I was thirty. Papa had been staying out the war with distant relatives in some awful village in the Ural Mountains, while I was the sole occupant of a penthouse in a Western hotel in Absurdistan. Papa had only his tears, while I had my Ativan. But I felt a kinship with him nonetheless. I had lost a mother, a father, and now, with Alyosha-Bob gone, a brother. I had been orphaned one more time. Thrown helter-skelter into a world that had no use for me.

Worse yet, something was wrong with my *mobilnik*. The Absurdis must have shut down telephone coverage in some misguided move to control information coming out of the country. Every time I dialed Alyosha-Bob's number, I got a recorded announcement: "Respected mobile phone user," a hoarse Russian woman said, "your attempt to make a connection has failed. There is nothing more to be done. Please hang up."

My attempt at connection had failed. What more could be said, really?

I didn't last for four days under my bed, as Beloved Papa had in 1943. In a matter of hours, hunger got the best of me, and I crawled out to order buffalo wings and a bottle of Laphroaig from room service. The world felt empty and silent around me. I turned on my laptop, but apparently the authorities had shut down the Internet as well. I was left with nothing more than television. The foreign news channels, having decided that the plight of the Absurdsvanï Republic seemed to the average viewer quite smelly and unpronounceable, had moved on to the warm Mediterranean waters off Genoa, where the G8 summit was under way, and sexy Italian protesters hurtling Molotov cocktails at the abusive carabinieri proved a great deal more photogenic. Even the Russian networks had decided to give Absurdistan a rest. The correspondents for the three main government channels could be seen half asleep by the Hyatt swimming pool, slumped over rows of Turkish beer bottles as early as ten in the morning. They, too, wanted to go to Genoa to swim with the dolphins and admire President Putin's compact, sportsmanlike physique and the happy impertinence of his American counterpart, Bush.

I looked down at the terraces beneath me. The morning glare of foam and pollution rising off the remains of the sea had coated the city in the bruised pink color of corned beef. With the cease-fire in effect, citizens, Sevo and Svanï, went about their lives, burrowing into the ready maw of the 718 Perfumery or gathering around taxis and failed minibuses to spontaneously drink Turkish coffee and spit sesame seeds at the sun. Armored personnel carriers bristling with armaments and antennae idled listlessly next to cafés, looking like the empty shells of dead insects.

I found a notecard from Larry Zartarian:

Dear the Guest,

Please Your Attention. Federal and SCROD forces are seiging the city. Airport is closed. Whilst the political Situation in our country is resolving ourselves, You may enjoy the historical beauty of Svanï City (which Frenchman Alexander Dumas calls "Pearl of Caspian"— Ooh la la!). Adjacent to Hotel is American Express Tour Company. It is only just for You.

I once asked Zartarian about the funny English he used in his letters to the hotel guests, and he confessed he was trying to represent himself as a wily local and not some middle-class brat from the San Fernando Valley. Poor Zartarian. When I closed my eyes, I could almost see his corpse laid out next to his mother's, ready for repatriation to Glendale.

I looked over the note and asked myself: *What would Alyosha-Bob do in this situation? He would always do* something. I put on a pair of gigantic square sunglasses and slipped into my roomiest vintage tracksuit, the one that prodded my stomach forward and held it prominently in place, so that altogether I resembled the infamous North Korean playboy Kim Jong Il.

It was time, as Dr. Levine would say, to go for a walk.

At the American Express office, two girls, one white and blond, the other sweetly brown and local, were lolling about their desks, applying nail polish and speaking quietly in English and Russian, their tongues clicking and clacking over all the right terms ("chick lit," "chill-out room," "Charing Cross station").

I warmed to them immediately, these sweet Western-minded creatures. I even managed to forget Alyosha-Bob's absence for a moment. "Hey," I said to the girls *en anglais*. "Whassup?"

"Good afternoon," the blonde chirped. "*Bienvenue*. Welcome to the American Express." She smiled genuinely, and the other—the dark one—cast her eyes down and grinned with her very full red mouth. The blonde was clearly an ethnic Russian; her name tag read Anna Ivanovna or something similar. I couldn't tell if I liked her or not. The way she huddled herself over her full bosom, she was neither particularly alluring nor entirely ignorant of the art of making young men suffer.

When I looked at the dark one, however, my thoughts immediately started to wander down below. She was dressed in a tan T-shirt and denims much too tight for her Southern hips. Often when I am compelled by a woman, my fantasies begin not with the brilliance of her smile, or the way she brushes back tendrils of her own curly hair, but rather, with the "great unknowable"—the way her reproductive complex looks when white workaday underwear is pulled over it in the morning, and whether or not certain hairs stray from the fold. For all this I can blame the collected works of Henry Miller, which I read during my internment at Accidental College and which coincided with my induction into hairy American multiculturalism.

"I'm a Belgian interested in the history of your country," I said, words that would have rung especially true if "Belgian" had been substituted with "Russian" and "country" with "vagina."

The blond girl started squealing about the different kinds of tours they had. Arts, crafts, churches, mosques, beaches, volcanoes, caves, stork habitats, oil fields, fire temples, "the world-famous Museum of Applied Carpet Making"—few cities could rival the Absurdi capital for the range of nonsensical crap on offer.

"The only problem with making a tour," said the blond one, "is that my grandmother is Svanï, so I cannot go to the Sevo Terrace, and Nana is Sevo, so she cannot go to the Svanï Terrace."

"What?" I said.

"As part of the cease-fire, there are restrictions on travel for Sevo and Svanï citizens," the blonde said. "As a foreigner, of course, you are completely exempt."

I noticed a large cutout of a locomotive bearing the American Express logo, upon which somebody had written, *All American Express luxury trains out of Republika Absurdsvanï are canceled by order of federal government and SCROD*. It seemed that I was left with nothing but stork habitats and the graces of two pretty women.

I turned to the dark Nana Nanabragovna (plucking her name from the pewter tag on her bosom), who was assessing me with her chestnut eyes and wry little mouth. I guessed that she had a robust sense of humor, or at least liked to laugh, and that once we were in bed I could provoke some ticklish giggles out of her. I could see myself kissing the warm, flat bulb of her nose and saying, "Funny girl! Who's my funny girl now?" This is what I used to do to Rouenna when the mood struck me.

Having been put in the position of choosing between the two American Express ladies, or at least between their ethnicities, I had to proceed diplomatically, lest feelings be hurt. "Where is the church that looks like an octopus?" I said, knowing full well that it was on the Sevo Terrace.

"That's the Cathedral of Saint Sevo the Liberator," Nana said. Her English, I noted, was authoritative and fully American, with a hint of consonant-free Brooklynese. *Sain' Sevah duh Lih-buh-rai-tah,* accent on the penultimate syllable.

I gave my regrets and a roll of cash to the blonde. Nana got her car keys.

Once she was in motion, it became clear to me that my new friend was a big girl. Not Misha Vainberg big, of course, but in the 70-kilogram (150-pound) range, factored into a height of about sixty-six inches. Despite the healthy country girl's body, urban fashion had not passed her by. She wore her denims lower than a Lower East Side *mami* and to the same devastating effect. Her tight tan-colored T-shirt canoodled her breasts. The space between her low-slung denims and high-slung T-shirt was taken up with a band of glossy sun-stroked flesh prickled here and there with dark hairs that stood on end, reminding me of the imported cypresses lining the Boulevard of National Unity. Remarkably, the transition from spine to posterior showed few color gradations—her entire dorsal area approximate to the hue of her upper arms, a solid gold tone. Her denims bifurcated a nice big ass. Her face was wide and emotive enough to accommodate the loves and losses of a dozen aristocratic Persian women, the particular nationality she most resembled. She had the barest of feminine mustaches, which, when covered with cream or froth, would remind me of myself as a twelve-year-old boy. The heat, which smothered me and made a sour borscht of my genitals, kept its distance from her, seemingly angling for a quick passing rub against her bosom. She drove a shiny black Lincoln Navigator decorated with a white-and-blue American Express flag, which, from a distance, resembled the less powerful standard of the United Nations.

When we were both locked into her truck, we turned to each other and smiled. There we were, two people, one a continent of flesh, the other a mere Madagascar, maneuvering onto leather, sliding our seats forward and back, folding ourselves into the car while mumbling things in Middle-Atlantic English, grunting and sighing like an old couple. We seemed, at least to me, *inevitable*.

I recited by heart the last e-mail Rouenna had sent me before the Internet was shut off:

Dear Misha, I am sorry you are in a dangerous place and people are dying but 1) your email was once again all about you, you, you (how about asking me about MY life for a change?) and 2) when are you NOT in a dangerous place where people are dying? Anyway, I'm sure you'll get out of your predigament just fine, because your a survivor.

P.S. You really should'nt hate Proffessor Shteynfarb who likes you a lot and has lots of wity and interesting things to say about you.

P.S.S. I should have told you earlier but I think your shrink is a real idiot.

In other words, I thought I was ready for a new love. I was ready to feel safe again in someone else's arms. I was ready to forget my Rouenna, at least for a while.

Nana and I drove down the Boulevard of National Unity, eyeing the commerce around us and sneaking looks at each other. A half-dozen empty KBR flatbed trucks idled in the middle of the thoroughfare, charged with some mysterious purpose we could only guess at.

"I thought the road between the terraces was impassable," I said.

"You are an important person, Mr. Vainberg," Nana said, smiling and showing off her lipstick-stained incisors, "and we are a hospitable people. My mother will be your mother, and there's plenty of water in my well for you to drink."

"If you say so, Miss Nanabragovna," I said. But as we approached a roadblock of jeeps and armored personnel carriers, I reached for the familiar plumpness of my wallet and felt up several US$100 bills, ready to be doled out to any teenager with a gun.

The soldiers manning the roadblock were taking an afternoon siesta beneath a tarp they had rigged between two of the APCs. I expected my tour guide to reach between her breasts and produce a Sevo cross for the soldiers to inspect, a prospect that made me dizzy with excitement, but instead Nana honked her powerful Navigator horn until a few rumpled youths languidly emerged from beneath the tarp.

Nana opened her window and leaned out as far as she could, in the meantime letting me look deep into the beginning of her ass crease and the tightness of denim against her caramel thighs. MISS SIXTY, read the label on her jeans, a new brand I was sure would catch on with the middle class.

"Boys, let me through," Nana shouted in Russian, the word "boys" sounding both coquettish and imperious.

"Yes, mistress!" The soldiers saluted and stood at attention. They ran back and started moving aside the tarp and their vehicles, cursing at one another to hurry along.

The salutes and ceremony were repeated at the Svanï Terrace checkpoint. I wondered aloud as to why Svanï soldiers would so honor a Sevo woman. "It is because we are flying the American Express flag," Nana said, although her ripe young voice sounded uncharacteristically false as she said it. She turned away from me, then put on her sunglasses, cursing as one of its hinges caught in the tangle of her arm hairs.

"We're almost there," she said, waving away the pain.

Our Navigator plunged down the winding road, and I soon found myself at the bottom of the world.

23

The Sevo Vatican

If the Svanï were made whole by their remote-control market and their association with Alexandre Dumas, the Sevo boasted a stranglehold on the sea. It loitered close by, gray and muted, peeking out from behind the faded mansions of the oil aristocracy that had decamped here a century ago, when the Caspian had first announced itself as a source of seemingly endless fuel and antagonism.

Instead of looking for a place to park, Nana simply abandoned her vehicle at a busy intersection. An elderly policeman crisply saluted her and rushed over to stand at attention beside it. He whistled to a passing soldier, who took off his shirt, dipped it into a nearby fountain, and began washing down the Navigator's sandy windshield. "You seem to be very popular," I said to my new friend, who merely shrugged. What the hell was going on here? I wished Alyosha-Bob would appear and explain things to me in his pedantic way. I felt vulnerable—susceptible—to anything without him.

Nana walked ahead of me, relating the peculiarities of the local architecture commissioned by late-nineteenth-century oil barons. "Really?" I said when told of the original owner of a massive neo-Gothic pile. "This was built by Lord Rothschild? The Jew?"

"Are there many Jews in Belgium, Mr. Vainberg?" my tour guide asked.

"Yes, quite a few," I said. "Personally I live in Brussels, but if you ever find yourself in Antwerp, you will see a funny sight sometimes—the local Hasids riding around on their bicycles, with their dark coats flapping along. We Belgians have quite an open society, you see."

"So you are a balloon?" she said.

I was hurt to the stomach by her frankness, by the idea that such a sweet woman could be a fat-baiter. "I do have a fondness for food," I admitted, "which may indeed make me in your eyes a balloon—"

"No!" She laughed. "Not a balloon. Oh, you poor man. A Walloon. A French Belgian."

"Ah, oui," I said. *"Un Wallon. C'est moi."*

"Parce que nous parlons français."

"Mm, no," I stammered, for I had never bothered to learn that complicated tongue. "No French, please. Right now I am trying to practice my English. Sadly, it is the language of the world."

Nana stopped and allowed me a nice look at her glistening body and face. If she trimmed herself just a little, she could be a chesty athlete; a swimmer, say, for I have heard that female swimmers rely on their massive bosoms for buoyancy.

"As you may have heard," Nana coyly told me, "the Jewish people have a long and peaceful history in our land."

"It is my understanding," I said in my most flirtatious and least reprehensible voice, "that they are your brothers, and whoever is *their* enemy is *your* enemy also."

"You say 'they,' " Nana said.

"I mean 'we,' " I conceded.

"It's pretty obvious, Monsieur Vainberg," Nana said. "I had a Jewish roommate in college."

"Here?"

"No, at NYU."

I must have appeared utterly blank-faced, for Nana felt the need to slowly explain. "New York University," she said.

"Yes," I whispered. "Yes, of course. I know it well. You are a graduate of NYU?"

"I'll be a senior this fall," she said.

I breathed heavily and embraced my own stomach, my *balloon,* if you will. She turned away and walked ahead of me. I followed her ass, stunned and queasy at the prospect of being so close to New York, the city of my dreams. So that's how it was! Another American cruelly trapped in a foreigner's body. Perhaps I could come with her

to NYU in September (if the war had ended by then). Perhaps the
generals in charge of the INS, in their Noahlike wisdom, would make
an exception for *two* hungry and fully consumerist post-Soviet bears.

We had started upon the Sevo Terrace's esplanade, which extended for a good kilometer toward the gleaming octopus of the so-
called Sevo Vatican. Despite the pre-lunch hour, despite this being a
workday, the promenade was choked with throngs of Sevo out for a
stroll, sucking up petroleum fumes and trying to re-create an old Soviet nostalgia for "the sea," which here consisted of gray snatches of
salt water lapping up to the barnacled bases of the oil derricks.

The promenade seemed to cater to the needs of the fertile fifteen-
to-twenty-nine demographic, but children also mature fast these
days. I witnessed a five-year-old in a bow and polka-dot dress dancing like an aged American slut to an accordion tune, as her parents
angled for photographs, shouting at the accordionist to play something a bit more lively.

How different my Nana looked from her countrywomen. There
was no mistaking her for anything other than a college senior,
twenty-one years old, swift, determined, and carefree, her body a wide
testimony to earthly pleasures sought and found, while all around,
barely pubescent girls were already consigned to a brutal, dolled-up
middle age spent at the hands of anxious relatives and dim-witted,
controlling young husbands. Nana had been privileged to leave the
former Soviet Union at just the right time in her psychosexual development. Her expectations were as enormous as my circumference.

At the end of the esplanade, the Sevo Vatican cast its eight tentacles trying to ensnare believers, the three-meter Sevo cross gleaming
from its hooded dome like an aerial antenna stacked on top of a satellite dish. "You have to admit, it does look like an octopus," I said to
Nana.

"I think it looks more like an egg," she said. "Like an egg that's inside one of those things they put them in. Like when you order a
poached egg."

"Like you get at a diner," I said.

"Yes, like you get at a Greek diner," she said.

"Yes, like you get at a Greek diner in New York," I said.

We smiled sadly at each other, bound by our use of the throwaway American "like," and I reached out my big, squishy hands, hoping she would reciprocate. But she didn't just yet. "Anyway," she said, "I am a Sevo, like it or not, so I have to feed you the official Sevo line. Here goes . . ."

And so for the next half hour, while I stroked her body up and down with my lurid male gaze, Nana told me many, many facts about the Cathedral of Saint Sevo the Liberator. I will try to relate to the reader some of the highlights (did I mention the orange highlights in Nana's soft brown hair?), but for a full appreciation of this weird octopuslike church, the reader should turn to the Internet.

The cathedral was built in either 1475 or 1575 or 1675; certainly there was a 75 in there somewhere. Around this time, the whole of Absurdistan suffered under the sway of the nearby Persians (or was it the Ottomans?), so naturally the Svaní claimed that the cathedral was originally a mosque, not a church, as it was built in brick rather than stone, the material of choice for those nefarious Mohammedans. But no! It was always a church, according to Nana (whose ass instinctively tilted upward whenever she exclaimed something), and anyway, who were the Svaní to talk? They had reached all kinds of accommodations with their Persian (or Ottoman) overlords during the Three Hundred Year War of the Footrest Secession, and they had the habit of putting stones around Sevo churches to claim them for their own. I'm not sure why this was significant, but the serious way in which Nana related these preposterous things only made me hotter for her, for when she talked her hooey, she resembled an actress longing to be recognized, a veritable American starlet with a full-moon face and the readiest of lips.

We entered the cathedral, which offered a nice break from the heat. Despite this amenity, it was largely empty, save for the old women violently crossing themselves by clusters of candles and whispering angrily at their missing god. No doubt about it, the church was an afterthought. The real action was on the esplanade, where commerce and matters of the groin held sway.

The head of the cathedral's octopus was taken up by a colossal dome, ringed by a circle of skylights that in turn lit up a fetching fresco inlaid upon the dome. "This was the original seal of the first Sevo potentate," Nana said. "A lion with a sword is riding atop a fish. This is to show that all power is ephemeral, and that even the mightiest ruler can lose his grip on the affairs of state."

"That's kind of nice," I allowed.

"It's my favorite symbol," Nana said. "I hate the whole business with the footrest, so I wear one of these instead." She withdrew from between her breasts a pendant bearing the lion-surfing-on-a-fish motif. I reached out to touch it. Its sweaty warmth, a product of her natural heat, made me feel wobbly and wet. I wanted to press my nose to it, too.

"Tell me, please," I said. "What *is* the difference between the Sevo and Svanï? You both look so cute to me. Why can't we all just get along?"

24

Why the Sevo and Svanï Don't Get Along

The Sevo and Svanï started out as one people, much maligned and forever in the shadows of the Persians, Turks, Slavs, and Mongols, who in different periods would come over to plunder and rape them pretty hard. And then along came Saint Sevo (the Liberator, mind you!), who, in the time-honored tradition of so many other religious personages, had a vision. What made this Liberator's vision particularly funny, not to mention oddly contemporary, was that he suffered it while high on a local herb called *lanza*. A fresco in one of the octopus's pre-tentacle alcoves showed a wiry peasant bent over a stone pot, nasally inhaling three strands of pasta, really the vapors of the *lanza* herb, which transported him temporarily into the next world (the ceremony of *lunzu*-sniffing is performed by Sevo monks to this day), where he met, of course, Jesus.

Jesus, rendered in the fresco as a spectral, bleary-eyed figure nearly as stoned as Saint Sevo himself, told our visionary that all was not right with his people, particularly the priests who had just last year excommunicated the saint for sleeping with their teenage daughters and forced him to live along the parched saltwater-blasted strip that would one day be known as the Sevo Terrace. "Look," said Jesus. "I'm a good guy, right? But enough is enough. After you come down from your *lanza* high, I want you to get your homeys together, get your pointiest utensils, and spear the bejesus out of all your enemies. And when you're through spearing, I want you to fuck every under-age cutie in town. I'm talking, like, *sodomy* here. Right in the dump-ster. Capiche?"

"Muh-huh," Saint Sevo replied. "So saith the Lord. And believe me, I'm all over it. But, Jeez, can you give me a sign? Something I can show my homeys. So that they know I'm, like, legit."

"Goeth you," said Jesus, "to the highest rise of the lowest terrace of your city. And then digeth you. Digeth and digeth, night and day, mornings and afternoons, skippeth you the lunchtime, and then you shall uncovereth that which you seeketh."

So the very next morning, Sevo the Liberator brushed off his hangover and ran to the highest rise of the lowest terrace—this, by the way, is where the octopus of the Sevo Vatican is presently located—and started digging. For many grueling days: nothing. And then, holy shit! A little piece of wood or something. But clearly very holy. The saint-to-be went back to his wretched hut, gathered a fort-night's stash of *lanza* from the backyard, and, with the piece of holy wood before him, got terrifically high. *Oy vei,* how many visions he had! Eighteen, to be exact, each represented in the cathedral by a primitive fresco (where did these poor, constantly pillaged people find the time for frescoes?). The most important vision of all, the one that would give birth to the entire Sevo nation, featured Christ on the cross, bloody and spent, whispering for Saint Sevo to get down on his knees like a doggie and lick the spilt blood pooling on the footrest. This our boy did gladly, only as he was lapping up the sacred corpuscles and pulling the resulting splinters from his tongue, a dirty, thieving Armenian crept up to the cross and chipped for himself a hefty chunk of Christ's footrest, tilting it to the position thereafter found on the Sevo cross.

Now, Christ is crucified along with two so-called thieves—a Good Thief, who defends him and is promised eternal salvation by the Son, and the Bad Thief, who pretty much goes straight to hell. The footrest of the Svaní cross, like the standard Orthodox cross, is slanted with the part on Christ's right pointing upward, so that Jesus is leaning toward the Good Thief. But in Sevo mythology, after the dirty Armenian chips away at the footrest, Christ leans in the oppo-site direction, that is, toward the Bad Thief. This has *all sorts of cru-cial theological implications,* none of which I can remember.

Anyway, back to the story. So the Armenian, chunk of footrest in hand, ran back to his native land, hoping to bless his co-nationals with the glory of the Footrest of the Lord. But God much detested the Armenians, clever bastards that they are, and He laid for the fellow a trail of golden coins, which the greedy Armenian naturally followed all the way to what is now the Sevo Terrace. Lost in that arid, inhospitable clime, the Armenian offered all his gold to Yahweh in exchange for His mercy, but the ever-mercurial Judeo-Christian God struck him down instead (and took back all His money to boot). The chunk of footrest was buried there in the sand alongside the Caspian, to await the day when a certain stoned Liberator would appear, pick up the holy wood, gather his homeys, and spear-fuck half the land. Those chosen homeys and their newly raped betrothed would become the Sevos of today.

I have laid out the tale of the Sevo-Svani schism in a hopefully entertaining hip-hop fashion, but it was related to me by my Nana in a less joyful manner. She used complex terms to describe the religious differences, such as "dyophysitism" and "monophysitism," along with frequent allusions to some Holy Council of Aardvark that rocked the region in A.D. 518, not to mention that whole Good Thief, Bad Thief hullabaloo. I do not wish to disparage her considerable knowledge of local prejudices, nor the faith to which she nominally belonged. I believe that when confronted with the irrational, we must not laugh, even when laughter is richly deserved.

We stepped out of the cathedral and onto the broad series of steps that connected the Cathedral of Saint Sevo the Liberator with the half-naked esplanade before it. "Look around you," Nana said. "Forget the religion crap. Look at the geography. We Sevo live along the coastline, and the Svani live in the mountains, the valleys, and the desert. For a thousand years, the Svani have been farmers and herders, and we've been the traditional merchant class. That's why there's the stuff about the Armenian in the tale of Christ's footrest—because the Armenians, not the Svani, are our traditional competitors. We're cosmopolitans trying to cuddle up to the West, while the Svani screw sheep and pray for salvation. That's why our churches are empty and theirs are full. That's why ever since trading became more important than farming, we're the ones with the big bucks."

"Good for you," I said. "I'm proud of you people. Merchants are more evolved than agriculturalists. That's a fact."

She ignored my comment, staring out into the oil fields silently tapping the seabed from the edge of the esplanade to the inky line of the horizon. She stared as far out as the violet-dappled halls of New York University, and, with one big, squishy hand shielding my blue eyes from the sun's glare, I stared along with her to the classrooms and cafeterias, the modern African-dance recitals and poetry slams, past the bustle of Broadway and Lafayette Street to the cast-iron triangle of Astor Place.

"Now, as part of your tour, Mr. Vainberg," Nana said, "I will take you out to a traditional Sevo lunch. Do you have any dietary restrictions?"

"Are you freaking kidding me?" I said, pointing to my stomach.

25

A Sturgeon for Misha

We walked down the esplanade, past a creaky bumper-car set imported from Turkey, festooned with indecipherable Turkic exhortations beneath a cartoon of a young brown woman being chased by a drooling gray wolf brandishing a knife and fork. To think how much of this world we don't understand. We pass it by and shrug. But if a Turk had appeared on the esplanade and explained to me why this cartoon was supposed to be funny, why it was attached to a bumper-car set for children, and why, pray tell, this particular set of bumper cars had landed here in the middle of Absurdistan and not in some dusty provincial Turkish amusement park—well, just think of how much more I would now know about this Turk and his nation, how much less prone I would be to dismiss his kebab-skewering, Atatürk-loving, repressive ways. Perhaps it would prove instructive for Misha's Children to spend their summers in a Turkish resort by the Black Sea, sunning themselves and learning about their dark Moslem cousins. I made a note to call Svetlana in Petersburg and tell her to make it happen.

Thoughtful and depressed after the history lesson, Nana and I walked along a pier stranded between two listing derricks and toward a mammoth pink clamshell. The clamshell, once in use as an amphitheater, had found more profitable use as a seaside restaurant called the Lady with Lapdog. We were the only customers despite the prime dining hour, the waitstaff having gone to sleep around a circular table, mostly middle-aged men in transparent white shirts, heads buried in their hands. They looked up at us wearily, displeased by the midday disturbance. We ordered the tomato salad, drenched in olive oil. It had been some time since I'd seen vegetables that colorful. I grabbed my gut, turned away from Nana, and started rocking back and forth, as if imitating my sworn enemies the Hasids.

"Mmm," Nana said. "Fresh, so fresh."

She poured herself a Turkish beer and I did the same, only adding a glass of Black Label to the equation. An old waitress in a filthy miniskirt and fluorescent panty hose approached, bearing in each arm a dish of eight perfectly square sturgeon kebabs. I glanced at Nana, but she hardly noticed me, lost as she was in the act of lancing her first kebab with her mighty fork.

My mind collapsed on itself, the toxic hump started humping, but it was unsure of the brand of toxicity to be released—either cold melancholy or the streetwise aroma of the Bronx. The sturgeon kebabs were the color of an Indian chicken tikka, their edges were charred black as the void, but their consistency was mealy and tender. "Fuck, fuck, fuck," I whispered in appreciation. The fish juices pooled over my chin and fell in oily yellow drops onto the plate, the tablecloth, my track pants, onto the ceramic floor of the Lady with Lapdog, into the barely breathing Caspian Sea, over the starving deserts of the interior, and into the lap of my beloved Nana, sitting across from me in silence, eating.

More fish came. I ate it all. I could feel my father's hands upon me. The two of us. Together again. Papa drunk. Myself timid yet curious. We would stay up all night. We would ignore Mommy's threats. Who could think of a school day in the morning when you could drop your trousers and pee all over the neighbor's anti-Semitic dog? I could feel my father's vodka breath in my mouth, in my nose, in my ears, my pasty body pressed to his prickly one, both of us sweating from the ghetto heat of a Leningrad apartment in deep winter, drowning in that strange atavistic stirring, shame and excitement in equal measure.

I ordered a batch of the Central Asian flatbread called *lipioshka*, using it to soak up the sturgeon juices shimmering on my plate. The beer and Black Label were gone; fresh cantaloupe had replaced them. The fruit was as bright and orange as the fish kebabs, only bursting with sugar instead of salt. I let the wedges chill against my inflamed gums, then breathed in the cantaloupe, which coated my throat with orange lather before dissolving into the center of my body, gone forever, like everything else I've ever eaten.

I looked up at Nana. She was shivering with delight. Her big, tough, cracked homegirl's lips were purple and flecked with all the juices on offer, except for mine. She was more alive than anything around her, and her aliveness distorted the oil derricks behind her and the Sevo octopus and the dingy esplanade and the Turkish bumper cars, and that made it all real and lovely and true. "There is a new seafood restaurant," she said.

"On Tenth Avenue," I said.

"Not far from—"

"—that new boutique hotel—"

"—they're gonna build."

"The one with the portholes—"

"—next to the Belgian place."

"The one thing you can't find—"

"—in New York?"

"Right—"

"—is a good paella."

"You need a very big skillet—"

"—the tapas bar."

"The one on Crosby—"

"—with the sherries."

"The *boquerones*—"

"—the olives."

"Zagat-rated—"

"—twenty-three for food."

"I went on a date—"

"—there?"

"Everyone does."

"Even you?"

"Me?"

"I wish."

"I wish right now."

"I wish I was—"

"Me, too."

I eased my elbows onto the fish-stained tabletop, sneaked my head into the crook of my arm, and let loose with the sadness. I felt Nana touch my soft wavy hairs with her hand, which was slow and methodical in its ministrations. Unconcerned about the snickering waiters, she was quiet and dry-eyed, a professional tour guide comforting her charge after he was robbed of his wallet and passport. "Sorry," I said.

"Sorry for nothing," she said, which may not have been her best English, but I understood what she meant.

"I'm drunk," I said, which was only partly true.

She settled the bill and we walked slowly, unevenly, at last hand in hand, down the pier toward the teeming esplanade. A SCROD billboard hung along the pier, a Communist-era-looking tableau of three middle-aged local men beneath an exclamatory slogan in the local language. All three had hooded gray eyelids, reminding me of a parade of turtles sauntering down toward the tide. One looked like a tired intellectual. He and another were distinguished by poorly made silver teeth, the third by a thick, feminine mouth and a daring young man's expression. A wheezing loudspeaker beneath them blasted the techno music of five years ago interrupted by snippets of angry Sevo oratory. "What does it say?" I asked, pointing at the billboard.

" 'The Independence of the People Will Soon Be Realized!' "

"I like that funny-looking guy with the girlie mouth," I said. "He looks like an Odessa singer. He must be the junior dictator of the bunch. 'Don't hate me. I'm not Stalin. I'm only in training!' "

"He's my father," Nana said.

I did not register what she had said at first; per the usual, I had been lost in thought about some aspect of myself. "Oh," I said finally. I stopped to examine my palms, the prominent green veins trying so desperately to bring blood to the fingers.

"I have something to tell you, Misha," Nana said in Russian, dispelling what was left of my Belgian identity. "My papa knew your papa well. They were in business together. He was a very dear man. When he came to Svanï City, to our house, he would bring me sugar cubes and mandarin oranges. As if there were still shortages, like in the Soviet days. As if I were starved for vitamins and sweets."

"Oh," I repeated in English.

I closed my eyes, trying to think of Papa, but what happened next trumped his memory. The ripe green papaya smell beneath the perfume, the feathery but strong feel of arms against my side hams, the soft kiss of downy lips against my forehead. Beneath the picture of her own father exhorting passersby to violent rebellion, my Nana was holding me close.

26

Food, Decor, Service

The next week I spent in love—with her, with the distant American city we held in common, and with myself for being able to so quickly recover from the post-traumatic stress of Sakha's murder and Alyosha-Bob's flight. We had sex practically on the same day we met; the myth of the conservative Eastern girl dispelled with a few slutty poses struck over a shared bottle of Flagman vodka at the Hyatt's Beluga Bar, followed by a trip up the glassed-in elevator, a five-minute bout of red-lipped fellatio, and then the sloppy application of a South Korean condom. These all proved fun activities, and I was able to stay hard for a while, even though I find condoms repellent, another attempt to smother and belittle my *khui*, only this time at the hands of the South Korean rubber barons.

She approached lovemaking as would many a big girl (and I mean *big*, not fat), with a sense of duty and equality and full-bodied joy that smaller, more rodentlike women do not possess. She giggled and playacted. She pushed me onto the bed, and I pretended to tip over, when in actuality that was exactly what I did, nearly snapping my fine Hyatt bed in two. "Come here, sweetie," I said, American to a fault. "Come to daddy."

"Whatchoo got for me, daddy?" she said, arms on her hips, young face shining with sweat, dark brown eyes glazed over with sexy drunkenness. "Show me whatchoo got."

"Yeah, you wanna see, sugarplum?" I said. "You wanna see what I got?" And for the first time since the Hasids snipped me, I was not afraid to bring it out to the light—the long scar, the patches of skin stapled to the stem, the general look of a rocket that had failed re-entry. Nana was not interested in the particulars. She shrugged, smiled, then went at it progressively—putting it in her mouth, turning it around, withdrawing it with a popping sound, some laughter at that, wiping her mouth with the inside of her elbow, then stuffing my thing back into the warmth of her oral cavity.

"Oh, that's nice," I said, all riled up by her easy middle-class Western ways: such a pleasant contrast from the seriousness of the Russian girls who approached my *khui* with the gravity of Leonid Brezhnev stepping up to the podium at the 23rd Party Congress in Moscow. "Oh, keep doing it to me, baby doll," I said. "Don't make me beg. Uh-huh. Aw, shit."

"You wanna pop me?" she said. This must have been some new-fangled youth term. The verb "to pop."

"I wanna bust a nut inside you, shorty," I said. "I wanna make you sweat, boo. Let's do this thing."

I'd like to say that she stepped out of her jeans, but in truth it took a while to maneuver two large dimpled buttocks and the accompanying vaginal wedge out of the hard shell of her Miss Sixty denims. We huffed and sweated; I had her hanging off the edge of the bed while I gripped the cuffs of her jeans; I nearly pulled a groin muscle getting her naked; but through it all I stayed hard, a testament to how much I wanted her. She kept her T-shirt on throughout the initial popping, which is just how I like my sex, infused with a little mystery. I slipped my hands beneath the cotton tee and felt the smooth creamery of her breasts while saving the visuals of those brown glossy globes for later. Her vagina was *all that*, as they say in the urban media—a powerful ethnic muscle scented by bitter melon, the breezes of the local sea, and the sweaty needs of a tiny nation trying to breed itself into a future. Was it especially hairy? Good Lord, yes it was. Mountains of kinkiness black as the night above the Serengeti with paprika shoots at the edges—the pubic hair alone must have clocked in at half a kilo, while providing the inspiration for two discernible trails of hair, one running up to the navel, the other to the base of the spine.

Naturally, considering my size, she got on top of me. But given her impressive overall body mass and natural resilience, I could see a day when we could broach the missionary position, not that there's anything special in attacking a poor woman that way. After we had fussed with the condom, I reached for her pubes, but she slapped me away. These preliminaries did not interest her. Instead, she just plain mounted me, holding on to my tits for balance, slipping me inside with no effort, both vaginal lips working to usher me into her tightness. I find it clichéd when couples insist that they have "the perfect fit," but between the busted-up, zigzag, Broadway boogie-woogie of my maligned purple *khui* and the all-encompassing nature of her Caspian *pizda,* we reached a third way, as it were.

That is to say, *she rode me.* It was all very classy and contemporary, like a modern-art survey course at NYU. I wanted to have the slogan I RODE MISHA VAINBERG imprinted on her T-shirt. "Yeah, do me," she kept saying, after issuing a few grunts so male and assertive they startled me into a brief homosexual fear, a fear compounded by one of her sharp nails digging into my tight rectum. "Do me, daddy," she said, her eyes closed, her thighs slapping against my upper and lower stomachs, my own tits making wet noises against my frame. "Just like that," she said, stealing a brief glance at me and then turning her head to the side so that I could lick her ear and plunge into her neck. "Just . . . like . . . that."

"Yeah," I said, "I'm fucking you, boo," but the words did not convince me. "I'm busting my nut tonight," I sang.

"My pussy *fills* so tight," she sang back in perfect ghetto English.

"Ouch," I said. She was crushing my pubic bone, grinding into it. "Ouch," I repeated. "Baby doll . . . ouch."

"Just a minute, pops," she said. "Just give me a minute. Do me right. Just like that."

"Move up a little," I said. "Move up. It hurts. My bone."

"Just . . . like . . . that," she said.

"My bone hurts," I said. "I'm losing it."

"AW," she shouted. "FUCK ME." She leaned back. I slipped out. Her thighs trembled before me, and I felt a warm, abundant liquid spreading on my own thighs, not sure which of us had issued it. My bedroom was filled with the smell of asparagus and related greenery. "Aw," she said again. "Fuck me."

"Are you all right?" I said. "Did I . . ."

"Did you what?" She laughed. Her mouth was long and equine, prickly around the edges. When seen in profile, her teeth cast their own shadows. She seemed to me then two bits silly and one bit dangerous, like a middle-class American high school girl stumbling upon the lechery of a Cancún hotel room. "That was it," she said. "You did it."

"I did it?"

"Just like that."

"Oh," I said. "So you came?"

She embraced me; I held on to her sweaty T-shirt, tracing circles around her surprisingly tiny shoulders. "Yeah," she said. "Didn't you?"

"Sure," I lied. "I busted a nut." The words were so stale in my mouth that I reached for a breath mint on the nightstand. I plucked off the empty condom and managed to throw it under the bed. I felt strange and happy, violated and possibly pissed upon. My asshole no doubt glowed red; my breast and stomach mounds were slippery with our combined saliva.

"Hold me," she said, even though I had been holding her all the while.

"Sweetie," I said. "Sweet girl of mine." These words made me sad with longing, but for what I could not say. For dessert, maybe.

"Talk to me," she whispered.

"About what?" I whispered back. The whispering inspired me to reach for the remote-control dimmer on the nightstand. As I lowered the lights, the distant constellations of oil rigs lit up the panorama beneath us, and the more our bodies faded from each other's sight, the more we could make out the world around us, the seaborne oil-pumping skyscrapers that stretched out in daisy chains toward Turkey, toward Russia, toward Iran, toward all the places for which we had no use.

"Tell me something," she whispered, her breath humid with the carbon smells of my *khui*, the saline waft of our afternoon's sturgeon, and the fading echo of an interim breath mint.

It was not the time to mention that I loved her, not before confirming it with Dr. Levine. Besides, there were things more elusive, symbolic, and somehow more important to share with her. I thought of what these things could be. I thought of that distant island lodged between two mighty rivers and the ways it had made us who we were—two fine people trying to overcome (we *shall* overcome, my friend). I thought of a possible future spent fucking, loving, and eating side by side. I thought of a little red book, not Mao's, exactly, but a volume of far greater importance, one I decided to quote to her from memory.

" 'This ain't your grandfather's Lower East Side,' say devotees of this 'cramped,' 'walk-in-closet-sized' temple of New American cuisine where Chef Rolland Du Plexis holds sway to a crowd of admiring dot-commers, local hipsters, and the occasional 'bridge-and-tunnel Visigoth.' Although some say the kitchen may have 'slipped on a banana' since 'the limos with Garden State plates rolled in,' a reasonably priced wine list and frequent celeb sightings 'keep 'em coming.' Food—26, Decor—16, Service—18."

I could feel her breathing hard against me. She grasped my toxic hump and rubbed it up and down. "That's that place on Clinton Street," she said. "I've been there."

"Muh-huh," I groaned. Her hands on my hump, kneading the dark, molten rock, were as natural as her vagina deep around my *khui*. I couldn't think of the English word, but when I did, I nearly cried out in recognition. *Soothe*. She soothed me.

"Go ahead," she said, "tell me some more."

"What do you want to hear?" I said.

"Go north," she whispered.

I walked with her down Rivington, making a turn on Essex Street; her hand on my back rubbing my hump; her erect bosom arousing the looks of Latino passersby, male and female, *papi* and *mami*, with its untrammeled young girl's freshness, its simple "I'm just Nana from the block" honesty.

Avenue A was ablaze with sordid colors. A tectonic shift, an influx of Eurotrash and computer money, had taken place in the past two decades, turning the neighborhood into a roaring volcano of hipness beneath which the cute multicultural citizens of the Lower East Side cowered like the Pompeians of yore. Soon the disaster would be complete, and the whole of Lower Manhattan would be covered by a lava slide of laptops and lattes, 1's and 0's standing in for the *khuis* and *pizdas* that once kept this 'hood pumping, the nights punctured by the wails of newborns hungry for nipples the size of caramels.

I swiveled my Nana around Sixth Street, past First Avenue, and up a flight of stairs. "Tell me," she said.

" 'It's always Christmas' at this reliable Curry Row standby lit up 'like your stomach after a bad vindaloo.' While dissenters call the cooking 'uninspired' and the harried atmosphere akin to 'life during wartime,' the cheap tabs and free mango ice cream make sure 'the party never stops.' Food—18, Decor—14, Service—11."

"Tell me more." She clutched me tight. One of my kneecaps, a solitary outpost of bone amid flesh, was wedged provocatively between her loins. I decided to walk her westward, pushing my knee into her moistness even as I chanted my singsong:

" 'Painfully long lines' take the 'Zen' out of this garden spot, but with sushi so fresh 'it water-skis down your tongue' and a sake selection as 'long as Japan,' even the 'most jaded downtown samurai' will scream 'Banzai!' Food—26, Decor—9, Service—15."

"More," Nana said. I rubbed my knee inside her, but she did not encourage my gathering lust. "More," she said. I walked her along the breadth of the city to the edge of the West Side Highway; I gave her everything I knew, Food, Decor, Service; I recited from memory, and when memory failed, I reached into imagination, cobbling together restaurants that didn't but should exist, bustling places where the tablecloths were a little dirty, the waiters a little dodgy, but the food was cheap and good and meant to fill you up through and through. And then, once the bill was settled, once the need of both toilet and bidet pressed into you from all sides, you would take a taxi back to your flat high up in the sky, falling asleep in your loved one's arms even before the elevator sounded its bell tone, announcing your arrival to the empty gray corridors, the churning waste-disposal system, the solid anonymous door with the apartment number you would so proudly write, with vestigial Cyrillic curlicues, on the back of envelopes bound for less fortunate lands.

The doorknob turned, the lights clicked, the cable television came on with a roar. And wouldn't you know it, Nana, my sweet brown rider. Just . . . like . . . that. We were home.

27

The Men from SCROD

I was feverishly filing my nails when there was a knock on the door. *A knock on my door!* The last two weeks on the town with Nana had convinced me I was in a sexy full-bodied thriller, but all that awaited me on the other side of the door was Larry Zartarian's balding head and that of his mother peeking out from behind an ice machine a few paces back. "We've got to talk," he said.

I offered him a bucket of buffalo wings, which he spurned. "Are you popping Nana Nanabragovna?" Larry asked me.

"Her body's mad ripe," I said in my defense. "I'm having dinner with her family tonight. All the SCROD bigwigs are going to be there."

The hotel manager walked over to the window and shoved the curtains aside. "Something's going on," he said.

"What now?"

"The airlift. Those Chinooks that landed at the Exxon. I thought they were evacuating everyone, but they were *bringing* people, too. Eighty-five foreign nationals, mostly U.K. and U.S."

"I don't understand," I said. "Even Josh Weiner got his little ass out of here."

"They airlifted out the embassy personnel and most of the oil majors—Exxon, Shell, BP, Chevron," Zartarian said, "but now I've got eighty-five *new* guests. And they're all . . ." He motioned me to come closer. He leaned over and whispered into my ear, "KBR."

I raised my shoulders and let out a heavy sigh to indicate that I had no knowledge or interest in the affairs of the ubiquitous Golly Burton. There was a civil war going on, or a cease-fire, or something—I was interested in *that,* in the ethnic strife and the killing, and in my own possible role in making things better for Nana's sweet absurdist people.

"There's a KBR rooftop luau planned for next week," Zartarian said, nodding meaningfully.

"A luau sounds like fun," I said.

"It's to celebrate the Figa-6 Chevron/BP oil fields coming on-line."

"Even the whores in the lobby have been talking about the Figa-6," I said.

The hotel manager poked a stubby thumb at the tinted window-pane. "That's Figa-6," he said, inviting me to look inside his thumb-print. I scanned the distant horizon until I made out another inevitable skyline of oil rigs. "That's the future of the Absurdi oil sector," Zartarian said.

"Looks good to me," I said.

"No, it doesn't look good at all," Zartarian said. "There hasn't been activity on those rigs for months. It's a Chevron/BP conces-sion, but most of the Chevron and BP oil monkeys flew out with the airlift. And now there are all these empty KBR trucks all over the place. KBR's buying trucks left and right, even the crappiest Russian Kamaz models. And they're just *sitting* there."

"The cease-fire is holding," I said. "They'll reopen the airport soon and get this Figa-6 thing going. This luau is a positive sign, Larry. Don't be such a worrywart. You're letting your mother affect your mood. I know what that's like, to have a parent. It's not easy." I gave him a friendly pat on the shoulder.

"Do me a favor, willya?" Zartarian said. "Nana's father pretty much runs the SCROD. See what he thinks about all this. Try to get a handle at dinner tonight."

"Okay, Larry," I humored him. "I'll try to *get a handle.* You try to get some rest. You're working too hard."

"Hey, if I survive this war, they're going to post me someplace big."

"If," I said, maliciously.

Zartarian's cell phone rang, and the Armenian mumbled something in the local tongue. "The SCROD men are here to pick you up," he said. "Remember, Misha, we're all in this together."

"Hey," I said. "How did you get your phone to work?"

"You can still dial inside the country," Zartarian explained. "It's the rest of the world that's verboten."

"Ah, so we're back in the USSR."

The SCROD men were actually two teenage boys in adjutants' uniforms. They were over by the glass elevator playing with a pair of submachine guns, pretending to mow each other down, then falling on the floor and grasping their stomachs, moaning in English, "Officer down, officer down."

"Boys, don't shoot anything," Zartarian admonished them. "We've got important guests here."

I was hoping for a BTR-70 armored personnel carrier, but the boys drove a Volvo station wagon, rusty around the edges. Feeling like an American high school student departing for the senior prom, I waved goodbye to Zartarian and his mother, who looked sternly at her watch, her bewhiskered countenance reminding me to return at a decent hour and to keep my nose clean.

We drove at an ungodly speed down the Boulevard of National Unity—jammed with sweaty bodies on a summer Friday night—and then plummeted down to the Sevo Terrace. The boys sat up front, chattering in their language and occasionally leaning out the Volvo's windows to shoot rounds into the still night air, a fearsome rat-a-tat that almost made me dip into my Ativan stash. "Boys," I said. "Act a little cultured, why don't you?"

"Sorry, boss," one of the lads mumbled in a farcical Russian. "We're just happy it Friday night. Everybody go dancing. Maybe you dance with a Sevo girl?" The other boy hit him lightly with his submachine gun and told him to shut up.

"I don't know how it is in your language, but when you talk to your elders in Russian, it is important to use the polite *vy* form of address," I instructed them. "Or at least you should ask if it's possible to switch to the familiar *ty*."

"May we switch to the familiar *ty*, boss?"

"No," I said.

The boys lapsed into a quiet moodiness for a few minutes and then went back to their barbarian chatter. I was not unhappy to be left alone. The rolled-down windows permitted a delightful breeze to enter the Volvo's cabin, thankfully skirting the young brutes up front with their leather-and-semen odors and instead tickling my nostrils with the smells of ocean and tropical trees—the tang of jacaranda, say. I took out my Belgian passport and, as I often did these days, pressed it to the hard nipple that stood sentinel over my heart. I was happy at the chance to see my Nana in her parents' house. For reasons all too complex and murky, the sight of children and their parents together aroused me.

The Sevo Terrace esplanade was ablaze with the flash and fizzle of makeshift fireworks aimed at the broad front of the Caspian. Most often these missiles failed to reach their watery target and fell instead upon the crowds of Sevo who had assembled by the edge of the sea and who now beat a panicked retreat from the aerial assault, children and elderly strapped to the backs of the working-age. "There's a war on," I said, "and these people gather to be shelled by fireworks. Unbelievable!"

"They just want to have fun, boss," one of my escorts told me. "We Sevo people like to roast the lamb and have a good time."

"There are many ways to spend an enjoyable evening," I said, "without getting maimed. In my day we drank port wine and talked well into the night about our hopes and dreams."

"We only *hope* and *dream* of moving to Los Angeles one day, boss. So what's there to talk about?"

"Yes—mm," I said, but I could not come up with an equally damning reply.

We circled the floodlit octopus of the Sevo Vatican and took a narrow road that led beneath the so-called Founders' Wall and into the oldest part of the city. Each terrace had its own Old Town, built at the time of either the Persian occupation or the Ottoman incursion, I cannot remember which. On the Sevo and International terraces, these were settled by the original Moslems whose beehive baths and stubby minarets had created two miniature Istanbuls quietly re-moved from the rest of the city.

But the Sevo Old Town was free of Moslems. Rising on a slight ridge, it was trellised by a set of winding roads, each charting a route between mountain and sea, and each eventually leading to a dead-end bluff upon which a formidable old house, squatting on timber chicken legs, reproached the driver for disturbing its solitude. The choicest homes were bored directly into the ridge and wore the frip-pery and ostentation of two centuries past. Their exteriors paraded soft colors, pale yellows and greens, and a ghostly azure that may have once mirrored the now-gray sea below. The houses were graced by long wooden balconies, intricate apertures that often hung from all three sides and were engraved with the lions and fishes of Sevo mythology. They were as beautiful as anything I had seen since land-ing in the country.

We were headed for a house that eclipsed the others in scale, a broad white structure punctured by the occasional skylight, while some of its neighbors were dilapidated to the point of lacking win-dows and roof tiles. As we neared the Nanabragov manse, it became clear that the house had been built of poured concrete. It was merely an expensive parody of the traditional Sevo home, a shell of cement that had grown balconies and winding staircases with the same cold resolve as it had sprouted the satellite dishes lining its roof.

My escorts had gone silent and slack as we pulled up to the house. They touched their weapons and breathed slowly through their noses. They craned their heads to better see the satellite dishes on the roof. They thought in tandem of their Los Angeles destiny, a fate that could not be articulated in words, only in gunfire and the hot-tub embrace of naked women.

A circular driveway surrounded a copy of Bernini's *Fontana del Moro*, the portly Moorish sea god at its center made out of marble several grades too shiny. I saw my Nana run out of the house, dressed in her usual fashion—tightness and youth, puckered flesh and hoop earrings, the hood of her clitoris clearly visible inside a pair of black sweatpants.

"Hey you," she said.

I trembled in response. "Hi-hi."

"Don't you look nice?" she said. I was wearing my tent-sized polo shirt and a pair of khaki pantaloons that I had bought on Dr. Levine's advice. "Yum," she said. "Gimme that sweet face." She kissed me long and hard, squeezing the nonentity of my ass, the pleats of my khakis billowing like two zeppelins in response. I glanced back at my stunned escorts as if to say, "See, this is what happens to cultured people who use the *vy* form of address."

"Come in," Nana said. "My pops is dying to meet you. Dinner's ready. They just shot three lambs." She took my hand and pulled me after her, her shoulders giving off a sweet peppermint concoction that the bodies of young women sometimes produce to make my life more difficult.

We strode into a vestibule the size of a good barn, four gilded mirrors reflecting the room's emptiness, creating the kind of vacant infinity I had always associated with the afterlife. An identical room followed, and then a third and a fourth. Finally we entered a chamber that contained a leather recliner, opposite which hung a flat-screen television. I was reminded of the homes of my former neighbors, the young investment bankers I had known in New York whose downtown lofts ("loft spaces," they proudly called them) maintained the air of a hasty wartime retreat.

"Look around you," Nana said, reprising her job as an American Express tour guide. "This is a traditional Sevo home. The layout is similar to that of any peasant's house, only a little bigger. In the old days, the rooms were arranged in a rectangular pattern around an open smoke hole. We're not so primitive, so instead of a smoke hole, we have a small courtyard." We entered the small courtyard, which properly should have been called a national forest, indeed the national forest of more than one nation, a combination of trees ranging from the palm to the mulberry, among which finches and sparrows caroled at one another, spouting their rapid, nervous gibberish like market sellers vying for a single customer.

The courtyard was so big that one often lost sight of the house enclosing it. All the empty gilded rooms we had seen before were merely a front, for the life of the house coursed solely through this warm green center, which was anchored, naturally, by a long table covered with enough aromatic food and dark red wine to stab me in all my needy places.

Nana's father, the master of the house, was surrounded by his many guests, their warble striving to outdo that of the birds above them. Once I was espied, he shouted, "Quiet!" and reached for what appeared to be the horn of a ram, such as the Judeans use in their elaborate ceremonies. Momentarily a similar specimen, jiggling with wine, was placed in my hand by an elderly servant, while the guests, upon discovering the proportions hidden beneath my billowing outfit, began to gasp and exclaim.

"Quiet, oh you throaty Sevo people!" the master shouted with a spectacular twitch of his entire tiny body, as if he had just been jolted by electricity or branded like a head of cattle. "A great man is among us tonight! We drink now to the son of Boris Vainberg, to our young dear Misha, formerly of St. Petersburg, soon of Brussels, and always of Jerusalem. Why, everyone knows the Vainbergs have a long and peaceful history in our land. They are our brothers, and whoever is their enemy is our enemy also. Misha, hear me and understand my words! When you are here among the Sevo, my mother will be your mother, my wife your sister, my nephew your uncle, *my daughter your wife*, and you will always find water in my well to drink."

"True! True!" the gathered throng shouted, and lifted their horns, as I did mine. A peppery concoction overflowed my mouth and dribbled down my chin. I looked in wet, alcoholic incomprehension at the little man who had supplied the seed that had birthed my Nana, a man who now stared into my eyes with the same fierce possessiveness I often cast upon my morning sausage. As he reached out his arms in a futile attempt to embrace all of me, Mr. Nanabragov's boyish body twitched yet again, nearly jumping out of his half-open linen shirt. He made a kind of peremptory snort and wiped his nose with his wrist. Another twitch followed, this one exposing part of his tanned chest, made stubbly by thick gray hairs but otherwise smooth and firm. Then he fell upon me and hugged me and kissed both my cheeks. I could feel him twitching and vibrating against me, not unlike the electric razor that denuded my chin each morning. "Mr. Nanabragov," I said, enjoying the florid warmth of the father nearly as much as that of his daughter, "your Nana has made me so happy here. I almost wish this war would never end."

"Me, too, dear boy," Mr. Nanabragov whispered. "Me, too." He let me go, then turned to his daughter. "Nanachka," he said, "go help the women with the lambs, my treasure. Tell your mother if she overgrills the kebabs, I'll feed her to the wolves. And we need more *lipioshka*, honey. Your new cavalier likes to eat, by the looks of him. How dare we leave him hungry?"

"I want to stay, Papa," Nana said. She put her hands on her hips and glowered with a teenage obstinacy. She looked so different from her father—he a tiny nervous snowflake, and she a great wide vessel of hope and lust. Only their full red lips bore similarity, the father's bubbly wedges endowing him with a drag queen's pouty glamour.

"This dinner is only for the men, angel," Papa Nanabragov said, and I noticed that indeed the courtyard was filled by exemplars of that one uninspiring gender. "Go have fun with your girlfriends in the kitchen. What nice lamb you'll make. Just don't overcook it. You want to keep your cavalier happy. What a fine man he is."

"That's so old-school," Nana said in English to him. "That's so, I don't know, like, medieval."

"What was that, my little sun?" the father said. "You know I'm not so good with the English. Even my Russian's an embarrassment. Now go. Fly away. But wait . . . Give me a kiss before you leave."

I had never seen my Nana stifle her anger before, mostly because she had never been angry with me (how can one be angry at a man of such few qualities?). She exhaled deeply, her loveliness settled from her round chestnut eyes into the vicinity of her slightly bowlegged lower half, and I thought she would soon start to cry. Instead, she went over to her papa, put her arms around him, and dutifully kissed him six times, once on each red cheek, once on each bald temple, and twice on the fleshy nose, curved downward like a comma. He tickled her. She laughed. He did his strange out-of-body twitch and simultaneously slapped her behind, imparting a squeeze. "You know, sir," I said, "it would be nice to have Nana and her pals at the table. Women are pretty."

"I respectfully dissent," said Mr. Nanabragov. "There's a time for prettiness and there's a time for seriousness. Let's eat!"

28

Dead Democrats

My dinner companions were an inspiration. They ate fervently. They ate with their hands. Their hands were always full. I occupied a large part of the main table, and they would reach over me, around me, past my nose, under my chin, to grab an oozing cheese pie or a warm hunk of pheasant or a stuffed grape leaf the size of a forearm. They inhaled their food into one side of the mouth while expelling Armenian anecdotes from the other. The food was good, the meat fatty and charred just right, the cheese lightly smoked, the soup dumplings coated with enough black pepper to make one cough and weep and thank our put-upon earth for all its spicy produce. I became nervous and discreetly slipped several Ativan tablets into my ram's horn, letting them dissolve amid the strong Sevo wine. But for all the Ativan in the world, I could not quell my anxiety. I started to rock back and forth, as I always do when confronted by food of this caliber. Mr. Nanabragov took this for a sign of Hasidity and started to make a toast to Israel.

"We Sevo understand your country's problems," he said, mistaking Israel for my country. "We, too, are the victims of our geography. Why, just look at our neighbors. To the south, the Persians, in the other directions the Turks, farther north the Russians. And sharing our country, the apelike Svanï. What problems we have. Just imagine, Misha, what would happen if, instead of occupying and subduing the Palestinians, the Israelis found themselves reeling under the Moslem yoke. I would compare both our peoples to a beautiful white mare saddled under a loutish black brute who digs his spurs into our tender flanks. Ever since Saint Sevo the Liberator found the piece of Christ's True Footrest delivered to us by that thieving Armenian— I'm sure my Nana has told you the story—we have been a nation apart from our neighbors, blessed by education and prosperity but cursed by our small numbers and the whip of our Svanï masters." He pretended to raise a whip high above his head and made a whooshing sound.

"Israel must support us, Misha, don't you think? Tell Israel that we should be as one. Tell them that we are both the last hope for Western democracy. If he were alive today, Boris Vainberg, your father of blessed memory, would be the first to run to the Israeli embassy and beg for their help on our behalf. And I know I speak for everyone around the table when I say that each of us would die for Israel as well."

"To Israel!" the gathered toasted.

"To the friendship of the Jews and the Sevo."

"Death to our enemies!"

"Well put!"

"Jesus was a Jew," volunteered Bubi, Nana's little brother, the youngest at the table.

"Certainly he was," his father agreed, cupping the young man's thick chin with one hand and rustling his dark mane with the other. They looked alike—Bubi was also a small, girlish-looking beauty who was doubling nicely around the edges, a victim of the Southern good life. He was free of his father's boisterous twitches, evidently content to live within his own cotton T-shirt, which bore the likeness of the famed Latin American guitarist Carlos Santana. "Yes, Jesus was a Jew," the father confirmed, nodding wisely at the fact.

"Alas, if you read Castaneda, you will see that he was not," someone said.

"Hush, Volodya!" another shouted.

"Don't mistreat the Jews," yet another volunteered.

I momentarily put down the soup ladle I had been using to shovel grainy osetra caviar into my mouth and looked at this Volodya. He was the only ethnic Russian at the table, an inflated, red-faced man with the sad, clear eyes and droopy ears of Vladimir Putin. I later found out that, like Putin, Volodya was a former KGB agent. Disgraced from that service after stealing above and beyond his allotted quota of amphibious jeeps and shoulder-fired rockets, he now worked as a security consultant for the SCROD. I decided it was best to ignore him. "I'm not interested in this man," I said, haughtily tapping my caviar ladle against my ram's horn.

But this Volodya would not let up with his quietly voiced Jew-bashing. Whenever my hosts toasted to the wisdom and financial muscle of the Jews, he would say, "I'm a good friend of the Austrian nationalist Jörg Haider."

Or: "It just so happens that some of my best friends are neo-Nazis. Good fellows, they work with their hands."

Or, more subtly: "Of course there is only one God. But that doesn't mean we don't have our differences."

The father twitched, nearly pulling off his shirt, then pulling it back on again. Bubi and the others loudly denounced the Russian and threatened to eject him from the table. But I would not oblige Volodya by becoming angry. "I am not much taken with Judaism," I announced. "I am a multiculturalist." Except there was no Russian word for "multiculturalist," so I had to say, "I am a man who likes others."

The toasts continued. We drank to the health of the pilot who would one day fly me to Belgium. ("But you should stay with us forever!" Mr. Nanabragov added. "We won't let you go.") We drank to Boris Vainberg, Beloved Papa of blessed memory, and the famous eight-hundred-kilogram screw he sold to a certain American oil services company.

Finally it was time to toast to the women. Mr. Nanabragov's hunch-backed Moslem manservant, who went by the name of Faik, was sent into the kitchen to gather the womenfolk. They emerged, greasy and sweaty and middle-aged, wiping their brows with aprons. Only my Nana and one of her school chums looked glossy and air-conditioned, as if they had spent their evening free of food preparation. (In fact, they had been toking up marijuana in Nana's room while trying on padded bras.)

"The bee is here because it senses honey," Mr. Nanabragov said, twitching and jerking and thrusting his hips. "Women, you are like bees—"

"Hurry up, Timur," said a sallow older woman, her sparse hair coated with flour. "You'll chatter until the sun comes up, and here we are with lamb to grill."

"That's my wife, everybody!" Mr. Nanabragov shouted, pointing at his spouse. "The mother of my children. Look at her carefully, perhaps for the last time, because if she overcooks the kebabs, I think I'm going to kill her tonight." Laughter and toasting. The women glanced back at the kitchen impatiently. Nana rolled her eyes but remained standing until the master of the house shouted, "Women, go! Fly away . . . But wait. First, my dear wife, give me a kiss."

Mrs. Nanabragovna sighed and approached her husband. She kissed him six times, on the cheeks, temples, and nose. She made to leave, but he got up, tipped her over, and kissed her loudly on the lips with a protracted *shoooo* sound while she whimpered and swung her arms about. "Papa," Nana said, "you're embarrassing her." Nana looked at me with brown-eyed despair, as if she wanted me to either separate her parents or inflict the same assault upon her. I was incapable of either. Meanwhile, the ravishing of Mrs. Nanabragovna continued.

"O-ho!" the gathered cried. "True love!" "They're inseparable." "Like something out of a movie." "Fred and Ginger."

Mr. Nanabragov let go of his wife, who fell to the ground and had to be helped up by her girlfriends. She shook the dirt off her skirt, bowed shyly to the men gathered at the table, and ran off to the kitchen, wiping her mouth with her sleeve. Nana grabbed her friend's arm and, with an exaggerated male swagger, followed the older women inside.

The excitement brought forth by the women abated. The lamb arrived, and its gristly, fatty consistency kept our mouths working hard. Faik the manservant, a half-visible Mohammedan gnome, appeared at our elbow to carve up new chunks of a giant kebab. "Eat, eat, masters," he said. "If you spit out some of the gristle, perhaps Faik will make a meal for himself. That's right, spit your gristle at me, excellencies. Am I not a man? Apparently not."

I could not believe a manservant could speak so brashly to his masters, and I almost expressed outrage on behalf of my host. But Mr. Nanabragov said only, "Faik, we are at your disposal, brother. Eat what you wish and drink as your faith allows." With that, Faik cut himself a few choice morsels and absconded with someone's wine horn.

Gradually the men began to regain some of their speech faculties. After they were done masticating the lamb and gargling their dessert wine, they picked up their *mobilniki* and started snarling orders across town or cooing to their mistresses. A group of older men who were clearly styling themselves after Mr. Nanabragov, with their half-open linen shirts and improvised nervous twitches, were having the same endless discussion that dominated the salons of Moscow and St. Petersburg that summer: whether a Mercedes 600S (a so-called *shestyorka*) was better than a BMW 375i. There was little I could add to that debate, other than my preference for a Land Rover, whose seats squished around me so pleasantly. Other men, including the taciturn anti-Semite Volodya, were talking about the oil industry in terms I could not follow—"light, sweet crude," "OPEC benchmark," things of that sort.

"You know," I said to Mr. Nanabragov, "I have a funny American friend who tells me this whole war is about oil. That it's all about whether a pipeline to Europe should run through Sevo or Svaní territory and who gets to profit from the kickbacks."

Mr. Nanabragov vibrated for a while. "You call that a funny friend?" he said. "Well, let me tell you, there's a difference between humor and cynicism. Do you think the Russian poet Lermontov was funny? Why, he probably thought so. But then he publicly humiliated an old school chum who challenged him to a duel and then shot him dead! Not so funny anymore . . ." He twitched silently and glared at me.

"I have another funny friend," I pressed on, "who says the Figa-6 oil field will never happen. He says the American airlift was just an old switcheroo and now there are all these new Halliburton people running around Svaní City for no reason at all. What's going on, Mr. Nanabragov?"

"You know," Nana's father said, "that Alexandre Dumas called the Sevo the Pearls of the Caspian. Now, there's a writer we respect. A Frenchman. Much better than Lermontov. He was funny but not cynical. See the difference?"

I was confused. Weren't the *Svani* called the Pearls of the Caspian? And why was Mr. Nanabragov bashing poor melancholy Lermontov and praising that overripe Dumas? Who cared about literature, anyway? Petroleum and hip-hop were the topics of my generation.

"Fine," Mr. Nanabragov said, "maybe some of us in the SCROD were upset that the Svani had control of the oil pipeline when traditionally we're the people of the sea, and they're the sheep-bangers of the interior. But we don't want to steal the oil like the dictator Georgi Kanuk and his son Debil. We don't want to spend the national patrimony in a Monte Carlo casino. We want to use the oil money to build a democracy. That's the operative word we all love here. Democracy. What do we call ourselves? The State Committee for the Restoration of Order and *Democracy*."

"I love democracy, too," I said. "It's great to have one, no question—"

"And democracy means Israel," said Bubi, winning himself another pat from his father.

"Even Primo Levi admitted the Holocaust figures were inflated," Volodya said.

"A few weeks ago," I said, ignoring the former KGB agent, "I witnessed the terrible murder of a group of democrats by Colonel Svyokla and the Svani forces. One of them had become a good friend of mine. His name was Sakha."

Upon mention of Sakha, the courtyard fell silent. The men began to open and close their *mobilniki*. Bubi quietly whistled "Black Magic Woman." A finch landed on a pile of lamb and began to sing to us about its golden life. "And," said Mr. Nanabragov, "you *liked* this Sakha?"

"Oh, sure," I said. "He had just gotten back from New York, from the Century 21 department store, and they shot him. Right in front of the Hyatt. In cold blood, as they say."

Mr. Nanabragov slapped his hands together and twitched three times, as if sending a coded signal to a satellite nervously circling the table. "We admired Sakha, too," he said. "Didn't we?"

"True! True!" the assembled sang into their cupped hands.

"See, Misha, the Svanï sheep-bangers think that by killing Sevo democrats, they can silence our aspirations. Oh, where are Israel and America when you need them?"

"But they weren't just Sevo democrats," I said. "They were Sevo *and* Svanï. A little of each. A democratic cocktail."

"You know who you should talk to?" said Mr. Nanabragov. "Our esteemed Parka here. Ai, Parka! Speak to us."

The gathered moved their chairs either forward or back until I saw a small, intelligent-looking senior citizen in a rumpled dress shirt holding on to a chicken leg. He turned his double-jointed nose at me and sniffed the air sadly. "This is Parka Mook," Mr. Nanabragov announced. "He spent many years in a Soviet prison for his dissident views, just like your dear papa. He is our most famous playwright, the man who penned *Quietly the Leopard Rises,* which indeed made the Sevo people rise up and pump their fists in the air. You could say he's the moral consciousness of our independence movement. Now he's working on a Sevo dictionary, which will show conclusively how much more authentic our language is when compared to Svanï, which is really just a bastardization of Persian."

Parka Mook opened his mouth, revealing two rows of poorly made silver teeth. Now I recalled where I had seen him: his image had flanked that of Mr. Nanabragov on the Sevo billboard by the esplanade. He seemed even more tired and depressed in person. "Happy to make your acquaintance," he said in slow, ponderous Russian that couldn't hide his thick Caucasus accent.

"Quietly the Leopard Rises," I said, "that sounds very familiar. Was it performed in Petersburg recently?"

"Perhaps," Parka Mook said as he regretfully let go of his chicken leg. "But it's not very good. When you put a Shakespeare or a Beckett or even a Pinter next to me, you will see how very small I am."

"Nonsense, nonsense!" the gathered shouted.

"You're very modest," I told the playwright.

He smiled and waved me away. "It's nice to do something for your country," he said. "But soon I will die and my work will disappear forever. Oh, well. Death should be a pleasant release for me. I can hardly wait to drop dead. Maybe tomorrow the sweet day will come. Now, what did you ask me?"

"Sakha," Mr. Nanabragov reminded him.

"Oh, yes. I knew your friend Sakha. He was a fellow anti-Soviet agitator. We did not share the same opinions as of late—"

"But you were still best friends," Mr. Nanabragov interrupted.

"We did not share the same opinions of late," Parka Mook resumed, "but when I saw his body on television, lying in the dirt, I had to shut my eyes. There was so much brightness that day. These infernal summer months. On some afternoons, when there is that much brightness—how should I put it—the very sunlight becomes false. So I closed the curtains and lost myself in memories of better days."

"And he cursed the Svanï monsters who had killed his best friend, Sakha," Mr. Nanabragov prompted the playwright.

Parka Mook sighed. He looked longingly at his abandoned chicken leg. "That's correct," he muttered, "I cursed . . ." He looked up at me with depleted eyes. "I cursed . . ."

"You cursed the Svanï monsters," Mr. Nanabragov said, twitching impatiently.

"I cursed the monsters . . ."

". . . who killed your best friend."

". . . who killed my best friend, Sakha. True enough."

We watched the old playwright go back to his chicken leg and nibble carefully. I felt the longing to comfort him and, by extension, the whole Sevo race. God help me, but I found their feudal mentality charming. You couldn't fault them for their ignorance, a small, impressionable people surrounded by nations lacking in intellectual rigor. They were young and ill-formed, like showy adolescent girls trying to win the affection of adults through prancing and coquetry and the deliberate flash of a skinny ankle. Forget my Petersburg charity. *These* were Misha's Children. I pledged my fealty to their sunny, prepubescent causes, their dreams of freedom and impossible happiness. "The world has heard of your plight," I said, "and soon you will have your dictionary and your oil pipeline."

"Oh, if only." The men began to sigh and blow unhappily into their empty wine horns.

"A tragedy took place yesterday," Mr. Nanabragov said. "A tragedy that will change everything."

"It's the end, the end," his co-nationals agreed.

"An Italian anti-globalization protester," Mr. Nanabragov said, "a young man, has been killed at the G8 summit in Genoa by the Italian police."

"How sad," I agreed. "If a pretty Mediterranean person can be robbed of his life, what chance do the rest of us have?"

"Just as our Sevo struggle for democracy was gaining some *market share* in the global media," Mr. Nanabragov said, "we have been banished from the *news cycle*."

"Just one dead Italian!" Bubi moaned, tugging at his T-shirt as if he wanted to join his father in a twitch. "We had sixty-five people killed last week—"

"Including your favorite, Sakha," Mr. Nanabragov reminded him.

"—and nobody cared," Bubi said.

"Unlike those rich, spoiled Italians, we're completely in tune with globalization," Mr. Nanabragov said to me. "We want capitalism and America."

"And Israel," Bubi said.

"We were getting live feed on BBC One, France 2, Deutsche Welle, Rai Due, and CNN, and now, one dead European later, you turn on any channel, and everyone's crying over the Genovese hooligan."

"How many such hooligans do *we* have to kill?" Bubi said.

"Shush, sonny, we're a peaceful nation," Mr. Nanabragov said.

They all turned to me and tugged their shirts in unison; Parka Mook put down his chicken leg and burped elegantly into his hand. "It's hard to define your conflict," I suggested. "No one's really sure what it's about."

"It's about independence!" Mr. Nanabragov said.

"And Israel," Bubi said.

"Saint Sevo the Liberator," shouted one of the elderly men.

"Christ's True Footrest."

"The thieving Armenian."

"Quietly the Leopard Rises."

"And don't forget Parka's new dictionary!"

"These are all good things," I said. "But no one knows where your country is or who you are. You don't have a familiar ethnic cuisine; your diaspora, from what I understand, is mostly in Southern California, three time zones removed from the national media in New York; and you don't have a recognizable, long-simmering conflict like the one between the Israelis and the Palestinians, where people in the richer nations can take sides and argue over the dinner table. The best you can do is get the United Nations involved, as in East Timor. Maybe they'll send troops."

"We don't want the United Nations," Mr. Nanabragov said. "We don't want Sri Lankan troops patrolling our streets. We're better than that. We want America."

"We want the big time," Bubi said in English.

"Please, go talk to Israel," Mr. Nanabragov said, "and then maybe they'll recommend us to America."

"How can I talk to Israel?" I said. "What can I say to it? I am only a private Belgian citizen."

"Your *father* would know what to say," Mr. Nanabragov told me.

We sat there quietly chewing on that fact like cud. The finches sang to the sparrows, and the sparrows returned the favor. There was a failure of the power supply. The house around us darkened, moonlit shadows appeared momentarily along the glassed-in verandas covered with trellises of grape. Finally the backup generators sprang to life. We could hear the women singing dolorously in the kitchen, my Nana's voice noticeably absent. A dog picked up their whimper somewhere in the distance.

Mr. Nanabragov was right. My father would know what to say.

29

Bad Manservant

The toasting reached a low ebb. Plastic jugs of sweet wine were brought in, and the men started to get drunk. I had never seen natives of the Caucasus put away so much. "In Soviet days, we used to drink from love and pleasure; now we drink because we have to," Mr. Nanabragov said, and this became the last, symptomatic toast of the evening. The men lined up to kiss me on both cheeks, their boozy, grizzly faces scratching me in a not unpleasant way. "Take care of us," some pleaded. "Our fate is in your hands."

"My mother will be your mother," others assured me. "There will always be water in my well to drink."

"Is it true," Volodya the former KGB man whispered to me, "that most of the pornography industry is in Jewish hands?"

"Oh, sure," I said. "Even *I* dabble in blue films now and then. Tell me if you know of any fallen Russian women. Or young girls, for that matter."

Mr. Nanabragov kissed me six times, on the cheeks, nose, and temples, just as his wife and daughter had him. "Good Misha," he said, slurring his words. "Good boy. Don't leave us for Belgium, sonny. We simply won't let you."

Nana emerged on the balcony, then swept me inside her air-conditioned bedroom, dropping me onto one of two small beds present. "Oh, thank God," she said. "Please fuck me."

"Now?" I said. "Here?"

"Oh, please, please, please," she said. "Do me, daddy."

"Pop you?"

"Just like that."

I assumed the position on the cold white sheets. I was not immediately erect; the stairs had winded me. But the sweet brown scent of recently exhaled marijuana, along with a general NYU laxity, prodded me along. She pulled up her shirt and unhitched her bra, letting her breasts fall into position. In the relative darkness of Nana's bedroom, which faced away from both the oil rigs and the corporate towers of the International Terrace, her teats were lit up by natural resources—the moon and stars—giving them a light gloss on top and a dark folded crease on the bottom. I squished them together and put them in my mouth. "Here goes," I said.

She landed on top of me, sticking me inside her in one lubricated motion, without the usual series of soft cries women produce upon being entered. I closed my eyes and tried to enjoy the pain. I imagined Nana and then another Nana and then a third, all of them on their hands and knees, their full-moon asses pointed toward me as I prepared to take them from behind.

"Just like that, Snack Daddy," Nana was saying, having recently learned of my college nickname. She leaned in to me and started rummaging through the curtains of back flesh as if sorting through the clothing bins of a fashionable secondhand store. Eventually she found what she was looking for.

"Please," I said, "I'm sore tonight. And I ate too much. I might—"

"Gently, gently," she said. "Look how gently I do it. I even trimmed my nails." And she hooked her finger into the mossy bull's-eye of my ass, probing deeper as she went.

"Ouch," I said, not so much in pain as in a general statement of who I was and how I lived my life. Gradually my eyes were adjusting to the darkness of the room, making out the posters on the walls—in one corner an announcement of a CUNY Graduate Center lecture by the famed Orientalist Edward Said, a very good-looking Palestinian; in another a picture of a teenage-boy rock-and-roll band, each kid tanned a perfect brown like my Nana, and as full-lipped and pouty as her brother, Bubi, or, for that matter, their father. As she continued to straddle me, I stared back and forth at these pictures, looking past one breast and then the other, until I assigned a value to each: left breast, Professor Said, right breast, boy band. What incongruous tastes my sweet Nana had, the kind of tastes that can mix only in the very young.

I heard a shallow moan, the sound of a belly too full.

I blinked. There was a second bed in the room. A girl was gently stirring upon it. It must have been the school chum I had briefly seen at dinner before Mr. Nanabragov sent the girls to the kitchen. Noticing my confusion, Nana leaned forward. "It's okay," she whispered into my ear. "When Sissey gets really high, she likes to watch."

"Ak, ak, ak!" I cried. I covered my breasts, my most humiliating part (together with my baggy forearms, they form four loose sacks of flour). I wriggled my ass until Nana's finger popped out. I tried to draw the sheets around us, but there simply weren't enough of them.

"Don't be scared, Snack." Nana laughed. "We're just bored and high, sweetie."

I tried to lift Nana off of me, but she resisted. Her friend's presence shamed and aroused me both. I grabbed the mattress, lifted up my ass, and started thrusting inside Nana, proactively, as they say. "Oh, shit," she cried. "Do it, Misha. Just . . . like . . . that."

Her friend moaned and rustled on the other bed. I liked hearing my name spoken aloud. I lifted up one knee, shifting Nana to one side, to let Sissey see what I doing to her friend's forest-covered reproductive complex, bouncing her ass cheeks and letting them clap against each other. I wanted to make her friend holler and address me using the polite *vy* in Russian. I wanted to make them both pregnant and then, for some reason, to leave them and go far away.

"Faik!" Nana shouted, and suddenly she scrambled off my bulk and threw a waiting robe around her curves. She pointed to the window. The face of Mr. Nanabragov's manservant was pressed against the glass, the crescent of his mustache floating above the puckered star of his lips. Nana waved a fist at him, and the manservant promptly disappeared, leaving only an outline of condensation and want. "That fucking Moslem piece of shit," Nana said.

I massaged the wet stump of my *khui,* hoping Nana's second mouth would come back to swallow it. I turned to her friend Sissey, who had brushed aside her copious hair to reveal two beautiful gray eyes, pupils dilated to match the scope of the Absurdi sun. "You're going to have to go pay him now," Nana said.

"I'm sorry?"

"Whenever Faik catches me with a boy, he wants a hundred dollars."

"But—" I didn't know whether to be more humiliated by the amount of money or by the fact that there were other so-called boys.

"He's in the courtyard. Go!" Nana said as she went over to her girlfriend and hugged her. Soon enough they were whispering in French, laughing their big horsey laughs and braiding each other's hair.

Faik was in the courtyard, sitting amid the dirty dishes pooled with punctured tomatoes and slicks of olive oil. He was casually smoking a pipe, the air filled with cloying apple-scented tobacco. I threw a US$100 bill onto his lap. He picked it up, inspected it against the moonlight, then folded it into the pocket of his checkered shirt. "I'd like another fifty dollars," he said, "because I saw Sissey watching while Nana was riding you."

Riding me. "If I ever caught my manservant doing what you're doing, I would have personally sent him into the next world," I said, letting a smaller denomination descend toward Faik's waiting hands. "I would have garroted him with my own hands, I swear."

"The next world?" Faik said, scratching at his stubbly sailor's haircut. "You know, some people look forward to the next world, but not Faik. In the next world, they'll ask me, 'What did you do in the previous world?' And I'll say, 'I worked like a horse to feed my family.' And they'll say, 'Good, you can work like a horse to feed your family here, too.' "

"You're lucky to be employed by such a prominent family," I said. "Children are starving in Tajikistan."

"A prominent family," Faik said. "Everyone at the table tonight was former KGB. Even Parka Mook the playwright was a collaborator in the end. Sevo nationalism! They're the same assholes who ran everything before. It took them two seconds to switch from the hammer and sickle to Christ's True Footrest. And that cretin of a son Bubi. With his Porsche and his hookers. What a disgrace."

I knew that Faik was right about the Nanabragovs. I knew I was getting into something ugly, or at least morally taxing, but I did nothing. I let it happen. Slowly, and then not so slowly, I was being pulled toward the SCROD. I was starting to believe in Nana and her family. I was falling in love with her father and his twitchy beliefs. I had been caught unawares by Parka Mook and his glorious Sevo dictionary. *Quietly the Vainberg Rises.*

At Accidental College, we were taught that our dreams and our beliefs were all that mattered, that the world would eventually sway to our will, fall in step with our goodness, swoon right into our delicate white arms. All those Introduction to Striptease classes (apparently each of our ridiculous bodies had been made perfect in its own way), all those Advanced Memoir seminars, all those symposiums on Overcoming Shyness and Facilitating Self-Expression. And it wasn't just Accidental College. All over America, the membrane between adulthood and childhood had been eroding, the fantastic and the personal melding into one, adult worries receding into a pink childhood haze. I've been to parties in Brooklyn where men and women in their mid-thirties would passionately discuss the fine points of *The Little Mermaid* or the travails of their favorite superhero. Deep inside, we all wished to have communion with that tiny red-haired underwater bitch. We all wanted to soar high above the city, take on the earthly powers below, and champion the rights of somebody, *anybody*. The Sevo people would do just fine, thank you. Democracy, it turned out, had the makings of the best Disney cartoon ever made.

"Would you rather live under Georgi Kanuk?" I shouted at Faik. "Gambling away the country's oil fortune in Monte Carlo? And no freedom of speech?"

"Freedom of what?" the Moslem manservant said. He blew a barrage of smoke at a lamb's head that served as the table's centerpiece and was already being picked apart by a squadron of flies. "They recruited half the boys in Gorbigrad for the last war. They put my son in an APC that exploded without any explanation and burned him from the waist down. He's twenty-three now, Bubi's age. How am I going to marry off a cripple? Do you know how much money I'll need to get him even a half-decent girl? Who's going to pay for all those German salves I coat his body with? He looks like a mayonnaise sandwich, my only son. But who cares about another mangled Moslem boy? We're all just fodder for the Kanuk family or the Sevo merchants. Maybe I should try to move to Oslo, like my cousin Adem. But what's the use? The Europeans shit all over him. Or maybe I can drive a taxi in one of the Gulf states, like my brother Rafiq. But those sandy Arabs treat us like Negroes down there, too. And you can't even get a decent drink because of those crazy Wahhabite mullahs. Wherever we Moslems go, it's the same *khui*. What's the use of living?"

"You should be thankful your masters are trying to give you democracy," I said. "Freedom is going to change your son's life. And if not his life, then the lives of his children. And if not their lives, then the lives of *their* children. By the way, I run a charity in Petersburg called Misha's Children—"

Faik waved me away. "Please," he said. "Everyone knows you're a sophisticate and a melancholic and that you slept with your stepmother. So what can be said about you?"

What indeed?

30

A Sophisticate and a Melancholic No Longer

I'll tell you something else. When I was four or five years old, my parents used to rent this wooden hut for the summer. The hut was about a hundred kilometers north of Leningrad, close to the Finnish frontier. It was perched on a yellowish hill featuring all kinds of decrepit vegetation and this rotting hornbeam tree that would take up human form and chase after me in dreams. At the bottom of the hill was a brook that made this characteristic *pshhhh* sound that I think all brooks make (they don't really burble, per se), and if you followed the brook around innumerable bends and cataracts, you'd emerge into this gray socialist village—which wasn't really a village anymore but some kind of depot for trucks bearing benzene or kerosene or another highly flammable gas.

Oh boy. Where am I going with this? Right. So Beloved Papa and I had this nautical theme going. He'd get these old beat-up shoes and he'd rip the tops off, so all you'd have was the rubber sole, and then he did some other things to the shoe—he made a kind of improvised sail out of paper and twigs—and we'd sail these shoe-boats down the brook. I think we ran alongside our sea-shoes, cheering them on, singing songs about ants and caterpillars and Mommy in her apron baking poppy cakes, my papa's face a jaunty combination of sparkling black eyes and wind-whipped bushy goatee. And if I try hard with my mind I can ascribe some kind of daily heroism or gentleness or even filial love to the scene of father and son following their rubber-sole regatta down the stream to a former village, now a base camp for idling benzene trucks, their sides stenciled with the fair warning: KEEP YOUR DISTANCE—TRUCK MAY EXPLODE.

Now, tell me, what was the point of all that? What am I trying to do here? *Why is it so hard to come up with a solid block of grief for a deceased parent?* Why can't I rehabilitate my papa the way Gorbachev rehabilitated Stalin's victims? See, what I'm going for is a kind of totalitarian triumph-over-adversity story with Beloved Papa cast in the role of wise, fun-loving, middle-class parent. I'm trying here, Papa. I'm doing my best. But the truth always seems to dampen my best instincts.

The truth is this: the damn shoe-boats never made it down the brook, they sank within ten seconds of becoming waterlogged or else were eaten by a hungry Soviet beaver. The truth is this: after a while, we ran out of shoes, and Beloved Papa would make boats out of walnut shells (same concept but much smaller boat), and these we would sail around our rusticated bathtub, only they also became waterlogged and sank pretty quickly, too. The truth is this: Beloved Papa had a very dim knowledge of flotation, a very faulty understanding of how physical objects are kept aloft by water, this despite the fact that, like every other Soviet Jew, he was a mechanical engineer by training.

The truth is this: on some level, Beloved Papa could not believe he had played his part in giving birth to a living, bumbling, farting, sentient creature such as me, and he would grab me fiercely enough to leave bruises on my arms and stare into my eyes with a kind of helpless fury, his budding love for me hemmed in on all four sides by fear. And self-knowledge.

He didn't want to hit me. He didn't want to swipe at my *khui*. Not this early on. But hitting young boys was the done thing ("If you don't hit, you don't love," his idiot relatives used to say), else they grew up cretins who couldn't pummel their way through grade school. Papa's stepfather had beaten him with a poker when he was seven, and by the time he was thirteen, Papa had celebrated his manhood by beating his stepfather half to death with the same poker. He then clocked some relatives pretty hard and also disfigured a local drunk suspected of ravishing children. He really went nuts with the poker. There was a nice kind of closure to that, although a few years later Beloved Papa had to spend some time in a sanatorium.

The truth is this: Beloved Papa had no idea what the hell to do with me. He lived in an abstract world where the highest form of good was not child rearing but the state of Israel. To move there, to grow oranges, to build ritual baths for menstruating women, and to shoot at Arabs—this was his lonely goal. Of course, after socialism collapsed and he finally got a chance to get drunk and happy-fisted on a Tel Aviv beach, he discovered a goofy, unsentimental little country, its sustaining mission nearly as banal and eroded as our own. I guess the lesson is—freedom is anathema to dreams nurtured in captivity.

Meanwhile, back at the Park Hyatt Svanï City, I was as free as I had ever been. I took my own ritual baths mornings, afternoons, and evenings, liberating my body from its degrading fat man's smells. I could not recall the last time I was so clean. The size of the Hyatt's tub (an artifact of Roman proportions) encouraged me to take to the water. *Splish, splash,* goes an American ditty. And I can't remember the rest.

I was a changed man. A sophisticate and a melancholic no longer, no matter what Faik would say. I loved my physicality, and I wanted to share it with the world, or at least the illiterate young maids who would stumble upon me, scream *blehlebhlebhhebhhhhheh!* or some other local expression, put up their skinny arms in protest, and run for the door. "Come back, little dopes," I would shout, throwing a wet sponge after their tails, "all is forgiven!"

The steam rose off my flanks as if emulating the incense crowding the dome of the Sevo Vatican. The water took responsibility for my sins. It absorbed the enormity of my dead skin, sloughing it off in reptilian layers, the sum of which, miraculously, did not clog the drain but evaporated to form a rainbow above the toilet. It buoyed parts of me I had long scorned, my necks, my chests, buoyed them one by one and made them brilliant and holy in the reduced, foggy light. It floated my legs upward until they naturally assumed the position of the pregnant Virgin in stirrups, until I could feel the smooth underwater kicks of the Son in my stomach. Overall, I found myself both beautiful and blessed. The mirrors arrayed above the bathtub showed me as I truly was—a tall man with a round, wide face, small blue eyes deeply set, the nose of a smart, predatory bird, a thicket of elegantly graying hair that had recently aged me into a long-denied maturity.

"What do you think of your son, eh?" I ask Beloved Papa, whose imaginary breakfast table I had placed directly beside my tub.

Papa was chewing a piece of hunter's kielbasa atop a piece of buttered bread, a morning treat his Swiss doctors had erroneously guessed would kill him. With the unsandwiched hand, he held his *mobilnik,* tipping it into his meaty mouth as if he meant to swallow it, too. "No," he said, eyes boring through the near-infinity of his bill-fold, dry alcoholic mouth puckering on every heavy word. "No, that's not it at all. If he dares . . . Why, I'll fuck him good. We've got everyone down—Sukharchik in Customs, Sashen'ka at Agricultural Import, Mirsky in Moscow, Captain Belugin at the precinct. Who does he have? Next time he comes up empty-handed, I'll throw his mother under the tram!"

"Papa! Look at me! Look how fine I've grown. Look how the water makes me so pretty and young."

Papa grabbed a teacup and drank down the hot liquid without so much as a snort of pain. He liked to think he was as strong as the bulls with the shaved heads and bad childhoods whom he had gathered around him. He liked to think of himself as a man for all seasons, as long as the seasons were dusty and dry. "Just wait a minute, Misha," he said. "I'm talking on the phone, right?"

How little use he had for me. But then why did you send for me, Papa? Why did you interrupt my life? Why did you put me through all this? Why did you have my *khui* snipped? I have a religion, too, Papa, only it celebrates what's real. "Asparagus," Papa said into his *mobilnik.* "If they're from Germany, the white ones, they'll sell. Just do what needs to be done this time or you'll get it in the *pizda* from me and mine."

"Get it in the *pizda,* Papa? That's not very nice. Children have ears, you know."

He shut off the *mobilnik* with an exaggerated click, the way he'd seen it done on television shows. He wiped the kielbasa and butter off his fingers with one of Lyuba's Hermès scarves. He walked over to the bathtub and stood over me, so that I shuddered and felt my nakedness before him. Is this why Isaac is always naked in the paintings while Abraham is safe and warm in his robe?

"Remember how you used to bathe me, Papa?" I said. "You bathed me until I was twelve. Until I got big, eh, Papa? And then you stopped. Too much work, you said. Too much to wash."

"I'm a busy man now, Misha," Papa told me. "The times have changed. Now everyone's got work to do. Everyone except you, it seems."

"I had an art internship in New York," I reminded him. "And a nice loft. I had my Rouenna to do laundry with. Why did you kidnap me, Papa? Why did you kill that poor Roger Daltrey from Oklahoma?"

"Fine," Papa said. "You want me to wash you? Where's the sponge?"

He put his hand on my neck. It was coarse and warm. He smelled reassuringly of garlic. As he cupped one of my breasts, I tried to see the disgust on his face, but his eyes were closed. He lifted up my breast and sponged underneath it. You have to keep all the crevices clean, he used to teach me. He scrubbed. Harder and harder. He went for my stomach, grabbing a fold, roughly sponging it until it felt raw and used, then moving on to the next. "Do you still love me, Papa?" I asked.

"I'll always love you," he said, moving along, moving downward.

"I want to believe in something, too, Papa," I said. "Just like you believed in Israel. I want to help the Sevo people. I'm not stupid. I know they're no good. But they're better than their neighbors. I want to avenge Sakha's death. Will you love me more if I do something important with my life?"

"You want to help someone, help your own kind," Papa said, scraping the dust and sand off my thighs.

"Mr. Nanabragov tells me I should talk to Israel. How do I do that, Papa? What's the trick?"

But Papa just kept rubbing along, his body rocking back and

forth, his jaws clenched, his lemur head bobbing along. "Think one person can change the world, Misha?" he said at last.

"Yes," I said. "I really do. Do you?"

Papa took off his shoe. He took out a pocketknife and, in a few frenzied motions, separated its sole, creating the preliminary outline of one of the childhood shoe-boats he used to build for me. He put the sole into the bathtub. It made a few seaworthy gestures, rolled along the waves caused by my deep breathing, then lifted its prow to the ceiling and promptly sank.

I looked around the empty bathroom. It was all quiet now except for the high-tech beeping of some Hyatt appliance. My papa was dead. Alyosha-Bob was gone.

I had work to do.

31

The KBR Luau

August came to the republic. An unpleasant warm wind materialized from the south—from Iran, I suppose—boxing Svanï City into a rectangle of hot air. The weather was so unforgiving, Timofey had to accompany me around town putting ice cubes between my tits in a desperate effort to refrigerate me. Being a Belgian, I began to appreciate what my fellow countrymen had to endure down in King Leopold's un-air-conditioned Congo.

The main event of the social season was the Kellogg, Brown & Root luau in celebration of the Chevron/BP Figa-6 oil fields. Everyone was talking about it—the white men by the Hyatt pool, the teenage soldiers manning the roadblocks, the young maids Timofey had arranged to scrub my feet in the afternoon. KBR was especially famous for its very generous "goody bags," and people were wondering what they would get at the rooftop luau (let me spoil the fun a little: it was a tin of beluga caviar accompanied by a mother-of-pearl serving spoon engraved with the Halliburton logo; a selection of scents from the 718 perfume store, including their new Ghettomän aftershave; and gold earrings shaped like tiny offshore oil platforms, which made a nice gift for Timofey's new girlfriend, one of the older Hyatt maids). The KBR luau was, without a doubt, the hottest ticket in town, and I saw my invite as a sign that I had arrived. If I was going to help Nana's father and the SCROD in their quest for Order and Democracy, it was important to keep my compass needle pointing true north, and in Absurdistan that always meant Golly Burton.

I heard the KBR people had a really easygoing Texas attitude (their company is headquartered in Houston), so I put on some checkered shorts and a banged-up pair of sandals that kept slipping off my sweaty feet no matter how much I tightened the straps. Nana, however, looked super-sexy in her flaming cowboy boots and a form-fitting Houston Astros T-shirt that finally made me appreciate the sport of baseball.

On the special Halliburton day, Nana and I made quick love in front of the CNN-tuned television, gave each other a tender, aromatic sponge bath, then took the elevator one floor up from my suite to the roof terrace.

We were greeted by a tall American soldier in Oakley sunglasses and a Kevlar helmet, armed with an enormous assault rifle, an unusual sight, given the cease-fire. A civilian female greeter put fragrant leis of orchid and rose around our necks and slapped a khaki KBR baseball cap on my head and a straw Halliburton beachcomber on Nana's, warning us of the effects of the blazing sun. "Are the goody bags inside?" Nana asked, craning her neck anxiously.

I could smell a thousand American hamburgers aflame, some exuding pure red meat and charcoal, others coated with a voluptuous layer of processed cheese. The roof was jammed with Halliburtonites and well-connected natives. The Absurdi men had dressed up in their traditional woolen pants and brown wingtips, their wives fronting thick gold necklaces and amber bracelets you could fit around a birch tree. The KBR folks were divided into two camps: British (mostly Scottish) employees in crisp white shirts and pressed trousers, and their more freewheeling Texas and Louisiana counterparts in Hawaiian shirts and knee-high black socks. Local cooks had formed a serving line to dish out steaming bowls of shrimp gumbo and crawfish étouffée, while more discriminating eaters were laying siege to the Svanï City Sashimi Company. The rooftop's open-air view was magnificent and all-inclusive, a front-row seat to the amphitheater that was the Absurdi capital, although a long banner covered the best parts of the skyline with the words KELLOGG, BROWN & ROOT + CHEVRON/BP = LIGHT, ENERGY, PROGRESS.

And below that, in smaller letters: GO, FIGA-6!!! IT'S YOUR BIRTHDAY!!!

I tossed a well-done hamburger into my mouth, inhaled some relish, got a Hyatt girl in a hula skirt to spray a sweet burst of perfume on my hands, and asked her to point me to the toilet. Along the way, I walked past a dozen two-meter-high tiki totem poles carved with various Pacific grotesqueries and wired to produce a kind of drumbeat Hawaiian-warrior sound (*Halla walla halla walla halla walla*), and a live palm tree studded with parrot cages. The parrots had been trained to say, "*Kwaaak!* Kellogg, Brown! *Kwaaak!* Halliburton!" along with phrases I had difficulty understanding, such as "LOGCAP! *Kwaaak!* LOGCAP! *Kwaaak!* It's a cost-plus contract! It's a cost-plus contract!"

The fact that the parrots knew more about Golly Burton's business than I did was distressing. I resolved to make myself more knowledgeable.

KBR had put up a fancy outhouse featuring a marble pissing trough for the men. As in grade school, cliques had formed among the pissers. In one corner, Sevo and Svanï were grunting along, trying to get their prostates to cooperate; in another corner, Scottish engineers were painting their initials on the creamy marble. But I didn't need a bright Halliburton parrot to know that the real power rested among the Texans and their ilk, so I waited for a slot to open and positioned myself in between two hulking Americans, their mustaches the off-white color of sandwich bread.

I shyly took out my *khui* and started making a puddle with it, whistling the famous American song "Dixie," hoping that would make me look legitimate. The men were all talking at once, their English both idiomatic and idiotic. I had to concentrate.

"Ends up we're throwin' Bechtel a bone," one of the men drawled past my head.

"I got a call from over there, askin' when the fun's gonna start. When those Ukrainian boys gonna start shootin' up the *infer*structure. I say, 'Don' worry 'bout the mule, son, just load the wagon.' "

"That's Bechtel for ya. Big hat, no cattle."

"You boys jes' wait till the cavalry shows up," someone shouted over to my pissmates. "We're gonna come out of this finer than frog hair. Remember the L-word?"

"You talkin' about them lesbian hookers again, Cliffey? Keep this man *away* from the Radisson."

"I'm talkin' L-O-G-C-A-P. What that spell?"

The men started to laugh, the fellow next to me tinkling on my sandal. "Cost plus!" someone shouted.

"Cost plus!" the others picked up.

"Blank check!"

"Indefinite delivery!"

"Indefinite quantity!"

"Indefinite *quality*!"

"Walk around and look busy!"

"Here come that four-hour lunch!"

"Here come that four-dollar blow job!"

"Here come Cliffey's sister!"

"Hey, sorry, big fella," said the guy next to me, his mouth exuding bourbon and fresh mint, as if he were a man-sized mint julep. "Looks like I jes' *tumped* all over yer foot."

"No worries," I said, shaking off my sandal. "My manservant will clean it up."

"Did you hear that, y'all?" cried the one called Cliffey, a short, beleaguered man who nonetheless seemed in charge. "His *man*servant gonna clean it up. I think we got a Bechtel senior manager here!"

"All them Bechtel people's up in San Francisco. Forget the manservants, they got man *lovers*!"

"I'm not from this Bechtel," I said timidly. "And I'm not a homosexual. I'm a Belgian. I represent Mr. Nanabragov and the SCROD."

"Nanabragov?" said my pissmate. "You mean Twitchy? Whut's up with that hombre? He looks like the dog been keepin' *him* under the porch."

"Naw, he a straight shooter," Cliffey said. "He's all about the LOGCAP. We do good business with him. And they love him over at DoD."

"What's DoD?" I asked.

"Department of Defense. Where you been, son?"

"Ain't I seen you with Nanabragov's daughter?" another pisser asked me. "That little Nana Nanny Goat of his. You were walkin' down the Boulevard ah National Unity with yer hand in her back pocket! You two hitched?"

I shook my head. "No, we're not married yet, sir."

"Thatta boy! He's eatin' supper before he even say grace."

"What's your name, son?" Cliffey said.

"Misha Vainberg," I said.

"Iner't yer daddy the one who sold us that two-thousand-pound screw?"

"Um, maybe," I said.

"Shoot, anyone who can pull the wool over *us* like that deserve to be the gov'nor. Your daddy was rarer than hen's teeth, son. You oughta be proud of him."

The others at the piss trough drawled their approval of my Beloved Papa.

"I *am* proud of my daddy," I said with a drawl of my own. "Excuse me, fellers. I think I'm all done pissing here."

I left the outhouse, relieved in every sense. The KBR people were all right with me. It was true that Halliburton in general was maligned among a certain American set, but perhaps these coastal liberals didn't understand the cultural relativism involved in being from Texas.

There was only one term I still didn't understand: LOGCAP. Perhaps I could get more information out of a Halliburton parrot. I found a particularly talkative specimen, his tail plumage the murky green of American currency. "LOGCAP," I said to the bird.

"Cost plus! Cost plus!" he squawked back.

"LOGCAP! LOGCAP!" I shouted at the parrot.

He lifted up his wing and did a number with his claw. *"Kwaak!"* he said. "DoD!"

"Department of Defense?" I said. "I don't get it, birdy. There are no American troops in Absurdistan. We're out of the news cycle. No one even knows this place exists."

The parrot started strutting purposefully from one end of his cage to the other. He lifted up his beak so that his profile mirrored my own. "Look busy! Look busy!" he said. "Cost overrun! *Kwaak!*"

Larry Zartarian sidled up to me. The poor hotel manager looked like he had spent the last week hiding out in a Finnish bunker. I was reminded of one of Ice Cube's lyrics: "I ain't down with the pale-face . . ." "It's no good, Misha," he said, nervously rubbing his hands against his trousers. His mother snorted assent from behind one of the totem poles.

"What's no good, Larry?"

"The SCROD has instructed me to clear off the rooftop by to-morrow."

"So?"

"I got a team of Ukrainian mercenaries just checked in to the hotel. And Volodya, that ex-KGB asshole, has been snooping around the roof with some kind of telescope. They're getting ready for something big."

I recalled what I had just heard at the pissing trough: *Ukrainian boys gonna start shootin' up the* infer*structure.*

"The parrot mentioned cost plus," I said. "What does that mean?"

" 'Cost plus' is one of the stipulations of the LOGCAP," Zartarian said.

"And what's this LOGCAP?"

Zaratarian rummaged through his pockets until he found a crumpled piece of paper. It was a printout from a U.S. government website, evidently from the days when the Internet was still allowed in Absurdistan. He pointed to the relevant section.

LOGCAP—the Logistics Civil Augmentation Program—is a U.S. Army initiative for peacetime planning for the use of civilian contractors in wartime and other contingencies. These contractors will perform selected services to support U.S. forces in support of Department of Defense (DoD) missions. Use of contractors in a theater of operations allows the release of military units for other missions or to fill support shortfalls. This program provides the army with additional means to adequately support the current and programmed forces.

Peacetime planning? Theater of operations? Programmed forces? "What the hell does this mean, Larry?" I asked Zartarian. "And what does it have to do with KBR or Absurdistan?"

"LOGCAP means KBR is the exclusive provider of support services for the U.S. Army in a time of war," Larry explained. "They had the same thing in Somalia and Bosnia. 'Cost plus' means they get a percentage of whatever money they spend. So the more KBR spends, the more they make. They can put in marble outhouses, monogrammed towels, endless training sessions, supply trucks just sitting around doing nothing. It's like a blank check from the Defense Department."

"But the U.S. Army isn't here," I said. "And this isn't Somalia or Bosnia. We've got oil here. We've got Figa-6. We've got a Sevo minority struggling against Svanï oppression."

"It's not my job to interfere in the affairs of hotel guests," Zartarian said, glancing briefly at his mother, still hiding behind the totem pole, "but I would just stay out of this whole thing, Misha. Don't get involved with the SCROD."

"Yes, you're correct," I said to the sweltering Hyatt manager. "It's not your job to interfere in my affairs. Please excuse me, Larry."

I went to look for my Nana. I found her arm-wrestling her father at a table reserved for the SCROD. Beneath her heavy face and round bosom, Nana had quite a sizable forearm, all muscle and heft. She looked like she had a lock on Twitchy, but at the last minute, her father pulled through and overpowered her, slamming her plump brown hand against the table.

"You're a brute!" Nana cried, pulling away and then rubbing her injured hand.

"Six kisses," her father said. "You owe me six kisses. Come on, now. Be a big girl. You made a bet, now pay up."

Nana sighed, forced a smile, and dutifully began to apply her mouth to her father's face. "Hello, friends," I said to my new family.

"Ah, it's Misha Vainberg, the hero of our time!" Mr. Nanabragov said, wiping off his daughter's saliva. He pulled up a big plastic chair and squeezed my neck paternally. "We've got some good news for you, little son. I'm about to give you as much joy as my daughter's been giving you. Would you mind if Parka Mook and I drop by your suite tomorrow? We'll have a nice talk."

"I would be honored, Mr. Nanabragov," I said. "There's always water in my well for you to drink."

"Very good," Nanabragov said. "Oh, look! Here come the hookers!"

Accompanied by roof-shaking applause, the Hyatt prostitutes, nearly twenty in number, were running up to a makeshift stage where microphones had been set up for them. For this occasion, the nocturnal butterflies weren't dressed in their usually slinky odes to the midriff and the hanging underarm. Some were wearing men's suits and cowboy hats, others U.S. Army camouflage and Oakley sunglasses, and still others appeared in blackface, holding cardboard spears, the word "Somalians" written across their tarred naked breasts. "It's like that Japanese theater," Mr. Nanabragov said. "Where the women play both genders."

The prostitutes were timidly smiling at us from the stage, brushing the hair from their full dimpled faces, and throwing kisses to their customers, who were recognizable by the loudest applause and by calls of "Fatima, over here!" and "Hey, Natasha, who's your daddy?"

Nana was laughing at the display of her fallen countrywomen, and I was wanting to join in the fun when I noticed a man at a nearby table solemnly staring into his bowl of chili, his hands rigid in his lap. I recognized that tanned peach head immediately. "It's Colonel Svyokla!" I shouted over to Mr. Nanabragov. "It's Sakha's murderer! Who invited him? Why is he here?"

"Shhh, sonny," Mr. Nanabragov said with a finger pressed to his lips. "It's a Halliburton party. We've got to be respectful. Let's deal with it later."

"I like it when you get all riled up," Nana said, circling one of my ears with her finger. "You're sexy when you stand for something, Misha."

One of the Hyatt prostitutes, a slim pretty one with naturally blond locks and eyes the color of pewter, was trying to get our attention. "Excuse me, gentlemen and lady!" she shouted. "Excuse me, please!" She waited for the noise to die down, then looked at a notecard and blushed terribly. "On behalf of the KBR Ladies' Auxiliary"—she pointed to her fellow sex workers—"and the various ethnic people of the Republika Absurdsvaní, I would like to say to Golly Burton, thank you for coming to our country!"

Wild applause from every table. Mr. Nanabragov got up to twitch. Nana's brother, Bubi, stuck his fingers in his mouth and whistled. I motioned for a passing waiter to bring me a crawfish.

"Golly Burton is famous company," the prostitute continued. "Everybody knows such company. And KBR is proud subsidiary of Golly Burton. We in Absurdsvaní are sometimes not deserving of KBR services. We fight among ourselves. We make violence. So stupid! Now we got Figa-6 oil field coming online, thanks be to Golly Burton. Now our children have many oils to make their future . . ." She looked at the notecard and tried to mouth the word. "Prosperous . . ."

"Preposterous!" someone corrected her.

"Take it all off, baby!" another shouted.

The prostitute instinctively tugged down on her gown to show off her perfect young shoulders. "And now," she said, "without further make do, I give you the Ladies' Auxiliary historical tribute to KBR!"

The girls told the story of Kellogg, Brown & Root through several clever musical numbers. The first, "We've Got Friends in High Places (Look at All 'Em Smiling Faces)," paid homage to Brown & Root's notorious influence peddling, from the first prime rib bought for a Texas roads commissioner to the decades-long wooing of Lyndon B. Johnson. Later, the girls celebrated Brown & Root's many military-service contracts overseas, from Vietnam ("Oh, me so horny!") to Somalia ("Oh, it's so thorny!") to Bosnia, where they broke into a note-perfect rendition of Queen's "Bohemian Rhapsody" ("I see a little silhouetto of a Serb / Golly Burt! Golly Burt! Will you do the fandango?").

But the most moving number of the evening was "Gonna Be Your Baby Daddy," a slow rhythm-and-blues duet between a "KBR worker" obsessed with his productivity at the Figa-6 oil fields and his long-suffering girlfriend, an Absurdi prostitute.

Prostitute: *BP, Chevron, Texaco,*
Why you treat me like a ho?

KBR Worker: *I'm out there, drilling away.*
I come home, and here I lay.

Prostitute: *I don't care 'bout all your regs.*
Why don't you drill between my legs?

KBR Worker: *You got light crude on my fingers,*
All night long your oil slick lingers.

Prostitute: *I can make a dead man rise;*
There's a gusher 'tween my thighs.

KBR Worker: *I'm too tired, I'm too spent.*

Prostitute: *Buy me perfume, pay my rent.*

Finally the alleged KBR worker (an older hooker wearing a fake mustache) turned away from her beloved to address the audience in a thick baritone: "Houston, we've got a problem . . ."

An offstage American voice: "Roger that, KBR employee. What's your problem?"

"I . . . I think I'm in love."

Our hero broke down and promised to marry the prostitute, make her "honorable," and pay for her to get Microsoft-certified at a Houston community college.

They say you're just a passport ho,
But they don't know you like I know.

Wasn't sure, but now I'm ready.
Gonna be your "baby daddy."

The finale loosened some tears from the older Absurdi ladies, deep into their dessert of cheesecake and baklava, and even Nana turned to me and said, "Aw, that's kinda sweet."

The lead prostitute thanked everyone for the thunderous applause and invited the KBR men to pile into a special suite on the fortieth floor, where they could "drill us good." With the roar of a Boeing breaking free of gravity, a hundred Texans and Scotsmen rushed the stage.

Nana and I headed for the goody bags.

32

The Commissar of Multicultural Affairs

I woke up early the next day and started squeezing myself into a Hyatt robe. It was difficult going at first (the robe was much too small), but eventually at least half of my body was covered in its downy softness. I felt whole and powerful, like the Reichstag must have felt when it was being draped by Christo. I ordered in large plates of fruit and pastry and steaming jugs of coffee and tea.

It was time for my sit-down with Mr. Nanabragov and Parka Mook.

At the appointed hour (plus another hour), they marched into the living room and took their places on opposite sofas, the playwright huddled next to me, glancing uncomfortably at his clutched hands, Mr. Nanabragov spread out, twitching brightly in the morning sun.

"We are here with excellent news," Mr. Nanabragov said. He stuck his hand down his shirt and jerked lively. "We just returned from a plenary council of the State Committee for the Restoration of Order and Democracy. We were all so impressed by you at dinner last week. You're every bit as cosmopolitan as your father. In some ways, you're even more modern than him and he was a very original thinker. Also someday you may marry my daughter and make her bear your children. And so, by a unanimous vote, we have decided to offer you a position at the ministerial level. How would you like to be the SCROD Minister for Sevo-Israeli Affairs?"

"Er," I said. "You know, my dear friends, I'm just a Belgian trying to get by. What do I know about running a government? My business is in the hands of others."

"What business?" Mr. Nanabragov said. "Our business is democracy, same as yours. Are you forgetting your martyred democrat friend Sakha? This is what dead Sakha would have wanted. Don't you think, Parka?"

The playwright was staring at the ceiling, methodically cleaning out his ear with a pinkie. "Parka!"

"What's the question?" Parka Mook said, wiping earwax against the seam of his pants. "It's early in the morning, gentlemen. I'm tired and sick."

"His martyred friend Sakha. The democrat—"

"Truthfully, he wasn't much of a friend," Parka said. "I met him briefly at a wedding, and then he was shot to death by someone or other. I knew him for maybe two hours."

"We're going to build a statue of Sakha the Democrat," Mr. Nanabragov said. "And use his likeness in our promotional materials. See, we're getting plenty of marketing ideas from you, Misha. You really are an inspiration. And there's another aspect to your becoming a SCROD minister. Everyone knows how much you love New York. Perhaps, after we have secured complete control over the country, we can appoint you our ambassador to the United Nations in New York. Then you can live there with Nana. How would you like that?"

I opened my mouth. The cold Hyatt air tickled my throat and dried out my tongue. "You'd do that for me?" I blathered.

Mr. Nanabragov smiled. Parka Mook, eyes closed, had started whistling "New York, New York." The whistles turned to snores, and the playwright gracefully tipped to the side, resting his warm gray head on a piece of my shoulder. "He likes you," Mr. Nanabragov whispered. "We should always honor the old."

I tilted my head so that I wouldn't scratch Parka Mook with my unshaven lower chin. An ambassadorship to the United Nations? Would the Sevo really take over the entire country? They seemed much more suited for leadership than those sheep-banging Svanï. Or was that just propaganda I had picked up at the dinner table? "You know the Americans have a visa moratorium against the whole Vainberg family," I said. "They won't let me in."

"We can get you diplomatic immunity," Mr. Nanabragov said. "And after you talk to Israel in your new role as Minister for Sevo-Israeli Affairs, the Americans will see you as golden. They'll do anything for Israel."

I was still confused by this "talking to Israel" business. How could I talk to anyone when my *mobilnik* couldn't even dial out of Absurdistan?

"You know, Mr. Nanabragov," I said, "Israel isn't really my country. New York is. I am very proud to be a Jew, but I am a *secular* Jew, like Baruch Spinoza, Albert Einstein, or Sigmund Freud. Indeed, the very best of Jews have always been assimilated and free thinking. The bearded Jews you see at the Wailing Wall, rocking back and forth, cowering before their god, those are fairly second-rate Jews."

Mr. Nanabragov accepted this fact with adult equanimity. "Fine," he said. "You're proud to be godless. But then tell me, Misha, who *would* you like to be?"

Who would I like to be when I grew up? This was a question that haunted people of my generation well into their forties. Momentarily I thought of Mr. Nanabragov's daughter, of her mottled brown breasts tickling my nose. "What about Minister of Multicultural Affairs?" I said.

"What's that?" he asked.

"I would be in charge of minority relations. I would unite all the different people living in Absurdsvanï. And together we would hold festivals and conferences almost every day. We'd celebrate our identities. It would look very good in the eyes of the world. *I would be a uniter.*"

"Hey, Parka, wake up!" Mr. Nanabragov said. "We're talking about the future here."

Parka stirred, wiping his mouth. He looked at the sleek gray surfaces around him and shrank farther into the sofa's distressed leather. "Where am I?" he said.

"You're in the land of the young and the fashionable," Mr. Nanabragov said. "Now, listen to what our Misha's going to be. He's going to be the Commissar for the Nationalities Question."

"Minister of Multicultural Affairs," I lightly corrected him.

"Mul-ti-cul-tu-ral. What a nice word, Parka, you should add that to your new Sevo dictionary."

"I add only real words," Parka said, rubbing his nose.

"Shush, old man," Mr. Nanabragov said. "Don't outlive your usefulness. Speaking of the young and the fashionable, Misha, do you know we Sevo have our own rap group? Would rap prove helpful to your new work?"

"Rap empowers everyone it touches," I said in English. "Tell me about this group."

"They're called the True Footrest Posse. Even I like their lyrics. Hey, maybe I'm multicultural, too!"

"It's easy to be—" I started to say, but my sentence would remain unfinished. An oddly personal boom, a rifle discharged past my head, shook the penthouse, then another, another, another, another, another, another, another, another, another. The windows reverberated in their frames, the flat-screen television slapped against the wall, and the sun itself was blinded by ten successive vapor trails, followed by ten distant bolts of thunder. Our lightweight skyscraper registered a weak sigh of exasperation as a veil of heavy smoke settled over the tinted windows with the grandeur of rolling fog.

Presently a sprinkler system activated, its high-pitched alarm reassuring me with its cloying, repetitive warble. Water was flowing somewhere, possibly on top of us. A good sign. In the end, I thought, civilization would win out.

"Well, how's that for you?" Mr. Nanabragov said, shaking his head and smiling. "The GRAD missiles work. The Ukrainian lads are bombing Gorbigrad!"

"GRAD missiles?" I said. "Those were GRAD missiles? Fired from the roof? We're shelling our own city?"

Dazed but excited, we strolled past the neighboring penthouse, which contained a Malaysian diplomat who was now screaming gutturally in his language. We hailed the elevator and pressed the button for the roof terrace. Everything worked in proper Hyatt fashion, bell tones rang to indicate the closing door, an LCD registered our ascent from 40 to ROOF TERR.

We emerged into the humidity. The vapor trails had dissipated,

leaving us with nothing but a perfect, scorching summer day to admire. The sprinklers refreshed us with steady cold showers, evoking
amusement parks and cheap excitement. All signs of the rollicking
Halliburton luau had been cleared away. A row of singed satellite
dishes pointed accusingly toward some faraway mecca. They gave off
an acrid burnt-rubber odor that I would soon learn to accept. The
spent rocket fuel, on the other hand, smelled like any other fuel,
sweet and sickly and masculine. The GRAD launcher was a slender
container sitting on a series of jury-rigged metal surfaces evocative of
a cheaply made bed frame. A half-dozen rockets were strewn about
the launcher, looking like loose crayons in an American kindergarten.
In the distance, we saw an F-shape of smoke rising over Gorbigrad. It
was hard to distinguish the fires that surely raged across the blighted
neighborhood; the sun itself painted Gorbigrad various incendiary
shades of orange and red.

Three tall, beautiful lads in camouflage uniforms were busy twid-
dling with a portable generator. Something inside me, greedy and
childish, broke loose. Despite the violence at hand, I wanted to talk to
these young Ukrainian mercenaries, to make myself known and liked
by them. All of us who grew up in the Red Army's shadow became
lifelong aficionados of destruction, enthralled by anything that could
bring swift ruin to the enemy. Like any empire in decline, ours was
becoming ever more brilliant at knocking things apart, at raising palls
of smoke over cratered school yards and charred market stalls. "What
have you got going here?" I said to the boys. "If this is a GRAD
BM-21 rocket system, why isn't it mounted on a Ural truck chassis?"

A hale-looking, blue-eyed fellow, his torso almost as wide as mine,
only layered with young muscles instead of lard, put down his wrench
and looked me over with measured surprise. "This is our own modified GRAD," he said. "It's not a BM-21, exactly. We couldn't bring
up an entire Ural truck to the roof, obviously, so we've reassembled
the basic chassis with two stabilizing jacks. Instead of four rows of ten
missiles, we've got two rows. But the basic firing capability is the
same—a fixed half-second interval. And we only need a three-man
crew instead of five."

"You brought all this up to the roof by yourselves?" I said, hopping from foot to foot with manly excitement. "In one day?" How competent these boys were! How well they handled themselves, whether trying to raise a family of four on eighty dollars a month or firing GRAD missiles off the roof of a Hyatt. "How clever, how very clever of you," I said. "And since you don't have a Ural truck, where do you operate the system from? Tell me everything!"

The fellow scratched at his armpits erotically and slapped on a khaki KBR baseball cap. "We've got a remote-firing device attached to a sixty-four-meter-long cable," he said. "We can fire from downstairs, from the thirty-ninth floor. And reloading time is less than five minutes, even with three people working. How do you know so much about GRAD missile launchers? Did you serve in the army?"

"Oh, no," I said. I tapped instinctively at my Jewish proboscis to show how unlikely army service would have been for me. "Sadly, that's not the case. I'm just an enthusiast."

"Our Misha knows everything about everything," Mr. Nanabragov said. "A burning intelligence."

"I'm called Vyacheslav," the mercenary said. We shook hands. His wrist was taut and narrow, like a leek.

"It is so wonderful to work with these boys," Mr. Nanabragov said as the soldier went back to his generator. "And look at the smoke over Gorbigrad! Now we've got a real war going. Smoke over the city! Take that, Genoa!"

I shielded my eyes to better discern the smoke, slowly shifting from a letter F into a series of O's and drifting toward the Absurdi interior. Another, unbidden series of letters was forming in my brain, starting with the letter C and continuing on to U, L, P, A, B, I, L, I, T, and Y. "Oh, God," I said. "Don't tell me you're shelling Gorbigrad because I told you your war wasn't exciting enough?"

"No," Mr. Nanabragov said, laughing and twitching at my silliness. "Well, fine, yes," he amended his answer. "But it's a harmless procedure. We've evacuated the areas to be shelled, so they're just blowing up empty houses. If you can even call those things houses. You know how awful it is over there. The whole place is a disaster. There's not even running water in some parts."

"Yes. But—"

"No one should have to live like that," Nanabragov said. "So we blow up a few neighborhoods, draw some attention to our war, and then we'll get USAID, or the European Bank for Reconstruction and Development, or maybe even the Japanese to pay for a new Gorbigrad. We've already got all the engineering firms we need, all those Bechtels and whatnot. Everyone wins. You should tell Israel about it."

"But it makes the Sevo look terrible," I said. "Like you're the aggressors."

"Do you think we have shit for brains?" Mr. Nanabragov said. "It's all worked out with the federal forces. In the morning our Ukrainian friends shell the Svanï parts of Gorbigrad, and in the afternoon they go for the Sevo districts. We take turns, see? But to outsiders, it looks like a real war. Like we're tearing each other apart. Help, help, U.S.A. Save our oil."

"Fine," I said. "But what happens to all the people whose flats you've destroyed? Where do they go until the Americans rebuild their houses?"

Mr. Nanabragov shrugged. "We're in the Caucasus," he said. "Everyone has an extended family in the countryside. They can go live with their relatives."

I turned to Parka Mook, who stood impassively, his hands folded over his crotch, his dry face and receding mustache drawn into the Russian letter Д. "Is this true?" I asked him.

"What do I know?" he said. "I'm an intellectual, not an urban planner."

I walked over to the edge of the roof and surveyed the red plains of Gorbigrad stretching into the sea, surrounded by the pinpricks of oil derricks, reminding me of a slain woolly mammoth encircled by cavemen with spears. Life could only get better for these people, I thought. How could it get any worse? There was a bit of American athletic wisdom that summed it up nicely: "No pain, no gain." I sighed, suddenly missing American television. What a nostalgic!

"So, Mishen'ka?" Mr. Nanabragov asked, grinning and stroking my hump. "What do you think? Want to join the SCROD, little son? We've got an office all set up for you. And a secretary crawling around on all fours."

"Let me think about it," I said, yawning heartily.

It was time for my afternoon nap.

I was having a pleasant dream about the Egyptian pyramids (for some reason, I was leveling them with a sledgehammer) when Larry Zartarian woke me up. He was standing over me, shaking me by the shoulder, shedding tiny velvet hairs all over my face.

He pointed at the tinted windows with his petite man-hand. Outside, the International Terrace stretched out before me, its skyscrapers silently reflecting the hills and the sea. "What?" I said. "How did you get in here, anyway? What about my privacy?"

"Look at Gorbigrad."

I let my gaze drop across the bay. "Yes," I said. "Gorbigrad has many problems."

"Look closer. That's the Blue Bridge Pass that connects Gorbigrad to the International Terrace. There are soldiers at the checkpoints so no one can get through."

"Fair enough," I said. "We need checkpoints. We're in a state of war."

"Do you see that gray chunk of rock over there? Look right next to it. That's the Alexandre Dumas Ravine. And see those black figures slowly going down the ravine? Like ants? Those are people. Trying to make their way down from Gorbigrad. They're trying to get onto the terraces. Many of them falling to their deaths, no doubt."

I examined these ants he spoke of, but I could barely make them out with my faltering, sun-blinded vision. What was he talking about? Dumas was a bad French writer. A ravine was a ravine. The Sevo and Svanï were not ants. Gorbigrad would be destroyed, then rebuilt anew. "Why would people fall to their deaths trying to leave Gorbigrad?" I said.

"Because Nanabragov and Debil Kanuk are firing GRAD missiles at them. From the roof of my fucking hotel. *Do you know what this will do to the Hyatt image?*"

"I thought the bombed-out people would go live with their friends in the countryside."

"The countryside is completely under siege. The borders are

sealed off by federal and SCROD forces. Your so-called bombed-out people are going to starve."

"How do you know all this?" I said.

Zartarian turned away from me. I focused on everything wrong with him—his premature baldness, the tight slacks outlining his monkey ass, and the small curves of his thighs. From this angle, stooped and small-shouldered, he looked even less suited for physical life than I was.

"Alyosha-Bob told me about you, Misha," he said. "He told me about your childhood. About your father."

I snorted. "I had a fine childhood. My papa made boats out of shoes. We pissed on a dog. Leave my childhood alone."

"You need to stop, Misha," he said. "You need to forget about trying to make things better here. You need to forget about the SCROD."

"Get the hell out of here, Zartarian," I said. But after he was gone, I took out my *mobilnik* and aimed it at the sky. I needed to talk to Alyosha-Bob. I needed to hear about my childhood. A lighthouse beacon revolved around the phone's screen, desperately looking for a signal. Finally the beacon stopped. "Respected mobile phone user," a hoarse Russian woman said, "your attempt to make a connection has failed. There is nothing more to be done. Please hang up." I shivered and hiccuped. The particular world of the Park Hyatt Svanï City floated around me—buffalo wings drumming against whiskey bottles, floral duvet covers suffused in CNN's lunar glow, and in the distance the people, threadbare and heat-stricken, playing out their imponderable dramas.

I wanted Alyosha-Bob back. I wanted to hold hands together, the way Arab men do, as we walked down the Boulevard of National Unity past perfumeries and Irish pubs, empty KBR trucks and armored personnel carriers.

But the hoarse Russian woman was wrong. There was definitely more to be done.

33

Ideas Away

The next day I was woken at ten in the morning by the sound of GRAD missiles being launched directly above my sleepy head. *Hey!* I thought, *what a way to start my first day as the SCROD Minister of Multicultural Affairs.* I put on my best tracksuit, had a bang-up sturgeon-and-egg fry at the Beluga Bar, then went back upstairs and flossed heavily.

The SCROD boys who had driven me to the Nanabragov residence were waiting for me in my official Volvo station wagon. I think their names were Tafa and Rafa, but that sounds rather made up. They were morons, that much I can vouch for. They spent the ride down to the Sevo Terrace addressing me in the familiar way, as if I were a greasy colleague of theirs, and chatting all the while about how a certain teenage American pop star would look with a pickle up her twat. I was ready to reach for my knout.

The State Committee for the Restoration of Order and Democracy gathered in an old House of Soviets atop a deserted bluff overlooking the sprawling octopus of the Sevo Vatican. The building looked very much like a Rhine Valley castle, and in fact had been constructed by German POWs in the forties. Their workmanship was evident. This was the only building of the Soviet era that did not look as if it had been continuously crapped upon by a flock of seagulls for the past five decades. In the dusty square outside the building, workmen were chiseling out a statue to Sakha the Democrat, holding aloft a torch in one hand and a Sevo cross in the other. His academic beard was trimmed down to nothing, and his face was aglow and expectant, as if he had just won a Century 21 shopping spree. "Well, at least he has the torch in one hand," I muttered to no one present. "That's democratic."

Mr. Nanabragov showed me to my office, a chamber the size of a barn brimming with dark wood and glass cabinets stocked with Armenian brandy, the typical privileges of a Soviet party boss. The title "Minister for Sevo-Israeli Affairs" had been crossed out on my door, and someone had written in English: "Ministry of Multiculti." Mr. Nanabragov pointed out the fact that I had twelve completely useless rotary phones lined up on my desk, more than anyone save himself, almost as many as Brezhnev had in his day (I assume his worked). I told Nanabragov that what I really needed was a computer with a working Internet hookup. He sighed and jerked around a little. "What's wrong, friend?" I said.

"I'm fighting with my Nana," he said. "I want her to quit her job at the American Express office so that she can become the mother of your children."

I had been privy to this argument when Nana had mounted me, sans condom (how wet her vagina, how flustered my *khui*), the previous night, bawling about her father's simple nature with each vicious straddle. "Children are like champagne corks," I advised Mr. Nanabragov, patting him on the back. "They should be pointed away and released."

"I don't understand," my potential father-in-law said. "Why are children like champagne corks?"

"Just get me the Internet," I told him.

We met in an airless conference room adorned with a series of warped walnut panels and a tremendous Sevo flag, a sturgeon leaping up over an oil derrick against a background of red and green—red for the blood of the Sevo martyrs and green for the color of American dollars. The men who had gathered around the conference table were the same ones who had come to Mr. Nanabragov's dinner party, only Bubi was missing due to a hangover. They sat there in white short sleeves, gray woolen slacks, and wingtips, their *mobilniki* parked next to their salads and glasses of fizzy mineral water, gossiping loudly in their own language. I might have been at a Lions Club ladies' lunch somewhere in Sinclair Lewis country if not for the bloody flag hanging above us, the oil derricks gleaming outside, and the occasional mumble of the special American word "LOGCAP."

The meeting started with a media roll call. According to Mr. Nanabragov, since the shelling of Gorbigrad had begun, Absurdsvaní was featured in thirty-four news reports, about half of them implicitly sympathetic to the Sevo people. "CNN, check," Mr. Nanabragov intoned, making a sweeping check mark with his twitching arm. "BBC One, check; BBC Two, check; MSNBC, check; Rai Due, check; Deutsche Welle, check . . ."

"What about people jumping into the Alexandre Dumas Ravine?" I asked. "Doesn't that look bad?"

"They're not jumping, they're sliding down," Mr. Nanabragov said. "Which reminds me, have you talked to Israel yet? Because there's good news on that front. Parka, tell us the good news."

The Cultural Minister, his morning face bristling with nose hairs, was staring out the window at the Caspian's lackluster tides. "Wake up, grandpa," Mr. Nanabragov said. "Tell Misha about the Mountain Jews."

Parka Mook fell out of his morning stupor and fixed me with his yellow eyes. He sniffed in my direction as if ascertaining my genus and specie. "Mr. Vainberg," he said, "good morning. How are you? Well rested? That's very nice. Now, allow me to play the fool's fool and tell you about our latest brilliant idea. Do you know who the Mountain Jews are? No? You don't? What a delightful man you are! How easy it must be not to know or care about your own people. Well, briefly, the Mountain Jews have lived among us probably since the time of the Babylonian exile. In the mountains, you see. Their mother has always been our mother, and they have always had water from our well to drink. And believe me, they drank and drank. They drank until our wells ran dry."

"Parka!" Mr. Nanabragov cautioned.

"In 1943 the fascist troops were headed directly for Svaní City, hoping to take control of the oil and the strategic port. The Mountain Jews turned to the local Sevo and Svaní leaders, asking to be hid among them in case the Germans came, or at least to secure their passage across the Caspian. I have found evidence, anecdotal evidence from several village elders, that the Svanï were lukewarm to the idea of saving the Jews, while the Sevo were mildly enthusiastic. So there you have it. Let the truth be known."

"But the Germans never reached Absurdsvanï," I said.

"Unfortunately not," Parka Mook said dryly.

"So who cares if the Sevo *might* have helped them. In truth, they didn't."

"Still, it's a beautiful story," Mr. Nanabragov said. "One minority willing to die for another. You should be shouting about it from a rooftop, Mr. Minister of Multicultural Affairs."

Meanwhile, the Minister of Tourism and Leisure was shamelessly picking at my salad. I gave him such a look, he nearly stabbed himself with his own fork. I reached in with one of my two big squishies and palmed a wedge of ripe, bleeding tomato. "The Holocaust is a serious business," I said. "It requires very expert branding or we'll all look like a bunch of idiots."

"Branding I don't know about," Nanabragov said. "But we can certainly build a statue to Sevo-Jewish friendship. Imagine a hundred-meter version of Misha and the dead democrat Sakha bent over a Torah scroll. And from the Torah scroll, an eternal flame comes shooting out."

"Fine idea! Let's build a Misha!" the gathered shouted.

"It'll take half the granite in the Dumas Ravine just for his head," some wise guy said.

I joined my fellow ministers in laughing politely at my unchecked gluttony. "But seriously," I said, "if you want to look good with the Holocaust, you have to do something original. Or if not original, then at least educational. Like a museum. And it has to be of the latest fashion, so every time a child taps a computer screen with his finger, some poignant fact about Jew-Sevo friendship pops up. Tap, tap, tap, fact, fact, fact."

"Can we build such a thing?" Mr. Nanabragov turned to the Minister of Finance.

The minister was nearly my size and likewise lived amid a tornado of hair and food particles. "Boys," he grunted, wiping sweat off his forehead and flicking it jauntily at the chipped mahogany table before us, "let me tell you about the state of our treasury." He proceeded to outline the rapidly decreasing state of a dozen offshore accounts, along with more informal financial institutions with names like "Big Sasha's Stash" and "Boris's Itty-Bitty Bank."

"What about all that oil you have?" I asked. "What about Figa-6?"

The room fell silent. The Minister of Tourism and Leisure to my right let out a series of short, difficult breaths. "How about this, Misha," Mr. Nanabragov said. "Why don't you ask the American Jewish community for some money?"

"I don't understand," I said. "You want me to ask the American Jews for money so that I can please the American State Department by making an overture to Israel?"

"That's right," Mr. Nanabragov said. "What's the American phrase? 'It's the thought that counts.' Hopefully they'll appreciate our initiative."

I considered my knowledge of American Jews. They always seemed to feel alone and unloved when, in truth, most of the American populace just wanted to kiss them on their shiny noses, bake them a casserole, shoot them some one-liners over dinner, and possibly convert them so as to hasten the Second Coming. Would these Jews respond favorably to a love letter from a small oppressed people somewhere between Russia and Iran? And what form would such a love letter take?

"I guess I can write some *grant proposals*," I said.

"We don't know what those are, but anything you do must be blessed by God," Mr. Nanabragov replied to general applause.

I took out my Hyatt pen and pad and wrote in moist excited letters:

MISHA'S TO-DO LIST
1) Get Internet installed in office.
2) Write grant proposals to build Holocaust Museum.
3) Encourage multiculturalism in everything I do.

"You see how hard Misha's working," Mr. Nanabragov said. "You see how organized he is. That's because he has an American education, like my Nana and Bubi. We old Soviet black-asses, we don't know what the hell we're doing."

The men around me were yawning and stretching. The lunchtime hour was knocking, and there were mistresses to spread at the Hyatt and steaks to dispatch at the new Tuscan Steak & Bean Company. Cigars were lit, followed by soft coughing and sleepy belches. Leave these good men to their idle pursuits. I, on the other hand, would return to my office to work out their country's future. Like the 3.94 student I once was at Accidental College, I would prove myself yet again.

34

The Situation Worries Me

Dear The Guest,

Please Your attention. Due to the worst-ening political situation, we are sad to inform You that many items on the Sushi/Sashimi menu will no longer be possible for You. (In particular we are out of mackerel.) We humbly beg You—forgive us!

Your Faithful Slave, Larry Zartarian, General Manager, Park Hyatt Svanï City.

I didn't want to admit it, but Zartarian was right. And not only about the mackerel. The political situation was "worst-ening." I couldn't get from one terrace to another in Nana's Navigator without getting stuck in a crush of Gorbigrad refugees. The faces of the blighted brushed up against our windows—I tried to spot members of the intelligentsia among them, maybe to offer them a ride, but all were coated with the grime of several days' travel, while the tinted windows of the Navigator erased any discernible signs of intelligence. The men, women, and children in front of me were tied to one another by invisible strings of kin and clan; they were stoic in their exile and loss, but they moved forward hand in hand as if their destinations were fixed, elders hanging on to the backs of their sons, sons cradling little daughters, the war veterans and the demented crouched ferally within wheelbarrows.

"It's just a temporary situation," I whispered to them. "Soon the international community will step in."

But I wasn't so sure. Panic was slowly creeping up the Boulevard of National Unity. Cases of Ghettomän aftershave from the 718 Perfumery and boxes of scruffy-looking Muppets with excited American googly eyes from the Toys "R" Us superstore were being pillaged left and right, squeezed into armored personnel carriers and waiting jeeps. For the first time since my arrival in Absurdistan, the armed forces actually seemed involved in their duties, officers calmly directing the looting, jotting dollar figures upon clipboards, and shouting at their inferiors to hurry their black asses up and load the fucking APCs already. A slow-motion military retreat seemed to be taking place, set to the occasional roar of GRAD missiles departing the roof of the Hyatt, followed by patches of rising gray dust and smoke at the line of the horizon. Only the KBR trucks stood silent and empty along the boulevard.

But mostly I was concerned about the gang activity. They called themselves the True Footrest Posses and they seemed to be on every street corner, hanging loosely like their Compton counterparts, some of them armed with sausage-thick Makarov pistols and AK-47s, others with rocket-propelled grenade launchers and light mortars that they listlessly dragged behind them, like some bothersome cleaning chore their parents had pressed upon them. They were kids, few over the age of consent, sunburned, depressed, malnourished, dressed in jerseys and sweatpants bearing the logos of the National Basketball Association. One had a blue Crips bandanna around his neck, another sweated terribly beneath a wool ski cap, a third had capped most of his teeth with gold and was bleeding around the gums. Almost all had ill-grown mustaches and sported pinkish sun-bleached sandals meant for some nonexistent third gender, along with buzz haircuts that spoke of either nationalism or retardation. Occasionally I would hear them rap in English about the violent, sexy life they wanted to lead in the Los Angeles metropolitan area and about what they would do to their Svanï or Sevo counterparts once their enemies were disarmed and bent over. One popular ditty I heard on the Sevo Terrace started like this:

Rollin' down Sunset
What do I see?
A bunch of hoey-ass bitches
Lookin' at me.
They got Christ's footrest all wrong
'Cause they asses are Svani.
I'm like, "Wassup, ho?"
She like, "My name is Lani."
That's an American name,
'Cause she got no pride.
Nut-draining Svani bitches,
They livin' the lie.
I line 'em up in front
O' they brothers
Put a gun to they head.
Svani bitch, you betta give it up anal
Or your brothers be dead.
The brothers cryin' like girls
While they sistas I'm fuckin'
I'm, like, slippin' and slidin'
They, like, flippin' and buckin'.

All this talk about forced anal sex worried me. This was *not* how you gained market share on MSNBC or even on the FOX network, and certainly not how you won the love of the world. It was time to take action. It was time to "talk to Israel."

And then a modern miracle happened. Nanabragov's men finally installed a high-speed Internet connection in my office. I whipped out my laptop, jammed its little dickey into a wall socket, and powered up the World Wide Web.

Reams of information eagerly floated onto my screen. Several dull websites demonstrated rather clearly what a grant proposal looked like. I learned about the soul-searching expeditions of contemporary American Jews from the banks of Poland's Vistula River to the extinguished *shtetl*s of Bessarabia. I learned about the average American Jew's curious if misplaced interest in something called "kabbalah." As for the Holocaust, few genocides were better documented. I drank some coffee, touched myself, and began my duties as the Minister of Multicultural Affairs.

35

A Modest Proposal

Project Name

The Institute for Caspian Holocaust Studies, aka the Museum of Sevo-Jewish Friendship.

Project Overview

The greatest danger facing American Jewry is our people's eventual assimilation into the welcoming American fold and our subsequent extinction as an organized community. Due to the overabundance of presentable non-Jewish partners in a country as tantalizingly diverse and half naked as America, *it is becoming difficult if not impossible to convince young Jews to engage in reproductive sex with each other.* Efforts to connect Jews of reproductive age through professional social networks and alcohol-fueled "meat markets" have had limited success. Israel, once a source of pride and inspiration, is now populated largely by an aggressive Middle Eastern people whose bizarre lifestyle is thoroughly incompatible with our own (cf. Greenblatt, Roger, "Why Does Hummus Leave a Bitter Taste in My Mouth?," *Annals of Modern Jewry,* Indiana University Press). It is time to turn to the most effective, time-tested, and target-specific arrow in our quiver—the Holocaust.

Even among the most thoroughly secular and unaffiliated young Jews, the Holocaust enjoys great name recognition. When asked to identify the following eight components central to Jewish identity— Torah, Mishnah, Talmud, Holocaust, Mikvah, Whitefish, Israel, Kabbalah—only Whitefish scored higher than Holocaust in a survey of thirty drunk Jews at a nightclub in suburban Maryland (cf. Green-blatt, Roger, "Oy! What a Feeling, I'm Jewish," *Annals of Modern Jewry*, Indiana University Press). The Holocaust, when harnessed properly as a source of guilt, shame, and victimhood, can serve as a remarkable tool for Jewish Continuity. The problem is the over-saturation of the Holocaust brand in media and academe, creating the need for a fresh, vibrant, and sexy (yes, *sexy*—let's keep our eyes on the prize) approach to the mother of all genocides.

The newly independent Sevo Republic, run under the democratic and Israel-friendly auspices of the State Committee for the Restora-tion of Order and Democracy (SCROD), is a small but attractive nation-state on the shores of the beautiful Caspian Sea. The history of Sevo-Jewish friendship runs as deep as the waters of the Caspian. Both are educated, entrepreneurial, and maligned people fighting with their much larger oxlike neighbors for their share of love, recog-nition, and adequate living space. In 1943, as Hitler's Operation Bar-barossa thundered toward the peaceful oil reserves of the Caspian, the Sevo populace began a voluntary campaign to transport the native Jewish population out of the Republic and toward safety in Stalin's Siberia. Today the country remains easily the most Jew-tolerant place on earth outside of Brookline, Massachusetts. This philo-Semitism, combined with an exotic location, the chance to enjoy the hospitality of a righteous people (finally an entire nation of *tzadikim*), and the opportunities of a temperate, beach-filled landscape most reminis-cent of Cancún, Mexico (only cheaper, much cheaper), creates the perfect environment for an education-based initiative that is a world apart from the hackneyed death marches of Auschwitz-Birkenau and Yad Vashem.

Methodology
A Striking Architectural Design

Some of the world's most remarkable recent architecture has been built in commemoration of the Holocaust, but much of it is too ab-stract and cerebral to inspire immediate Continuity in the loins of a frigid Jewish woman in her thirties. The Institute for Caspian Holo-caust Studies will take the shape of a giant broken matzoh, in reference to the tragedy that befell our people and as a reminder of the Passover meal, which, among all the traumas of a Jewish upbringing, consistently rates as the "least scarring" (cf. Greenblatt, Roger, "Why on This Night of All Nights Do I Take Only *One* Milligram of Lorazepam?," *Annals of Modern Jewry,* Indiana University Press). The main exhibition space of the broken matzoh will lead to a titanium-clad lamb shank (hint: Frank Gehry) symbolizing both the forearm of the Almighty and our own newly found brute strength.

The New Tribalism

Identity politics are a great boon to our quest for Continuity. Identity is born almost exclusively out of a nation's travails. For us— a prosperous, unmolested people safely nuzzled in the arms of the world's last superpower (as of this writing, anyway)—this means Holocaust, Holocaust, Holocaust. The twin halves of broken matzoh will be infused with the spirit of the New Tribalism that is captivating young people across the Western world as an angry response to global homogenization. The first half will show the past travails of the Jewish people (a parallel series of walk-in closets will do the same for the Sevo), and the second half will show how easily we forget how much they hate us (ditto, Sevo). To be a bit reductive: first half, unpronounceable—Kristallnacht, Kindertransport, Kraków ghetto, Chernowitz, Wadowice, Drohobycz; second half, guilt-inducing— towering videos of Jewish college boys at fraternity mixers hitting up demure Korean girls, while pretty suburban Jewish *maideleh* fetishize their urbanized African American counterparts at a Smith Barney softball game. Subtext: *six million died and you're twirling around a bar stool with some* hazzar?

Holocaust for Kidz

Studies have shown that it's never too early to frighten a child with images of skeletal remains and naked women being chased by dogs across the Polish snow. Holocaust for Kidz will deliver a carefully tailored miasma of fear, rage, impotence, and guilt in children as young as ten. Through the magic of Animatronics, Claymation, and Jurassic technology, the inane ramblings of underqualified American Hebrew day school teachers on the subject of the Holocaust will be condensed into a concise forty-minute bloodbath. Young participants will leave feeling alienated and profoundly depressed, feelings that will be partly redeemed and partly thwarted by the ice-cream truck awaiting them at the end of the exhibit.

The "Think It Can't Happen Again?" Annex

Yeah, you think so? Well, think again, friend. This daring conceptual space will feature dozens of French Arab youths throwing rocks at passing museumgoers, threatening, "Six million more," while passive French intellectuals stand by in the shadows, smoking and drinking, smoking and drinking. For safety reasons, the "rocks" will be made of 100 percent recyclable paper, and the French Arab youths will be caged.

The Titanium-Clad Lamb Shank

We end the museum on a high note, celebrating the achievements of cutting-edge American Jews through life-affirming exhibits such as "David Copperfield: The Myth and the Magic" and "Onward and Sideward: The Death of Literature and the Birth of the Sitcom." A room or two can be devoted to Israeli cultural achievements. Or not.

The Tent of Consent

This is where it all comes together, where Continuity gets its capital C. Upon entering the Tent of Consent and submitting a blood sample and credit check, Jews of reproductive age (thirty-four to fifty-one) will show Hitler and his goons just where they can stick their Final Solution. Here the word "no" is not an option. Here there is no diaphragm. Note: Tent should be rugged and green to denote summertime reproduction. No circus tents! This is serious business.

And Now a Word from Our Sponsor . . .

As an opportunity to reach out to the true hellmouth of American political power, evangelical Christians will be given their own (much smaller) tent from which they can proselytize to reproductive Jews emerging all sweaty and wobbly from the Tent of Consent. We estimate only 1 to 2 percent of our most expendable stock will actually fall for this crude *goyishe* siren song. A small price to pay, and our lobbyists will thank us.

Outcomes—First Year of Operation

1) Two hundred thousand Jews will sow an additional one hundred thousand Jews on the shores of the Caspian Sea.

2) Two to four thousand lackluster Jews will become born-again Mormons (or whatever the hell) and will stop pulling the rest of us down.

3) Twenty thousand Jewish children will learn that it's somehow their fault.

36

Comidas Criollas

As I sent out my Holocaust proposal to the members of the new SCROD listserv, I was shocked to discover an electronic message from rsales@hunter.cuny.edu parked in my mailbox.

Dear Misha,

Whats up Pa? House it going where you at?

I know I'm probably not your favorite person right now but I dont know who else to turn too. Proffessor Shteynfarb left me. He won a scolarship in South Of France and he just up and left in the middle of the semester. I sent him an email but he never wrote back and then I call his publisher and this really obnoxous bitch told me that their not doing the Anthology of Immigrant Writing any more either.

I think I may be Pregnant from Proffessor Shteynfarb. I'm pretty sure I am because I vomited up. But whats worse is how hard I worked on that essay about how they set our building on fire in morrisania and now no one will read it or care about how I felt growing up. I thought I was Different and had a Special Story to tell but I guess I'm not and I dont. Honest that hurts me more than even the fire and the Pregnancy because for a second there I had Hope my life would be differrent.

Your probably saying ha ha, I told you so. Dont denie it! But I know you always had Hope for things too. And I know I was one of your Hopes and I let you down. Your probably already seeing somebody new by now so it looks like I'll get my Pay Back.

Anyway I dont know what to do about the baby and I guess I should

have it because its a Sin otherwise. I wish you were here Misha. I wish
none of this had ever happened. If you still love me even just a little bit
please tell me because it would mean a lot right now.

Hugs & Kisses,
Rouenna

P.S. I know your safe because you get through everything okay. Your
smarter than you think.

P.S.S. I got the last tuition check, thank you. I am going to study
extra hard now to become an amazing admin assistant.

P.S.S.S. I'm gonna do laundry in a minute and I aint wearing
nothing!

I don't usually feel revulsion (everything in my world is kind of re-
volting in its own way), but Rouenna's message brought me to the
brink. A lifetime on the streets of the Bronx, and after all that pain
and horseshit, she gets pregnant by Jerry fucking Shteynfarb. Who
the hell had sex with a Russian writer without using a condom? What
was she thinking? But in the end I couldn't help myself: I felt sorry
for her. For the sad goateed presence in her belly, yes, but mostly for
the beaten-down tone, the way she had been stripped of everything
vital in just under two months. What could I tell her? Was it still my
duty to comfort her? I responded with two messages. First:

Rouenna, I think it's time to stop calling Jerry "Professor
Shteynfarb."

And then:

You should go see a doctor first thing in the morning, and if you are
pregnant then you should get an abortion as soon as possible. I don't
care what your abuela Maria says, you are not ready to have a child
without a father.

I looked out the window of my office. It was raining for the first
time in days. With the loathsome sun finally extinguished, the city appeared nearly as glamorous as Hong Kong, its shortish row of sky-

scrapers rising above an anthill of government buildings, its port studded with idled cargo containers. Only the oil fields filling the bay, their singular ghostly luminosity, reminded me of my location.

But I wasn't there.

I was on that stretch of East Tremont Avenue in the Bronx, *our stretch,* which starts from the El Batey Restaurant near Marmion Avenue and then swelters down to the Blimpie franchise on Hughes, where, back in '98, Rouenna's favorite cousin was busted by the cops for some complicated, non-sandwich-related offense.

East Tremont Avenue, solid purveyor of attainable dreams, where stores will sell you *todo para* 99¢ *y menos,* 79¢ gets you a whole chicken at Fine Fare, and $79 will land you a flowery upright mattress with a "five-year warrenty"; where a 325-pound Russian man with a hot *mamita* on his arm is respected and accepted by all; where dudes wheeling by on bicycles and young mothers languidly window-shopping at She-She Juniors & Ladies will subject me to the same breathless local query: "Yo, Misha, ¿qué ongo, a-ai?"

At El Batey Restaurant, specializing in *comidas criollas,* the phallic jukebox is playing a phallic song, and everyone has their attention fixed on each other's asses, and Rouenna is gossiping with some friend about which of the waitresses is pregnant and whose boyfrien' has just been sent upstate for ten years, but all I can see in front of me is a plate of glistening limes, a little red prick of Tabasco sauce, and a bottle of Presidente beer, the top of which comes perfectly wrapped in a sweaty napkin—the small pleasures of a beleaguered world. And I'm waiting, waiting, waiting for the metal pot filled with *asopao de camarones,* or "soupy shrimps," as the menu calls them, waiting to surrender to *ajillo,* for there is more garlic in the pot than water or rice or shrimp even. And soon I am filled with cold Presidente, hot Tabasco, and the basso profundo reverberations of garlic in my *estómago.* I rise from my chair, grab the gossiping Rouenna, and carry her to the impromptu dance floor in back, beneath the television set perpetually tuned to the exploits of the local baseball team, the *Jankees.* We try to dance, the slowest dance in history, but mostly we just stand there and stare at each other, making little animal noises, the purrs of set-upon cats, the steady whine of basset hounds, which the jukebox all but drowns out with its thick salsa beats. And we kiss. Garlic and sweat and pure love, we kiss.

I'm a little drunk as Rouenna helps me back to her place on 173rd Street and Vyse, past the senior-citizen troublemaker in the Chicago Bulls wife-beater who always threatens to kill Mister Softee, the rather innocuous mobile ice-cream vendor, and past the Jehovah's Witnesses Hall, now being reverently approached by women with tinfoil-covered platters of pigeon peas and rice. There's a wedding on, and Rouenna winks at me, meaning *When, already?*, and she smiles at me with just the hint of gentle mockery that I've always appreciated, that in and of itself manages to reduce me a little, manages to cut out the shrimp and rice and boil me down to my essential desires—a girl, a city, a libertine but tender way of life.

I thought I was Differrent and had a Special Story to tell but I guess I'm not and I dont.

Oh, my poor sweet baby.

37

The End

I found myself at a party at Nana's house. With drugs, no less. A cauldron of black infinity smelling like the back of a public bus. This was *lanza*, the local drug that had inspired Saint Sevo the Liberator to his visions of Sevo brotherhood and Svanï annihilation, the trip that launched a thousand trips, mostly to the grave.

We were in Nana's bedroom, sitting around the cauldron, which was perched atop a hot pot, waiting for the miniature shrubs to boil over so that we could all breathe in the fumes. When a thin mist appeared, I started inhaling with gusto. I was trying to forget the electronic message I had just received from Alyosha-Bob, telling me to stay the hell away from the Nanabragov family and to get out of Absurdistan *now*. A disaster was imminent, according to him. I decided not to worry myself too much. One of the teenage True Footrest Posses had just plundered the Emporio Armani. How much worse could things get?

Nana had invited her best friend, Sissey, who had recently watched us make love, and Anna, the mediocre Russian blonde who worked at the American Express office. The girls were in a brilliant mood. They were doing their best Gorbigrad accents, pretending they were hookers trying to pick up KBR workers at the Hyatt's Beluga Bar. "Golly Burton! Golly Burton!" they hooted. "You buy me Coke! You have lucky lady back home? I better. I wear thong-*g-g*. Thong-*g-g*. I wear thong-*g-g*. Up my ass I have thong-*g-g*."

I tried to imitate a swashbuckling American oilman. "Up your ass?" I said. "I know somethin' else I can put up there!"

The girls exploded with mirth. They lifted their legs in the air like dying bugs and convulsed rhythmically. As they were all lying on the same bed, opposite the one that supported me, I could see *their* young asses, all in jeans, forming a tight row: in this pantheon, Nana's was the biggest, spilling over and beyond the Miss Sixty label, then came that of her dark-haired friend Sissey, with a passable half-moon, then the pert, tiny cantaloupe of the Russian's behind. "Fat Uncle on the bed," Sissey shouted to me. "Fat Uncle on the bed! Come on over and visit us, Fat Uncle!"

I rolled right over and into their waiting arms, and they grasped me the way young girls tackle a puppy. "Fat Uncle loves you," I croaked, and we all started giggling. I eased into the mass around me; there were breasts and a piece of earlobe, not Nana's. We breathed in and out together. The breasts were warm and the earlobe needed sucking. It struck me: we were high.

The idyll was interrupted by a knocking. I looked up. Faik the manservant had pressed his ugly mug to the windowpane. "Oh, go give him some money," Nana said.

It was a terrible imposition, and yet I could hardly care less. Doing one thing was as good as doing another. I decided to put on my legs, but they were already attached, rather roundly, to my thighs. Now it was time for my feet. There they were! "There's a lucky break," I said. "I have two feets and two leggies." The girls started giggling once more, their laughter dissipating into breathy French sentences that I could not understand.

Man, was I high.

Outside, Faik was perched on a unicycle. A tuba was attached to the handlebars in place of a horn, and his sailor's cut had given way to a spotted leopard's scalp. In fact, he may have been a leopard-man of sorts, Faik. Who knows with the Moslems—they really are different from us. "I saw you and Nana and Sissey and the Russian girl, and you were all touching each other," he said.

"Oh, God," I said, "you're right. We *were* touching each other. Ears and breasts. It was so loving and tender. I wish the rest of this fucking country were more like that. Those girls are just so great. You're so great, Faik. Yes, you are. A great, *great* leopard."

"I want three hundred dollars," Faik said.

"See, that's great, too," I said, ladling out the money. "Other people would have asked for four hundred."

"Are you drunk?" Faik asked. "Did you and the girls smoke *lanza*? Then I want another hundred dollars."

"That's absolutely fair," I said in English. "I can do business with a leopard-man like you."

I noticed, in a kind of roundabout way, that I was losing verticality. "Are you following me?" Faik said. I looked around. I had apparently walked him down the stairs and into the inner courtyard.

"Oh," I said. There was a palm tree and a plane tree in the courtyard. Which tree would win in a race? I wished I were an environmentalist. "Hey, Faik," I shouted, but he was quickly pedaling away on his unicycle. "Where are the girls? I want to go back to the girls. Where are you going, you leopard? Take me with you!"

"Wow," I said to myself. "This is turning into one Sergeant Pepper's kind of day." I whistled a few bars of "Lovely Rita." Maybe I was back in the States already, but this time armed with a journalist's visa. Now I just needed to write everything down and file my story before the deadline. "I wonder where the grown-ups are, anyway?" I said to the palm tree. "You can talk to me. I won't use your real name."

The palm tree wasn't talking. Probably protecting the plane tree. "I want girls," I said, and with the fair sex in mind, I started knocking on the heavy wooden doors around the courtyard. No one answered. I walked into one of the rooms and saw a dying middle-aged woman spread out over a golden duvet. It was my mother. "Oh, poor girl," I said. "Poor girl." I couldn't believe I was calling my mother a girl, but there it was, the feeling that she was younger than me and in need of my help. I cradled her face, trying to make out the familiar features, but her entire head was covered by a giant tube sock, two blue stripes around where her mouth should have been. "Good," I said. "You got the American socks. The search is over." My mother put her cool white fingers between my neck folds and made a quizzical sound through the tube sock. "Last eighteen years?" I said. "Many things happened. First, communism died. Then Papa got rich. We went to the Alps. I got circumcised something bad. Then they put Papa into the ground. A pretty Jewess brought gardenias. Then I ended up here." The alabaster hand wiped my mouth and skirted the edges of my lonely nose. A gust of sock air emerged out of my mother's neck and formed a series of inverted Cyrillic letters, like when Americans try to learn Russian. "What?" I said. "Sure, I've got a girl, but she's nothing like you, Mommy. I mean, it's like you always said: you get what you pay for."

My mother snorted her assent. I tried to cradle her head in my hands, remembering how, as a five-year-old, I used to braid her hair while she napped, trying to make her look like a little girl whom I could cuddle and kiss with impunity. I noticed that her smells had changed, that there was a lustier, dirtier aroma about her: the scent of an unclean kitchen. And it wasn't a tube sock over her face, but rather an onion skin, beneath which an alien face hissed and contorted. She started speaking in a coarse Southern tongue. A thin ribbon of hate flitted through my heart. *Why didn't you protect me from him?* The frying pan! Nothing made sense. *Why did you feed me so much?* Bowls of condensed milk for breakfast, midnight snacks of raw pig fat spread over black bread, cold veal and mayonnaise salads in the hot afternoons, poppy seed cakes crowned with clotted cream, rounds of cervelat smoked sausage and cheese squares atop slices of butter as thick as my thumbs. *Why did you let me get so fat, Mommy? So that he wouldn't roll around with me anymore? So that he would stop loving me? I was all alone after you died.*

Saddened, I left the mysterious Mother Room. The sun burned me like an ant under a telescope. Tired of stalking the premises, I let the house do the walking—it pivoted around me, dozens of empty, sunlit rooms flashing past, until I was standing by the front gate, nudging it open with two disembodied hands. I was free!

I walked down the street. The two imbecilic boys assigned to me, Tafa and Rafa, were sitting in my Volvo station wagon soaking up precious air-conditioning. I knocked on one of the windows. "*Vy* or *ty?*" I shouted to the boys. "Polite or familiar? Ach, I ought to knock your heads together." To my surprise, my adjutants actually did have hairy brown coconuts on their shoulders. "I ought to buy

myself a hovercraft," I opined to them rather loudly. "New technology. Gonna invest in."

The road followed a curvy downward path toward the sea, past the
pretty Sevo houses with their carved balconies, their overgrown front
gardens rustling with barberry shrubs and creamy milk flowers. I
caught sight of a broken rosebush peering out of a chain-link fence
and was swiftly dispossessed of all my fundamental worries. "It's like
being back in Yalta," I shouted. "With my *mamochka*!" The winds of
that particular resort town, with their Chekhovian overtones, side-
swiped my ass. I hopped and skipped down the road (not really possible, but so it seemed at the time) until I found myself at a kind of
border crossing. Armed men in tight sweaters stitched with the word
DYNCORP were blocking the path. I imagined what it would be like
to try to tear the assault rifles out of their hands, hundreds of bullets piercing me, *ouch, ouch, ouch* a hundred times over. "Watchoo
doing?" I asked them.

"Protecting the neighborhood," they said in these South African–
sounding accents. "From the looters. You live here?"

"I'm Nana Nanabragovna's boyfriend."

"Really? What are you called?"

"Fat Uncle. Snack Daddy. Misha Vainberg. Call me what you like,
but please let me through."

"Be careful out there, sir. The people have lost their senses."

"That's the people for you." I pressed on toward a gallery of heat
and sound. After a few solitary meters, I was accepted into a crowd of
around a million persons gang-pressed into the dust bowl of the Sevo
Terrace. Hands burrowed into me; little hands, big hands, sea-wet
hands, sun-dried hands. Everyone was looking for my wallet but kept
coming up with my balls. "They look and feel almost alike," I hinted
to my friendly assailants. "Keep looking. Ooh, you're very warm. No,
no, no. I don't like tickling."

The crowd passed me around, squeezing and poking. *This is what
Jesus must have felt like on a good day.* I was relayed under the tentacle-
arches of the Sevo Vatican and toward the sad greenery of the waterfront. There was rumbling above us. A deep groaning sound. Then a
couple of *pop-pop-pop*s. Small-arms fire. I looked up, hoping to catch

sight of my favorite GRAD missiles. Nothing doing. The teenage members of one of the True Footrest Posses were scrambling up a hill with their mortars and surface-to-air missiles. *Good luck, kids!* I hit something hard and stony. An old woman was laid out on an enormous marble conch shell, part of some defunct art nouveau fountain. Her whole family was crying over her, children by her feet, grown-ups at the head. "Is she dead?" I asked them.

"We'll never forget her," the relatives wailed.

"Don't be so sure," I said, trying to be sympathetic. "What may seem like a terrible loss today may be just an uncomfortable memory tomorrow. She was old. Hard to carry. Use this opportunity to move to America." But after I spoke, the sobbing only increased. A fist waved through the air attached to some glandular epithets. I moved away, shaking my head. The people *had* lost their senses. It was all just jungle emotions now. They couldn't wait to start mourning one another. That was the one thing they knew backward and forward. Death from above, death from within. Tyrants and heart attacks. The three most popular words in the Russian language: "*Stalin. Gitler. Infarkt.*"

What the hell? Everyone was screaming at me now. I turned this way and that, toward the sea, away from the sea, and wherever I turned, I saw gleaming gold teeth and infected tonsils ululating in hatred and terror. "I didn't do anything," I said, looking at my feet. "Just let me be," I told them. But the screaming only grew louder. And then the deep groaning sound resumed, and I heard a steel drum played over a second-rate loudspeaker. *Pop,* someone said. *Pop pop pop. Shhhheeeeeouuuuuuu!*

I looked up. The people had put up their fists and were crouching fearfully on the ground. And then I understood. They weren't angry with me. I wasn't the problem. I looked into the people's eyes. Their eyes, it would seem, were watching God. I followed them up to the Svanï Terrace. Nothing. Then upward to the International Terrace. Nothing still. No, wait. Something. Something unusual was happening up on the International Terrace. Something not quite right but beautiful still.

The skyscrapers were dancing.

Not with each other, but with each other in mind, like flirtatious poor folk sizing up each other's hips across an equatorial dance floor. The Hyatt danced. The Radisson danced. So did Bechtel. BP was practically making a fool of itself. Only ExxonMobil stood aloof, nodding its head a fraction, tapping its feet, barely keeping up with the beat.

And then the Hyatt decided to cut loose. She—for there was a slender femininity about her—lowered her hazel eyes, ignored the spaghetti strap that had fallen promiscuously off her pretty shoulder, and then, in a move of such dazzling brilliance that the enraptured sun turned rainbow every glittering piece of her broken heart, she jumped across the sea.

38

My Mother Will Be Your Mother

Someone was fondling me, and I didn't like it at all. I turned over on one side and felt a moist clam crunch beneath me. A disgusting male mouth, all turmeric and bad teeth, was breathing down my nose. "My hand!" the mouth said. I opened my eyes to face a man I can only describe as polluted. And in pain.

"Sorry, fellow," I said. I rolled off his hand and he clutched it, crying and trying to unbend the fingers, which, in my dazed state, seemed as green and squirmy as the legs of a grasshopper. "Ooofah," I said, rubbing my eyes with my intact pale squishies. Was I still on the Sevo Terrace? What the hell had happened? The *lanza,* for one thing. And then . . . Some strange memories swished about, filling my head with vapor trails. But the trails all led to one place: to the tentacles of the Sevo Vatican unfurling outward, as if to embrace me, one orange clump of stucco in particular somersaulting toward my happy, stoned, unflinching face. I raised my hand toward the bridge of my nose and felt a dark, deep, caved-in nasal pain. A hump had swollen on one part of it, but there was also a new emptiness underneath, a concavity, making me feel, in some ways, like a gentile. I stopped playing with my nose and looked upward at the city around me.

The city was finished.

The skyscrapers of the International Terrace were still standing, but their facades had been entirely stripped of glass, leaving only the joist-and-girder skeletons underneath. In their new incarnations, the buildings looked like charred model showrooms for disposable Western furniture. The Hyatt was no longer a magical destination for the city's priciest hookers, but rather, an open-faced checkerboard of five hundred squares, each marked by an identical queen-size bed, cherry-wood dresser, and marble-topped desk. The office towers, on the other hand, were a complex geometry of scrambled workstations and blasted modular units, a dizzying white-collar crush akin to the world's most difficult flowchart. But beneath this sophistication lay a simple, exposed fact: the West, when stripped bare, was essentially a series of cheap plastic components, pneumatic work chairs, and poorly framed motivational posters. The towers that had risen over the city as a watermark of Euro-American civilization were work hives and nothing more. As quickly as they had been put together, they could be taken apart. Already, teams of adventurous local alpinists were mounting the shorn facades of the towers and hauling down flat-screen televisions and gleaming Hyatt toilet fixtures by means of an ingenious pulley system they had rigged up in a matter of hours.

Beneath the International Terrace, the Svanï Terrace had taken the brunt of the falling debris, the Moorish-style opera house covered in glistening shards of green glass and splattered dark blue by an infinity of exploding toner cartridges. Six Svanï churches had been set on fire and were smoldering evenly across the terrace like the smoke-stacks of some previously undiscovered industry. On the Sevo Terrace, the dome of the Sevo Vatican resembled an egg cracked down the middle by means of the world's heaviest spoon. The tentacled columns had crumbled entirely; from this day forward, the church's storied octopus shape would exist only on the pages of Soviet-era guidebooks and the reverse side of the hundred-absurdi (US$.001) note.

I got up and walked toward the waterfront, thinking, improbably, of washing the blood from my face amid the oily swirls of the Caspian. I moved along carefully, for there were people everywhere in various stages of injury and distress. I didn't know it yet, but the Hyatt and the office buildings had been evacuated completely before being hit by an afternoon's worth of rocket-propelled grenades and artillery shells. Most of the casualties were Gorbigrad and country-side refugees trying to take shelter in the terraces below. I avoided the eyes of the gently rocking citizens still crouching instinctively on the ground. The scene around me had reached a perfectly abject equilibrium among those quietly bleeding to death and those stumbling ahead looking for water and some trace of authority.

I walked toward the docks, the sun either setting or rising over the oil fields, it was impossible to grasp which. A woman in her forties approached me. She had gold teeth and a clean Russian accent. "How do we get out of this circle?" the woman asked, her tone as soft and ponderous as the big bosom that she proudly held aloft. "This karma that's been dealt to us?"

"Good question," I said, looking up at the high-rise remains of the International Terrace. I didn't want to mention the fact that I never really believed in karma, that I thought most events were simply the outcomes of discrete actions taken by individuals, corporate entities, and nation-states. But how do you say that to a common person without sounding like a wisenheimer?

The woman followed my gaze up to the rump of the defunct Daewoo Building. "Oh, those," she said. "I don't really care what happens to the foreigners. Our lives will be hell with or without them. Do you want to hear my story?"

"Um," I said. I was coming off my *lanza* high, and I wanted to get right back on.

"Don't worry, it's a short story. I can tell that you are an important man and that you are expected all over town. Generally speaking, I earned thirty dollars a month working for the railways ministry. Until the trains stopped running. Then my son got drafted into the Sevo forces before he could take his *magister* exams. And we're ethnic Russians. What do we care who wins, the Sevo or the Svanï? And then my husband left me. I want to marry again, but there are no more normal men left. If you know of a good man, please tell me." She looked up and down my well-fed profile and brushed her sparse reddish hair back seductively. Did she consider me a good man? Given her circumstances, maybe I was. I tried, as a common courtesy, to picture her with her skirt hiked up to her waist while I took her from behind, but nothing was registering. Where was my Nana, anyway? Safe at home, I assumed. Surrounded by armed men.

A little girl ran up to us and clutched at the woman's leg. She was of that age when all children get to look sleek and confident, a tanned summertime face and a bun of straw hair held back by a bonnet, and yet there was something mousy and unkind in her smile. I noticed that her feet were dirty and unshod. "Where are your sandals, dear?" I murmured. "There's broken glass everywhere."

The woman started whispering violently into the girl's ear. "Talk nicely," she said. "Talk intelligently to the good man. Don't be a stupid little one. Don't make things up."

The girl turned away from me and shook her head. She buried her face in her elbow and made some indecent noises. "What a cute one," I said. "What's the matter? You don't want to talk to your Fat Uncle? Well, don't be scared. The war will be over soon, and then we'll all go home and play with our kittens."

The woman gave the child a nasty bump forward with her knee. "Yulia, talk to the nice man!" she commanded. "Children are difficult," she said to me, "but at least you can teach them things. She's my youngest. Five years old. She's a bit slow. My two sons, now, they're a real treasure. One has a bronze medal in school, and the other is clever like an oligarch."

"I know a fairy tale," the girl said in her syrupy little girl's voice. "It's about a fishee that gets caught in the sea and then the fisherman plucks the fishee's eyes out so she can't swim back, and then he cuts her stomach open to take out the caviar—"

The mother reached down and swatted the girl's tender neck. "That's a stupid story," the mother said. The girl did not cry out. She merely touched her neck and whispered, "Didn't hurt at all."

"Listen," the mother said. "You're a nice man. Too nice to be talking to us, or to such a stupid girl with her ugly stories. My boys are starving. If you give me fifty dollars, we can go beneath the docks, all three of us. I know a little space where no one can see us. You can do whatever you want."

"What?" I said.

My body floated up, like a balloon, like a Walloon or what have you. I was gone from this place; I was in New York, with Nana, on a park bench. The sun was setting. A day of commerce was at an end.

I could smell frankfurters and homeless men. I could smell myself on Nana's smooth brown hand.

"What?" the woman repeated, as if mocking me.

"What are you saying?" I said.

"Just that if you wanted to," the woman said evenly, "if you had the money, we could go beneath the docks. All of us, or just you and Yulia. It would take fifty dollars, and we wouldn't ask any questions."

I swung at her. I had no plan of attack, but almost immediately, my fist found its way inside her mouth and was working to dislodge those hideous golden incisors. To no avail. She bit down on me, but there was no blood. Neither of us screamed. I breathed out the word "bitch" but heard only its stinging falsity. I raised my other hand, trembling, into the air, as if I were an A student trying to draw the teacher's attention. I formed a second fist and brought it down on the woman's head, co-opting all the weight at my disposal. The woman crumpled. She just lay there on the broken, glass-strewn concrete, shaking feverishly and trying to mouth a single word, which may have been "police."

As if there were any police left.

My ankle throbbed. Yulia, the little girl, was biting me, digging her nails into my flesh. At first I didn't shake her off. I stood there and let the pain accumulate, willing it to shock me into action, into a new state of resolve. But the little girl couldn't do it. She had neither the strength nor the sharp teeth to change me, to make me see differently. I turned around and started to walk away, loosening her grip on me with each hard-won step, dragging her silently across the concrete and broken glass. "Papa," I heard her cry after she had finally fallen off my ankle. I didn't look back.

I wanted to go back to my bed in the Hyatt. I wanted to take a long bath in the Roman tub. I wanted my allergy-free pillow and a mindful note from Larry Zartarian by my bedside. The farther I walked away from the pier, the more I hated the little girl. A part of me—a hideous part, to be sure—wished I had punched her instead of her mother. Wished I had killed her. A brick to that mousy smile, to all our mousy smiles. *Let us all die,* I thought. *Let this planet be free of*

us. And then, a hundred years later, let the resurgent earth sprout wispy
dandelions and delicate hamsters and five-star hotels. Nothing will ever
come of the human race. Nothing will ever come of this land.

I was walking, or so it seemed, toward the International Terrace, toward the 718 perfume store, and toward the Hyatt—but
those three things existed only in a very abstract sense. I was walking
toward the ideal of the Hyatt. Toward the memory of a 718 perfume
store. Toward the faint outcropping of the burnt-out International
Terrace. What I was really doing was walking away from the girl,
whose screams for Papa followed me down a road stained with the
blood of others.

"Friend," a voice called out to me. "Friend, where are you going?"
A spry old man, an amiable clown, was running alongside me, his feet
barely keeping up with my long, desperate strides.

"To the Hyatt," I said.

"It's gone," said the old man. "The Svanï bombed it. Tell me,
friend, who are you by nationality?"

I told him. Out of the corner of my eye, I saw the man crossing
himself. "Some of the best people in the world are Jews," he told me.
"My mother will be your mother, and there will always be water in
my well to drink."

I continued staring ahead, walking briskly, and trying to recapture
my solitude. Everyone talked too much here. No one left you alone.
What if I didn't want the man's mother? What kind of stupid imposition was this ritualized mother-swapping?

We walked for a while without a word between us. And then the
man took several authoritative steps that were actually the prelude to
a halt. Without knowing why, solely through the power of his suggestion, I lingered as well. I looked into his face. He wasn't old at all.
The thick zipperlike creases forming an odd parallelogram across his
face were the strokes of a large knife wielded with impunity. His nose
had absorbed so many uppercuts that it had taken on the retroussé
shape of a New England debutante's. And his eyes—his eyes were
gone, replaced by small black cylinders that could see only the target
in front of them, the pupils reflecting but one frightening idea

trapped in a single cone of light. "Let me shake your hand," the man said as he took hold of my limp arm and squeezed. "No, not like that. The way real brothers shake it."

I did my best, but the air had gone out of me. His fingers were covered by a jumble of numerical tattoos, testifying to a life spent in Soviet prisons. "Yes, I've been to jail," he said, noticing my gaze, "but not for thieving or killing. I'm an honest man. You don't believe me?"

"I believe you," I whispered.

"Any enemy of yours in Svanï City is an enemy of mine," the man said. "What did I tell you about my mother?"

"That she's my mother also," I stammered. I could feel fat bloody pain in my right hand, and the world tilted toward the left, as if to compensate. If I was going to die, I wanted my Rouenna near me.

"My mother . . . no, *our* mother is in the hospital—" the man started.

"What do you want?" I whispered.

"Just hear me out," the man said. "I could have done wrong by you. I could have called my friends who are waiting around the corner with their *kinjals*. Just like this one." He turned his torso to let me see the glint of the short Caucasian dagger glowing dully in its wilted leather scabbard. "But I didn't."

"I'm the Sevo Minister of Multicultural Affairs," I sobbed, feeling the weight of humiliation settle around my shoulders, cloaking me as it had never done before. "I run a children's charity called Misha's Children. Won't you please let go of my hand?"

"Our mother is in the hospital," the man repeated, tightening the grip around my big, squishy hand as my vision turned a new shade of purple. "Are you so heartless that you won't help her? Do I really have to take out my *kinjal* and slice your stomach open?"

"Dear God, no!" I cried. "Here! Here! Take my money! Take whatever you need!"

But in the single opportune moment when he let go of my hand so that it could find my bulging wallet, I felt the fear fall away and the humiliation lift. It wasn't the money. No, it wasn't the money at all.

But after thirty years with my head on the scaffold, after thirty years of cheering on the executioner, after thirty years of wearing his stifling black hood, one thing was certain: I no longer feared the ax.

"Fuck your mother!" I said. "I hope she dies."

And then I ran.

I ran with such speed that people, or what remained of people, silently fell away before me, as if I had been expected all along, like mortar rounds and destitution. I collided with burning cars and burning mules, and I felt the smoky air dissipate around me, creating the conditions for my salvation. For I wanted, more than anything, to be saved. To live and also to take vengeance for my life. To shed my weight and to be born anew.

I ran and ran, my heart and lungs barely keeping up with the ridiculous imposition of such motion. I ran past an overturned T-72 tank propped up on its own barrel and a burnt-out chess school featuring a mosaic of children playing around an elderly master, pink dots delineating their rosy cheeks. As I looked behind me to see if the man with the dagger was still on my heels (he was not), I stumbled over something, a twisted shape with what looked like a charred paw sticking up from its torso, a pool of blood radiating in one direction like a badly drawn arrow. "Poor puppy," I whispered, daring myself to take a closer look at the animal.

Right away I was heaving over the red earth and chopped concrete.

It wasn't a puppy at all.

I backed away from the little corpse. And then I noticed the familiar socialist edifice beneath which I had chosen to stumble.

I walked into the moldy temple of the local Intourist Hotel, one of the concrete monstrosities where foreigners had been lightened of their hard currency during Soviet times. A dusty painting showed Lenin cheerfully disembarking at Finland Station, beneath which a banner warned in English: NO CREDIT CARDS. NO OUTSIDE PROSTITUTES, ONLY HOTEL PROSTITUTES. NO EXCEPTIONS.

A *babushka* was weeping into her scarf at the reception desk, something about her poor dead Grisha. "I want a room," I said.

The woman wiped her eyes. "Two hundred dollars for the deluxe suite," she said. "And there's a whore already waiting for you."

"I don't want any whore," I mumbled. "I just want to be alone."

"Then it's three hundred dollars."

"It's more *without* the whore?"

"Sure," the old lady said. "Now I got to find her a place to sleep."

39

Living in Shit

I spent the next two weeks and US$42,500 at the Intourist Hotel. Each day the price of my so-called deluxe suite would go up by 50 percent (my last night alone added up to US$14,000), while two additional refugees would be pressed into my damp bicameral digs. What could one do? Outside the hotel, the situation—as it was still called—grew more absurd by the hour; gunshots and mortar rounds rhymed with my snoring at night and cleaved the daytime into shooting and nonshooting hours, the latter coinciding roughly with dinner and lunch. The only reason the Intourist Hotel remained unscathed (and insanely expensive) was the fact that nearly everyone shooting had a relative cowering between its thick concrete walls.

The first to show up were Larry Zartarian and his mother. The old lady in charge of our floor—black socks up to the calf, followed by a bouquet of varicose veins—positioned the Mother and Child in the living room. When the Zartarians' historical enemy, a stray Turkish oil executive with vast sums of cash, arrived, they were slotted directly beneath my bed. At night I could hear the mother cursing her progeny in some difficult language, while Larry tearfully rocked himself to sleep, his big head sending shock waves through the mattress springs.

Timofey had the second bed in the room, a wet moldy pillow and a sheet made of wrinkled cardboard, but was soon forced to share it with Monsieur Lefèvre, the Belgian diplomat who had granted me my European passport, and Misha, his McDonald's concubine. The two tried to have sex next to Timofey, but my moralistic manservant punched them both in the face and they bled silently onto the bedspread. Lefèvre, upon seeing my bulk spilling over the tiny Soviet bed so that each leg and arm hung suspended like a ham at a Castilian tapas bar, started laughing with every atom of his marinated red face. But the joke was on him several days later, when he committed suicide in our bathroom.

Meanwhile, well-connected Absurdis who lacked secure housing in the capital were settling the living room and threatening to burst into our private chambers as well. Uncultured and rich, dressed like flamingos on parade, they reminded me of the first Absurdis I had seen pushing their way onto the Austrian Airlines jet what seemed like a lifetime ago. Among them, they had several swaddled, dark-lipped children who teethed day and night but remained oddly quiet and mesmerized by the RPGs puncturing holes in nearby buildings with the roar of perfectly calibrated thunder. Three times a day, the ugly hotel whore—dressed every bit as piquantly as the other female occupants of our suite—made her rounds. In deference to the children, a towel was draped between two glass-covered bureaus (each containing a corroded silver bowl with the insignia of the 1980 Moscow Olympics), so that whoever was interested could squat with the whore in measured privacy. The lovemaking sounds, however, were not easy on the ears, as if the principals were making a baby out of clay. "This is how we used to live in our communal apartment when Brezhnev was still in charge," Timofey noted nostalgically.

The whore came and went, but I was not horny. Or hungry. Or anything. From the first day—when the hot-water tap came off in my hand, releasing, instead of water, a spray of frightened baby roaches— I had been completely disinvested in my own existence. Everything was happening to others: to Timofey, to the whore, to the ego-fucked Larry Zartarian and his many-moled mama. "Others suffer, but does Vainberg suffer?" I asked Malik, the mysterious green spider who lived in the corner of my bedroom and whose eight silky legs terrorized Mrs. Zartarian throughout the night. The arthropod had little to say.

As for sustenance, one could still eat well in Svanï City, despite the complete collapse of everything. A shy little Moslem boy brought in sesame seeds and hunks of black bread and threatened us with a blade if we didn't pay. Every morning Timofey crawled out of our room, ran through the gunfire, and brought back yellowish eggs just released from some contraband chicken, and creamy Russian ice-cream bars with the White Nights logo, which made me wistful for my pastel-hued St. Leninsburg, the city I had fled only two months ago, hoping never to return.

But I couldn't bring myself to eat. To do so would have required the eventual use of the toilet, a greenish husk rising out of the cracked bathroom floor, the seat of which was home to enterprising mosslike bacteria that were trying to survive the attack of hungry roaches and the daily slap of a hundred round Absurdi bottoms. Like the toilet bacteria, I, too, had my natural enemies. My former Volvo drivers, Tafa and Rafa, had discovered my presence at the Intourist, and one bloody Sunday, when all my roommates had gone to forage for food, they woke me up to a volley of kicks aimed at my stomach and face. "*Vy* or *ty*?" the teenagers were shouting. "Polite or familiar? Who's uncultured now, bitch?"

I grunted, more from being roused out of a rare slumber than from any actual pain. My stomach had been receding of late but could still take an assault by a pair of skinny brown feet in cheap flip-flops. "Polite," I lowed. "You should always use the polite form of address with your betters."

Predictably, the next kick worked its way right into my mouth, which quickly filled with the taste of metal and nutrients. "Baargh," I spat. "Not the mouth! Oh, you ruffians."

I would have come to a bad end if Timofey hadn't shown up with a Daewoo ink-jet printer he had stolen somewhere. Centimeter for centimeter, the device was a perfect match for Tafa's (or Rafa's) head, which cracked (informally, I should say) beneath it. After his companion fled, Timofey sat down to nurse my poor mouth.

While he ministered to me, I stroked my manservant's balding head, the kindest thing I had ever done for him. "You stiw wike me, don't you?" I said to Timofey through a slightly remodeled row of front teeth.

"When my master is down, I only love him more," Timofey said, dabbing and bandaging.

"What a kind Wussian soul you have," I said. I thought of Faik, the Nanabragovs' Moslem manservant. "These Southern types are weally woothless," I said. "You awen't woothless at all, huh, Tima?"

"I try to live like it says in the Bible," my manservant told me. "Other than that, I don't really know."

"Intwesting," I said. I realized I knew next to nothing about my manservant, despite two years of having him clothe and feed me every day. (He had been a homecoming present from Beloved Papa.) What was wrong with me? Suddenly I was overcome by a surge of universal man-love. "Why don't you tell me ewything about yo wife fwom the beginning," I said. "Fwom when you wuh just a wittle wad."

Timofey reddened. "There's nothing to tell, really," he said. His Polish polyester sport jacket was missing half a lapel and had been stained by a bowl of tomato soup. I resolved to buy him a brilliant suit at the earliest possible date.

"Oh, pwease," I said. "I'm cuwious."

"What's to say?" Timofey said. "I was born in Bryansk Province, village of Zakabyakino, in 1943. My father, Matvei Petrovich, died in a tank battle with the fascists under Kursk in the same year. In 1945 my mother, Aleluya Sergeyevna, contracted tuberculosis and soon met her end. I was moved to my aunt Anya's house. She was nice to me, but she died of an untreatable case of shingles in 1949, and my uncle Seryozha beat me until 1954. Then he died from drink, and I was sent to an orphanage in the city of Bryansk, province of Bryansk. I was beaten there, too. In 1960 I sinned terribly and murdered a man with my bare hands after drinking. I was sent to a labor camp in the Solovki Islands from 1960 to 1972. There a warden was kind to me and found me a job in a town in Karelia in the cafeteria of the executive committee of the local Communist Party. My life was happy until 1991. I had my son, Slava, and we played soccer and *gorodki*. I continued to drink and was hospitalized. After communism, I lost my job but discovered God Almighty. I stopped drinking. In 1992 the party cafeteria became an expensive gym, but I had a spare key and slept beneath the basement in a warm ditch. Your father found me in 1997. He told me he was happy to see such a sober Russian face. In 1998 he took me home with him. And so this is my story."

Timofey had clearly become tired after giving the longest speech of his life. I, too, felt woozy from the mouth pain and from the sharp pangs of incredulous love. He leaned his head on the pillow, while I leaned mine against the hard, bitter-smelling half-lapel of his Polish sport jacket, and in this way we went to sleep.

40

Talking to Israel

September came, and with it my Nana bearing apologies. "Where the hell have you been?" I scolded her. "I was frightened to death for you."

According to Nana, the Nanabragov manse was filled top to bottom with relatives and fellow clansmen fleeing the countryside, leaving no room for me and my manservant. Mr. Nanabragov had told her that once we were married, I would be entitled to take up residence with them, but at this stage the actual Nanabragov family took precedence. "Oh, my poor Misha," she cried, throwing her hands around my neck. "Yew," she said. "You smell like you work at the enamel factory."

"There is no hot water, and roaches live in the showerhead," I explained to her, working my wounded mouth around the r's and the single l.

"And you've lost so much weight," Nana said, feeling up my new fat-free pouches and the nascent outlines of actual body parts—one stomach, individualized compartments for lungs and a heart, the ironwork of ribs coming to the foreground. Despite the escalation of hostilities, Nana herself was as thick and glossy as an otter.

"Do you like my new skinny look?" I asked, rubbing my hands all over her booming chest, my toes curling from excitement, as I made a mental note to commence masturbation the moment she left. "I'm like that famous actor. Something-von-something."

"To be honest, I liked you better when you were a big prime rib," Nana said. "Fat is the new look for guys."

"No limits," I said.

"Uh-huh." She reached over and cupped my genitals. I cried out in happiness, but an elderly snort brought me short.

"We mustn't," I said. "The Hyatt manager and his mother are under my bed."

"Oh," Nana whispered. "How disgusting. Listen, Misha, my father would like to talk to you. He eats a long lunch at the Lady with Lapdog every single day. My mother says he no longer loves us."

"Is it safe for him to be out there?" I asked. "What about the war?"

"He's got a whole new posse to protect him," Nana said, tapping at my privates with an index finger while I impotently flared my hips at her. "But listen, Misha. No matter what he says to you, remember—we have to get out of this place. I'm already missing a whole semester at NYU. How's that going to look on my transcript?" She leaned in closer to make sure the somnolent Zartarians couldn't overhear. She had eaten mutton kebabs for lunch, mutton kebabs with the gristle still on, dunked into a dish of dill yogurt sauce. "I know a way out of Absurdistan," she whispered. "American Express is gonna start running that luxury train to the border again. Now go to the Lady with Lapdog and talk to my father. Tell him 'Goodbye, already.' Tell him 'We're out of here.' "

From a chink in the cardboard blocking my hotel window, I watched her squeeze in behind the wheel of her American Express–flagged Navigator (the passenger seat had been taken up by a man in a fine V-neck, hunched over a Kalashnikov) and speed off toward the part of the Sevo Terrace that best resembled Santa Monica. She was so beautiful when in motion, tough and bejeweled like a poor Mediterranean woman just come into money. I had been angry at her for neglecting me, yet every time I saw her, I fell in love again. The air around me was light and feminine, filled with the promise of mango-scented moisturizers and duty-free.

I sat on the living room divan, letting a mysterious male baby-child crawl over my legs, farting profusely and making a desperate hacking sound out the other end. Better him than the roaches that used my body like a caravanserai all night. I poured myself a glass of somebody's contraband Hennessy and lit up a contraband cheroot. My hands trembled, and not only from the hunger.

I had a problem. I wanted to do right by Nana, but I didn't want to go to the pier to see Mr. Nanabragov. Don't get me wrong, it wasn't the gunfire and the mortar shelling but the prospect of seeing that little girl whose mother I had clocked, that little Yulia. Did I do right by leaving her with her momma? Should I have taken her with me? Are we best off with abusive parents or no parents at all? Some days, I tell you, I just want to break this world in two.

The baby-child quietly choking on my lap was starting to smell unnaturally, and my lap wasn't doing any better. I stole some perfume from one of the sleeping Absurdi dames and, thus scented, walked out into the sunshine.

A pall had settled over the city. Looking up, one could discern a scrim of dust particles above the ravages of the International Terrace. This dust, which one hoped would have deflected the sun, instead locked in its heat so that the atmosphere sizzled with instant brush fires, magenta oil slicks, and the deep blue waft of office chemicals. The air was so alive and full of instantaneous reactions that the city's remaining citizens looked beaten and lost by comparison. A few of the more active men crawled out of the rubble and offered me packs of Russian cigarettes for US$10 apiece. "Not a smoker," I let them down gently.

The rest of the populace was too tired to shoot at me, too tired even to acknowledge such a large presence among them. For the first time since my arrival in Svanï City, no one appreciatively followed my stomach with their hungry eyes, no one silently congratulated me on my good fortune. Walking in this peaceful manner, I soon crossed over to the waterfront esplanade, whose grassy medians had assumed the look of an urgent Red Cross appeal. Hectares of tents made out of blue United Nations High Commissioner for Refugees tarp lined the former strolling ground; the graying grass and the sickly palm trees had been eaten by man and mule; the Turkish bumper cars had been stripped down to the chassis, their crude mechanical essence exposed.

I looked around apprehensively. Satisfied that Yulia and her dastardly mother were nowhere in sight, I walked down the pier toward the pink clamshell of the Lady with Lapdog. Mr. Nanabragov and Parka Mook were lunching beneath a faded SCROD poster that featured their faces along with the threatening tagline THE INDEPENDENCE OF THE PEOPLE WILL SOON BE REALIZED! At present, the two friends looked even more satiated than their own beaming visages above them—Mr. Nanabragov, lost in concentration, was spearing a sturgeon kebab with one fork and brandishing a green pepper with another, while the playwright dabbed his chin in a raspberry compote, his hooded eyes half closed. They were surrounded by men in black T-shirts with blue-veined biceps, their hands crisscrossed in Soviet prison tattoos. A speedboat bearing the Russian tricolor bowed and scraped along the pier, her hold being emptied of enough cigarette cartons to kill off the remaining population.

Mr. Nanabragov dropped his pickle with a twitch, ran over, and kissed me on three cheeks. He had a new nautical smell about him— sea urchin, sea damp, and sea salt—and his muscular Southern nose stabbed me in all my soft places. "Dear one, dear one," he cried. "You've spoken to my Nana. You're not upset with me for not letting you stay with us? Family comes first, no? If there were more room in my house, yes? Or if you married our Nanachka, finally, hmm?"

"I'd marry her just to get out of the Intourist," I joked.

"Would you?" Mr. Nanabragov said seriously. "We could have a small private ceremony. I suppose the political circumstances are not the best right now. But as you can see, we've regrouped a little." He pointed to the bandits chewing on toothpicks around the half-comatose figure of Parka Mook. "We're replenishing the SCROD coffers through the booming cigarette trade."

"Would you like to buy some?" a young maritime thug asked me, brandishing a carton of something called Business Class Elite, featuring an Aeroflot plane plummeting to the ground. "Eighty dollars."

"That's my future son-in-law you're talking to," Mr. Nanabragov objected. "Give it to him for forty."

"Not a smoker," I said.

"Oh," Nanabragov and his new friend sighed.

"How's the SCROD going?" I said. "Any media interest?"

"It's still very hard to convey our message to the world," Mr. Nanabragov said. "Of course, the Russians are all over us. Look at this!" From Parka Mook's lap, he snatched a week-old copy of a popular Russian newspaper called *Arguments and Facts*. Next to a picture of Putin blandly conveying displeasure to his cowering cabinet, I spotted the grainy likeness of three Ukrainian mercenaries and the former KGB agent Volodya hanging off the terrace of the Hyatt. Their snapped necks had been tied to the charred remains of four satellite dishes, their arms spread out at modest angles like the swept-back wings of an airplane. It was a lousy likeness. The poor Ukrainians appeared heavier and more menacing than they had when they were alive, and the long shot didn't capture the peasant-blue equanimity of their eyes.

"Jesus Christ," I said in English, exhausting the last thimbleful of compassion that remained.

"The Russians are threatening to bomb us for this," Mr. Nanabragov said, "as are the Ukrainians. Now, if only the *Americans* would bomb us, then we'd really be somewhere."

"What about the UN?"

"They sent over some tarps. Nothing much we can steal. Listen, Misha, you should go talk to Israel. It's time. We know exactly who you should see. There's a Mossad agent in the Intourist Hotel. He's pretending to be a Texas oilman named Jimbo Billings. Go chat him up. As your future father-in-law, I'm begging you on my knees." To the contrary, he remained standing.

"I would do anything for you, Mr. Nanabragov," I said. "Alas, I had typed up my proposal for the Museum of Sevo-Jewish Friendship on my laptop computer. I'm sure it was destroyed when the Svani bombed the Hyatt."

"Actually, we have your laptop right here," Mr. Nanabragov said, pulling the sleek gray device from under his chair. "Some of our boys paid a visit to your room after the attack. Just picking up some odds and ends."

"I'll do my best, Mr. Nanabragov," I said. "But you must know that Nana wants to leave the country. She's a young girl. She's got her NYU to consider."

"Go! Go!" Mr. Nanabragov twitched. "The SCROD first, and then our Nana."

I dutifully heaved my way back to the Intourist, where I was informed that indeed a Jimbo Billings was on the premises. I ascended to the top floor, outmaneuvered the portly floor attendant, and knocked on Jimbo's door. "Excuse me." I coughed. A perfectly Russian voice promptly sent me to the *khui*.

"I am Misha Vainberg," I said. "I come in peace."

"Vainberg!" the voice trilled, and then, switching to Texan English: "Well, shoot, come on in, buster!"

The room must have been the tidiest in the entire hotel, free of giant green spiders and petulant Absurdis, save for the hotel hooker fixing up her mustache by the vanity mirror. Mr. Jimbo Billings, a short, muscular man in denims and short sleeves, looked vaguely Levantine or Greek, sun-wrinkled and drained of blood, with perfect blue and green eyes (one color each) and fast-moving hands made of fine leather. I could see how, after a fifty-hour immersion in the iconic American show *Dallas,* the Mossad agent could begin to pass for a middle-aged Texan. "Darlin'," Billings said to the whore. "Do me a favor, willya? Scram." The young lady pouted and made a show of her hips but quickly left us alone.

"So," I said, "my sources tell me we share a certain religion in common. Although I'm fairly lapsed and modern. In any case, *shalom*."

"Sources?" Billings said. "Sha-*lome*? Shoo, doggie! That's some imagination you got on you, boy." His mood rapidly shifted downward; he shook his gray head and said, "Hot damn, what we gon' do with you, Vainberg?"

"Nuthin'," I said, falling for some reason into his ridiculous accent. "I'm all fine and dandy right here."

"How you reckon?" Billings asked.

"I got somethin' for you," I said. "It's good for Israel, good for the Jews. A Holocaust museum. Gonna make some old-fashion' synergy happen. Gonna make people believe again." I held out my laptop for him to examine.

" 'The Institute for Caspian Holocaust Studies,' " Jimbo read,

" 'aka the Museum of Sevo-Jewish Friendship.' " He pursed his thick sunburned Sabra lips and read on a bit longer. "You know what ain't good for the Jews, Vainberg?" he said after a while. "You ain't."

"Screw you," I said. "I'm just tryin' to help."

"You tryin' to help Nanabragov and his daughter, so don't play me the fool, son," Billings said.

"And so what?" I said. "So what if I want to help an oppressed people other than my own? I'm a new kind of man. And you better hope, for everyone's sake, there are more like me."

"A new man? And what kind of man that be?"

"A man that ain't got no racial memory."

"Sure you do. You the biggest Jew of us all. You cain't help yerself. You cain't help where you come from. Just lookit your papa. He had you cut by Hasids when you were eighteen. God*damn*, son."

"My papa loved Israel."

"Your papa . . ." Billings stopped. He looked into my eyes, lifted his shoulders, then lowered them to reveal himself a man of very small stature and a generation older than I had thought. "You can call me Dror," he said in a Mid-Atlantic accent tinged with something phlegmy and Hebrew. "Although that's not my name."

"What were you saying about my papa?" I said.

Jimbo-Dror shook his head. "Look, Misha," he said. "In the seventies, a drunk, charming *refusenik* was sort of poignant. *Shabbat Shalom in Leningrad* and all that. But by the nineties, your father was just another Russian gangster . . . an antisocial personality with limited impulse control. I'm quoting from his file now."

The official Mossad characterization of my papa—so small-minded and bleak—did little to provoke me. The dried patch of snakeskin that had been my toxic hump was depleted of toxins. The anger was gone. My papa was long dead, relegated to Israeli files and the receding nighttime shadow play of his hands upon me.

"Maybe he was what you say," I told Jimbo-Dror, "but I doubt he loved Israel one *shekel* less than any of you Mossadniks. He gave three million dollars to some rabbi who wanted to drive the Arabs into the sea."

"We're not required to *love* it," Dror said of Israel. "Just to make sure it exists." He reached into his shirt pocket and pulled out a pair of wire-rims, looking like a tired Indian merchant relentlessly pushing his stock of goods across the oceans. He unfolded a piece of paper. "There's an American Express train that leaves Svanï City September seventh, arriving at the border on the eighth. AmEx has bribed the border guards so that passengers can get out of the country. I'll be on that train, if you need my help. The next train leaves on September ninth, arriving on September tenth. I suggest very strongly that you get out while you can, certainly before the Russians start bombing next week. You can get your Nana to help you with the ticketing. I think it's fifty thousand a person. But don't take her with you! Her father will kill you if you take her away from him. You know how these black-asses are about their daughters."

"You're leaving, too?" I said. "Goddammit, Dror. Nobody cares about this country at all. And the Sevo support you against the Palestinians, you know. Doesn't Israel need friends?"

"This requires a two-part answer," said Jimbo-Dror. "Yes, we need friends. And no, we really don't care about this country at all."

"Fine," I said. "But what about the oil? Don't you at least care about the oil?"

"Oil?" Jimbo-Dror took off his glasses and looked me over with his keen polymorphic eyes. "Are you joking with me, Vainberg?"

"What joking?" I pointed a bloated index finger at the window, beyond which I assumed the Caspian seabed toiled and bubbled. "The oil," I said. "Figa-6. The Chevron/BP consortium. KBR. Golly Burton."

"You're serious, aren't you?" Dror said. "Son of a bitch. I thought Nanabragov would let you in on the secret. You know, sometimes, after all these years of playing urban cowboy, I still have the capacity to be amazed."

"What secret? Tell me!"

"Misha, you poor fat *shmegegge* of a man. There *is* no oil."

41

Birds of Prey

"No oil," I said. To make sure I had understood correctly, I repeated the words in Russian. *"Nyefti nyetu."* I felt as if something dear had been taken away from me, as if a flotilla of my papa's rubber-sole boats were sailing away from me and over the horizon. I had gotten so used to the oil; one could almost say I had gotten close to it. Everywhere and everything was *nyeft'*. The modern world was composed entirely of petrol.

I walked away from Jimbo-Dror and toward his window to look at the stubby, sea-lapped orange legs of the nearby oil platforms and the skeletal derricks idling above them.

"Empty," he said.

"But what about Figa-6?"

"Let me give you the big picture," the Mossadnik said. "There are supposed to be fifty billion barrels of oil reserves in the Absurdi sector of the Caspian. In truth, there isn't *one percent* of that left. Figa-6 will run out by the end of the year. It doesn't make sense to start pumping it. The Absurdis have been lying to the investors from the start. Most of their hydrocarbon reserves were tapped out during Soviet times."

"But how can that be?" I said. "What about the KBR luau? What about the pipeline to Europe? Wasn't that the reason for this whole Sevo-Svanï war? Wasn't that why they shot down Georgi Kanuk's plane?"

"Georgi Kanuk's plane was never shot down," Dror said. "The old man's living in a villa near Zurich, quite nicely, from what I've heard.

Kellogg, Brown and Root bribed him with two-point-four million dollars and gave Nanabragov the same. And that was just a down payment. There was supposed to be plenty more once the LOGCAP contract got started."

"I don't understand."

"When they realized the oil was almost finished, Kanuk and Nanabragov needed something else. The sturgeon's nearly extinct, and the only thing this country grows is grapes. *Awful* grapes. Now, Exxon, Shell, Chevron, BP, they understood they'd been taken for a ride, and they started cutting back on what was left of production, but they did it slowly, so as not to scare off their shareholders. Just look at all those fancy skyscrapers they built." The Israeli gestured toward the extinguished skyline. "But then the Absurdis and their friends at Golly Burton had a better idea. Let's get a massive U.S. Army presence in here. We'll do support services, build marble outhouses, overcharge the hell out of the Department of Defense, 'cost plus' all the way, and all we have to do is get our oil services staff out and replace them with our military support people."

"I don't understand—"

"Just shut up and listen. So now all KBR, Kanuk, and Nanabragov need is a reason for the American army to pull in. This place is strategically located. Iran is next door. What about an air force base? Well, you've got a problem. The Russians still see Absurdistan as their backyard. They might get mad. And anyway, how much can you skim off a little base like that? You need something big. You need a huge U.S. Army presence doing peacekeeping and humanitarian work. Now, KBR was set to score a ten-year LOGCAP contract starting in 2002, but what good is all that if there's no heart-wrenching genocide around the corner? 'Think Bosnia' became everyone's motto. 'How can we make this place more like Bosnia?' I mean, you've got to hand it to Halliburton. If Joseph Heller were still alive, they'd probably ask him to be on their board."

I took a deep breath. There was a bottle of Hennessy on the counter, and I helped myself without asking. Jimbo-Dror motioned for a glass as well. "And so," he continued after a taste of the cognac, "the so-called civil war began. Only two things went wrong. The war got completely out of hand. These glue-sniffing True Footrest Posses really started blowing the crap out of the place, which may be good for a civilian engineering outfit like Bechtel, but it scares away all the Western workers, and more importantly, it scares away the Department of Defense. And then something much worse happened. Nobody cared."

"You mean the Western media."

"I mean the American people. See, we knew this was going to happen. We did a focus group—"

"The Mossad does focus groups?"

"We're open to all kinds of methodologies. And we're very interested in how genocides are perceived by the American electorate. So we did a focus group in suburban Maryland. Right away I knew KBR was in trouble. We do a sample space of three troubled countries: Congo, Indonesia, and Absurdsvanï. Okay, first part. We give these American *schmendricks* a map of the world and say, 'Point to the general area where you think Congo is located.' Nineteen percent point to the continent of Africa. Another twenty-three percent point to either India or South America. We count those as correct answers, because Africa, India, and South America all start out wide and then taper off at the bottom. So, for our purposes, forty-two percent of respondents sort of know where Congo is.

"Then we do Indonesia. Eight percent get the actual country. Another eight percent hit the Philippines. Fourteen percent go for New Zealand. A surprising nine percent aim for the Canadian Maritimes. We count all those as correct answers, because the respondents essentially know that Indonesia is an archipelago or at least that there are islands involved.

"Finally we do Absurdistan. *Nobody* gets it right. We start offering clues. 'It's near Iran,' we say. *Huh?* 'It's on the Caspian.' *Whuh?* 'Alexandre Dumas wrote about it after he visited Russia.' *Yuh?* Complete disaster. We show pictures of Absurdis, Congolese, and Indonesians at play, picking fruits, frying goats, and so on. More problems. The Congolese are clearly black, so that strikes a chord with all the respondents. Like them or not, you got plenty of blacks in America.

The Indonesians have funny eyes, so they're Asian. Probably work hard and raise dutiful children. Good for them. Then you get the Absurdis. They're sort of dark, but not really black. They look a little Indonesian, but they've got round eyes. Are they Arabs? Italians? Persians? We finally settle on 'taller Mexicans,' which is another way of saying we're fucked.

"Then we really let the cat out of the bag. We tell them, 'Look, there's a genocide happening, and the U.S. can invade one of the following ten countries.' We give them a list of countries, real and imaginary. We've got Djibouti, Yolanda, Costa Rica, Eastern Tuchusland, Absurdsvanï, and so forth. Guess what came in dead last, even behind the reviled Homoslavia? That's right. See, the way 'Absurdsvanï' is pronounced and spelled, it's utterly impossible for an American to feel anything for it. You have to be able to use a country as a child's first name to get anywhere. *Rwanda* Jones. *Somalia* Cohen. *Timor* Jackson. *Bosnia* Lewis-Wright. And then you got this *Republika Absurdsvanï*. Hopeless.

"So I call my friend Dick Cheney—he was still CEO of Halliburton back then—and I say, '*Hamoodi*, this isn't going to work. This country's a complete zero. You can maybe do Iraq in a few years, depending on who wins the U.S. election, or blow up Panama one more time, but stay the hell out of the Caspian.' But Cheney, you know, he doesn't listen to no one. It's 'LOGCAP this' and 'LOGCAP that.' Well, look out the window! There's LOGCAP for you!"

I took another sip of cognac. I looked out the window at the sterile Figa-6 oil fields and the false industrial sunset breaking out across the water. I scratched myself in a place where I had no itch, somewhere between my lower stomach and infinity. And then I understood. *I'd been had.* Utterly. Completely. They'd used me. Taken advantage of me. Sized me up. Known right away that they had their man. If "man" is the right word.

"Do you think . . ." I started to say. "Do you think Nana Nanabragovna knew about this all along?" But before the Israeli could answer, I was already out the door, heaving myself down the pockmarked esplanade toward the Lady with Lapdog.

. . .

"Maybe you shouldn't have talked to this Jimbo-Dror," Mr. Nana-bragov said, jerking severely, one hand angrily pulling on the gray tuft of hair between his still-muscular tits. A dead sheep was being hoisted from a newly docked speedboat and into the waiting arms of the Lady with Lapdog staff. It was nearly dinnertime at the Lapdog, and the menu promised mutton. "This Jew seems to be a propagan-dist for the other side."

"Which other side?" I said.

"Who knows?" Nanabragov shrugged. "*Some* other side. Every-one has always been against us. The Russians. The Armenians. The Iranians. The Turks. Look who we're surrounded by. We have no friends here. We thought maybe Israel would like us and then the American public would be our friends. That's why we reached out to you."

"You lied to me, you twitchy bastard," I whispered. "The oil . . . the fucking LOGCAP!"

Nanabragov made a lightning twitch to starboard, as if rehearsing for some new Latin dance. "Did I do something wrong, Misha?" he asked. "Did I do anything to hurt my people?"

"The people . . ." I said. I looked to the refugees clustered beneath blue UNHCR tarps by the waterfront. I was worried they would catch wind of the mutton and sturgeon grilling several meters out to sea and then storm the Lapdog. Had they any strength or anger left? "You've destroyed them," I said. "The country is ruined."

"Well, what can be done?" Nanabragov shrugged.

"I believed in you," I said. "I thought we would make something better. All the people really need is a little hope and encouragement. They're hardworking and clever."

"This country is nothing without oil," Nanabragov said. "Sevo, Svanï—it makes no difference. We're a feudal nation. We have a feu-dal mentality. It was all perfectly fine during the Cold War. We were taken care of by Moscow. But now the world changes so quickly that if you're even one centimeter behind, you'll be behind forever. When you compare us to all those Chinese and Indians, you know we've got no business being in the race. We need to find a new patron."

"But the young people aren't like that," I said. "My friend Alyosha says they can burn hundreds of pirated DVDs in seconds. They can hack into anything."

"Sure, they can burn and hack," Nanabragov said. "Give me a torch and I'll set the whole place on fire. I'm telling you, anyone who's the least bit smart around here fled to Orange County a long time ago."

"So you destroy a country because it's not competitive. What kind of reason is that?"

"It's the best reason, Misha. Nowadays, if you don't have natural resources, you need USAID. You need the European Bank for Reconstruction and Development. You need Kellogg, Brown and Root. If only we could get on America's top-ten list and score big like Jordan or Egypt. Or Israel."

"Why did you kill Sakha the Democrat!" I shouted. "He wasn't just some third-rate peasant. *He was one of us.*"

"Federal forces killed Sakha. It wasn't the SCROD."

"You planned it together with the Svanï. First thing you did was get rid of the democrats."

"A lot of good they were. Rotten intelligentsia. Couldn't tie their own shoes. What are you doing, Misha? Oh, for God's sake. Stop it! Men don't cry. You look funny. Such a big man in tears . . . What would Nana say if she saw?"

I shook down to the most ridiculous parts of me, tears flying in every direction but upward, like the oil gushers that had failed to materialize. I could still hear Sakha's tender bleating, his last words, which had been addressed to me. *Mishen'ka, please. Tell them to stop. They will listen to a man like you. Please. Say something.*

Mr. Nanabragov came up to me. He raised his hands as if to embrace me, but they twitched out of position. He stood there jerking silently. "Misha," he said. "Don't take my Nana away from me."

"What?"

His eyes were filling up with water and rainbows. "You don't understand what it has been like without her," he said, sniffling. "When she was at NYU and my Bubi was studying Ethnic Musicology at UCLA, there was nothing for me . . . nothing to live for. People like your father and me, we're of a different generation. Family is what we know. We can't live the way people do now, one child in San Diego, one in Torrance, one in the Valley." He wiped at his eyes.

"Surely you don't mean to leave her *here*," I said.

"You can both stay. Get married. After the Russian bombing next week, things will settle down. You'll see. I'll give you a piece of the cigarette action, not that you need a piece of anything."

"But we'll die here," I said, wiping my raw nose.

"Not necessarily. Don't you understand? I'll do anything to keep her. You're your father's son. He killed an American just to make sure you wouldn't leave him."

Seagulls were circling low over the dead sheep, and the Lapdog waiters were fingering their pistols. I remembered the seagull attacking the British kid on the videotape of my father getting decapitated. Everywhere I went, birds of prey were looking for an in. I stared at the smoke-gray sky above us, black smoke from the Lapdog grill, the haze wafting from the still-burning city. "Misha," Mr. Nanabragov said. "Misha. How can you fault me? Your father killed an Oklahoman to make sure you couldn't go back to New York."

"I know," I said simply.

"He wanted to keep you near him. He missed you so much. Is there anything more important than a father's embrace?"

"Nothing," I whispered.

And then Mr. Nanabragov was around my neck, crying and jerking and humping my leg. They still couldn't stop smelling of rancid sweat, our old men. All those French colognes and moisture gels, but that fundamental rank still lingered in their armpits. "Misha!" Mr. Nanabragov cried. "You have to promise me that you won't take my Nana away from me."

I felt him contracting around me, twitching in time with the slowing thump of my own heart. "I would be very angry if you did, Misha," he said. "So you have to promise me she won't leave."

I felt his bitter drool on the back of my neck. "I promise," I said.

42

Saltines and Fresca

We left a few days later. It was September 9. The day was light and airy and spoke of deliverance from the summer's heat. The train station was on the Svanï Terrace, but we didn't bother with any precautions. The SCROD and federal checkpoints had disappeared completely, and Svanï and Sevo citizens staggered around without hindrance, free to die on any terrace they chose.

We stood in the waiting room beneath a fading picture of the Svanï dictator Georgi Kanuk, upon whose grave octogenarian visage one commentator had written #1 TERRORIST and another FATHER OF THE NATION. Nana's mother had sneaked out of the house to say goodbye to us. Removed from the courtyard and the kitchen, she was a surprisingly different creature, feisty and emotional. The afternoon sun had touched her pale homebound cheeks. While she wept prodigiously at her daughter's departure, she did so with an almost reticent delight. "God will bless you," she kept saying to me and Nana. "In Brussels, in New York, wherever it is that you go, God will follow your footsteps with a father's eye."

"Tell Papa my heart is breaking," Nana said. "Tell him I'll come back as soon as the war is over, so maybe they should try to wrap it up by the Christmas break. By the way, is there any money in the Citibank account? I still haven't paid the bursar."

Mrs. Nanabragovna wiped her tears. "Now you're with Misha," she said, pointing to the general area around my wallet. "Misha will be your father, and there will always be water in his well for you to drink." Mother and daughter smiled and embraced each other.

I was angry and disgusted with the Nanabragovs, but I couldn't help being moved by their parting. "Be careful, little mother," I said to Mrs. Nanabragovna. "The Russians are planning to bomb the city next week. You must take shelter in your basement."

"Oh, they'll never bomb *our* house," Mrs. Nanabragovna said with a dismissive wave. "They'll just make a loop around Gorbigrad."

We were escorted onto the train by an army of men wearing home-made fatigues with the words AMERICAN EXPRESS RAPID REACTION FORCE. Our self-appointed protectors handled us roughly, like the soldiers they were, banging our laptops against the gravel and pulling us by our sleeves. We cursed their mothers under our breath and yet rejoiced at the presence of their formidable armaments, in particular the tank-busting cannon being dragged ahead of us.

The platforms were deserted. All the rail lines had been bombed into torqued ellipses of the kind made popular by a certain American sculptor, save for one upon which the American Express loco-motive and two wagons idled. They were old wide-gauge Soviet cars brought up to gleaming Western snuff. The locomotive sported a silk-screened AmEx logo. Absurdi children had painted the wagons with scenes of a better life for themselves, earnest depictions of dark-haired boys and girls wearing Svanï and Sevo crosses, flying happily between the Eiffel Tower, the Houses of Parliament in London, and the Leaning Tower of Pisa. YOU'VE GOT TO PLAY TO WIN, the children had written in large green English letters beneath their impossible fantasies. The roofs of the train cars were occupied by more members of the American Express Rapid Reaction Force nailing down their RPG launchers and waving a Colorado's worth of small arms at the sky.

We were handed over to a relatively pleasant group of Nana's for-mer American Express colleagues, who immediately told us that the soldiers were merely "volunteers" and not affiliated at all with the American Express company. We were given a stack of documents to sign, denying the company's responsibility for our likely deaths at the hands of desperate starving folk marauding along the train tracks.

One of the wagons had been converted into a plush Irish pub called Molly Malloy's, a branch of which used to service multinational oil execs on the International Terrace (its taps, in retrospect, had gushered better than the oil wells). The wood paneling had been artificially aged and warped; only the authenticating smells of piss and meat pies were missing. The bartender, an imported Tatar in a jolly green hat, bade us to return for happy hour at six, when top-shelf drinks were reduced to US$20.

I sent Timofey off to bed down in the service quarters, then retired to our compartment. The comforters and pillows were plush and hypoallergenic, the overhead racks had a built-in DVD player, a plasma screen, and a docking station for our laptops with Internet access that actually worked. "This is better than the Hyatt!" I told Nana as we fondled each other beneath a tasteful print of Svanï City at the turn of the last century, a wooden tram running past an onion-domed church, men in crisp czarist uniforms bidding each other good morning.

I had nearly removed her bra and liberated one nipple when the conductor meekly came a-calling. "I'm paying for both of us," I told the old man trembling in his AmEx regalia and visored cap. "And for my manservant, too."

"Three persons, all told," the conductor said, showering us with his spittle. He was yet another aficionado of the local breakfast favorite, sheep's head and trotters dunked in garlic broth. "Er, all told, one hundred and fifty thousand dollars, please, sir."

I proffered my American Express card, and the conductor excused himself to run it through the system. "Just slide it under the door when you're finished," I told him, and went back to sampling my Nana's sugar and sweets.

She had blessed the entire train crew with the sounds of her tumultuous nine-part orgasm when the locomotive whistled and our train sprang into belated motion. Nana dismounted, licked her fingers, then pressed her plush nose to the window. "Are you sad to be leaving your homeland, sweetie?" I asked, pulling on my underpants and giving a last tussle to my still-swollen organ.

"There's not much of it left," Nana said. She made an outline with her pinkie against the missing shape of the Central Mosque in the distance. The moistness of her digit against the glass left a pretty arabesque in place of the minaret's defunct silver cupola. The train passed through a tunnel, and we reemerged on the far end of the Gorbigrad peninsula. From this vantage point, the wrecked skyscrapers of the International Terrace had lined up in such a way that you could see clear through their looted interiors to an Ottoman fortress in the background that had been cleaved more or less in two. Nana lowered the shades.

"They'll build it anew," I said. "Maybe USAID or the European Bank will come through after all. Won't they, Nana?" I watched her face closely, trying to see how much she knew of her father's exploits.

"Misha, you're *cute,*" Nana said in a way that would brook no dissent. She put her head on my lap and yawned. "I hope your optimism carries me through life, little father. Want to play Food, Decor, Service?"

We did that for a while, and then I logged on to the Internet to check the weather in Brussels, my future home, and in New York, where Nana was headed to begin her NYU semester. "You're going to have some great weather in the city," I told her. "Wow, from the tenth to the sixteenth, we're looking at temps in the seventies, clear skies. You're so lucky."

"Someday the Americans will let you back in," Nana said, yawning again. "They'll forget that your father killed the Oklahoman and welcome you for your money." She burrowed into the comforter and started to snore dramatically. I most likely did the same, rocking our carriage with my sleep apnea.

Around six o'clock, I woke up and adjourned for a drink. The bar car was decorated with many Irish proverbs celebrating the wisdom and hilarity of unchecked alcoholism, the remaining space given over to large placards that said HERE CAN BE YOUR ADVERTISING. Retreating KBR men in pleated shorts and extra-large T-shirts were lounging on the tartan couch by the window while the bartender served them luscious pink lobster rolls and thick, oily American potato chips. The men were raucous and drunk. One of the Scotsmen was apparently trying to have a literary conversation with his Houston counterpart. "Evelyn *Whuh*?" the Texan was shouting. "Get outta here, mister! That ain't a real name!"

The train moved slowly to make sure our protectors would not fall off the roof. Outside the window, the country people had gathered by the tracks to try to interest us in their remaining possessions—the leftovers of their mules, their wives' silver brocade work, plumbing fixtures that looked like mud-caked saxophones, gilt-edged portraits of Georgi Kanuk in happier times presenting a drooling Leonid Brezhnev with a fist-sized diamond.

In the background, the Caspian Sea was fighting an encroaching salt bed, while in the foreground, a lake of slurry and waste butted up against a dehydrated stretch of grass; between the two, the remains of the oil industry were being minutely disassembled, sections of old nodding donkey pumps now offered for sale by the men lining the railroad tracks.

The smell of fresh excrement penetrated the bulletproof walls of our wagon, and we could hear members of the AmEx Rapid Reaction Force stomping about on the roof, threatening the dying men outside with the laser scopes of their rifles or else picking off the rare Daewoo steam iron in exchange for packets of contraband saltines and warm cans of Fresca. As the sun set, the impromptu trading lessened in tempo, and the men lining the railroad tracks began to decompose into clay shards and clumps of sand mixed with grass. Their humanity ended so swiftly that one moment I could discern the subtle glow of the whites of their eyes against the blue and black of the fading desert and sea, and in the next instant I saw only yellow on black, gray on black, black on black—nothing.

My *mobilnik* rang. The St. Petersburg telephone code appeared on the screen. Apparently international calls were possible this far out of the capital; we had outdistanced the Absurdi censors.

The familiar number blinked impatiently on my phone. It was Alyosha-Bob. I wanted to tell him that I was safe and leaving the country, but I was too embarrassed to go into the particulars of what had transpired—how the Nanabragovs had taken my honor and how one of them—granted, the most gentle and sympathetic—was now snoring away in my train compartment. Instead, I picked up one of the Russian papers and tried to distract myself with the news. The death toll from the Absurdi conflict was approaching three thousand, the American electorate still couldn't find the Caspian Sea on a map, while the Russian president Putin was promising both to bomb the warring parties and to mediate between them. I put the paper down. My stomach and mouth were suddenly hurting from the beating Tafa and Rafa had given me. Or perhaps I had merely channeled the suffering of the nation around me.

I pictured my life in Brussels. The days passing slowly in that quiet European indeterminacy. The price of living amid civilization, away from the bustle and treachery of America and Absurdistan both.

The older Scots were trying to teach the Texans the chorus to one of their bagpipe songs, soused with melancholy cheer and the impossibility of ever really saying farewell. Potato chips flew out of mouths and beer steins clanked together as the Tatar barman tried to keep the beat with a pair of coasters.

> *So whenever friendly friens may meet*
> *Wherever Scots foregather,*
> *We'll raise our gless, we'll shout*
> *Hurroo,*
> *It's Carnwath Mill forever.*

The sun had set entirely, and the AmEx men were shining their flashlights at a yellow corpse stumbling alongside the tracks, its hands waving madly for a moment's notice. We pulled down the shades before the gunshots began.

43

The Faith of My Fathers

I was rightfully hungover the next day, whiskey being one of my more problematic tipples. Something was blocking the busy neural pathway where my neck had set up a Customs post with my head. "Oh, dear," I moaned, kissing Rouenna's face, or, as it turned out, the doughy pillow where she had left her scents. Did I say Rouenna? I meant Nana, of course. And then I realized I had been dreaming of Rouenna all night long, about the time she and I, along with her little cousin Mercedes, had taken a tour of Hunter College. As we passed through the library, the lively ten-year-old Mercedes had said, "Ai, *mami*, look at all them fucken books!" And Rouenna, who had misguidedly dressed herself in a business suit for the informal college tour, very solemnly replied, "Why you cursin' in an educated place, Mercedes?"

Was it the word "educated" that was scraping away at my heart? The respect for book learning from a woman who, up till that point, had thought Dickens was a porn star? Was it the cheap business suit that could barely contain Ro's figure? Why did I miss her so much all of a sudden, my traitorous Bronx girl with the tough hands and the bleeding gums?

"Breakfast is here, *bobo*," Nana said. "Get it while it's hot." The train crew had set up a small table for us upon which a heap of croissants and muffins exuded the nauseating smells of butter and cranberries. I propelled myself to the table, nearly knocking over a silver tray bearing a notecard with the AmEx logo. A train happily chugged past an indifferent sun; below, a message written in a woman's dainty, practiced hand:

Good morning, respected passenger!
Today is Monday, September 10, 2001
We are passing through northern Absurdsvani, where today's temperature will be a maximum of 28 degrees Celsius, with sunny conditions prevailing along the Staraushanski Valley and into the Griboedov mountain range.
Lunch in the bar car will be a caviar sampler with blini and just-picked country leeks followed by elderberry-cured roast beef (a northern Absurdi specialty) with fingerling potatoes and cavalo nero.
We will be arriving at the Red Bridge border checkpoint at 15:00 o'clock. Please have your passports ready.
My name is Oksana Petrovna, I am proud to work on this train, and I am here only just for you!

"Such a nice girl, this Oksana," I said to Nana. "She's even more professional than that poor Larry Zartarian." I winced at the thought of the Hyatt manager and his mother, still trapped beneath my bed at the Intourist Hotel.

"She's a slut," Nana corrected me, pouring three creams into my coffee, which is how I took it.

I raised the shades. What a difference a night made! The oily sea-desert had been replaced by a near-alpine vista. Fields of yellow late-summer grass (or was it really hay in disguise?) rolled down the hills. Rills fed brooks, which nurtured distant lakes, which in turn drank from the whitecapped mountains straddling the horizon. A bird that might have been an eagle or a pigeon (my eyesight is not so strong) circled above the distant skyline of these promontories. And something was mercifully absent from this unfurling of nature's green, blue, and white tricolor, something beaten and raw, scorched and unkempt, vulgar and blackened with rot. "Where are the people?" I asked Nana. "Why don't they come eat all these eagles and hay instead of dying in the desert?"

"The people have been moving off the mountain for decades," Nana said. "They follow the oil."

"But there's no oil left," I said. "Right, Nana? The whole war was cooked up by your papa and Golly Burton because they ran out of oil. Isn't that true?"

Nana shrugged. "What do I know?" she said. "I'm just a senior at NYU. You gotta try this excellent honey! It's soooo good. And not too sweet. Taste the difference?"

I tasted it, all right. "That is really great," I said. "Where does it come from?" We started turning over the honeypot, trying to find a label. "Ah, it's from Turkey!"

As I was finishing up the croissants, the train came to a halt. "Yum, yum, yum," I said, glancing out the window. Some vendors had gathered beneath my window, and the AmEx soldiers were jumping off the roof to bargain with them. The country folk had set up a wooden bench piled with cartons of Newport Lights, spinach leaves, and fresh cherries. "The lunch menu didn't say anything about dessert," I said to Nana. "Maybe I should buy some cherries."

The sound of a local tongue brushed up against my window with gravelly insistence. Already voices were being raised in anger even as U.S. dollars changed hands along with cigarettes and spinach. It was then that I noticed a strange phenomenon—the vendors had little blue and white circles pinned to their dark heads. *Yarmulkes?* "Nana," I said, "are these the Mountain—"

The door to our cabin slammed open. A presence almost as large as my own took up the space between Nana and me, immediately overturning our breakfast table. "Vainberg!" the creature barked. "Oh, thank God I've found you! You have to get off the train now! I'm a friend of your late father's. Avram."

I backed off into a corner and raised my hands in protest. Avram? My father? Not again! "What's this about?" I said weakly.

The man was of late middle age, dressed in a leather cap, along with designer shirt and pants that his wife had nicely matched to his proportions. He had a pitiful and worried mien, yet the rest of his appearance was strong, sweaty, and powerful. He was clearly a Jew. And such a Jew! A prehistoric Jew, as I've said before, a *Haimosaurus rex* with the flabby little hands, the big roaring mouth, the broad muscular legs and sensual hindquarters. *So this is how we all began,* I thought to myself. "Mr. Vainberg," the Jewish dinosaur was saying, "they will kill you at the border. They will take Miss Nana back to her father. We have no time. You must get off the train without delay."

"Oh, hell," Nana said. "My father must have found out I left with you. He probably ordered the border guards to kill you in revenge."

"Not *probably*. Exactly so!" the intruder cried. "I'm a Mountain Jew, Mr. Vainberg. There was a Mossad man, a Dror or a Jimmy, who came through here three days ago, and he warned us that you were coming and that there would be trouble if the Nanabragov girl was with you. We've set up a diversion outside with the American Express hooligans. We must get you off the train. These thugs will soon tire of bargaining for cherries, and then they're liable to shoot us all."

"The American Express train crew works for Nana's father?" I said.

"Everyone works for Nana's father in the end."

The particulars were starting to settle around my broad shoulders. Goddammit. Another pogrom. There would be no caviar for lunch. There would be no hypoallergenic lovemaking. "Wait!" I said to Avram. "My manservant is bedding down in the service quarters. I must get him, or *he'll* get the bullet at the border."

The dinosaur tapped on his watch. "We haven't the time."

"He's Jewish," I lied.

"Your *manservant*? Jewish?"

I was running down the empty corridor, petite French doors swinging aside in anticipation of my arrival. Finally I stumbled upon a beautiful Russian girl rouging her considerable cheeks. This must have been the very Oksana Petrovna who had left us that thoughtful notecard. True to Nana's words, there was something sluttish in the girl's comportment. "Miss," I said in English. "I need my manservant to help make my toilet. Rouse him from his slumber. And quickly!"

The girl hurriedly snapped shut her compact case, leaving one freckled cheek bare of pomade. "I am here only just for you!" she cried as she leaped into a nearby cabin, dragging out my befuddled Timofey by his ear. I thanked her, grabbed Timofey by the ear myself, and yanked him to the passenger car.

Avram had unlatched a side door and was already scurrying down with my luggage. As Nana approached with her 718 cosmetics bags, the Mountain Jew put a hand out in front of her breasts. "I know she's your girlfriend," he said to me, "but if we take her off the train, there might be trouble for our community. What's left of the SCROD might attack our village. It might not be good for the Jews."

"She's my Nana, and she goes with me," I said, knocking back Avram's hand. He sighed wearily, prehistorically, and followed us out onto the golden grass. We ran down the slope of a nearby hill falling away from the railroad tracks, our urban feet struggling to make sense of the uneven and uncemented terrain. "Aif!" I cried as a mushy patch of earth nearly sent my ankle in a different direction from the rest of me. Timofey grabbed me before that fatal moment and started pushing my body with a coarse countryside vitality. "Very good, Tima," I huffed. "In nature, *I* will be *your* manservant. Good boy."

"Past those bushes," the Mountain Jew instructed. Nana cried out from the sting of branches and twigs; I grabbed her behind, hoping to shield myself from the worst of the thicket's ravages. Having cleared this chamber of horrors, we emerged onto a cool dirt path beneath a canopy of oaks. A small Daewoo sedan awaited us. The driver was a tall, skinny youth snug beneath a helmet of greasy hair. "My son, Yitzhak," the Mountain Jew said. "My one and only. Well, drive already, you idiot!"

Yitzhak rumbled down the dirt road with teenage abandon. Nana was trying to stanch a bloody cut to her forehead, Timofey was picking brambles and berries out of my hair, and all of us were heaving with exhaustion and bewilderment. I looked back at the barely visible railroad tracks upon which the AmEx train was still idling, wishing the world were a better place.

We lapsed into a moody silence, our eyes on the road before us, never on one another. "Are you fleeing to Israel?" Yitzhak asked me in the same accented, barely comprehensible Russian his father spoke.

"I'm going to Brussels," I said. "Nana is flying to New York."

"New York!" Yitzhak said. "It is the city of my dreams."

"Really?" I said. "What a good kid you are."

"Forget about it," Avram said. "We have relatives in Haifa. You want to go somewhere? Go visit them. A free bed you'll have."

"You'll love New York," I said. "It's like having the whole world on one small island."

"I understand you can play basketball with blacks on the street," Yitzhak said.

"Very true," I said. "I like the way your mind works, young man."

"Don't encourage his stupid dreams," the Mountain Jew said. "Several times it has happened to us—the young people leave for L.A. or Brooklyn, they marry an outsider, and after a few years they won't come home for *Pesach seder.* They won't even fly back to piss on their grandfathers' graves. But when things go bad with their gentile wives or with their half-breed children, they run back to us. 'Papa, *papochka,* what have I done? I've forsaken my people.' And we welcome them back, and kiss them, and love them like they haven't stabbed us through the heart. Because for us it's simple. If you're a Jew, even if you're a sophisticate and a melancholic, you will always find a home here."

"Thank you for saving us," Nana said, putting her hand on Avram's shoulder. "You've risked your own lives. We won't soon forget your kindness."

Avram shrugged her off. "Well, who else would do it?" he said. "The Mossad man came and said, 'There's a Jew in danger.' We knew exactly what to do. A Jew in danger, so let's save him. This is how our minds work."

I sighed wearily. An anger was developing inside me, the anger of a man with a growing debt. I tried to position my face in the rearview mirror so that I could smile in encouragement to the nice Yitzhak. His curious brown face smiled back at me. We were passing a ramshackle village populated solely by stray dogs and scruffy chickens past childbearing age, a barber sitting lifelessly by his shack, the word "barber" misspelled in English and Russian and possibly a third language. We noticed the paisley domes of three similar mosques and the sharp bayonets of their minarets aiming at the innocent sky. "Do you get along with the Moslems?" Nana asked in her new supplicant's voice. "You live in such close proximity."

"We're fine with them," Avram said, doffing his leather cap and fixing his comb-over. "They don't bother us, and we don't bother them. They're not very bright, that's for certain. Just look at how they live. These houses haven't been painted in decades. Is that supposed to be a market? Just turnips and radishes and nothing imported? Wait until you see *our* village."

"Now, Avram—" I started to say sharply, but Nana was already pressing her elbow into my hide.

"Don't you dare, Misha," she whispered in English. "Don't you realize what he's done for us?"

"What he's done for *me*," I whispered back. "I'm the Jew."

"Who cares why he did it. I was gonna get sent back to my father. I was going to miss another semester at NYU. So shut it, willya?"

We were driving down a steep gravel path lined with gilded Soviet statues of supple female volleyball players and fierce badminton gods groaning in midswing. "They were going to build an Olympic training center here," Yitzhak said. "But someone stole all the money."

"Yeah, someone," I murmured to myself. The gravel path ended in a smarmy river of unknown provenance. Beyond it lay a clump of newly built towers capped by silver spires and satellite dishes, along with enormous redbrick manses, some surrounded by miniature cranes hoisting fourth and fifth stories or the gleaming skylights that covered them, a kind of storybook village with a relentless microwave sheen.

"Our humble hamlet, Davidovo," Avram said. "Our little paradise."

After the desolation of the Moslem town, we found ourselves on a modern thoroughfare lined with crowded storefronts labeled HOUSE OF FASHION and PALACE OF HAPPINESS and 24 HOUR INTERNET CLUB, their parking lots gridlocked with Toyotas and Land Rovers. In a nearby residential area, old people, withered and Oriental-seeming, sat impassively on wood-carved front porches, their bodies slowly drying out in the sun while children of every age scrambled around them in a flurry of tanned legs and glistening Versace belt buckles. "Where are all the grown-ups?" Nana asked.

"Trading," Avram said. "In Israel or in Moscow. All kinds of goods and household products. We import half the things you find in Svaní City. We even have our own 718 perfume shop."

"So you're a merchant people," I said, my words sour with distaste.

We were coming up to the village square, at which point I squinted in disbelief. A sunlit replica of the Wailing Wall in Jerusalem took up an entire side of the square, green moss authentically growing from between the cracks in the equally genuine brickwork, a set of Israeli date palms arrayed in front.

"And what the hell are those?" Nana said. She was pointing at two statues made out of some kind of fiberglass, one a strange mishmash of three men dancing over what looked like a broken airplane and the other of a man with a torch holding on to his belly, as if stricken with gas.

"That's Sakha the Democrat holding the torch of freedom after being shot at the Hyatt," Yitzhak explained. "And the other one is Georgi Kanuk ascending to heaven after his plane was shot down, with his son Debil and Alexandre Dumas holding on to his legs, trying to keep him here on earth. See, if any renegade Sevo or Svaní gangs attack us, we're good either way."

"And here comes the welcoming committee," Avram said. We were surrounded by a bunch of playful children. A little kid in a too-large yarmulke and an acid-washed T-shirt that said NAUGHTY 4EVER ran up to the car and started knocking on my door.

"Vainberg! Vainberg! Vainberg!" he shouted.

"Help me out of the car, young man," I said. "There's a dollar in it for you." As the child's prepubescent compatriots made their dervish circles around me while shouting my family name, I ambulated toward a gaggle of men smoking fiercely in the shadow of the Wailing Wall. Upon inspection, half of them were no more than

teenagers, their heads draped in silken white yarmulkes, their un-
combed black hair reaching down to their eyes, their gangly bodies
slack from village life. "Is that your girlfriend?" one of them asked,
pointing to Nana, bouncing ambivalently toward us. "Is she Jewish?"

"What, are you crazy?" I cried. "That's Nana Nanabragovna!"

"We can get you a nice local girl," another recommended. "A
Mountain Jew. Pretty like Queen Esther, sexy like Madonna. After
you marry her, she'll do all kinds of things. Half of them on her
knees."

"Dirty little kids." I sniffed. "What do I care for religion? All
women are equally good on their knees."

"Suit yourself," the teens replied, parting deferentially before an
old man who was leaning against Avram, his dark face drowning in
the white fuzz of a beard gone awry; one of his eyes was forever
closed to the world, the other blinking a bit too insistently, his mouth
producing squirts of slobber and happiness with the speed of an
American soda fountain. "Vaaaainberg," he crooned.

"This is our rabbi," Avram said. "He wants to tell you something."

The rabbi gently spat at me for a few seconds in some incomprehensible local patter. "Speak in Russian, grandfather," Avram said.
"He doesn't know our tongue."

"Whooo," the rabbi said, confused. He rubbed the yellowing
sponge that covered his brain and made an effort at the Russian language. "Your fardur woooze a great persons," he said. "A great persons. He help us get built this wall. Looka how big."

"My father helped build this wall?"

"Give us moneys for brick. Buy palm from Askhelon. No problem.
He hate Arabs. So we make plaque."

One of the smoking men by the wall moved aside and tapped an
index finger at a handsome brown sign upon which I could immediately discern the eagle swoop of my father's strong nose, the unhappy
hieroglyphics that the artist had shaped into his left eye, the bramble
of crosshatching that outlined the joy and sarcasm of his thick lower
lip. TO BORIS ISAAKOVICH VAINBERG, the plaque read. KING OF ST. PE-
TERSBURG, DEFENDER OF ISRAEL, FRIEND TO THE MOUNTAIN JEWS.

And below that, a quote from my father, in English: BY ANY MEANS NECESSARY.

The smoker extended his hand. I noticed his fingers were covered with faded blue-green tattoos, testifying to many lengthy Soviet prison terms. "I'm Moshe," he said. "I spent many years with your fardur in the Big House. To us Jews inside, he was like our fardur, too. He was always love you, Misha. He talk only about you. He was your first lover. And nobody will love you like that never again."

I sighed. I was feeling wobbly and teary and overcome. To find my father's face looking down at me in this antediluvian outpost of Hebraity . . . *Look, Papa. Look how much weight I've shed in the last few weeks! Look how much we resemble each other now in profile. There's nothing of my mommy left in me anymore. I'm all you now, Papa.* I wanted to trace the outline of his face with my finger but was intercepted by several of the middle-aged Jews, who also wanted to shake my hands and tell me in their broken Russian what gay, thoughtful times they shared with my Beloved Papa, both inside and outside the Big House, and how, after the Soviet Union had collapsed, they worked together to make "bigger and bigger moneys day after day."

We heard a strange teakettle sound from the rabbi, the rumble of phlegm trying to pass through a nose bent by age. "He's crying," Avram explained. "He's crying because he's honored to see such an important Jew here in his village. There, grandfather. It's all right now. Soon everything will pass. Don't cry."

"The rabbi's getting a little lost in the head," one of my father's friends explained to me. "We sent for a new one from Canada. Twenty-eight years old. Fresh as a radish."

"Vaaaainberg," the rabbi sang once more, touching my face with his hand, a clump of earth and garlic.

"This poor man lived through Stalin and Hitler," Avram said of the rabbi. "The Sevo had him sent to a labor camp in Kamchatka when he was twenty. Seven of his eight sons were shot."

"I thought the Sevo tried to save the Jews," I said. "Parka Mook told me—"

"Are you going to listen to that fascist?" Avram said. "After the war, the Sevo tried to have all of our men sent to the gulags so they could take over our villages. We had the plumpest cows, and our women are freckled and have very thick thighs."

Nana had clasped her hands around the rabbi's crinkly, fragrant body and was happily interrogating the old man in Russian: "Is it true, sir, that the Mountain Jews are the descendants of the original Babylonian exile?"

"We are-a?"

"Well, that's one theory. Don't you keep a written record, Rabbi?"

"A what-a?"

"Aren't you Jews supposed to be the People of the Book?"

"A who-a?"

"Don't bother the old man," Avram said. "We Mountain Jews, we're not known for our learning. Originally we raised livestock, and now we trade goods in bulk."

The rabbi resumed sniffling, the criminals smoked down their Newport Lights, the teenagers gossiped about the world's sexiest Jewesses. I looked at my father's profile. I looked at his former prisonmates (*He was your first lover*), at the kind, flummoxed old man clinging to my elbow, at the sacred brick wall in front of us, and at the last quote my Beloved Papa had left for the Mountain Jews. BY ANY MEANS NECESSARY.

Had my papa known that he was plagiarizing Malcolm X? Papa's racism was a thing to behold, impenetrable, subsuming, all-encompassing, an epic poem. Could he have independently reached the same conclusion as a black leader of the Nation of Islam? I thought of what my father had told me when I returned to St. Leninsburg. "You have to lie, cheat, and steal just to make it in this world, Misha," he had said. "And until you learn that for a fact, until you forget everything they taught you at that Accidental College of yours, I'm going to have to keep working as hard as I can." I thought of my Rouenna, piling all her hopes upon my warm fat body, and then, after I had been imprisoned in Russia, trying to make a life with Jerry Shteynfarb. I thought of the Mountain Jews and their side-by-side statues of Georgi Kanuk and Sakha the Democrat, the murderer and the murdered. I thought of all that I had seen and done in my last two months in Absurdistan.

A shard of crystal broke in me. I fell to the ground and threw myself around one of Avram's prehistoric ankles. The Jews turned to look into my dumb blue eyes, and my dumb blue eyes looked back at them. "Thank you," I was trying to say, although nothing came out. And then, with increasing levels of pleading and helplessness: "Oh,

thank you.

Oh,

thank you.

Oh,

thank you!"

The Corner of 173rd Street and Vyse

Our hosts put us up in a half-built mansion that resembled a four-story crenellated doghouse with a satellite dish hanging off the roof. Our bedroom was cavernous and empty, like a train station right before dawn. Nana's face lay against my shoulder—despite her youth, she was already suffering from the mild stages of sleep apnea, her throat muscles clenching, her pretty face vainly biting at pockets of cold mountain air.

In a corner of the room, a lime-green musical insect was starting up Stravinsky's Symphony in C. Otherwise all was silent. I crawled to my stomach, then crawled to my knees, then crawled to my feet. I walked out of the house. The cobblestone alleys were empty of all creatures. The lights in the modernistic synagogue had been extinguished, and the flag of the 718 Perfumery beat silently against the store's weathered facade. The main street was also devoid of life except for the 24 Hour Internet Club. Inside the club, as one would find in a similar establishment in Helsinki or Hong Kong or São Paulo, a dozen overweight teenage nerds typed away on their keyboards, one hand held tight against a carbonated beverage or a meat pie, their thick oversize glasses aquariums of gray, green, and blue. I said *shalom* to my fallen brethren, but they barely grunted, not willing to interrupt their electronic adventures. I bought an aromatic crepe rolled with cabbage, parsley, and leek and tore it to shreds with my teeth.

Dear Rouenna, I typed when my turn came.

I'm coming for you, baby girl. I don't know how I'll do it, I don't know what terrible things I will have to perpetrate against others to achieve my goal, but I will come to New York City and I will marry you and we will be "2gether 4ever," as they say.

*You've done me wrong, Rouenna. It's okay. I'll do you wrong, too. I can't change the world, much less myself. But I know that we are not meant to live apart. I know that you're the one for me. I know that the only time I feel safe is when my little purple half-*khui *is in your tender, tangy mouth.*

You're touching your belly as you read this. If you want to have Shteynfarb's child, go ahead. He will be my child, too. They are all my children as far as I'm concerned.

What else can I tell you, baby bird? Study hard. Work late. Don't despair. Get your teeth cleaned and don't forget to see your gyno regularly. Whatever happens to you now, boo, whether you carry to term or not, you will never be alone.

Your porky russian lover,
Misha

Back in the mansion, I tried to stir Timofey to his senses, but he refused to let go of his precious sleep. I slapped him lightly. He looked at me with sleep-crusted eyes. His breath tickled my nose. "At your service, *batyushka*," he said.

"We're leaving Nana behind," I said. "She can cross the border the next day. We're flying out of here without her."

"I don't understand, sir," Timofey said.

"I've changed my mind," I said. "I don't want her. And I don't want her people. We're not going to Belgium, Timofey. We're going to New York. By any means necessary."

"Yes, *batyushka*," Timofey said. "As you wish." We sneaked into the bedroom to fetch my laptop and tracksuits. I looked at Nana's contorted face, her plump tongue rolling back into her throat, her arms spread out like the Good Thief on his cross. I still loved her very much. But I wouldn't bend down to kiss her.

• • •

An hour later, we are wading through a gray sludge-filled river, the failed nation of Absurdistan now entirely at our backs. In the distance, beneath the sliver of the young moon, a similar Moslem crescent flies over the sentry tower of a neighboring republic. I carry my laptop high over my head; Timofey sweats beneath my heavier luggage; Yitzhak, the nice boy who wants to play basketball with blacks in New York, waves a white flag and shouts something in the local tongue, a string of consonants that quarrel with the occasional stray vowel. When we hit dry land, we start running toward the sentry tower, waving our white flag, my Belgian passport, the recognizable gray square of my laptop.

Rouenna. With each step I am getting closer to you. With each step I am racing toward your love and away from this irredeemable land.

Let's be honest. Summers in New York City are not as romantic as some would think. The air is stagnant and stinks alternately of sea, clotted cream, and rained-upon dog. But early September is still warm and succulent in your arms. I've been thinking, Ro. We should buy one of the few remaining row houses on Vyse or Hoe Avenue, something grand and decrepit, Victorian or perhaps even American Gothic, a wide veranda beckoning the children of the nearby housing projects.

Look around us. The old men playing dominoes for money; five-year-old Bebo, Franky, Marelyn, and Aysha kicking around a dusty football; their older cousins skipping the world's most artful double Dutch; teenage moms and dads talking sex at each other across the stoops, calling their little ones *tiguerito,* "little gangster"; the sneakers hanging off the telephone poles; the tricked-out Mitsubishi Monteros pumping salsa across the streets; the moms reading the coupon pages like newspapers; the stores with no name but PLAY LOTTERY HERE; the roses sticking out of the iron grilles of housing-project windows.

In our basement, the laundry machines and dryers are spinning. You pass me a rolled-up ball of baby socks, warm to the touch. Our household is large. There will be many cycles. Oh, my sweet endless Rouenna. Have faith in me. On these cruel, fragrant streets, we shall finish the difficult lives we were given.

ACKNOWLEDGMENTS

I want to thank the following New Yorkers: my friend Akhil Sharma for exceeding duty's call and for his careful shearing of this manuscript; Daniel Menaker, my brilliant editor and mensch nonpareil, for shepherding me to greener pastures; Matt Kellogg, a young man who knows his words, for assisting in Dan's shepherding; and Denise Shannon, my agent, for a keen critical eye and for keeping me solvent all these years.

The Ledig House International Writers Residency in upstate New York has always been there for me when I needed a green place to write and think.

The best parts of this book, such as they are, were written under the care of Beatrice von Rezzori and the Santa Maddalena Foundation, her remarkable writers' retreat near Donnini, Italy.